Also by Milena McKay

The Headmistress

The Headmistress

Magdalene Nox

Standalones

The Delicate Things We Make

The Perfect Match

A Whisper of Solace

These Thin Lines

Copyright © 2024 Milena McKay
All Rights Reserved

ISBN: 9798338493168

No part of this book may be reproduced in any form or by any electronic or mechanical means, including information storage and retrieval systems, without written permission from the author, except for the use of brief quotations in a book review.

Cover art & design by Jenifer Prince
Interior design by Landice Anderson
Edited by Heather Flournoy

For content warnings and contact information, please visit www.milenamckay.com

Reverence

MILENA MCKAY

For my grandmother…
Who survived camps and prisons and yet loved through it all…

"True love begins when nothing is looked for in return."

ANTOINE DE SAINT-EXUPERY

Adagio

One
Of Blood & Satin

Her first ever glimpse of Katarina Vyatka was one of cold eyes and bloody satin ribbons. Juliette wasn't certain what shocked her more—the absolute steel in the charcoal gaze or the droplets of crimson that splattered the prima ballerina's slippers and the studio's mirror.

The soloist, a guy Juliette never had any time of day for, was wailing in pain, covering his cheek. The rest of the dancers were petrified. The mythical Soviet prima, the Empress of Moscow, Katarina the Great, the one whom the entire world had heard of yet had never seen—save for the odd video snippet, stolen and smuggled across the Iron Curtain—stood tall and proud, her regal shoulders thrown back, watching the spectacle unfold before her without a sound.

In fact, it was something Juliette had heard ever since the announcement was made that Bolshoi, the main ballet company of the Soviet Union, would be touring in Europe. *Katarina Vyatka will not be speaking.* If this entire incident was anything to go by, Katarina Vyatka did not need to speak. She was lethal without a word.

If Juliette had been directing this scene, she would have set it to unfold in slow motion. A random man extended his unwelcome hand, and a second later, a slap resounded, followed by screaming. She'd have staged the entire piece in bloody colors and silence.

It was shocking. It was unnerving. And yet, under the projector lights or in real life, had Juliette been in Katarina Vyatka's position, the show would have unspooled along similar lines. However, there would be two deviations. First, nobody would dare. And second, she'd be heard. She was Juliette Lucian-Sorel, and not a soul in Paris ever forgot that. Even if Juliette herself very much wished these days that they would.

Her train of thought was interrupted quite rudely by Gabriel, who bumped into her from behind. She almost turned to mock his unusual clumsiness but belatedly realized that the collision was entirely her fault. Juliette had been the one to stop abruptly. To watch. To stare, more accurately.

Juliette had played it cool all month since learning that, for the very first time, the otherwise well-toured Bolshoi was bringing out their legendary current star. Probably the most iconic ever, if anything Juliette had seen of Vyatka on those bits of tape was correct.

As the Princess of Paris, she couldn't jump up and down and clap her hands from excitement and curiosity. But she had wanted to. Oh, how Juliette had wanted to. There really wasn't a bigger mystery in the ballet world than Katarina Vyatka.

And that was when Juliette had suffered her first disappointment. They were told the prima was not to be approached. By anyone. The second letdown came on the heels of the first. Everyone was to stay as far away from the entire Soviet company as possible. Juliette had wilted a little.

She hadn't let it show. Again, Princess of Paris and all that. And she had maintained her poker face even with Gabriel, who could barely keep himself in his Lycra leggings from the sheer exuberance. Granted, it did not take much to get her dancing partner out of his pants to begin with. So Juliette had paid Gabriel no mind.

But she herself had been disappointed. She couldn't pinpoint exactly why. She spoke absolutely no Russian, outside of the occasional profanity picked up during her own tour of Moscow and Leningrad two years ago. And she highly doubted the Bolshoi prima spoke English. So she couldn't explain her dejected reaction.

Juliette had resigned herself to watching, as it was more than the rest of the world was afforded. The tickets for the Bolshoi tour—all three performances—had been sold out in minutes and were being scalped for ungodly sums. This was history in the making, after all, and Juliette got to see Vyatka closer than any of the people who stood in lines for hours to throw obscene amounts of money at skimpy paper stubs ever would.

Juliette and the rest of the Paris Opera Ballet company observed the touring dancers rehearse in the space usually reserved for their own classes. And that alone was quite a privilege.

Except, it looked like not everyone at the Palais Garnier was aware of the history, the making of it, or even the common courtesy of not being a letch. Michel certainly was not, because he seemed to have taken one look at the main attraction and swaggered in during the short break while the Bolshoi choreographer was busy giving instruction on some less than perfectly stretched arm on a plié. Her back turned to him, Vyatka was in the middle of fixing a ribbon on her slipper when he placed a hand on her waist and tried to pull her up and closer to him.

Perhaps the issue was that Juliette expected no sound. After all, the entire week had been governed by something akin to religious sacrament. Silent and exulting. Vyatka did not speak, she did not even breathe out loud, from what Juliette had so far observed. She was silence herself. In motion or in repose, Katarina Vyatka seemed to be surrounded by a shroud of inviolability. She wore her greatness, her talent, and her status like a shield. Or a hazmat suit, which she apparently actually needed, since men like Michel breathed the same air as she.

And that's what made the open-handed blow deafening. Juliette didn't know what had scratched Michel's cheek, but while the blood was unexplainable, it was also absolutely expected. The second Katarina had raised her hand, Juliette somehow knew.

This woman would leave bruises.

What a strange thought. Juliette shook her head at her own wandering mind and focused on the ensuing chaos.

All hell had broken loose. Michel was howling as if Vyatka had castrated him with a rusty spoon instead of giving him much less than what he deserved. Had he touched Juliette like this, he'd be fired on the spot. She assumed he would be, anyway, hence the histrionics. Not that they would dissuade—

"What in the hell and damnation is going on here? Michel, you absolute jackass, come with me!"

Thundering through the storm of crying, screaming, and whining, a booming voice settled everyone. Because no matter the theatrics, Michel, for all the blood, tears, and howls, could not fool Francesca Bianchi. The fearsome and no-nonsense director of the Parisian ballet company had one hand on his wrist, dragging him to the side of the studio.

With everyone focused on the squealing Michel and the cursing-in-three-different-languages Francesca, Juliette braced herself and finally took Katarina Vyatka in.

She felt like the bracing was very much warranted. Because the sight was sublime. Katarina Vyatka watched the kerfuffle around her with a slight smile.

Juliette almost gasped. Talk about the unfairness of the universe. She was certain that whichever divinity had created this woman, they must've had a really good day all those thirty-something years ago. In fact, when they were done putting the final touches on that ethereal face, said divinity must've wanted to show off, imprinting the decisively unfair dimples on those chiseled features.

The dimples were an astonishing surprise, and then just as suddenly as they had appeared, they were gone as the Bolshoi prima's face went impassive and then completely expressionless. Marble statues a block away in the Louvre displayed more feeling.

It was like watching pencil being erased off paper, except the effect was instant. From mild amusement, barely noticeable unless one was paying close attention, to abject nothing.

As the smile disappeared off the angular, pale face, in the depths of the stark emptiness Juliette gleaned an emotion that she herself had never known. Oh, she recognized it when she saw it, but she was far too blessed and sheltered by her privilege and status to ever experience this kind of fear.

And it was fear. A glimpse of terror that etched into Juliette's imagination even deeper than Vyatka's hand had marked Michel's cheek. Juliette wanted to cross her arms around her chest, to contain the shock of it. Instead, she took a deep breath and followed Vyatka's eyes to the source of the dread.

A man in a wrinkled brown suit was walking up from the corner of the rehearsal room. He was so visually nondescript that Juliette didn't even wonder she hadn't noticed him before. Yet, once his presence was anything but insignificant, she couldn't quite look directly at him. A visceral reaction of distaste overwhelmed her.

A hideous little man with a very shrill voice in an ill-fitting boxy suit. So very out of place in the airy, high-ceilinged space of the studio among these graceful, sculpted bodies in ivory tulle and satin.

"Madame Bianchi, allow me to apologize on behalf of my comrade. Mademoiselle Vyatka is unused to such elevated company, being a simple working-class woman, and so she is unaccustomed to attention from sophisticated gentlemen."

Without waiting for a reply, the man grabbed Vyatka's elbow and escorted her to the far corner of the classroom where he proceeded to speak to her in an animated whisper. The prima must have been exceptional at poker, because after the initial imprint of fear, her face remained impassive as anger and spittle flew her way. Juliette felt nauseated.

"Ouch!" Gabriel's voice was faintly amused and a little sleepy next to her ear. "I mean, she's been nothing but rude and standoffish with everyone since she arrived. And she drew blood for a grope, so talk about an overreaction. But whoever this suit is, he really didn't need to humiliate her like this. Good thing she doesn't speak English, otherwise I bet Vyatka would have his head, just as she had Michel's cheek."

Any other day, Juliette might have agreed with him that the slap was perhaps an overreaction, if undoubtedly justified, and the subsequent discreet smile of clear enjoyment of putting the fool in his place spoke volumes. But the humiliation she had just witnessed was so completely out of place.

Working class? Vyatka was the modern-day Michelangelo of ballet, and in Juliette's world, Michelangelo behaved the way Michelangelo wanted to—as long as he drew and sculpted the way he did. Yet here was this little man, in his brown suit…

Gabriel yawned. "Did I tell you, rumor has it she killed some unfortunate prima in Moscow?" Juliette turned to him so sharply, he chuckled. "My darlin' girl, you are so easy. So maybe not killed, but you know the Bolshoi gossip is always so damn cutthroat. She was third in line for the main prima title. One of the other primas ended up maimed, and the other—pregnant. I'm almost certain Vyatka is not responsible for the latter. Though, look at her. If anyone could, it would be her." Gabriel shrugged and Juliette had to suppress a shiver. Yes, if anyone could manage such a feat, it would indeed be this woman.

Gabriel yawned again and went on. "You know how it goes with rumors. The tongues wagged about her injuring the first one. Badly." He sobered up, and the second shiver Juliette felt was of a different nature. Gabriel seemed to not notice either of her reactions as he leaned against the wall and continued.

"They hushed it up. She's the commies' darlin', some rags-to-riches sob story there. The reviews and the gossip from Bolshoi's London performance last month are raving. The Empress of Moscow is everything they said she would be. Perhaps more. Maybe that explains the bloodthirst. Still, it does not excuse whatever this fool, this insult to fashion, thought he was doing."

Juliette ventured an attempt at more details, though why she'd want them escaped her. "Well, you know how Russians are."

Gabriel shook his head. "But she's not. Someone mentioned the other day that even her first and last names aren't Russian. I don't remember exactly, but I think she's from one of those Baltic countries. And you can't expect me to actually differentiate those three socialist republics at this hour."

She wanted to berate him for the lack of respect given to the Baltic states, but Gabriel's jaw almost creaked as he yawned again. Lecture abandoned, Juliette gave him a thorough once-over. Her best friend and confidant, her ballet partner of seven years, Gabriel Flanagan looked tired. With the season not having yet started and their own tour over weeks ago, the sleepiness in his eyes told her that the exhaustion was not related to dancing. Or not the ballet kind of dancing.

"I take it you had a long night?"

Gabriel laughed, happy and carefree, throwing his blond hair back, attracting attention from pretty much everybody in a ten-mile radius. He made the impossible look easy.

Tall, with broad shoulders, sculpted arms, and a bearing that was admired and envied by everyone he crossed paths with, he was a modern-day Apollo with his golden locks framing a face that was sinfully handsome.

As the principal dancer of the Paris Opera Ballet company, and with his unbelievably good looks, Gabriel could've been genuinely despised by quite a number of people. However, once they met him, they were charmed and disarmed. He was kind and gentle and should have been everything Juliette desired in a man—if only she desired men. She categorically did not, and so they had been inseparable friends since their school days.

"I wish I could tell you. A gentleman never does, though." Gabriel smiled brightly and a little too nonchalantly for Juliette's taste.

"I hope you were careful." She did not intend to infuse her voice with concern, but every day the rumor mill brought more and more distressing news from their male acquaintances near and far.

The smile stayed on the striking face, but Juliette knew her words registered as the light in those brilliant eyes dimmed slightly.

"I've known him for years, and I was as careful as I could've been. Jett, if I can't trust this man, I can trust no one."

He was quiet for a moment, and they watched as the Soviet dancers arranged themselves for the next movement of the rehearsal.

Instantly forgetting Gabriel, Juliette felt a chill running through her. The Soviet prima had returned. The wrinkled suit followed her. That naked fear was back in the now-ashen depths of Vyatka's eyes.

And despite being surrounded by a crowd, amidst the whispers and the gossip, for some reason Juliette's hands itched to wipe away the out-of-place emotion from the marble features. She shivered again, and Gabriel took off his lopsided knitted sweater, draping it carelessly over her shoulders, the gesture practiced and cherished. But this time it was too practiced. A bit too deliberately kind.

"The hallways are always drafty, darlin'." At her narrowed look, he just waved his elegant hand at her. "Please don't worry about me, Mom, I know what I'm doing."

Juliette smiled up at him at their inside joke, and they shared a moment like so many others in the past seven years since both of them landed in Paris from the London Royal Ballet where they had studied together.

They had both been too talented and their futures had been too bright to be held back in the corps de ballet or to even dance solos behind the well-established English principal dancers, and so when Paris had called, they'd answered in the blink of an eye.

Juliette had been reigning for seven years as the biggest talent the Paris stage had seen, earning her the title of "Princess of Paris." She had never fully embraced the adulation. It lay awkwardly on her shoulders. All that glitter. All that ass-kissing.

And maybe the past few years had been a touch darker, the luster of gold dulled by the string of failures the company's productions had faced, but Juliette felt her crown and her throne were secure. So why was she shivering in the doorway of the studio, wrapped in Gabriel's sweater, watching the Empress of Moscow with such trepidation?

A question for another time, perhaps. Juliette tightened the familiar-smelling wool around herself and allowed her mind to take in the ongoing rehearsal.

Saying that the Bolshoi company was very good was an understatement of grandiose proportions. The Soviet ballet was magnificent. That wasn't a surprise, as the dancers were drilled from very early childhood. Their discipline and methods rivaled military schools. What was a surprise, however, was that the main star, the principal attraction of the entire company, looked and acted unlike anyone in the crowd surrounding her.

Juliette had expected to see perfect movement, skill, and precision. Those things would be par for the course. She hadn't expected this level of vulnerability.

On the other hand, as Gabriel kept pointing out to her, maybe it wasn't vulnerability at all. Perhaps Vyatka was simply arrogant and unpleasant, and Juliette was ascribing her own feelings to the Soviet prima.

She certainly often felt vulnerable in the crowd. They didn't teach you in ballet boarding schools what happened when you attained your dreams. They didn't teach you that once you became the star, people would be covetous of every aspect of your life. They didn't teach you that everybody around you would have an agenda. They didn't teach you to be aware that nobody was your friend once you reached these heights.

Betrayal made one distant, standoffish. And as Juliette's eyes followed the Soviet prima around the room, observing the small mannerisms, the near disgust she showed every time anyone so much as came close to her, Juliette thought that perhaps Vyatka was, indeed, just arrogant. Nothing wrong with that.

And then, despite watching, despite paying attention to every move of the pale limbs in front of her, Juliette almost missed the jump.

While she had been woolgathering, the company had warmed up to move past the adagio stage, and Katarina Vyatka was performing grands jetés. A pin would have dropped with more sound. The big jumps, as they were known, were technically complex. The extension of the legs in a perfect split, the grace of the arms, and the famous landing. One of the most complicated parts of the movement—the landing—should be quiet. In Katarina Vyatka's case, it was entirely soundless. Juliette's breath caught in her chest. Next to her she could sense Gabriel's jaw drop.

The boards trembled ever so slightly under Juliette's own feet, but other than that, nothing. How was it even possible? Surely, the laws of physics… Her thoughts running haywire at what she was witnessing in the complete silence of the room, Juliette caught the ice-blue gaze on her as the Soviet prima was in mid-jump, and her heart stopped for just a moment. Something… Something in that look, in those eyes—

"I'll be damned, Jett!" Gabriel's whisper contained so much hungover admiration, Juliette smiled. One thing about her partner, she'd never met a dancer less full of himself, so quick to praise those around him. "I didn't think I'd ever say this, but she just might be better than you are at this, darlin'."

Well, that was a bit much, even for him. But he wasn't wrong. Juliette's jumps were a standard-bearing feat in their industry, but even she could be heard on her first alighting.

Gabriel ducked, expecting her to smack him, but she could not tear her eyes off the scene in front of her. Vyatka was in full flight now, and the boards creaked slightly with every subsequent landing as her jumps gained speed and power.

It happened when Vyatka wrapped up her routine. Juliette was distracted, still tangled up in her thoughts, when the révérence was executed. The showy bowing sequence was one of the least important movements, one that was almost an afterthought, and yet it caught her eye. In fact, it slashed across her consciousness with the blunt force of a wrecking ball.

Wrong, was all she could think. Katarina Vyatka's révérence was technically incorrect and quite obviously eliciting some amount of pain to the prima. The head was bowed at an unnatural angle, a flaw so stirringly obvious yet strangely ignored by everyone around them. Juliette tensed, her entire being demanding that she rush forward and correct the stance that was surely causing discomfort.

Damn, she looks in pain…

Gabriel's hand squeezed her shoulder for just a second, dragging her back to reality. Belatedly, Juliette realized that she had not managed to keep her thoughts to herself and had broken the decree of never addressing the Empress of Moscow, who, now standing tall once again with no sign of any discomfort, was glaring at her with what looked to be hate in her cold, lifeless eyes.

Two

Of Ruined Bows & Traded Blows

*I*n the thundering silence that followed, Juliette felt as if she had been lifted to a scaffold. All eyes were on her, including the slicing ice-blue ones that held palpable weight. No wonder this woman never spoke. If she inflicted this much damage with her eyes alone, Juliette shuddered to imagine what she could do with words.

They held each other's gaze for a second longer, Juliette putting all her courage on the line, biting her lip and raising a hand to her chest, desperate to atone for her hasty remark and a rather boneheaded mistake. One never commented on another dancer's form or injury. It simply wasn't done. What had possessed her to speculate about Vyatka's pain out loud?

Juliette, however, knew what it was that had taken over her mind and, subsequently, her mouth. For years she had dedicated what little free time she had to working with injured dancers, correcting their form to ensure they'd bounce back to painless performances. And Katarina Vyatka's form had been off. Juliette's trained eye had caught the slight variation in the movement. She was perhaps the only individual in the room who could see it, but see it she did. A few degrees off perfection , the révérence had been spectacular, but Juliette could swear it had been painful.

Was it the desire to help? Or the hope to prove Katarina Vyatka had not been perfect?

What a notion!

Gabriel's earlier remark about the Soviet prima being better than Juliette had her dander up, but surely not to this extent. Then it occurred to Juliette that despite being contemporaries for almost a decade, they had never been compared to each other. Not even in Moscow and Leningrad during Paris Opera Ballet tours. It was said that they were too different.

The instructor demanded the jumps be demonstrated again, and the dancers took their places with the prima setting up in the middle of the room. The piano soared, and so did Katarina Vyatka. As she aced another perfect landing, Juliette could feel her heart beat in rhythm with the movement, earlier embarrassment set aside.

Yes, they were indeed too different—in style, in deportment, in looks. And yet, her own chest was rising and falling as if they were jumping in parallel, Juliette knew the dancer she was watching more than matched her. After all, an empress was a couple of rungs above a princess.

She shivered again, suddenly feeling the cold sweat on her back. With one last look at the tall, magnificent figure, Juliette turned and stepped away from the rehearsal studio.

The draft was getting under her skin and so was this ballerina. Juliette's mistake aside—and that was embarrassing enough to never want to face the Bolshoi prima—there was something about Vyatka, and the immense talent was only half of it. Sure, a rather obvious and impressive half, but…

The fear. That caged-animal look was so out of place on a woman who owned the world. Or at least her part of the world behind the Iron Curtain. Why did it tug at Juliette's thoughts? Why was it making her curious? And was it curiosity? Or was it something that Juliette refused to acknowledge as being anything but what it really was?

She shook her head. Sure, Juliette had always had an eye for beautiful women. And while this one was among the most beautiful she had ever seen, Juliette also had the brains to know when to leave well enough alone. Especially after her blunder. Katarina Vyatka came not just with her own red flag—an actual one—but with a political quagmire in the form of KGB agents following her every step.

No, it wasn't the austere beauty. Juliette could and did have any attractive woman she wished. It was the terror behind it, an emotion so incongruous with anything a prima should have felt. This emotion made Katarina Vyatka not just a beautiful and talented dancer. It made her a mystery—

"You're not serious, darlin'."

She had completely forgotten about Gabriel, who was observing her very closely, his eyes sparkling with mischief.

Juliette turned away from him and made her way down the corridor and into one of the smaller rehearsal rooms. It was time for her own stretches and to get ready for a day of planning the season ahead of them.

"I have no idea what you're talking about."

He fell in stride with her, and once the door closed behind them, he leaned back against it, arms crossed over his broad chest, a bemused smirk on his face.

"Gabriel…" She sighed. "Don't even start. It's not what you think. There is just something about her."

The smirk was gone, and he narrowed his eyes, suddenly solemn.

"Sure, darlin', there's a lot about her. There's the five foot ten—to put it in measurements your Yankee and my Irish selves understand—of supreme specimen among goddesses. I don't think I've ever seen anyone built that way. And I don't think anyone in my presence ever landed a jump with no sound. No offense, Jett."

Juliette scoffed and waved him away, "None taken, and you

might be right, though I am not ready to admit all that just yet. Still, it wasn't the jump. Nor the fact that she is indeed gorgeous. If you're into cold, distant, arrogant older women. I just think I saw something."

"Well, I am not into either cold, or distant, or arrogant, or women, but I know one particular prima who is. A good friend of mine. You might know of her? The Princess of Paris?" Juliette swatted at his shoulder, and he ducked away, laughing. When he stopped, he eyed her closely. "And what about this *something*? Is that why you made such an uncharacteristic blunder? Even you know better than to say stuff like that out loud, darlin'."

Juliette tsked and turned away from him, only to be hoisted off her feet and tickled.

"I will use every advantage I have on you, Jett! You may be the smart and skilled one, but I am stronger and prettier." Gabriel smiled and held her tight till her own fit of giggles subsided. He could always make her laugh.

When he finally put her down, she glanced at him in the mirror as they stood side by side. They looked good together. Better than good. The yellow gossip magazines—and some of the not-so-yellow ones—kept pairing them up. The rich donors and those who didn't know them very well asked if they were planning for children. No, they had no plans and why would they, a lesbian and a gay man? Not that their closets were even that tightly shut. In the homophobic world of the eighties, their profession blessed them with a freedom rarely attained these days.

But he was her best friend. And he knew her better than anyone else. So of course he'd seen through her, of course he'd read her. Because he was just so very good and so very perceptive. Which made him lovely but also occasionally inconvenient when Juliette wanted to keep some things to herself.

"Are you all right?"

Yes, very perceptive. And very inconvenient. She wasn't

ready to confess to anything regarding the Soviet prima and the sense of premonition that was like the cold sweat on her back, distracting and ominous. Hence, a diversion was in order.

"Helena called."

"Ah." His hands gently squeezed her shoulders in a gesture that had become familiar between them, comfort given and comfort taken. "I miss her too."

Juliette tended to forget that Gabriel and Helena had been close and that losing her ex-lover had been hard not only on her, but on her best friend as well. She patted his warm hands before stepping away.

"I don't know why she still calls."

It wasn't necessarily a lie. She had been with Helena for three years. The loss was no longer as acute as twelve months ago when they had said their goodbyes. It had been Helena's choice to say those goodbyes in the first place, so why was she the one still calling?

"I have this tiny little hunch that she didn't really believe you wouldn't follow her, Juju."

The use of her childhood nickname meant Gabriel was being gentle with her. She lifted her face to meet his gaze, and yes, the radiant green was tinged with a tenderness that made her own eyes sting. Which only angered her.

"I feel like you should have been the one to leave everything behind and move to New York with her, Gabriel. The way you have been carrying on since she left."

She softened the blow by cloaking the words as a joke. But even she heard the slight whip of viciousness in her own voice. Still, he smiled.

"I'm not the lonely one, darlin'. You are. Lonely and wounded by Paris."

Before she could find the words to slap him all the way back to Belfast, he was gone, leaving the door to her rehearsal room ajar in his haste. Well, one thing he always did know was that her wrath wasn't one to be trifled with, especially not when he'd hit a very painful spot.

And painful spot be damned! She was the Prima Ballerina Assoluta desired by every company, and her options and her calling card were full to the brim. Her title, one of the handful of such honors in the entire world, had been bestowed by the French Government. A unique distinction for a foreign ballerina in Paris. In Europe, in fact. A Prima Assoluta was usually someone local, someone of their own. Juliette was very much an alien among Parisians, and yet she had cemented her place. She needed no one, least of all her ex, who had scampered to New York and who had also had the audacity to believe that Juliette Lucian-Sorel would meekly follow her. Juliette Lucian-Sorel followed no one. She led. Ballets, companies, productions, partners, dances. No, Dr. Helena Moore knew better. Or should have known—

A commotion in the hallway drew her out of her indignant thoughts. Someone was running, fast, but the sound was that of pointe shoes. What kind of fool would run in those? One wrong step would cause a twisted—or worse, broken—ankle.

Juliette was by the studio entrance in an instant, but it was the second set of footfalls that stopped her in her tracks. Heavy, definitely not those of a dancer. This second runner was faster, and when a litany of Russian erupted just outside of the door, Juliette flinched. The woman was clearly distraught, though her tone was quiet and Juliette could not distinguish any individual words. The male voice was loud and cutting, angry to the point of enraged, and it sounded frightening.

"Nyet!"

Even with her very limited understanding of Russian, Juliette knew this one. *No.* She was out in the hallway like a bullet. The wrinkled brown suit had his arm raised, ready to strike, and Katarina Vyatka's eyes were huge, the blue completely enveloped by the black of the pupil.

Juliette straightened to her full height. She matched the Soviet ballerina and towered over the suit. When she spoke, she deliberately lowered her voice to make him strain to hear.

"I assume you were about to remove that speck of lint from Mademoiselle Vyatka's shoulder, Mister…"

She let the lack of name dangle and demonstratively reached out to beat him to the imaginary grain of dust on the black sleeve of the leotard. A subtle scent of orange blossom perfume reached back, momentarily hypnotizing her senses with the sweetness that felt both perfectly fitting and entirely out of place for this woman. Juliette almost staggered back with the surprise of the effect such a simple scent had on her. What hadn't surprised her was Vyatka flinching under her cursory touch. Juliette had insulted her earlier, even if she doubted the Soviet prima understood her words, but being interrupted during her practice was bad enough and now the touching—

"It's Ivanov." His anger did not dissipate as he sneered and bit the name out, spittle flying. Juliette did not recoil, but it was a close call.

"Of course it is. Next thing you'll tell me your first name is Ivan." She offered him one of her fakest, meanest smiles. He smiled back, just as fake, though his wobbled a touch at the corners, clearly uneasy at being caught in the act. Then, as if a veil had lifted, his eyes cleared of the rage and he changed tack.

"How did you know?" His loud, out-of-place laughter echoed in the narrow bowels of the Palais Garnier.

"Lucky guess. Now, Mademoiselle Vyatka here doesn't seem to require any more of your kind and generous help—"

"On the contrary. Do not trouble yourself. She is my ward, you see, and it is my duty to make sure nothing bad happens to her. France is a dangerous place. All these sexual deviants…"

This time his smile was sly, knowing, slimy, and Juliette wanted a shower. Her sexuality had never been a secret, but to have it thrown in her face like this was jarring, to say the least.

She took a step closer, her anger, which she so rarely allowed to gain the upper hand, taking over.

A quiet voice from her right interrupted whatever clearly foolish thing she was about to profess. To her absolute astonishment, Vyatka opened her mouth and actual sounds came out. Juliette was at first taken aback and then miffed at herself for being startled. Of course Katarina Vyatka could speak. Juliette's earlier assertion of her being shrouded in silence was just that, a fanciful assertion, so why did the low sound have such an earth-shattering effect on her?

Juliette was still staring when, after a few words in Russian and a shake of her head, Vyatka left, graceful steps taking her down the winding corridor and out of sight. The suit threw Juliette another lascivious look before attempting to follow, but not before spitting one last warning.

"You have no clue what you're getting in the middle of. Stay out of this. You have no power here."

Juliette watched him go too, his bulky shoulders encased in the ill-fitting garment filling the narrow corridor, giving it a claustrophobic feel. She did not return to the rehearsal room until his heavy steps stopped echoing between the walls of her dominion. As he turned to look at her before disappearing, Juliette inexplicably felt compelled to speak.

"You're wrong, Ivanov. I am the only one who has any true power here."

His widened eyes were her clue that every lie she intended as a blow, landed.

Three

Of Observed Vulnerability & Defections

"*I* look good in a tux."

Gabriel's forearm under her fingertips flexed as he preened a little. He did look good in anything, though, and Juliette rolled her eyes at his antics. He was also an admirable shield from adoring fans, peers, sponsors, and other assorted hoi polloi invited to a grand reception such as this one.

Gabriel drew the unwanted attention away and all Juliette had to do was offer a graceful nod or a barely there smile, which made him the perfect partner. After years of both dancing together and attending these sorts of events, they had the routine down to a T.

They made their rounds, Juliette repeatedly steering Gabriel away from the Bolshoi company, as she could feel the KGB agent's slimy gaze on her. There was no need to cause a scene, no matter how much she wanted to do so just to wipe that dirty smirk off his ugly, pockmarked face.

After speaking to a number of people and dropping Gabriel off with some of his opera friends, Juliette found herself drawn to the de facto host of the reception, the president of the Republic, whom she had met before and who, she knew, was a big fan of hers. She allowed him to offer her a glass of champagne and ply her with compliments and assurances that he and his wife would both attend every opening night this coming season, no matter the reviews. That last one set Juliette's teeth on edge.

Smile and nod, smile and nod.

And so she did, and he prattled on about the new productions that were going up on the company's roster. He knew what he was talking about—Juliette always gave him credit for that—and so her next fifteen minutes were not boring, despite them being regularly interrupted by the president's staff for "matters of the Republic." When she finally excused herself after a particularly long interruption, Juliette found the way he was so deeply disappointed adorable.

"I have to say, you have him entirely wrapped around your finger, Mademoiselle Sorel."

The manner of the man speaking to her was familiar, and Juliette took her time turning, giving herself a head start to place him. After a second, as the face came into focus, so did the position. The newly named Culture Minister. He was familiar because of his previously held title. They called him the "Budget Czar," and everyone feared him. His power of decision over government spending extended far and wide. Yet to Juliette, he had been just another man. One she hadn't liked at all. His use of her name—the wrong use, to be exact—cemented her opinion of him.

She pursed her lips and exhaled, counting to ten. Of all her battles, this one was tiresomely predictable.

"Lucian-Sorel. It might've meant nothing to my American parents, but I have learned that here in France, I'd rather avail myself of my full name, if only to avoid any Stendhal associations."

The minister smiled, a common reaction to a running joke Juliette had always used to her advantage. When she continued, she sensed him relaxing a fraction. "As for the president, the admiration is mutual." She refused to hide that she didn't know the minister's name. She'd been in Paris seven years, and these men came and went along with the Seine's water.

"The Soviet company are his honored guests and are here only because he personally made it happen, Mademoiselle Lucian-Sorel."

Even though his features were alight with good humor, she knew a warning when she heard one. What was it with men warning her off today? At least he deigned to use her proper name.

Juliette was certain the minister's focus on the word *honored* was quite deliberate. She kept her face impassive as he went on, clearly choosing his sentences carefully, his tall, thin frame storklike in both look and demeanor, all bony knees and assumed dominance. Too bad for him, Juliette didn't particularly care for birds.

"I watched you tonight, Mademoiselle Lucian-Sorel. You have hardly spoken two words to the distinguished guests. I'm sure some of them are quite displeased with your lack of warmth. After all, you are the face of Paris Opera Ballet. Surely after so many years in Paris, you've learned how to act according to your place in this city, and not as a touring American."

Ah, so the complaints of a brown wrinkled suit were not the reason she was getting a governmentally sanctioned scolding. This was a chastisement for not playing nice enough hostess.

Juliette set her jaw. She had been spoiling for a fight ever since the early morning. Wishes really did come true. And while she knew that the bulk of her anger lay with the owner of the shit-colored tweed, this perfectly tailored suit would have to do. He was providing her with an outlet for all that pent-up rage. She was getting tired of men telling her what to do.

"I assure you, Monsieur le Ministre Lalande, Juliette has been the soul of welcome to the dancers of the Bolshoi company."

Wishes be damned. Like a figment of her imagination, the voice interrupting an impending upbraiding of a French government stooge sounded absolutely disjoined from the body. And then, slowly, graceful despite the cane, Francesca Bianchi materialized at Juliette's side.

The Director of Paris Opera Ballet, once a distinguished ballerina in her own right, walked with the same aplomb she had used to glide over the floorboards of the stage. A torn meniscus and a botched surgery had ended the Argentinian's career quite prematurely, one of a series of events that, in turn, had ensured Juliette's place at Palais Garnier.

Now the esteemed Madame Bianchi ruled over them all, coming up with ways to balance the delicate politics of the main French ballet company and occasionally finding herself in Juliette's bed. Neither made a big deal out of either event. Francesca took her leadership over the dancers as a given and over the occasional night with Juliette as a fun diversion. Juliette chose not to dwell.

Except in moments like these, when Francesca was the cavalry over the hill. One that Juliette hadn't summoned. She didn't need protection, but it was nice to know that her back was well and truly covered, even when she was the one about to unleash the hounds of hell.

The man gave them both a long look, as if trying to figure out whether he was being dismissed or if Juliette had been firmly taken in hand. Perhaps seeing what he wanted to see, with a nod, he departed.

"Before you say anything to the contrary, amor, I could smell you getting ready to draw blood and was solely doing my custodial duty of overseeing the talent in my care."

Francesca pushed back the too-long fringe on her stylish pixie cut and gave Juliette an appraising gaze. When she spoke again, her voice lowered into a whisper.

"Lalande is irrelevant. He likes to think he controls access to the president when it comes to arts, and that is neither true nor important. What is concerning to me is your morning adventure into saviorhood. The KGB people, or as they like to call themselves, 'administrative officers for the Bolshoi troupe,' have expressed their displeasure with your behavior."

Juliette bit her lip to hide the smile that was trying to break through. So she *had* made an impression on the miserable little man, and he had run tattling to Palais Garnier leadership. Coward.

"Sadly, not even a magician like you can have it both ways, Cesca." She infused her voice with as much sincerity as she could. No, Francesca wasn't buying it, but they both enjoyed the game. "You can't have me play nice and be welcoming to our guests and, at the same time, not displease the suits. I fear my mere presence is displeasing enough to them. A woman existing independently of their rule is an insult to them."

It was Francesca's turn to bite on her inner cheek, eyes full of mirth.

"Oh yes, because being hospitable and minding your own business usually don't go hand in hand for you, amor. You're a troublemaker, and you know it. Angelic face and all this black Lucifer hair make you even more of an alluring little devil, Jett. You have always been trouble. It's one of the many reasons why the public adores you. You get away with anything. Everything, really."

The compliment should have pleased her, yet it scratched at an old wound, the scab still occasionally tender. Juliette was usually much more careful not to rip it open again, as the blood was rather difficult to get out of the gauze and chiffon of tutus and leotards.

"The public appreciates me because I'm exceptional at my job, Francesca." She tried to sidestep the oodles of failures that had marked both their careers in the past few years before realizing that her voice had slipped into that tone—the low, dangerous one—and she brought herself back to the present. The wounds, old and new, would have to wait.

"As for our esteemed, poorly dressed guests"—she allowed sarcasm to slip in—"and I mean 'esteemed' in the broadest of ways, so broad in fact that I leave no trace of any kind of real respect in that term…" She drew a breath, trying to calm her unexpectedly racing heart. Why was she getting so unnerved by this? "Cesca, you'd have done the same thing. He was manhandling her, and I wasn't going to stand by while a woman was being abused five steps away from my rehearsing room."

Francesca made a face, one that spoke of being torn and thoroughly disgusted. Then she closed her eyes and her shoulders drooped.

"You can't get involved, Jett. Neither of us can. The issues surrounding Vyatka, Bolshoi, and KGB are so above any of our pay grades, they might as well be in the stratosphere. With Rodion Foltin defecting in London two summers ago, Bolshoi is under tremendous pressure to not lose another principal dancer."

Juliette gritted her teeth but allowed Francesca to continue.

"They will be gone tomorrow, amor. And I will drink an entire bottle of chianti to celebrate never seeing them again. I call you a troublemaker, but this guest visit has been nothing but trouble to us as hosts. Not even my Prima Assoluta has ever caused me this much headache."

She smiled to take the tiny sting out of the joke, and Juliette found herself vacillating between wanting to retreat into her usual indifference and actually caring and respecting this woman—and not just because they chose to share a bed on occasion. In the end, she allowed herself to extend a hand and give Francesca's forearm a gentle pat.

"You look tired." At least she could still be truthful in some matters with Francesca. The past two weeks had clearly been brutal, and they showed in the faint lines on the face Juliette knew so well. Eighteen years her senior, Francesca was gorgeous, tired or not.

"I need sleep. I might need you, too. Though I heard from

the grapevine that Helena has been calling, and I will not add more lesbian drama to your plate."

Well, Francesca had always been very direct. And Gabriel had always had a big mouth.

"Oh, don't blame the boy, he worries about you."

"Why is it that he gets to be a boy, and I get to be the troublemaker? We're both twenty-five." Juliette raised her chin higher and turned away from Francesca, who chuckled behind her.

"I know you hate the title, but you are the Princess of Paris, amor. They don't call you that for nothing. And he never got to be crowned as Prince. The press merely calls him 'the Irishman.' So I get to remind both of you of your places and of the ways of this ballet company."

With a thin smile even she knew was not sincere, Juliette left Francesca to her nicknames and gossip.

For the next hour, she managed to be the soul of the party. She talked to people, schmoozed the important ones, and stayed away from the Bolshoi company without being a cold fish. Still, it was getting late, and she had done more than enough to assuage any of her detractors.

There. Mission accomplished.

Juliette thought of her cozy apartment on Rue de Rivoli, warm from the evening sun slipping through the massive windows overlooking the Tuileries Gardens. She would kick off her high heels and pour herself two fingers of Aberlour.

With one last look around, Juliette turned to go, only for a gaggle of Bolshoi ballerinas to catch her eye, giggling and pointing in the direction of the balcony. They were looking at Gabriel, who was busy charming one of the soloists. Of course he was. Despite not being attracted to them, he had a good eye for women. The Russian was beautiful. Not a match for Katarina Vyatka, but then there probably weren't many who were. Juliette was quite grateful for that.

She tried not to think about the prima. Or the vulnerability she kept witnessing in those massive eyes. How sad and lonely they looked when Vyatka thought nobody was watching. And how angry they were when they met Juliette's. But sad or angry, they tugged at something in Juliette, some kind of recognition that she desperately tried to ignore.

And speaking of sadness, something tickled the back of her neck, like a feather, tender yet inescapable, and Juliette couldn't resist turning, her own gaze running smack into the ice-blue eyes she kept telling herself she was not thinking about.

Vyatka was alone, standing in the corner, her long, slim fingers wrapped around a champagne flute that appeared thoroughly flat. Her knuckles white, her lips in a thin line, and her chin raised, she had an air about her that Juliette recognized all too well—the "leave me alone" vibe where any and all approach would be immediately prevented. She looked tense, a sprinter preparing for the starting gun. And something in that steady dark glare pulled at Juliette yet again.

Time stood still for a moment, as did they, and then suddenly, like a thread tangled and knotted, their connection became taut. Juliette had a feeling that if she were to turn and run, that thread would pull, tearing flesh with it.

The image was rather gruesome, and Juliette almost rolled her eyes at her own foolishness. Except she couldn't, not really. Not when the tug of the thread was so real, just as real as their eyes steadily looking at each other.

A large group of guests passed between them, and by the time the last straggler moved along, Vyatka was gone, the lonely flat flute of champagne on the sideboard the only piece of evidence left behind.

Finally free, Juliette did roll her eyes. She was acting out of character. And she'd had enough of being on display. Juliette passed her own flute to the closest server before making her way toward the side exit. There would be photographers outside, and she had already run the gamut of them on her way in.

It would not do to appear to leave alone when she had arrived with Gabriel. They weren't in the business of fooling anyone; those who wanted to look closer would easily see that both of them were quite queer. Americans detested the word, but Juliette had not been an American in over twenty years, since her parents put her on the plane to London, and so she quite enjoyed shocking everyone by using it blatantly.

Loud laughter sounded behind her, and she turned her head to stare at whoever was making a spectacle of themselves. The next thing she knew, in her forward motion toward the door, she had collided rather painfully with someone, knocking knees and shoulders.

The wide eyes were familiar, since Juliette kept telling herself she wasn't thinking of them at all, and the scent, the clean, subtle yet unmistakable perfume, the same orange blossom from earlier, was unmistakable.

She had her hands full of Katarina Vyatka. Now that was a sentence Juliette had never believed she'd be able to put together in her thoughts, yet here she was.

Except, the silent, arrogant, brilliant, and unapproachable prima was shivering in her arms. Juliette was quick enough to find her footing despite holding double the weight, and, as she was ready to let go, she squeezed the other woman's shoulders for encouragement to do the same. But Vyatka only held tighter, clinging to her for a long moment before Juliette felt more than heard the deep inhalation.

The image of a sprinter getting ready for the start of the race popped into her mind again, and just as she was about to ask if she could help in any way, Katarina exhaled and then, in very clear, perfect if quiet English, without the barest of accents, uttered four words.

"I wish to defect."

Four

Of Reckless Deals & Promises Made

In the immediate aftermath of the collision, several things became clear to Juliette. First, Katarina Vyatka had been gearing up for the race of a lifetime, because as Juliette tugged her along the winding corridors of Palais Garnier, she kept up with the ease and poise of a seasoned runaway. No hesitation, no sign of regret. The hand in Juliette's was warm, steady, and slightly callused from the barre. It didn't shake, and its owner no longer trembled.

Second, Juliette remembered her earlier thought and Francesca's decree that she couldn't get involved. Well, the evening had proven them both wrong. Hearing Vyatka's plea, there was no force in either the known or unknown universe that would have stopped Juliette from gently untangling their gowns and proclaiming loudly that they needed to go to the bathroom and set themselves to rights after Juliette's unexpected and uncharacteristic clumsiness. That she led them instead past the bathrooms and through the labyrinth of hallways, away from the pursuing crowd of brown rumpled suits, was the logical choice, given their predicament.

The office of the Director of Paris Opera Ballet, ensconced on the third floor in the deep bowels of the Palais Garnier building, became their sanctuary. And it was in this sanctuary that they faced the first consequences of their escape.

"You did what?"

Francesca's voice rose to a shrill. Cane in hand, she was breathing heavily, having been summoned hastily by a member of the corps Juliette had managed to snag from the party before they left and sent after Francesca under orders to come urgently to her own office.

"Your assumption is incorrect, Madame Bianchi, Mademoiselle Lucian-Sorel didn't, actually, do anything at all."

Juliette and Francesca both turned to gawk at the deadly calm, if a bit paler than usual, Vyatka, who was sitting regally—a queen receiving peasants—in the director's chair, speaking in that utterly unnerving low, cultured, slightly gravelly voice.

Was it that Juliette was still coming to terms with the fact that the Soviet prima could speak? Or was it the perfect American English, down to the absolute lack of any kind of geographically placeable accent? Just textbook. Juliette blinked and saw Francesca shake her head as if to ascertain she was indeed hearing the Empress of Moscow utter words. Then Francesca propped the cane against her desk and settled unceremoniously on top of it with a whisper of an *oof*.

"I have to preface this with an apology, Mademoiselle Vyatka, and I am sorry, but we will deal with you in due time." The clipped tone and the blazing eyes she turned to Juliette told her that there would be no apologies to preface what was coming her way. Francesca inhaled deeply and then unleashed her infamous temper.

"I am speaking to my current Prima Assoluta, my Étoile, who was under the strictest orders to stay away from you and your entire godforsaken company!"

Shrill no longer covered the volume of Francesca's screaming.

"Cesca—" Juliette cursed under her breath at being interrupted, as Francesca was having none of it and simply barreled over her protestations.

"Don't you dare, Jett! You think because we sleep together

you can pull stunts like this, well, let me tell you—"

Vyatka raised an impeccable eyebrow at the intimate confession, but before Juliette could prevent further details of her life being disclosed, it was Francesca's turn to curse at the interruption as the door to her already crowded office opened and Lalande stepped in, equally thunderous.

"I assume the word on the street is correct? Katarina Vyatka attempted a defection?" His brow was furrowed, and he seemed to want to be anywhere but the space and the situation he was finding himself in.

"The president sent me to handle the incident. This is embarrassing on so many levels. He guaranteed that nothing of this sort would occur in Paris. He personally promised the Soviets."

From the corner of her eye, Juliette could see Vyatka's already impassive face turn to stone. The massive eyes filled with sheer resolve and stubbornness. Juliette expected her to speak. To scream. To argue. To defend herself. For goodness' sake, to ask how dare all these people treat her as if she was a mere commodity, an object. God, to demand to be treated as a ballerina of her stature deserved to be, Soviet or not.

But then, just like in the rehearsal room, something appeared to have suddenly broken inside her, as if a doll had ruptured the string pulled to make her dance. Vyatka sat immobile and silent, eyes dry and empty. All signs of stubbornness from seconds ago, gone. She was the unfeeling statue once again.

The starkness of the transformation was physically painful to witness, and Juliette remembered the third thing about tonight.

She had been ready to take on the world ever since a slew of insignificant men deemed themselves worthy to either berate her or tell her what to do. And here was her brawl. She had not chosen it. In fact, she'd done everything to avoid this situation. But the vision in front of her, the brilliant, talented, oh-so-alive woman transformed into a colorless, lifeless version of herself, a mannequin for all intents and purposes, because the worthless men were deciding her fate yet again.

Well, then... Here we go.

"I wish to speak to the president."

Both Lalande and Francesca turned to her, their faces comically different in their expressions—the latter a picture of resignation, and the former of pure disbelief.

"You think you can convince him, don't you?" Lalande's expression was slowly turning into the same powerless one Francesca was sporting.

"I will try. I witnessed the abuse this woman was forced to endure, and while you can sleep just fine at night knowing that you could do something but didn't, I chose differently. I chose to try."

She took a step closer to Vyatka, subconsciously positioning herself between the ballerina and the rest of the world. This was foolish. And dramatic. Juliette had no idea what she was doing, not a single clue of what kind of mess she was getting herself involved in. If anything, the faces of Francesca and Lalande should've been a strong enough deterrent. But Juliette never had much good judgment when it came to being bullied into submission. Even if submission was the correct way to proceed.

Her very American upbringing of never letting bullies win was deeply ingrained. Moreover, she just really disliked these people. Sticking it to Ivanov and his KGB cronies while helping this woman? A bonus, in her mind.

"You think I'm unfeeling." Lalande, obviously defeated now, paced back and forth in the confines of the office.

"I think you don't want to have more on your plate than you already do. And I think you detest that I am a woman wielding considerable influence."

He shook his head, but before he could answer, Juliette simply spoke over him.

"I will spare you the trouble of going to the president. I

will take all responsibility. But I will not stand idly by. And you won't stop me."

Francesca clambered down from her desk, but Juliette wanted none of her lecturing either. It was time to change her strategy. Threats were only mildly successful. Promises might be a different story.

"Think of the headlines, and think what a coup this would be for the Paris Opera Ballet. If nothing else, think of what this could mean for this company."

As Francesca's eyes turned just a touch avaricious, Juliette knew she had landed a blow to the opposition and gained an ally. Nothing fired up Francesca Bianchi more than the betterment of her company. And scoring a hit like Katarina Vyatka, the greatest Russian dancer since Maya Plisetskaya, was the chance of a lifetime. Especially in the times they were weathering.

"Would the two of you stop scheming and just consider that this is an international scandal? The Brits are still being smacked around by the fallout from Foltin's defection!"

Juliette waved him away.

"That's for you to deal with, Monsieur Lalande. For you and for the little men like you. And then, when all is said and done and taken care of, you will sit in the parterre and watch the new *Swan Lake*, or whatever production Francesca deems suitable, and give a standing ovation from the president's right. Because it will be amazing, a once-in-a-lifetime show."

Juliette took a breath and gave him a direct look, their eyes meeting, and she knew she had won.

"The ovations, Monsieur Lalande. It's what I do. My specialty, if you will. Now it's your turn. What is it that you do exactly?"

He ground his teeth loudly, the muscles in his jawline working as he glared at her. Then he stormed out of the office.

Juliette had a distinct feeling she had pushed just a bit too hard. Oh well. She would not have gained him as a friend anyway. She didn't need him as her friend. She needed him to make sure her demands were met, no more and no less, friendships be damned.

In the end, Juliette didn't have to speak to the president. Lalande came through. The Bolshoi people were incensed, the fallout was immense. Enormous. Whatever measurement came after those to signify how absolutely, terrifyingly, and exhilaratingly big the size of the outcry was.

Juliette reveled in it. Quietly. She and Vyatka sat for hours in Francesca's office, which was now under guard of several officers of the French police, and waited. They didn't speak. Juliette had learned early, in the noise box that was her London boarding school, that quiet was a treasure, and Vyatka seemed made for silences.

She stared at nothing, moved very little, and if not for her very stillness, Juliette would have felt completely alone in the confines of the small space.

In contrast, Francesca was a whirlwind of motion, words and gestures every time she came in to relay messages, bring water, and give updates.

"The Soviets are enraged."

The blonde, perfectly groomed eyebrow arched up again, a gesture so immaculately fitting to the occasion Juliette wanted to admire it for a few hours. She almost asked Vyatka to do it one more time before she caught herself and quickly turned to Francesca to avoid further embarrassment.

"Of course they are. Let them be enraged. They can't do anything about this anymore. It is entirely out of their hands."

Juliette could hear the calmness in her own voice even if she wasn't exactly feeling it. She let her tone project serenity, but the more time passed, the less certainty she felt about the outcome of this operation.

It was starting to slowly dawn on her, the sheer magnitude of the politics she had ventured into. Juliette closed her eyes, and when she opened them, she was met by the perceptive azure gaze. Vyatka was looking directly at her, as if she had been reading her thoughts. Juliette half expected the other ballerina to lick her finger before turning another page of Juliette's psyche.

She smiled awkwardly, feeling the tips of her lips curl upward slowly, trying to project some sort of assuredness, but Vyatka just looked on, no sign of letting Juliette get away with anything.

Juliette cracked her knuckles and forced herself to not avert her own eyes. After a while, Vyatka moved her gaze away, perhaps a gesture of acquiescence rather than submission, and Juliette slowly exhaled. Maybe she did pass whatever test the Soviet had just been conducting? Maybe she had given the other woman enough reassurance?

Francesca threw her hands up, muttered a few chosen curses in Spanish, and left again in a cloud of anxiety and freshly applied perfume.

Juliette stood and took a few steps toward the dark window. Paris stretched in front of her, the city asleep, the avenue quiet. The witching hour indeed, when things occurred that could never happen in the sharp light of day, in the fantasy-piercing reality of the sun.

So Juliette chose to blame the dream-weaving night on the other side of the cold glass under her fingertips, and without looking at the pale woman behind her, simply uttered, "I won't let anything bad happen to you."

She felt more than heard her own foolish words. And they were foolish. In the darkened window that was now acting like a mirror, Vyatka looked nothing like a damsel needing rescue. If anything, she bore a striking resemblance to the villain of the piece, that arrogant eyebrow up again, the penetrating gaze burning a hole in Juliette's back.

So her protectiveness wasn't entirely appreciated. Juliette didn't mind. It felt out of place anyway. She was a good ten years younger than Vyatka, so of course her presumption would not go over well.

Still, somewhere in her chest, the promise burrowed in and laid its head on her heart, both light as a feather, as it came out so naturally, and heavy as lead, because what the hell was she doing promising something she had no idea how to pull off?

When Vyatka spoke again, the effect of witnessing a miracle still lingered. Juliette wondered if hearing this voice would ever not feel like magic.

"I'm aware they call you the Queen of Paris. Is it true? And does your heavy crown have the power to alter lives?"

Again, Juliette was enthralled by how much of a mystery this woman was. Her days in Paris were engulfed in silences and profanity, if Gabriel was to be believed. In arrogance, in boorishness, general standoffishness, and lacking in the sophistication a prima of her stature was expected to exhibit.

Yet, here she was asking Juliette about the powers of her crown, employing metaphors. The cultured notes of the low voice carried such depths of worldliness that Juliette wondered if she herself could ever match them.

"It's princess. The French tend to be cavalier with their queens." Juliette smiled at her own joke, but the dark eyes simply narrowed, and she cleared her throat before adding, "Though, I never once used that term for myself, Mademoiselle Vyatka. Étoile, maybe. After all, Paris Opera Ballet has a special title for its principal dancers. A star. It's both fitting and overwhelming. As for the royal designation…"

The mesmerizing eyebrow lifted again, either at the trailing off or at the confession, Juliette was not entirely certain, so she forced herself to finish her thought.

"Truth be told, I don't particularly enjoy the title. It comes with a price, and you said it yourself—that crown is heavy. And like most valuable things, it's very fragile."

Her interlocutor bit her lower lip. Juliette's heart sped up, her breathing grew shallow. Had she revealed too much? Why couldn't she stop speaking?

However, when she replied, Vyatka's voice held a tremulous note. "You don't act like anything about you is fragile. Certainly, you give your opinion freely. Maybe too freely."

The glare was back, and Juliette ducked her head. Was the Soviet ballerina speaking about Juliette's ill-advised remark about her révérence?

"Ah, I just wanted to…" Juliette trailed off, stumbling over the thought. She had no idea what had possessed her earlier when she couldn't keep her mouth shut, or where she wanted to take her comment now.

"I think the words you're looking for are, 'I'm sorry for jumping to conclusions.'"

Vyatka tightened her see-through shawl around her, and Juliette licked her lips before answering.

"I work with injured dancers… And obviously, a neck injury like this… It's my job—"

Vyatka's glare stopped Juliette dead in her faltering explanations.

For a few seconds neither spoke, the sound of Juliette's breathing the only one permeating the room. Then she exhaled and gave Vyatka her most winning smile.

"To borrow advice from the indomitable Madame Bianchi, I should stay out of your business. My apologies."

"And yet you made me your business. And are risking that aforementioned crown for me. You are not what you seem. Nor are you what they say you are."

Juliette laughed sincerely for the first time this evening, and it felt good to just be able to release that tension she had been holding on to.

"Neither are you. What a surprise you turned out to be, Mademoiselle Vyatka."

"Katarina, please. And nobody is what they pretend to be." Something suspiciously similar to ice settled around Juliette's heart. The voice held the same notes Juliette had heard filtering in when Vyatka was chased by the detestable KGB agent. Juliette wondered about the reason behind this tone. She wondered about so many things, yet the woman had fallen silent again, and Juliette realized the conversation was over.

The door opened, and this time Lalande was back. If his face was anything to go by, there had been a breakthrough and Juliette's very long evening would finally be coming to an end.

"Mademoiselle Lucian-Sorel? If I may have a word?" He held the door open for her, and as they both stepped into Francesca's secretary's space, he gave it a cursory glance as if making sure that they were alone. Then he looked Juliette square in the eye.

"Let's put our cards on the table. I will arrange for Katarina Vyatka's defection under two conditions. It's only going to happen if you agree to both of them. I don't want you to argue. Just say yes and she will remain in Paris, granted full asylum under French law."

So, this man had turned out to be exactly like the rest of them—an opportunist. Juliette knew when she was being played. But she could still feel that vise around her heart, restricting her breathing, reminding her of the foolhardy promise she had made. And those dejected eyes had sliced just as sharply as they had the moment Juliette had seen them turn empty the very first time.

"I assume you will outline your conditions, Monsieur Lalande? Or am I to agree blindly?"

His sudden smile was sharp, teeth gleaming too brightly. "Would you?"

Juliette sighed. She was tired. A brilliant and beautiful woman just a few feet away was being used as a pawn in a political tug-of-war, and this worthless man had the gall to play games.

"No. But since this is nothing but a farce to you, let me try and guess what the next steps in this charade would be." Juliette crossed her arms over her chest and took a deep breath, Lalande watching her warily. "If I say no, the life of an exceptionally talented ballerina would be endangered. After attempting to defect, she can't go back to Moscow. Her career would most certainly be over, and we have no way of knowing if she would even be able to keep her freedom. So I must say yes. But also, if your demands are such that my 'yes' is impossible to give, we both know that my next move is to less-than-respectfully go over your head and demand an audience with the president."

She pursed her lips. Lalande remained silent. Finally, he shrugged his shoulders, obviously surrendering whatever high ground he thought he was holding. "My first condition is that Vyatka must join the Paris Opera Ballet company."

Juliette bit the inside of her cheek. It hadn't even crossed her mind that Katarina would not be joining them. What else would she be doing in Paris? If she had wished to join the Royal London Ballet, she would have defected last month during Bolshoi's tour of England.

"And the second demand?"

"Condition." He coughed awkwardly before proceeding. "As the new Culture Minister, I will be taking a more involved role in the administration of the Paris Opera Ballet. In fact, this was part of why the previous minister was replaced and I was elevated to the position. To fix things." He applied harsh focus to the word *fix*, and Juliette pursed her lips. He was making it sound as if Paris Opera Ballet was broken. Still, she lifted her chin slightly, indicating that he should go on. His tone was even more wary when he proceeded again.

"Both companies are not living their best days. My predecessor reserved his influence for the budget only, and I think it was a mistake to allow things to get out of hand as much as they have. With both the opera and the ballet troupes."

Juliette narrowed her eyes. She was aware of the financial difficulties the companies were going through. Truth be told, any ballet company in the world that was subsidized by governments never had quite enough money for everything it needed, no matter how generous their budgets were. And their recent reviews weren't worthy of those budgets. Juliette Lucian-Sorel's name could be papered over many cracks, but not all. And even she was beginning to get beaten up in the press.

She chewed slowly on her lower lip. Bureaucrats were nothing but trouble, and dealing with them on a daily basis was not something she'd look forward to. But Katarina Vyatka getting a second lease on life and gracing the stage of Paris? No, Juliette would deal with what came from Lalande when she approached that bridge. And moreover, it would likely be Francesca who'd have to handle the fallout anyway.

"So, what do you want from me, Monsieur Lalande?"

"I want your word that when the time comes, you will not contradict my decisions regarding the running of Paris Opera Ballet. That neither publicly nor privately will you undermine me and my decisions."

A particular note in his speech raised the hairs on the back of Juliette's neck. He was gearing up for something. This wasn't just an offhand request. He knew what he was asking her to agree to. This wasn't a conversation in hypotheticals. Not to him. Dread stirred in the confines of Juliette's mind. Something was coming.

The door creaked, and Katarina stepped into the small office, looking for all intents and purposes as if she were climbing the stairs of the scaffold to the guillotine. The worry lines Juliette had not noticed before on the pale, sculpted marble face were much deeper than a thirty-something-year-old's should be.

"Katarina?" Juliette reached out a hand but was met only with a questioning look. She remembered the earlier flinch and wanted to chastise herself for being a fool.

"I'd rather be told if I am being denied asylum. I would need to prepare myself for my return to Moscow. And for the consequences." Katarina's voice did not tremble, and her eyes were hard. The kind of hard that came from years and years of disappointments, of torment and struggle.

Juliette's premonitions would have to take a step back. "You won't be denied asylum, Katarina. You're staying here. In Paris. And at the Palais Garnier. You will be joining the company." She smiled and this time did not attempt to touch the other woman, who clutched the flimsy shawl around her shoulders and was now quivering quite visibly.

Next to her, Lalande cleared his throat. *Ah, of course…*

"You have my 'yes,' Monsieur Lalande. Now go do what the French taxpayers are paying you quite a generous salary for."

He shook his head, and then it was just the two of them in the much smaller, cluttered space, filled with papers and files and smelling like cigarettes and yesterday's coffee.

Katarina was watching her with wide-open eyes, huge on the colorless face, framed by the longest inky lashes that periodically fluttered like butterfly wings, painting long shadows on diaphanous cheeks.

"You made a deal. For me. With him."

Juliette smiled briefly at the perceptiveness.

"I've made worse deals in my life, Katarina. And for much less, at that."

Katarina took a step closer but then faltered, stopping halfway. They were inches apart. The orange blossom scent spellbound Juliette's senses. When Katarina spoke, it was the quietest of whispers delivered with the finality of a person sentenced to death.

"I hope you don't regret it."

Juliette felt the words on her skin, the exhalation of breath required to utter them.

And then Katarina was gone, back to the safety of Francesca's office, away from Juliette, who was dizzy on the scent and the warmth of the presence no longer inches away from her.

The room, tiny and cramped as it was, suddenly felt empty, the disarray reflecting the tangled mess of emotions Juliette was confronting. She touched her cheek, where Katarina's words seemed to have branded her, and remembered the blood on Michel's skin, in exactly the same spot, drawn by this very woman. Juliette also recalled her prescient thought that this woman would leave bruises. She honestly hoped she was wrong.

"Well, then, for both our sakes, we'll have to keep the promises we've made today." As her words disappeared in thin air, Juliette realized hers was the only promise made, and Katarina's sounded more like a warning.

Five

Of Unwanted Royalty & Assuming Power

Years later, when asked about the deal she had made that saved Katarina Vyatka's career and possibly her life, Juliette Lucian-Sorel would confess that she thought very little of the logistics of it. Not about where Katarina would live, what exactly she would be doing at the Paris Opera Ballet, how she would be taken care of, and a myriad of other questions.

Hell, Juliette hadn't even considered how they would get out of the damn building, since they had caused quite the ruckus leaving the reception and she was fairly certain the Bolshoi reaction to their prima defecting had not been kept under wraps. Francesca didn't tend to exaggerate such things, and she had mentioned the rage, the anger, and the screaming.

The commotion had indeed caused quite a stir with the photographers already following the high-level dignitaries and other celebrities to the reception. They had been aligned outside of the Palais Garnier, waiting for the opportunity to capture a few run-of-the-mill candid shots of departing guests. Instead, they had gotten a bombshell to cover.

The news of the defection had quickly reached beyond the confines of the building on Place de l'Opéra, and in the blink of an eye, the number of photographers had doubled, in addition to all the news outlets sending reporters with cameras and recorders to the grand stairs. Peeking from behind the half-open exit doors, Juliette cursed the nosy Parisian press and their omniscient presence.

In her seven years here, she had gotten used to them, and more importantly, they had gotten used to her. Her pictures were rarely taken without her permission anymore, as her wrath was generally well-known, and after so many years and so much success, she was no longer a novelty.

She'd almost forgotten what being in the eye of the storm looked like.

"You've unleashed the Kraken, darlin'. Well, both of you." The mangled reference to a four-year-old movie did nothing to impress her, but then Gabriel wasn't trying to. He stood next to her, a comforting presence due to his size but also because when finally told of what was happening, his only reaction was to shrug his shoulders and squeeze her elbow—as if rescuing Soviet defecting ballerinas was something Juliette did regularly. She wanted to laugh, though she knew the tiredness and the weirdness of the circumstances were more than likely to turn her laughter hysterical, and if she started, Juliette wasn't certain she'd be able to stop.

Still, it was good to be able to count on her best friend to never make a big deal out of her exploits.

Katarina watched them impassively, and once Gabriel got to his usual volume of rowdiness and humor, warily, the haughty glare glided over him with a mix of skepticism and dismissal. A sleek and graceful cat watching a golden retriever be his rambunctious self. And that did cause Juliette to choke on a giggle, the imagery too comical yet too precise to help reign in emotions running amok. She recovered quickly under the suspicious dark glare, masking her laughter with a cough. "Not fond of men?"

The gaze did not waver and the eyebrow stayed down. Juliette felt as if her question had won her a gold medal.

"Someone has to do the lifting in a pas de deux. Even if it's on stage only."

Gabriel choked on whatever nonsense he had been spouting, and Juliette smiled. Humor was so unexpected coming from the severe figure of the Soviet prima.

Still, the snubbing of men was no surprise, the way her compatriots were constantly manhandling her. Jokes aside, that protective chord of Juliette's, the one that had started this entire mess, twanged in sympathy and wrath. Well, no more. Katarina Vyatka, with all her fury, her haughtiness, and that sadness Juliette tried to convince herself she had not imagined, would be safe here in Paris.

Everyone seemed lost for words for a long moment, watching the journalists settle in a loud gaggle outside. The Paris night, the normally quiet and placid time, was fully abuzz now, the commotion causing hundreds of darkened windows around them to light with people rubbernecking at the scenes unfolding before them on the Place de l'Opéra.

Katarina drew a deep breath, her chest rising and falling visibly. Juliette tensed. After all, she had seen it before, and that one bracing breath had been followed by one hell of a turn of events. Yet nothing came, just another breath and then another, deep, rhythmic inhalations. Juliette knew calming breathing when she heard it. She'd done it plenty before performances. Was Katarina gathering her courage?

She was still pondering why the other woman felt the need to brace herself when Katarina's quiet voice penetrated her focus.

"I apologize for all this." All traces of earlier humor gone now, Katarina pointed in the general direction of the braying crowd of photographers, reporters, and gawkers. Then she dropped her arm and lifted her face to Gabriel. "I won't apologize for trying to save myself."

The revelation seemed so immense, the honesty and the rawness of it so profound, that Juliette feared its consequences.

Especially knowing Gabriel's penchant for nonchalance. His usual reaction to most everything was to laugh things off. She steeled herself for the familiar guffaws, because then Katarina would claw his eyes out and Juliette would have to intervene.

Gabriel, however, surprised her. "Jett here wouldn't let you do that anyway, even if you tried."

Katarina looked puzzled for a moment before the right corner of her mouth twitched and a small smile played there. Juliette tried not to stare at how such a tiny emotional display transformed the austere features. Humor looked good on Katarina Vyatka. Hell, Juliette suspected joy looked amazing on Katarina Vyatka, and despite every single warning sign blaring in her head, she wanted to make this woman smile fully, self-preservation be damned.

"Jett?" Katarina's voice was incredulous.

And now Gabriel did laugh.

"Yeah, she has been Jett ever since we crossed paths in the London boarding school as ten-year-olds. I mean, have you seen her fly?" Gabriel's face was full of such honest adoration, Juliette's eyes stung. "It was Juliette or Jett, and pretty much nothing else since. I teasingly called her 'Juju Baby,' and she bloodied my nose. I dropped the 'baby,' and she stopped hitting me. How did you think we ended up as best friends? A man respects a woman who can beat him to a pulp. Hence you, Mademoiselle Vyatka, and I are going to be the very best of friends."

Katarina gave him a sideways glance. "Are we now?"

Gabriel winked at Juliette. "Oh yes, because you can probably wipe the floor with me any day, ma'am."

He leaned on the doorjamb, a picture of insouciance, and gave Katarina his most angelic smile.

"Twice on Sundays," was the husky reply, and then the dimples Juliette had observed from afar the other day were on full display as Katarina gave a short peel of laughter, startled and honest and rusty.

Well, damn.
Juliette almost covered her eyes. Someone should issue a warning label of some sort, because these were definitely lethal weapons on an already drop-dead gorgeous face.
Do not look without protective eye gear. Risk of damaging one's eyesight... And one's intelligence.
Juliette could actually feel her intellect plummet to the level of single-cell organisms. Though parameciums, amoebas, and other eukaryotes were asexual beings and probably not taken by a set of unexpected dimples on a magnificent face.
Gabriel and Katarina kept up their quiet banter, and Juliette wondered at herself. She was never shallow, never prone to objectifying a woman, and she certainly never allowed herself to sexualize an almost complete stranger. She shook her head, dislodging the cobwebs of tiredness and temporary insanity. If she carried on this way, she'd have to apologize to Katarina... who was giving her a very strange speculative look from under those butterfly-wing eyelashes of hers. Juliette bit her lip to hide a charmed smile before schooling her features and glaring at Gabriel.
"Before you give away all our secrets, maybe try and figure out where our escort is and why we're still standing here at eleven p.m.?"
Gabriel booped her nose, but before he could try anything even more inane, they were finally joined by Lalande and a few people Juliette didn't recognize. Francesca was not far behind.
"Mademoiselle Vyatka, as you can see, the news of your defection has spread rather rapidly, I'm afraid. You cannot return to your hotel, though we will try to retrieve your belongings. And there will be no opportunity for you to say goodbye to your Bolshoi friends."
"I have nothing of value in my suitcase. And I understand, given the vehemence of my country to deny me the opportunity to remain in France. As for friends?" The shadow so often

marring Katarina's face returned in full force, contorting the flawless features into a mask of simmering rage. "I have no friends, Monsieur le Ministre."

Juliette felt the strum of premonition hit the chords of her heart yet again.

A storm is coming.

On cue, lightning tore the night in half, a crash of thunder on its heels shaking the sky. Juliette knew her life had been very much demarcated now. Before tonight, and after.

Perhaps Francesca had been correct in her assessment that Juliette had no idea what she had wrought. The multitude of logistical details about this defection were becoming apparent and quickly overwhelming. And one of them loomed larger than all the others.

Lalande, ever the political pragmatist, had not let the issue escape him, either. "The Paris Opera Ballet has apartments and dorm rooms our dancers can occupy while working for the company, but none are currently ready and I would hesitate to take you anywhere alone while the Bolshoi and the KGB agents are still on the ground—"

"She can stay with me."

There, now nothing loomed anymore. Settled. Juliette wanted to pat herself on the back, despite every head in the room turning toward her. Granted, this gesture was so uncharacteristic of her that she was certain she'd lie in shock that very night in her cozy bedroom on Rue de Rivoli. This saving business must've gone to her head if she was offering her own apartment, her veritable sanctuary, where not even Gabriel had free entrance, to a virtual unknown.

Francesca was the first one to find her voice. "The apartment next door to yours is being renovated. It was slated for our new star soprano, but she will not join till January and so this gives us enough time to find her different accommodations. It will likely take a few weeks to a month to finalize it for Mademoiselle Vyatka."

Juliette shrugged. "Then we shall revisit this in a few weeks. In the meantime, I think we have been kept prisoners in these walls for a bit too long?"

Lalande cleared his throat before gesturing outside. "The car is ready, Mademoiselle Lucian-Sorel. The police will be posted in front of your building for a few days, just in case. I've already arranged for that, since the KGB knows it was you who spirited Mademoiselle Vyatka away from the party. As for getting out of here, I don't think there is any chance of avoiding the crowd. The story is out there, the public has been drooling over Mademoiselle Vyatka from her first performance, and she is the biggest star that has graced the floorboards of Garnier since… well… you. And you were not a Soviet ballerina shrouded in mystery and intrigue and quite a lot of rumors." He smiled lasciviously, and Juliette was grateful for skipping dinner.

"Your point, Monsieur Lalande?"

He dropped the smile and was back to his irritable self. "My point is that I believe we do this once and we will never have to do this ever again. The public wants to see and to know. The order of asylum has been signed. There is no going back and there is nothing to lose. We come out, Mademoiselle Vyatka gets photographed and waves to the public, I will make a short statement, Madame Bianchi will concur, and we all go on our way. Sneaking out will only cause more questions. We have nothing to hide here."

Juliette could certainly see the reasoning behind his plan. And she had to give it to him, it wasn't all bad. In fact, feeding the hungry monster that was the French press would probably end up the wisest decision they could make under the circumstances, even if all she wanted was to disappear quietly into the night. She had never enjoyed curtain calls as much as her peers did.

But this was not her decision to make, and so she turned to the one who would have to do the proverbial curtsying to the press and to the French public.

"This is a very small price to pay for my freedom, Monsieur le Ministre." The steel was perfectly audible in Katarina's words, and everyone exhaled, clearly relieved they'd be doing the right but also the expedient thing. It was getting late. Juliette's feet, encased in the stiff leather of her high heels, were not going to be happy tomorrow.

They exited together, a group of ten people, Juliette and Katarina surrounded by ministerial staff with Gabriel and Francesca close by, and just as they approached the area where photographers and gawkers were cordoned off by the gendarmes, the rumpled brown suit that could only belong to one man, whom Juliette thought she'd recognize even in her sleep, the pockmarked face that was sure to haunt her nightmares, materialized to their right. The crowd of photographers swallowed the Russian for a moment, and to her dismay Juliette lost sight of him in the avalanche of questions being hurled at them.

Some photographers were respectful, some were presumptuous, yelling out her first name only, some were shouting for Gabriel, but most were targeting Katarina. Several even attempted to ask her questions in extremely broken Russian.

Katarina stayed above the fray, her apprehensive expression from earlier gone, the seasoned, arrogant, and cold prima front and center. She answered questions with brief precision, her words measured and sparse. She disregarded the ones that were too invasive and kept her tone remarkably neutral.

The cameras kept rolling and the flashes were bright and blinding, yet Katarina Vyatka stood tall and proud in front of what pretty much amounted to the entirety of France—and the whole world through the live TV broadcasts—and without disparaging her own country, simply held the line of "I wished to dance my best years in Paris," which was diplomatic but also extraordinarily mild considering that she was escaping a deadly dictatorial regime, even if it had mellowed slightly in the recent years.

A shout of "Are you defecting because of a man?" from the back of the crowd was laughable. Yet, to Juliette's astonishment, Katarina was visibly taken aback, turning slightly to face her, seemingly seeking guidance or perhaps reassurance, and Juliette found herself giving her a little smile and a nod. Their gazes held on each other a second longer, the air filling with an intensity and an energy that Juliette was not entirely unfamiliar with, but the tether of realization was just out of her reach and she couldn't grasp it, distracted as she was by the crowd of vociferating reporters.

"I am here precisely because I won't allow men to influence my life anymore. No woman should." Katarina's answer only seemed to amplify the noise. Yet she looked completely unperturbed and after a few more minutes stepped back, allowing Lalande and Francesca to take center stage again.

And just as she thought they had finally escaped unscathed, with Francesca and Monsieur Lalande reciting the standard diplomatic statements about human rights and talent and freedom, the pockmarked face appeared right in front of Juliette.

"I told you, you have no idea what you're meddling with. The game here is way above you. You are out of touch, woman. Who do you think you are?" He spat every word, and this time she did not hide her revulsion, demonstratively wiping her face, fully aware that the entire world would be capturing this footage. Even the shouts of the reporters seemed to have quieted down, focusing on the exchange, cameras rolling.

Next to her, Katarina froze, the proud and even haughty dancer vanishing, a shaken woman left in her stance, eyes wide and the already pale face now almost ashen. Juliette felt Gabriel move closer to her, no doubt with the intent to shield her as he often did in situations with rowdy or overzealous fans. But this wasn't one of those cases. And Juliette needed to slay this particular monster, no matter how much she hated the way she was about to do it.

"I am the Princess of Paris, Agent Ivanov. And nothing in this city is above me."

Juliette very demonstratively reached out her hand, knowing that the risk was very high, since Katarina had rejected her just a few hours earlier, and that her apprehension at being touched was visibly strong. But Juliette also knew that there was only one way of taking one's power back. And that she couldn't do it for Katarina. She had already done more than her share.

And then, in the middle of Place de l'Opéra, with hundreds of photographers and the whole world watching, Katarina, graceful and in full prima mode, made the perfect ballet hand—thumb tucked and middle finger slightly lower than the index—and extended it toward her.

Juliette took it gently but firmly and felt it steady, even if ice-cold, in hers.

The Minister of Culture's people cleared the way, and from the corner of her eye she could see them taking the agent away. It was over. Ivanov shouted more threats in their direction, but Juliette ignored him. After the little interlude, the two ballerinas reached the car with no issues, the crowds parting in front of them like the Red Sea.

As the car door shut behind them, Juliette found herself exhaling and closing her eyes.

"For what it's worth, Mademoiselle Lucian-Sorel, the title, and the role… It's natural for you. And it becomes you." Katarina's voice was quiet again, yet neither distant nor lifeless, the hand Juliette hadn't realized still rested in hers warming slowly.

"It goes with the territory, Katarina, but I find the entire spectacle ridiculous. The veneration, the adulation."

"You don't love that part?"

Juliette opened her eyes to a curious pair observing her closely. Did she love that part? She loved to dance. The dance was the very essence of her. The applause and attention were par for the course. And yet… Did she really love them? Nobody had ever asked her before. What a strange night. What a strange woman.

"From afar," was all she said, and Katarina nodded. Juliette looked at the pensive features for just a moment longer, recognizing belatedly that she wasn't the only one finding a deep understanding in this moment. Did she want to be this transparent? After all, this woman was a stranger.

Yet when this stranger spoke next, Juliette realized that whatever efforts she might think to undertake in the future to keep more of herself closed off, they would probably be in vain.

"The papers will portray you as Parisian royalty, putting a nobody who dared to cross you in his place. They will relate how you vanquished a foe with the magnificence of a few words and the flaunting of your crown. They will be in awe and sing your praises. And you will hate that. Because you did neither of those things."

Juliette blinked. "Oh?"

Katarina slowly intertwined their fingers for just a second, their palms coming flush against each other before she gently tugged her hand free.

"No. You did all of that to save me, Your Highness."

The earlier premonition of nothing ever again being the same in her life returned tenfold, even as Katarina turned away from her and Juliette was left alone with her thoughts and the lights of the streets to keep her company on the very short drive. At least she would always have Paris.

Six

Of First Impressions & Midnight Calls

Neither Gabriel nor Francesca followed them up the four floors to the penthouse on the Rue de Rivoli. Juliette was grateful for it. Lalande had assured them that they would try to get at least some of Katarina's things back from the hotel, since she had nothing with her but the evening gown and high heels she was wearing. By the end of the night, the shawl she had wrapped herself in looked more like a rag from all the twisting.

Juliette felt very much like that shawl. And above all, exhausted. Also, not a little awkward. There was a woman in her apartment. No one had been here since Helena had left, her boxes picked up by professional movers a few days later. There had been a lot of those boxes, and Juliette had always marveled at how many items a person could accumulate in only three years of cohabitation.

Cohabitation. The term sounded strange. A cold, detached, sterile word. Helena would probably like that. She loved to analyze their relationship in the cold, detached, and sterile light hanging over a therapy couch. Juliette initially laughed it off as a professional defect and then she stopped noticing it altogether, until she simply couldn't ignore it anymore. Until every word between them was cold and detached and sterile. Analyzed to death and spoken with clear precision.

When had they become that couple?

At the small cough behind her, Juliette closed her eyes, chasing away the remnants of memories. Helena and she had royally messed up a beautiful thing, and no amount of reminiscing was going to fix that, no matter how many times her ex called.

But that was in the past. In the right here and now, there was another woman in the apartment on Rue de Rivoli, and Katarina Vyatka felt entirely extraneous here. She made no attempt to move farther into the hallway from the front door, no sound other than the slight clearing of her throat, perhaps perturbed by Juliette's woolgathering, however her presence seemed to change the entire place. The emptiness had suddenly vanished, replaced with a waiting of sorts, like the coiling of a spring, only not tight enough. Not yet. Fanciful as she might be, Juliette felt the palpable straining of the steel.

Trying not to ascribe nonsense meaning to her own melancholy mood, Juliette pointed to the spare bedroom.

"This will be your room for however long it takes Francesca to finalize the renovations. There's a robe and some toiletries and necessities in the bathroom, and I'll lend you a pair of pajamas. We'll see what the situation is with your clothes tomorrow, and if need be I'll find something for you. Knowing Francesca, she will have the apartment next door ready in no time, and then you will have more privacy."

Katarina smiled, the stretch of lips crooked and a bit unnatural. "I don't know what privacy is."

Juliette's eyebrows rose of their own accord before Katarina continued.

"Dorm rooms are funny that way. And after… I had to share." There was so much more to those words, Juliette could tell. Innumerable saids and unsaids, at the same time. *I had to share.* Not *I shared.* Bolshoi had truly guarded their prized asset. And yet, here she was. Free from them.

"Well, you will only share with me for a bit. And I am rarely home. So it might not even feel like sharing."

Katarina opened her mouth as if to ask something and then bit her lip, visibly reconsidering before taking a longer glance beyond the open door of Juliette's spacious bedroom.

Ah, Katarina must've taken the statement of rarely being home as her seeing someone. Juliette tilted her head to the side, giving her new roommate a closer look. Francesca had all but thrown her sexuality in her face during their screaming match at Palais Garnier, so Katarina, no matter how sheltered and guarded she might be, was fully aware Juliette had relationships with women.

She wasn't ashamed of who she was. Her profession and her status blessed her with not needing to hide herself too much. And London and Paris had been exceedingly accepting of whom she loved. Would this woman be the one exception? Would she judge?

Before Juliette could refute her perceived busy social agenda as nothing but work commitments, including working with the younger dancers at the Ballet Academy, Katarina found her voice again.

"I don't wish to pry. And you owe me nothing. You've already done so much for me. For an unknown."

Despite the words being in the realm of gratitude, the tone was acerbic as ever, as if Katarina knew she had to be thankful to Juliette yet couldn't quite bring herself to fully express it. Or maybe she simply didn't like her. Nobody had said you had to like those who saved you. Juliette bit the inside of her cheek. Yeah, nobody said that, but for some reason, Juliette wanted her to. Like her, that is. Just a little.

Then she realized what the hell she had been thinking and blushed, taking a steadying breath. Time to take care of issues at hand instead of entertaining these foolish notions.

Hearing Juliette's earlier assertion—about letting a stranger into her life and her home—being echoed back at her was eerie. And so she said nothing, just stood there as Katarina took the first few steps into her space.

She was tentative initially, something Juliette had come to recognize as natural reservedness, perhaps indeed refusing to pry into the affairs of a woman who owed her nothing.

Juliette wondered what Katarina saw, how this sanctuary looked through the eyes of someone who had lived an entirely different life. She had been to Moscow and Leningrad twice. Paris Opera Ballet toured regularly, and even though Francesca preferred to travel anywhere else but the Soviet Union, they still occasionally stopped there en route to the much more hospitable hosts in Asia.

She remembered the regimented buildings, all alike, square and boxy, concrete slabs standing huddled together in exacting neighborhoods. Rows and rows of the identical structures lining the equally similar streets. Scarcity and order were everywhere, even if the touring ballet company was always sheltered from the everyday lives of regular Soviet people. Still, some things slipped through, and the reality of the daily grind was harsh and sobering.

How did Paris, with its frivolity and its freedom, its gauze and lace, look to this woman after an existence of standing in line for a loaf of bread? For sausage? For tights? An existence she couldn't leave without causing an international scandal? They didn't call it the Iron Curtain for nothing; escaping was akin to breaking through metal barriers.

The apartment on Rue de Rivoli was Juliette's pride and joy. Years of collecting art and books. Years of lovingly arranging the space to fit her needs, to reflect her style and her moods. Some posters of the dancers of old. Her idols, looking down at her from the aged paper, encased in glass and carefully crafted wooden frames. A tiny Monet. A large Bellcourt. Several paintings by lesser-known French and English contemporary artists.

A slew of sculptures and small knickknacks. All thoughtfully selected.

Juliette looked around, and when she turned back Katarina was no longer observing the space. She was watching her.

"It's beautiful."

From those lips, the praise felt effusive. Juliette smiled. Was she really nervous about this woman liking her apartment? How ridiculous. How absurd! But she had already admitted to wishing to be liked, so what was one more indignity?

What was it about this creature, encased in silence and derision, that tugged at something in Juliette's chest? Since she had no answer, Juliette turned away, her heels dangling from her fingertips as her bare feet followed the familiar track toward the bedroom and its walk-in closet. Just before she closed the door, she heard Katarina's murmured, "It suits you."

Well...

Juliette lit the few lamps scattered around the room, detesting the overhead light, and found herself sitting on the bed, the shoes falling down with a muted *thump* at her side. She could sense the scent of orange blossom in the room, despite Katarina never having crossed this threshold. Juliette thought she could get used to the sweet fragrance, so unlike the woman herself yet now so intimately linked to her in her mind.

The phone rang, pulling her harshly out of her stupor. She felt like she had been caught with her hand in the cookie jar.

Busted.

Oh, what nonsense. Busted? For what? For the second time this evening, Juliette thought how ridiculous she was behaving.

She lifted the handset off the hooks and schooled her voice.

"Hello?"

There was only a small beat of silence before the line came alive with a familiar chuckle.

"Your Highness."

Juliette could have recognized this voice anywhere. For three years it had been the sound of her happiness.

"Helena."

Juliette didn't know if she was upset, sad, or just flat-out irritated at her ex calling at this hour. Calling again. Calling at all.

"I loved it. TF1 interrupted their news program and had it live. I caught the tail end of it."

The wonders of modern live television. Juliette was still weirdly unaccustomed to something being broadcasted live across the ocean. And for that something to be ballet-related news, of all things. When a few years ago her own performance had been televised, she'd felt like she'd stepped into one of Isaac Asimov's books. The future was right here. What was next? Portable phones?

Helena would have a field day with Juliette's thoughts going anywhere except to the matter at hand. But avoidance had never been her style.

"Why do you still watch French television? And TF1, of all the channels?"

Helena laughed again, the warmth and familiarity of the sound enveloping Juliette in a languor that wasn't entirely unwelcome. She tugged the diamonds from her ears, dropping them on the nightstand, and then simply stretched on her bed, gown and all.

"Is this an actual question, Jett? And it wasn't the actual TF1. NBC, CBS… one of them re-broadcasted. Does it matter?"

No? Yes? Maybe? Juliette didn't know. So much left unsaid between them. So much pain and hurt, and now? Now just small talk. How strange.

"You're spending a fortune on these calls, Hels." The nickname slipped from her tongue, the force of habit too strong for her to be able to stop it.

"I worry about you. And I feel guilty for leaving you. Hence, I assuage my feelings with these exorbitant transatlantic calls that bring nothing but old regrets to us both."

Well, Helena Moore was always honest. To a fault, in fact.

The same fault of honesty that had driven them apart at the first real hurdle of their relationship.

"So you're checking in, for both our sakes? You've seen on TV, my day has been pretty full. I do appreciate the concern, Hels. But you know I don't wilt under the bright lights of the Palais Garnier." Juliette chewed on her lower lip, wondering when her normal latent irritation with Helena had turned into mild affection. They were the perfect lesbian cliché. Exes and friends.

"Yes, that was spectacularly done. But, lights of the Opera aside, it was still very much unlike you. You never used to claim the moniker, even if half the world says it to your face. I assume you needed to make a statement. And she is pretty."

Juliette laughed, then remembered that she was not alone in the apartment and quickly lowered her voice.

"C'mon now. We both know she is more than just 'pretty,' but that is neither here nor there. She needed help and yes, I needed to make a statement. These people think that if they subjugate one country, they rule everyone everywhere. Well, they don't rule me. Nobody does. I do as I please."

There was a sigh on the line, and Juliette belatedly realized what she had said. No, Helena had never wanted to actually rule her, but a little cooperation on Juliette's part would have gone a long way toward averting a rather bleak end to a beautiful three-year relationship.

"How did Francesca take it?"

Juliette was grateful for the slight change of angle, if not of subject.

"Fine. She is gaining one of the brightest stars in the ballet sky. So she will have to figure out how to corral her into the fold without stepping on anyone's toes."

"Your toes?"

Juliette, in the process of rolling down her stockings one-handed, stopped. The thought hadn't even crossed her mind.

"We're not the same, Hels. And the season is long. I can't dance all the leads anyway."

Even to her own ears, her words sounded weak. Should she have considered that the addition of one of the best ballerinas in the world—one whose talent rivaled only Juliette Lucian-Sorel herself—to the company would have a direct impact on the Prima Assoluta? Probably.

Helena gave voice to the next thought before it even properly materialized in Juliette's mind.

"Either way, Jett, it's done now. And you're right, the two of you are not the same. From everything I've seen of her, and I saw her in *Sleeping Beauty* on a bootleg tape smuggled from Moscow, she is your exact opposite. You're like light and dark, and not only due to your coloring."

Juliette held her breath, waiting for her ex's next words. Helena Moore had once been a very promising ballerina in her own right. In fact, they had met at the London academy first, before Helena decided that her real calling was psychology. Their paths had diverged for years, and they only reconnected when Helena surprised Juliette at the back door of Palais Garnier after the season opener. She was pursuing her master's at the Sorbonne at the time.

They had been inseparable for three years. Then Helena received an invitation to pursue a PhD and teach at Columbia, and for some reason she was absolutely certain that Juliette would simply pack her things and follow her to New York.

Except, Juliette entertained no such ideas and was in turn absolutely certain Helena Moore would choose to do her PhD at Sorbonne University and stay with her.

Well, it turned out their absolute certainty was worthless. They were both wrong. Bitterly so. And for the past twelve months, Helena had been making these ridiculous calls. They talked about nothing, and certainly not about not loving each other enough to alter their own lives for the sake of the couple they once formed.

But Helena was still one of the most trusted voices in Juliette's head. Something wooden fell down on the other end of the line, and Juliette smiled. Chess and ballet. Not much changed with Helena.

"Are you playing by yourself again?"

Helena chuckled. "I'm merely lining the pieces. I have a new set. Trying to see how this entire ordeal of yours plays out. You put a target on your back, White Queen. And not just by embracing the Black Queen."

"Coloring-wise, your metaphor doesn't work, you know. Blonde, brunette, it's the other way around. And are you saying I should be wary of her?" It sounded surreal to even put it into words. Katarina seemed entirely detached from everything around her. And she was still Juliette Lucian-Sorel. And the much-detested crown was hers.

"I don't know, dearest. Metaphors aren't the point here. Watch your back. Though I'm sure Francesca does more than watch it." With that parting shot, even though it did not hit its target in the slightest, Helena hung up. Very carefully, as if the phone would shatter in her hand at any moment, Juliette placed it back on the hooks and then just sat on the still-made bed, listening to the city falling asleep around her.

The darkness blanketed the street outside, not unlike a comforter, one of calm and ease. It was her favorite time of the night, a few hours before it would slowly morph into twilight. The moment felt magical, as if anything was possible, as if reality was split in halves of fables and myths. She got up and slowly made her way toward the open window.

A stone's throw away, the impregnable walls of the Louvre Palace held secrets and treasures. In the distance, the Tour Saint-Jacques speared the night sky, its stark height and Gothic appearance in contrast with the modern mortar of Rue de Rivoli. In front of her, past the Tuileries, the river stitched the two banks of the City of Light like a ribbon piecing together a broken costume. The city that had lived through the plague, conquests, revolutions, war, occupation, and more war was at her feet, deceptively tranquil and quiet.

And then in that very quiet, Juliette heard a tiny sound, one that did not belong to the night, nor to the city. It was coming from her own apartment. A sob. Heavy silence followed the echo of misery.

Juliette almost took off in the direction of the spare bedroom, yet a moment later the oppressive silence was broken by barely audible footsteps, and to her left Juliette saw Katarina step fully onto the small balcony. The slim hands—blue rivulets of the veins, the only color on alabaster skin—reached beyond the rail, extending palms up into the night, and Juliette realized it was raining. The hands were now getting splashed by raindrops, and from her vantage point, her companion unaware of her presence, Juliette could tell that while the water on the long fingers was all rain, the angular face was tear-stained.

So she had heard right. Katarina had been crying. Just like the earlier fear and sadness in the blue eyes had opened something in Juliette's chest, the tears went even further. They sliced, a jagged edge of pity and helplessness splitting Juliette's ribs to the deep empathy within.

She was about to head back, grateful that she had remained unseen and thus sparing both of them the embarrassment of witnessing someone so prideful fall apart, when the silence was broken once again. Just before Katarina disappeared from the balcony, quietly closing the wood and glass doors behind her willowy form, she whispered, looking up at the clearing sky, at the shy stars peaking among the storm clouds.

"Thank you."

Juliette did not sleep the rest of the night, the warning from Helena warring with the tearful vision of Katarina thanking her stars.

Variations

Seven

Of Mornings After & Settling In

"So, the night went well, I take it? No blood on those amazing parquet floors of yours?"

Gabriel was bent over his bag, looking for his water bottle, sweat dripping off his face. They had just finished their morning class, with Francesca taking over the duties of wiping the floor with them.

The core dancers had departed, and the soloists were congregating in their usual corner. Most of them rarely spoke to Juliette and the other principal dancers. Gabriel was an exception, but then he always had been. He winked at them as he straightened and swaggered exaggeratedly closer to where she was pulling on her leg warmers.

"You are being ridiculous." She threw a slipper at him, which he caught with his free hand while chugging water. Juliette could absolutely hear the swooning happening in the soloists' corner.

"About the blood?" He puffed out his chest, taking a deep breath, and then sat down next to her. "It isn't unreasonable to ask, you know. All things considered."

"Am I missing something, Gabriel? Because first Helena was all up in arms about me making space for another prima who would come to stab me in the back, and now you?"

Juliette reached for the towel, if only to have something to do with her hands, while Gabriel took his time answering. When he did speak, he sounded thoughtful.

"That is actually not what I meant at all. Mostly, I was making a terrible joke about the total ball-buster that is Katarina Vyatka. But now that you mention it, or should I say now that Helena mentioned it—"

"And what did our esteemed Doctor Moore mention?" Francesca made her presence known, her tone pure venom.

Juliette felt the corners of her mouth twitching. *Ridiculous* was the word of the morning, that was for certain.

"You, for what it's worth."

Francesca gaped but then waved exaggeratedly.

"Disparagingly, I'm sure."

"Just to imply that whatever happens, you will watch my six. Literally."

It was an old joke between them. Francesca smirked.

"On my watch, it has only gotten better. You are welcome, amor. As for the esteemed doctor and the point she was making, I am sure you of all people saw all the possibilities and all the angles in this entire affair."

Juliette bit her lip. Her reputation as a cerebral and methodical dancer extended to her life choices, and she had never been impulsive. How was she to explain to Francesca and Gabriel that yesterday had been very much an aberration for her and, for once, instinct had taken over?

A change of subject was required. Because as Gabriel had, Francesca was bound to ask questions. And Juliette would much rather not answer some of them.

Especially the ones about how her morning with Katarina had gone. Or what Katarina looked like in just a towel with water droplets running down her long neck, chasing the blue veins down that translucent expanse of skin. Or how Juliette forgot how to breathe and executed the most perfect imitation of a deer in headlights. A very flustered deer that turned all beet red at the revelation of the longest legs barely covered by the aforementioned towel. Or how Katarina's chest rose and fell under Juliette's flustered gaze.

Or how Juliette turned away as if slapped when their eyes met and she realized that surely she was making this woman uncomfortable. She distinctly remembered mumbling something about the time and it being the perfect hour to go for a run before grabbing her shoes and sprinting out the door. No, gun to her head, she'd never be able to say what time it was, but it was exactly the proper time to disappear from the apartment and maybe the face of the earth and what had she gotten herself into?

After tossing and turning for a few hours before dawn, Juliette had chosen to eschew the struggle and attempt breakfast. But with the shower and towel and, well, all that skin, she found herself on the warm, still-wet-from-the-rain Paris streets that met her with birdsong and sleepy pedestrians. She didn't push hard, just enough to brush off the cobwebs of the sleepless night. But the vision of freshly showered Katarina, smelling of Juliette's shampoo, was something this run—even if she had chosen to set new speed records—would not be able to erase. That image was branded into her brain.

So after all that, being subjected to questions from Gabriel and Francesca was decidedly not ideal. Even before either of them sensed blood in the water. Or whatever it was that was making Juliette act like a schoolgirl with a crush.

Crush? Holy hell.

Juliette almost smacked her forehead. So much for being cerebral. So much for being rational. So much for… No, she was all those things. Once she'd get over herself and over whatever possessed her and on with her life and most especially with this conversation, because Francesca—

"Jett?" Damn, Francesca was standing right over her, leaning on her cane, looking for all intents and purposes as if she knew exactly what Juliette had been thinking about. Or whom she had been thinking about. Damn, indeed.

"How did it go earlier, with the minister?" There. Juliette wanted to pat herself on the back. She had uttered words. Cogent words that were not out of place and entirely appropriate to this very morning. Because long, muscled, pale legs were absolutely not. Not for this morning, and not for any other time of the day.

After casting one of those meaningful, piercing looks her way, Francesca sighed. "It was fine. Vyatka is… strange."

The speed with which Juliette lifted her face from her leg warmers was dizzying. It was also probably a dead giveaway, considering she was being watched for exactly such a tell, but when she met Francesca's narrowed amber eyes, it was too late.

"Strange?"

Juliette knew her attempt at keeping her tone as neutral as possible had probably failed when Gabriel and Francesca exchanged knowing glances, before the cane was dropped to the floor rather unceremoniously and Francesca hopped on the windowsill closest to Juliette's prone form.

"I have seen her dance. I have seen her rehearse. She is a live wire, a raw, abraded nerve, alive. Yet in the past twenty-four hours, I have seen no life in her. A marble statue could bleed before a life sign could be drawn from this woman. It's like these are two different people."

Juliette thought back to the night, the tear-stained face, the quiet thanks given to the stars, the lingering looks, and the vulnerability in those eyes. No, not a statue. Not by a long shot.

"Her strangeness aside, Jett, we are getting a new prima. And the good doctor is not entirely wrong."

Francesca brushed a speck of lint from her silk sleeve, not meeting Juliette's eyes.

Gabriel's laughter was just a tiny bit forced. "Oh please, Cesca. You run this place, are you saying you are not certain of the Princess of Paris's place at Palais Garnier? It's all in your hands, after all."

Juliette appreciated the attempt at levity, despite the false note of surety in her best friend's voice, and the question.

When Francesca finally met Juliette's eyes again, something in those golden depths was cagey, hidden, and the sense of premonition that had not left since she had first seen Katarina Vyatka plucked at her heartstrings, harder this time, with a pull that made her wince.

"My hands…" Francesca's smile was tinged with an emotion Juliette was unable to read, but then it was gone, and the usual hauteur was back on those full lips. "Well, thank God, my hands are stronger than my legs these days. And no, nobody would dare usurp the throne of the Princess of Paris, not even the Empress of Moscow. I am so very partial to the former, you see."

And now the eyes looking down at her were kind and teasing, and Juliette had no choice but to smile back.

"You are so very lucky I am very good, Cesca."

The three of them laughed, Francesca's merriment by far the loudest.

"Oh please. As if anyone would say anything if I chose the most talentless member of the corps. Nobody tells Hollywood directors whom they can feature in their films. Nobody will tell me, either. But yes, you being the best dancer to ever walk the Opera floorboards definitely helps."

"I really wish I could take exception to that last assertion." Gabriel pouted a bit before continuing. "But I can't. Hence, my asking earlier why everyone is suddenly worried about Jett. Yes, her charity and savior complex is a weakness of hers. But she has the crown, the throne, and the talent to back them. And she has you to stage the ballets that will showcase all of the above. Plus, she has the most majestic arms in the entire city to be showcased on." Gabriel flexed his impressive biceps and in one swift motion picked Juliette up from the floor, gathering her at his chest.

Francesca smacked said majestic arms.

"Put her down, you fool. If you damage my prima before I reveal my master plan, I will demote you to the Moulin Rouge, not just to the corps."

"I fear that is not something that Monsieur Flanagan would consider punishment, Madame Bianchi."

Juliette stilled in Gabriel's arms, another tell she was certain he would notice, but the voice had materialized seemingly from thin air, even in a room full of mirrors.

The woman was ethereal, standing in the doorway in a pair of ankle trousers and a gauzy blouse. Juliette nearly lost her breath. The towel had been quite a shock to her system, but seeing Katarina Vyatka wearing her clothes, the linen that caressed her skin now lying open over the translucent expanse of the long throat… Juliette coughed and averted her eyes. Gabriel gave her a reassuring squeeze before gently putting her down. If there was any doubt that he had figured out her predicament, it was gone now. Not when he was literally propping her up with that little smirk playing on his smug face.

Juliette bit her lip and looked at Katarina again. Despite them being of a similar height, the clothes didn't fit exactly right, and yet the way she wore them—with that debonair nonchalance of someone who knew she looked amazing even in ill-fitting castoffs—was more than making up for the incongruence.

Juliette was suddenly aware of the subject of the conversation that surely Katarina overheard. Talk about embarrassing and awkward. She closed her eyes and said a little prayer to whichever divinity was listening that Katarina had missed the charity part.

Gabriel, perhaps having had enough of his triumphant glee, was the one to find his voice first.

"As I said yesterday, I have a feeling you and I will be close friends, Mademoiselle Vyatka. And I promise not to correct your already perfect posture, unlike Michel."

One corner of the unsmiling mouth twitched. Juliette broke into a light sweat.

"Scared of blood, Monsieur Flanagan?" Katarina's words were dry as a bone, and yet the glint in the hooded eyes spoke volumes.

Gabriel played along. "Terrified. And completely in awe of the blood-drawing prowess."

The corner of the mouth that had twitched earlier was allowed to lift slightly more in an enigmatic half smile. "Then you have nothing to be afraid of, Monsieur Flanagan. Awe is an appropriate emotion."

Jumping off the windowsill, Francesca winced visibly, cursed, then picked up her cane and thumped it on the floor once, the customary attention-grabbing gesture as effective as ever. "This is all very cute, but we have work to do."

Juliette saw Katarina pull on her blouse, clearly needing to change, and wondered what she could change into, to begin with. The thought of lending her some spare leotards, which really were like second skin—

"I need the three of you in my office. Vyatka, you missed the morning class and will need to catch up in the afternoon. Jett, you'll figure out her clothes situation after we speak. Gabriel, grab some food for us from the cafeteria and then come upstairs. This is a longer discussion, and I don't want any ears. I have a feeling that with the three of you, the gossip will spread anyway." Francesca gave Gabriel a sharp glare before turning and heading in the direction of the exit and the staircase.

"Why does she think I will be the one to spill the beans on whatever harebrained scheme she is concocting this time?" Gabriel pouted and picked his bag off the floor.

"Maybe because it's always you?" Juliette tried to act as naturally as possible, still not meeting Katarina's eyes. Gabriel guffawed and threw his bag her way.

"Since I'm on lunch duty, you can carry my stuff, Jett." Only a swift maneuver saved her face from being smashed by whatever heavy and smelly items he lugged around in that sack, and Juliette sighed before setting it on her shoulder.

"I see you are doing his work again."

Juliette almost jumped, the voice and the comment so

unexpected despite her being so focused on how she appeared to Katarina. Katarina, who seemed to be seeing right through her act.

"I'm not certain I get your meaning."

"Even in your pas de deux, you carry his weight. He is one of the best male dancers I've ever seen, but he is just that—a male."

There was so much rancor, so much bitterness, and yet the tone was neutrality itself, a mere observation.

Juliette wanted to ask questions. To prod just a bit. After all, the former Soviet prima had been rumored to have been engaged. There was some kind of affair attached to her name and that of the dancer who had defected a few years ago in London. Foltin.

Juliette had seen him a few times. He'd been much older than her, by a good twenty years, which put him about a decade ahead of Katarina herself. He was… not attractive. Something in him held that small note of sliminess that Juliette could not pinpoint. Still, they had exchanged only a sentence or two after his performance, and while she did not like him as a man, as a dancer he had been in a class of his own. Gabriel was amazing. Foltin was better.

Moreover, last night when Francesca's outburst had inadvertently outed both of them, Katarina had seemed… not shocked, exactly, but a shadow did pass in those cold blue depths and Juliette did not think it had been an approval.

And why was she thinking about Katarina and homosexuality to begin with? Juliette rolled her eyes at herself and marched forward, lengthening her stride.

An efficient maneuver with most people, it failed to reach its intended results, as Katarina matched her step in the wide corridors of the Palais Garnier, the faint orange blossom scent slipping under the ever-present and ever-familiar smells of rosin and sweat mixed with industrial cleaner. Somewhere close by, piano notes mingled with the rhythmic movements of a warm-up, the perfect backdrop for this stroll through the building.

Everything was safe and familiar and very much hers. Except for the orange blossom, and the occasional sensation of warmth whenever Juliette took a step that brought her just a few inches closer to her companion.

Her skin tingled on her left side, and she was reasonably certain her palms were perspiring. She was behaving like a fool. Another shake of her head, this time assuredly at herself, and Juliette felt she could speak without giving away whatever strangeness possessed her.

"Gabriel is the best of men."

Katarina did not even attempt to hide her exaggerated eye roll. "Men have their uses."

Juliette bristled, all sense of warmth and familiarity gone, the orange almost cloying now. Still, even as she was about to open her mouth, she admitted the day had not yet come when Juliette Lucian-Sorel would be the one staunchly defending the male cause. Katarina could have this round. Juliette waved her hand to indicate as much.

She got a purse of the full lips as a reply to her wave after what seemed an eternity. Or for the length of the entire second floor. By the time they took the turn toward the stairs leading up to the administrative offices, Juliette surmised that was all she was going to get.

A gaggle of ballet school students passed them by, most of them nodding or saying good morning to her. Juliette did her best to reply and call out a few names. The girls preened at being noticed and giggled as they skipped on their way, undoubtedly to join the corps de ballet for one of the bigger productions. The season was starting, and rehearsals were in full swing.

A perfectly raised eyebrow was all she got for her interaction with the juniors, and while she did not mind defending Gabriel—he was occasionally a scoundrel—Katarina's reaction to the kids rankled.

"I teach evening classes, usually specialized lessons for the girls who want more instruction to catch up to the rest of the pack. I work with dancers who require correction of poses and movements that injure them."

The words spilled out before she even realized she had been explaining herself. Katarina's eyes widened a fraction at the last sentence. The silence that followed stretched and their footsteps echoed in the now-empty hallway.

"The corps has its uses too, I suppose. I guess it's another example of your charity. Or lack of ability to mind your own business."

Well, whatever divinity Juliette had been praying to earlier clearly gave no credence to her pleas. Katarina had heard the exchange with Gabriel. And she had not forgotten Juliette's révérence faux pas.

Still, Katarina's response had been predictable for someone who appeared so proud in the light of day and under bystanders' curious gazes. There was more of that… pragmatism, for lack of a better word. And if she was honest with herself, Juliette had no words at all. It was a bleak and dark outlook that her companion was espousing, and Juliette had never been one for the shadows.

She had no way of knowing what Katarina's lived experiences were, of course, but she was beginning to suspect whatever they had been, they had rendered the former Soviet prima closed off and maybe a touch unfeeling. Which went to contradict the woman who, last night, hid her tears in the rain and thanked the stars.

Francesca's door appearing in front of them was a welcome relief from Juliette's confusion. She had been thinking too much about Katarina Vyatka. Delivering her to Francesca and never having to deal with her again, especially once she'd vacated Juliette's apartment, would be exactly what she needed to stop this feeling that she was off her rhythm. She was a ballerina, after all, and she needed her balance more than anything. Stealing one last glance at the ice-blue eyes shielded by indifference and detachment, Juliette mentally added "especially now" to all of her previous thoughts.

Eight

Of Lust & Fear

"I am dancing *what* with her?"

Well, so much for dumping Katarina on Francesca and never having to deal with her ever again.

"*Swan Lake.*"

Two words in Francesca's heavily accented tone sounded like a verdict. A capital one.

"I'm sorry, you want Jett and Kat here to dance *Swan Lake*? Together?"

A sharp glance in his direction from the narrowed cold blue eyes and Gabriel immediately lifted his hands palm up.

"Katarina, Katarina the Great, Empress of Moscow, my apologies, Your Majesty."

Katarina ignored his buffoonery entirely. She had made her point. A good point, too, because knowing Gabriel they'd be "Jett and Kat," or whatever annoying, ridiculous moniker he'd make up for them, in no time.

Still, Gabriel's question landed like a lead balloon and surely, with its weight and consequence, broke some of the lacquered antique parquet pieces on the gorgeous office floor.

Francesca didn't deign to look at him, instead meeting Juliette's questioning gaze head-on. "No, otherwise you'd not be here, querido."

Gabriel pinched the bridge of his nose and then simply stared at the Director of Ballet in complete stupor.

"Jett, you said it yourself when you were staging your little coup d'état last night. *Swan Lake* is the most famous production in the world by far, and your fiery speech gave me the idea for a perfect reinterpretation. A reinvention of the old and boring."

Francesca's face, tipped to the ceiling as if in the middle of a solo performance, was alight with a maniacal kind of passion. Then she finally looked back at Gabriel and deflated. When she spoke, sarcasm came loud and clear in her tone.

"From the intelligent and understanding look on your face, and the clearly delighted ones on the ladies' visages, I take it you are all on board, fully supporting this, and will work your exquisite behinds off to ensure standing ovations every night. Right? Amazing. Dismissed."

Francesca threw her cane in the office's corner and turned her back to the dancers standing motionless and in total astonishment. When she reached her chair and plopped down behind the immense desk, she pursed her lips before regaling them with a very displeased string of curses. Once she was done, she blew out a breath and rolled her eyes before speaking.

"I have the best prima in Paris and the former face of Moscow ballet, and you want me to stage what? *Giselle*? Spare me. That horse is so dead, beating it seems grotesque. We need a revolution!"

"People tend to lose heads after revolutions in this town, Madame Bianchi." Katarina's words were dryness personified. Juliette couldn't help but smile.

Francesca wasn't impressed, and her frosty, unamused voice said as much. "Cute. Always knew you were a cute one."

Katarina curled her lip but said nothing, and Juliette suspected nobody had ever dared call her cute in her entire life. Francesca dismissed her with an exaggerated shrug.

Juliette felt the need to intervene, if only to avoid bloodshed.

"Cesca, the same ballerina always dances Odile and Odette—"

"Oh, yawn, yawn. Of course one ballerina dances both. *Swan Lake* is about transformation as much as anything else. However… Can't you see? Blonde and brunette? Can't you grasp my vision? Light and dark? And the blonde here dancing the dark swan of evil and the brunette being the Goody Two-shoes? Tell me, if you're the public, aren't you running and selling your firstborns for a ticket to the opening night?"

"Evil?"

"Goody Two-shoes?"

Both Katarina's clear objection to being immediately cast as the villain and Juliette's reaction to being essentially slotted as the boring one would have been comical if they hadn't also been visibly uncomfortable.

At least, Juliette was. Ever since this morning—and honestly, who was she kidding, ever since last night—she had just not been feeling like herself. That sense of premonition, of an extended déjà vu of sorts, that kept tugging at the corner of her conscience was rather exhausting when all was said and done.

Since Juliette always tried to be as sincere as she possibly could, at least with herself, it didn't feel like things were actually done at all. It seemed that whatever was looming over them all had only just begun its ominous approach.

She told herself it was the deal she had made with the Culture Minister. She told herself it was the stranger in her apartment. Juliette told herself many things, but she couldn't ignore her own distinct discomfort and a state of alertness that was so out of character. She felt boxed in, in this office full of light and old librettos.

Music sheets were scattered on every surface, some amongst dust bunnies and some covered in empty mugs. And yet even here, with scents of stale coffee mingling with Francesca's bespoke Dior, the orange blossom teased at Juliette's senses, making her extra aware of the presence to her right. Making her extra aware of her own reaction to said presence.

Not that Katarina needed much to be noticed. Or remembered. Ramrod straight, shoulders thrown slightly back, she was the picture of a thunderstorm in complete stillness. For someone who was so unreadable damn near all the time, today of all days those sharp angles of the pale face showed exactly what she was thinking, and Francesca's call for a revolution clearly did not resonate. Maybe as a person whose country boasted to have undertaken quite a bloody one, she just wasn't a fan?

Juliette grinned at her own joke before schooling her features. She had her own objections to voice, chiefly among them—

"I shall not, under any circumstances, be taking any parts off Mademoiselle Lucian-Sorel's plate."

Yeah. That one.

Katarina had beat her to the punch, and it was like a weight had lifted. Juliette stood taller. Helena had planted a seed last night, one that Juliette did not want to necessarily nurture, but with Francesca already making moves to split roles, it was hard not to become a touch paranoid.

Francesca pursed her lips and laid her hands, palms down, on the antique desk.

"I was not going to stage *Swan Lake* at all. Not this year. The company's repertoire was getting predictable, and what can be more predictable than the little swans? Now, shaking it all up, two ballerinas being the centerpiece, doing an extensive pas de deux between the shadows and the light? Now *that* is something that has never been done before. And that is something that I could have never even dreamt of doing, simply because no one—absolutely no one—who walks these hallways could ever be on the same stage as Jett as an equal and belong there."

Juliette could feel her own eyebrows rise toward her hairline. Francesca was never effusive with her praise, perhaps wary of giving her too much leverage in their already murky relationship, but this was decidedly nice to hear. Even as her cheeks turned pink, Francesca went on, pointing a long bony finger straight at her.

"She is my prima. My principal dancer. Nobody in my company dares to take her parts. Not even me. But she cannot dance opposite herself, and in you, I finally have a puzzle piece that will match my star." The up-and-down look Francesca gave Katarina would have probably made a lesser woman spin around and run. Katarina didn't so much as flinch.

"You helped me get asylum because—"

"I *allowed* you to stay at Palais Garnier, Mademoiselle Vyatka, against my better judgment and under duress, because the powers that be forced me to and because you are the second-best dancer I have ever seen on the floorboards of this theater. But please don't mistake my self-interest as approval of you being here."

Juliette almost gaped and managed to school her features only at the last second. This was harsh. Yes, Katarina had caused a lot of trouble for everyone involved, but surely Francesca saw—

"I do see the advantages of having you with the company. And I would have been a fool to not grab this chance of capitalizing on your fame, your considerable skill, and your even greater scandal. But make no mistake. If not for Juliette, you'd not be here, and she will always be my number one."

Francesca's dark eyes bore holes into Katarina's, and Juliette felt like she was intruding on a very personal conversation. She had more often than not been on the receiving end of praise, applause being very much her milieu, yet this felt different. Territorial. And thus all the stranger.

A few more seconds of the staredown and Francesca was the first to avert her eyes. When Katarina spoke, her words had the finality of a death sentence.

"You have your Odile, then."

She took a step back and leaned against the wall, leaving Juliette space to stand alone in front of Francesca, alone with her argument, alone with her decision. Even Gabriel, stretched out on the futon by the bay of windows, was quiet.

She tried to sift through the multitude of questions that kept popping into her head. The original pas de deux was iconic for its physicality, and neither ballerina would be able to so much as lift the other one an inch off the floor. But that seemed somewhat moot, especially when Francesca's eyes were shining with that maniacal light of obsession.

"I will dance the parts I'm given, Cesca, you know that—"

A clap of hands, then a fist pump, and Francesca was on her feet, cane forgotten, limping her way across the office and sweeping Juliette into a bone-crushing hug.

"Excellent. Most excellent indeed. And Gabriel is still your Prince, and he loses nothing—"

"Just the most beloved part. The audience will lose its collective mind!" Gabriel's face was a comical mixture of a pout and the brightest eyes ever. Honest to a fault in both his disappointment for himself and excitement for her. For the potential of the production. Because in one thing Francesca was absolutely right, despite her brashness: Two ballerinas dancing *Swan Lake* was a revolution. And that meant butts in seats and a revamp of Paris Opera Ballet's reputation, from predictable and stale to unexpected and unprecedented. And in their business, that meant everything.

Still, the issue of the pas de deux was a logistical nightmare. That and the lifts.

"No lifts." Francesca made a sweeping gesture with her arm, not unlike flicking off a cape.

Both Juliette and Gabriel gawked. Katarina remained impassive, arms crossed over her chest, looking from one participant of this conversation to the other with visible boredom.

"Cesca—"

"I have made myself very clear and I will not be reconsidering my decision. The pas de deux is not a gender flip, amor. It's a vision of the movement. I am reinventing it, not massacring Tchaikovsky. Plus, you two are already wearing each other's clothes. How much more lesbian do you want this entire experience to get?"

Juliette felt more than saw the stiffening of Katarina's willowy arms, and the bored expression lifted for a moment before the clearly practiced detachment returned to the chiseled features. This was the second time Francesca had brought up her lesbianism in front of Katarina and the second time the former Soviet prima reacted in a way that Juliette could only guess was a recoil. Too bad. But maybe just bad enough to have Juliette overcome the stupor she entered every time she had to come face-to-face with her. Bigotry wasn't attractive.

Except, Katarina was. Even now she was breathtaking. After being thrown to the wolves of her judgment on the subject of sexuality the way Juliette had been, Katarina's allure sadly didn't dim. She remained the epitome of gorgeous. Juliette watched, mesmerized, as her future dance partner pushed off the wall and took a few steps toward the exit, clearly done with this conversation since it had turned to matters disturbing to her. Nothing seemed to detract from the allure. Juliette pressed a steadying hand to her abdomen and got a narrowed-eyed look from Gabriel.

In the meantime, Katarina had reached the door, with her long, unfaltering stride crossing the room in just a few steps.

"If this is all." Despite the supposed inquiry, there was no question mark in her tone, and it felt very much like she was the one dismissing them all. To Francesca's nod and careless, "Yes, yes, go take class, make up for the lost morning," she simply closed the door behind herself without a backward glance.

A second passed, two, the clock on the wall measuring time and the beats of Juliette's heart, which suddenly felt like it was beating itself out of her chest.

Here it comes...

"No way, Jett! You do not!" Gabriel was on his feet and by her side in the blink of an eye.

Juliette sidestepped him, but apparently also sidestepping Francesca, who was smirking at them, was not an option.

"Oh, if I was a betting woman, I'd put a considerable amount of money on the fact that yes, she very much does, querido."

Juliette shook her head at their shenanigans.

"Last I checked, you *are* a betting woman and I have no idea what either of you two clowns are talking about."

"You and the walking icicle over there, amor, of course." Francesca pointed to the door and made a show of looking for her cane. Gabriel jumped to help her. Once he had delivered the ebony oak, he gave her an elbow bump, as always mindful of her balance.

"I see now why you are staging the pas de deux between these two. All that talk about great ballerinas, matching Jett, so bogus. It's all about the sizzle. And while we fake sizzle as well as can be expected from two gays, even I can't act at that level."

Francesca laughed, and Juliette felt like she had taken a walk through the magic mirror. For surely this must be a parallel universe of some sort. She had probably been inhabiting it since yesterday because the entire ordeal had to be a figment of her imagination. Especially the way she acted around Katarina. Which had to be some kind of aberration, one she would deny till death. And speaking of denying...

"What level is that, Gabriel? Because I see no level—"

"It's really serendipitous that you are a dancer and not a sharpshooter, amor. Your eyesight leaves quite a lot to be desired. You couldn't see Helena roping you into that relationship, nor goading you to go to New York. And that's fine. Part of your charm. All that brain and all this nearsightedness. To your own importance, to your own attractiveness. It doesn't matter. It's enough that I see it. And the public will see it."

Juliette rolled her eyes and looked down at her fingernails. It was time for a manicure.

"And what is it that you and the public will be seeing?"

"Lust and fear, amor. And these are unique emotions to play *with* and play *to* when dancing. Nothing comes close to that."

With those words, Francesca took Gabriel's arm and left Juliette alone in the now-empty office among dirty mugs, scattered music sheets, and a faint trace of orange blossom.

Nine

Of Pink Light & Night Terrors

Okay, so maybe Francesca was a tad correct. Only a tad, mind you. Juliette wouldn't go as far as lust, because that was way off base and she just didn't want to wade into that quagmire. However, to be fair to all involved, Juliette decided to cautiously admit to attraction. Fine. Francesca could have attraction.

Juliette was miffed about it, but the feeling wasn't foreign. She was experienced, after all, and knew how to handle it without making the object of said emotion uncomfortable. And Juliette was convinced that Katarina would not be just uncomfortable, she'd be utterly disgusted by it, since she had shown nothing but contempt every time Juliette's lesbianism had been mentioned.

Juliette, however, felt that her usual woman-about-town savoir faire in matters of women had abandoned her. She had already been thoroughly inappropriate to Katarina by getting caught ogling her as she exited the shower, dripping wet, in a flimsy towel.

Juliette wanted to smack herself upside the head for being so obvious. So devoid of tact and self-control. In her defense, Katarina could stop traffic on any day. Katarina covered only by a patch of cotton would have paralyzed Paris's entire infrastructure. Juliette was only human.

Well, human or not, days passed and she felt like an alien in her own space. They would exit the apartment on Rue de Rivoli and walk seemingly together yet without a single word past Rue Saint-Honoré toward Place de l'Opéra. A fifteen-minute walk on her regular days, Juliette would make this one in ten because Katarina stopped for nothing, not even red lights, although there weren't too many of those. So Juliette kept up, even if she wasn't entirely sure why. They weren't speaking. They weren't even acknowledging each other.

Arriving at Palais Garnier, they would take class, and Katarina would finally talk, her words precise and concise and none of them directed at Juliette. She would usually address either the pianist or the janitor and then retreat to the ever-characteristic silence.

Even her silence held weight. And took space. Juliette could never quite shake her awareness of the other prima—despite Katarina positioning herself out of her line of sight and occupying the farthest corner of any classroom. Juliette had become so attuned to Katarina's presence, predicting when she was in the rehearsal room before she herself even entered it. The air itself felt charged.

Juliette more often than not chastised herself for being foolish. The woman clearly disliked her. Whether it was that gauche ogling incident, or the constant reminder that Juliette had been her savior, or that after a lifelong career as the biggest star and attraction of one of the world's most prominent ballet companies she was now very deliberately playing second fiddle to someone much younger than her, or some combination of all of the above, remained to be seen.

And on top of everything, Francesca and the rest of the administration seemed hell-bent on never quite letting Katarina forget how indebted she was to them all—and especially to Juliette.

Juliette wasn't entirely certain that despite her impassive

assurances that she did not wish to take her parts, Katarina wouldn't drop some sturdy piece of decoration on her just to end the litany of "you wouldn't be here without her." Something in the way Katarina watched her every move made Juliette's skin feel too tight and her palms break out in sweat.

With each day that passed, Juliette was increasingly reminded of the age-old adage about the road to hell and the good intentions that paved it. Her good intentions, her savior complex, in this very case.

Still, their days went on, and after class they would sprawl on the floor till Francesca arrived and made them rehearse until they were so tired they could barely stand.

Then Katarina would disappear, and Juliette told herself she'd immediately forget her very existence. Juliette would have lunch and continue with the rest of the company. She'd attend more rehearsals for *The Nutcracker* and *Don Quixote*, which were the productions she was headlining this season. She would try extra hard for *Don Quixote*, since it would be the season's flagship ballet. The number of heavy expectations riding on its success was enough to break even the strongest of backs.

Despite Juliette herself having doubts about everything in connection to the old Spanish tale, Francesca was still staging it.

"You said you would keep your reservations to yourself, Jett." Francesca offered her a towel and leaned on the wall opposite the mirrors.

"I haven't said anything." Juliette wisely hid her face and her opinion in the folds of cotton, but Francesca was not deterred.

"You don't have to say anything. The way you come in for rehearsals, as if this was Place de la Concorde and the old single blade was still standing on the scaffold, is telling me, nay, shouting at me, that you're not enthused." Francesca gave her a bilious look.

"I don't have to be enthused, Cesca. I have to sell the ballet. And I shall. Don't I always?"

Even to her own ears, her words sounded hollow. The production was lacking. She knew it. Gabriel knew it. And Francesca's excessive bitching told her as much. All they had to do now was bite the bullet and bear it. With the programs printed, the company was committed. *Don Quixote* would be danced, consequences be damned.

Where Juliette didn't have to fake excitement and enjoyed herself immensely was in Tchaikovsky, even though they would reserve *The Nutcracker* for the holidays. It was one of her favorite ballets, perhaps because she and the entire world associated it with Christmas and cheer. She loved dancing it and looked forward to it every year.

The one show Juliette had no idea what to make of was Francesca's *Swan Lake* revamp. The ballet had been in production with the company two years prior, but the choreography and interpretation had been deemed stale and thus poorly received. Her own press was stellar, per usual, but Francesca and the company itself were lambasted heavily for lack of inspiration. In fact, that was when the string of terrible reviews had begun, and try as they all might in the years that followed that fiasco, Paris Opera Ballet had been unable to dig itself out of the hole of the steadily expanding negativity.

Their tours were resounding successes, but once they set foot back in France, the press was like rabid dogs on them and nothing they staged rose up to expectations. Nobody had been spared, and even Juliette's amazing reviews had turned lackluster soon enough. Her technique was lauded, but she was deemed "lost and spent on stage" in more productions than she cared to remember. Francesca would rage and throw things and call the French all manner of names, but Juliette knew something had to give, and soon.

"Is she compensating, do you think?" Juliette was draped over the barre, her legs leaden and her breath coming out in short pumps.

Gabriel, a few feet away from her, gave her a look from under heavy eyelids and dropped his head back to the floor with a loud *thump*.

"Jett, who the hell knows with Cesca? Can you ever predict what bee will get under her bonnet? Just the fact that she was so vocal about not wanting Kat here and is now staging a production that caters to her presence and strengths…"

"You're lucky she's not here to take a few swipes at you for calling her that."

He shuddered playfully and then sat up, hugging his knees.

"What she doesn't know can't hurt me, Juju, and you won't tell on me, will you?"

Gabriel gave her an angelic smile before grabbing his water bottle and continuing pensively.

"Something has to give. The company is in a sorry state, and neither of us have been able to move the needle even a little despite our clearly superior efforts. It's like we're cursed. No matter the production, it's one bad review after the next. The crowds are thinning, the budgets are getting smaller. So, why not try something outlandish? Risky and maybe foolish under normal circumstances, but what does she have to lose?"

He wiped his brow and flopped back down.

"So, a Hail Mary…" Juliette turned to face him and caught the grimace on his face that usually followed whatever saying she used that was quintessentially American.

She ignored him and mulled his answer. For all his flighty affairs and apparent superficiality, Gabriel was too attuned to the company to be completely ignorant. And he was probably right, even if little about this situation was evident or straightforward.

And even if Juliette was still mesmerized by Francesca's dislike for Katarina. In fact, everyone but Juliette herself and Gabriel showed nothing but contempt for the former Soviet prima. It made Juliette inexplicably angry.

"You're making the face you usually make before mounting

some ill-advised crusade, Jett." Gabriel's chuckle brought her back to the present. "Are you upset on behalf of Vyatka? She seems to be taking the animosity in stride, and if anything, is completely unbothered by it. Why are you?"

That was the million-dollar question, and Juliette bit her lip, holding back what was on the very tip of her tongue. None of these people saw Katarina, none of them understood her. Then Juliette realized how silly her thoughts were and shook her head. Katarina seemed impervious to everything around her, including Juliette, and they were all better off leaving well enough alone. Katarina didn't need her protection.

As the rehearsals started in earnest and Juliette had to make more and more room in her schedule for an extra afternoon session to work with Francesca and Katarina on the pas de deux from the second act of *Swan Lake*, she knew her face showed mostly apprehension. The steps and the moves were more than risky. They were downright risqué.

She said so one evening when Katarina had long departed after a strenuous and demanding rehearsal and she was alone with Francesca, who kept adding more components to the movements.

"You just don't see what I see," Francesca answered, pushed her chair toward Juliette, and perched on it, looking down and not even disguising her perusal of her former lover.

Juliette wasn't so sure they were former anything anyway. Could they be exes if they'd never been together properly? Francesca didn't seem to be bothered at all, neither by the fact that their arrangement seemed to have ended, nor that neither of them had acknowledged that it had.

"You're about to tell me that you are betting on the lust that I refuse to acknowledge, aren't you?" Francesca's smirk in response was decidedly lurid, and Juliette slapped the knee closest to her. "Don't. I am not protesting anything, but do you not see that she hates me?"

The teasing was gone, and a thoughtful expression took over the beautiful features.

"Amor, Katarina Vyatka doesn't hate you. She's a cold fish. I doubt she'd work up the energy it takes to have that strong of an emotion for anyone. I'd watch my back for sure, but more because she seems highly feral to me. I guess living your entire life behind the Iron Curtain under unmitigated control of a totalitarian state and being the politicians' favorite plaything and prisoner would do that to anyone."

"Plaything? Prisoner?" Juliette refused to regret asking, even if Francesca's face was glowing with something akin to "gotcha."

"She's been kept under wraps for over a decade, amor. Despite being the absolute best ballerina the Soviet Union has ever produced. Don't you wonder why? She had to beg for her life, humiliate herself in front of you, me, Lalande. What was she escaping, the biggest star of her country, with hundreds of thousands of clamoring fans? Whatever she was running from that warranted such humiliation must have been quite something indeed."

It took Juliette a few seconds to process Francesca's words, who, undeterred by her rumination, continued with a grin.

"Or maybe she is just a garden-variety bitch. A superiorly gifted one, but a bitch nonetheless."

"I don't think she can be garden-variety anything, Cesca. And wasn't it her own countryman Pushkin who said that genius and evil are incompatible?"

Francesca laughed out loud and leaned forward to give Juliette a one-armed hug.

"My darling, darling girl. I often forget that underneath all your talent and all your otherworldliness, a twenty-five-year-old is hiding. Keep thinking your thoughts and believing your Russian poets, but I would not stop checking my shoes for glass, amor."

Juliette tsked. "Is this why you treat her like she has the plague?"

The silence that met her question stretched for longer than Juliette would've liked. She'd much prefer that Francesca dismiss her query as nonsense. When the answer did come, Francesca's voice was all steel.

"I'd treat her better if she had the plague, Jett. I'd know what to expect. Fever, sores, imminent death. With Katarina Vyatka? I have no idea, and that is what I don't like about her."

The words rang in Juliette's mind all through the afternoon and her evening class with the injured dancers.

That night, Juliette was particularly late returning home. A young ballerina, once a very talented prospect, seemed to have lost her sumptuous skills despite numerous tutors and classes. Juliette knew the issue had to be an old hamstring injury, but so far, her endeavors to discover the extent of its remaining impact on the range of motion and the correctness of steps, especially the tendus, were futile.

The ballerina was moving perfectly, but in the middle of the extension something was shifting almost imperceptibly and the next step would be out of alignment, disrupting pose and range. Juliette had a feeling that the calf was affected by the weakened hamstring, thus derailing everything. But the girl was stubbornly rejecting every attempt at assessment of the entire leg, insisting there wasn't any issue.

The eerie similarity with Katarina dismissing any kind of injury with the viciousness of an angry—yet graceful—blonde mongoose gave Juliette pause. The image her tired brain had conjured made her grin, then she caught herself. Her entire day had been spent trying not to think of Katarina. She needed a hobby of some kind.

As she exited Palais Garnier, her luck stayed rotten. The sudden storm, so out of season, left Paris—and by extension, her—soaked and moody. The Rue de Rivoli was quiet, the luxury of a wealthy neighborhood silent at night with the absence of tourists. In a few hours, the hotel next to her building and the world-famous Angelina, the neighboring tearoom, would begin their preparations for the day. The sumptuous gardens across the street would awaken from their slumber and welcome throngs of people. Joggers would muddy their running shoes. The construction workers would yell and gesture as they broke ground on the Louvre Pyramid. Pigeons would clamor for crumbs, and Paris would shake off the rain and the thunder.

But for now, everything slept. Juliette very much wished herself to be in a similar state. The day had been long, and the emotional toll of having someone in her space, in her classes, in her rehearsals—dammit, in her head—was beginning to weigh heavy.

The key turned smoothly in the lock, the darkness around her scraping the already abraded nerve endings raw.

"I was told the apartment next door will be ready in three weeks and then I will be out of here."

Juliette nearly jumped out of her skin.

"My fucking… Jesus! Vyatka, what the hell?"

Arms wrapped around her chest, back against the far wall of the foyer, Katarina stared at her with visible displeasure.

"I can ask the same."

Juliette took off her shoes, not bothering to keep the noise down. They were past pleasantries.

"No clue what you could be saying. I'm exhausted, I'm hungry, and I'm drenched. In case you haven't noticed, there's a torrential downpour outside."

Her stockings were next. Juliette's balance still off and her breathing erratic, she did not bother going to her room. Katarina had seen her in a leotard. She'd have to deal with her tired, naked legs.

Katarina's way of dealing was to have her eyes follow Juliette's every move and glare at the expanse of skin on display. Juliette merely shrugged. Ballerinas were rarely afforded the luxury of privacy, and nudity was par for the course for their profession.

They showered and changed in front of one another all the time. And she was past caring what this prude had to say, if she had anything to say at all.

"You'd be none of those things, if you endeavored to be home at a decent hour. Then maybe both of us would be getting a modicum of rest and not be exhausted for tomorrow's rehearsals."

Ah, so it turned out that Katarina did have things to say. Juliette took her time getting up from the little footstool and made her way across the room till they were face-to-face. Of similar build and almost identical height, every day Juliette understood more and more what Francesca saw in them as the perfect Odile and Odette. After all, the Prince did confuse the two of them, falling for the wiles of Odile and forsaking his love for Odette.

"What I do with my time to cause me to be as exhausted as I am is nobody's business but my own, Katarina."

The words were like puffs of smoke between them, and Juliette very much craved a cigarette. Maybe the stench of tobacco would exorcise the orange blossoms once and for all. Why had she never really gotten into the habit? And was it too late to start now?

An inch separated them, and Juliette ignored the little voice in her head that told her that playing with fire—or ice, in this particular case—was bound to leave her with burns. But she didn't step back, and to her vicious delight, neither did Katarina. In fact, she showed no reaction at all, her face as inscrutable as before. The only signs of what Juliette interpreted as wariness were those unreadable eyes narrowing slightly and the chiseled nostrils flaring.

They stood for what seemed an eternity, darkness like a shawl around them, no longer a distressing sight for Juliette. When had that happened? When had she stopped being afraid of the dark? Something must have shown on her face, because Katarina narrowed her eyes further and then finally, with a slight bow of her head, stepped to the side and toward her room.

"Your time is your own."

Katarina's voice held a note of resignation, and as she took a few more steps away, Juliette whispered, "Obviously." As retorts went, it was pathetically weak, but a flinch in Katarina's shoulders told her that she nevertheless hit her mark.

Talk about pathetic. Bickering like children. So they had all this… animosity between them. Big deal. Juliette made her way through the dark apartment to the kitchen, where the small lamp was waiting for her. With a touch of her fingers the space was illuminated by the tiny pinkish light she left on every night.

Small, but mighty…

It chased the shadows away, and with them, her fears. She opened the fridge, more out of habit than with any determination to eat. A few wilted leaves of spinach and some kind of brown concoction in a glass that might have been her milkshake from three days ago made for a sorry sight. There would be eggs at the Opera cafeteria in the morning to give her an energy boost.

In her bedroom, the silence deepened. So did the solitude. It was her space. Nobody, not even the stranger in the next room, had access. Except, the usual familiarity and comfort of her room didn't soothe her tonight. Restless, she crossed to the bedside table and the phone that stood there.

One breath… This was a bad idea. She should not be calling Helena just because she was lonely and her feathers were ruffled by a woman who seemed hell-bent on doing more of that every single day.

Two breaths… Time stretched, a spider's web, so precariously fragile yet simultaneously deadly. Was she simply a fly trapped in it?

Three breaths… The shrill ringing of the phone made Juliette jump out of her skin for the second time in the space of twenty minutes.

She knew instantly who it was. As if she had summoned her into this dark, lonely night. Like magic. Like that previously described very bad idea.

"I had a feeling you were not asleep." Helena's voice was like smoldering embers in an otherwise empty hearth.

"It was a long day, longer evening." Juliette sat on the bed, then reconsidered and stretched out, the phone call a blanket against the chill of the earlier rain.

"I hear you are pulling many of these lately, darling. *Swan Lake* with two ballerinas is quite an undertaking."

There was no innuendo nor judgment in Helena's words, maybe just a touch of curiosity. After days of being antagonized, Juliette could live with that. Still, they had a rhythm to these nocturnal conversations, and Juliette knew her part.

"Is there anything Gabriel keeps to himself these days?"

Laughter on the line told her she had made the right choice by not giving in just yet.

"Gabriel is a treasure. And he is both elated and worried about you. He says it's like herding two cats. Two angry cats. Is it true?"

Juliette thought about the confrontation in the foyer and wanted to confess. To simply tell Helena everything. They had always been absolutely honest with each other. But the apartment was quiet, flakes of pink light slipping under her door from the kitchen, and something held her back.

"You should come over for the opening night. Francesca promises that it will be quite a show."

"And what do you think, Jett?"

"I think—"

Somewhere nearby, a wretched sob pierced the stillness of the apartment. A sound so full of fear and desperation, Juliette thought for a second that it couldn't be real. Surely nobody felt these levels of horror. On the line, Helena's voice sounded concerned.

"Jett?"

Another sob, a little less loud but all the more terrifying in its stringency, followed, and Juliette was on her feet and hanging up the phone before she even knew what she was doing. In the next moment, she was by Katarina's door.

Should she knock? The silence deafened her for a second, suggesting she had imagined the crying. Surely she had. The sounds were so horrific, so full of pain and devastation. She must've imagined them, she must've—

"No!" Katarina's voice was much louder here, and Juliette forwent the knocking, throwing the door open and stepping into the dark room. The bed dominated the space. It was perfectly made, Juliette's earlier thoughts of bouncing a coin totally justified. It was flawless. And empty.

Ten

Of Dark Closets & Dusty Staircases

The third cry wrenched Juliette out of her horrified stupor and directed her steps toward the closet. It was much smaller than her own, built into the tiny alcove in the wall between the two bedrooms, and yet when she slowly drew the flimsy door ajar, it managed to house what looked like decades of terror and sorrow.

Katarina, knees pulled up to her chest and arms clutching them tight, was rocking back and forth, her face awash with steady streams of tears that seemed to drown out the blue of her eyes entirely. Hollow and expressionless, they appeared unseeing. She did not flinch when Juliette pulled the door fully open, nor did she appear to even realize she was no longer alone.

She seemed to be in a trance, consumed whole by the nightmare. A cry was followed by a hiccup, then another.

Juliette felt useless, powerless to stop the flood of sorrow and unable to just walk away, even if she knew that if Katarina had been aware of her presence she wouldn't be happy. Well, happy or not, Juliette was not leaving, not when the sheer horror was etched on features that barely an hour ago had looked so arrogant.

After a moment of deliberation and remembering how Katarina still recoiled from touches, Juliette opted for sound.

"Shhh… It's just a dream. It's over now. Just a dream… A bad dream." She infused her words with all the calmness she could muster while being completely overtaken by the same grief that seemed to permeate the room, turning contagious. Juliette wanted to weep and couldn't understand why. She was home and she was safe, and yet watching this haughty, brilliant woman sob as if death had opened her rib cage and nestled there, was breaking her heart.

Emboldened by the absence of rejection, Juliette sat down, just outside of the closet yet close enough to feel the warmth of the huddled form.

Katarina's unseeing eyes looked past her, and the tears kept falling, but Juliette sat still and, for lack of a better idea, whispered into the chilly air of the night flowing in through open windows, still saturated with petrichor and thunder.

"I don't dream. Not really. Neither good nor bad." She swallowed around the lump in her throat and went on, hoping that her mere presence, the sound of her voice, would pull Katarina out of the haze she seemed gripped in. "I am not afraid of much, so maybe that explains my lack of dreaming. Though I have to confess to disliking the dark. Ever since I was a child, my mother used to leave candles burning everywhere until I fell asleep. After a while, my father replaced them with little night-lights."

A long inhalation next to her was the only sign that she was not speaking into a void. Katarina was coming around.

"I keep one on, you know. Or I used to, before you arrived."

She settled more comfortably, the floor a familiar surface after years of being sprawled on almost every piece of parquet, floorboard, or linoleum of the Palais Garnier.

"The little pink lamp in the kitchen."

Katarina's voice was hollow, devoid of any emotion or intonation and much lower than what Juliette was used to. As if she had been screaming for a long time. Or sobbing.

"I usually light it in the morning before I'd leave for the

Opera." Juliette ducked her head, burrowing her face in her hands. The chill of her palms was a balm on her rapidly heating face. She couldn't quite believe what she was sharing. Helena barely understood this and was only peripherally aware of Juliette's strange habit. Gabriel used to tease her good-naturedly about it, and Francesca had never had the chance to learn it existed. Yet here she was, sharing her weirdness with this virtual stranger. And a thoroughly unpleasant one at that.

"So you don't walk into darkness when you come home."

This stranger, despite the existential crisis she was clearly going through, understood more than her closest friends combined.

"Yes, that." Juliette touched her sternum, the pressure of the truth too much, yet she didn't stop speaking. "And because when I walk at night, I always look up from the street, and seeing the light on makes me imagine someone is home. And that someone left the light on for me. In that moment, I matter. I matter enough to make an effort."

Another sigh was her only answer for a long while, the quiet settling between them comfortably this time, like fog, blanketing the earlier fear.

"She wouldn't leave the light on for you?"

For a woman who looked as if she drank pure lemon juice when Juliette's sexuality was thrust front and center, Katarina was rather casual about speaking of Juliette's past. And the woman who lived there.

The stab of loneliness, that shard of being left behind despite the love and the trust, the one that periodically twisted under her heart, popped up again, and Juliette knew it was time to end this conversation. The weight crushing her chest was making it difficult to breathe.

Nothing ever came from talking in the witching hour, in the sea of tears and grief. So she wiped her own with the back of her hand and got up.

"We didn't live together for very long, and it doesn't matter." Even as two lies in one sentence left her lips, the phone rang. Its shrill call, the timing of it, and the universe conspiring against her once again meant only one thing. Helena was worried and Helena was on the other end of the line, spending fortunes and wasting lifetimes on transatlantic phone calls. The least Juliette could do was answer. The most—apologize for hanging up abruptly earlier. But she had nothing left in herself to give. As she stepped out of the spare bedroom, a parting shot of, "Seems to me she still lives here," was the last thing she heard out of the tiny closet and the woman huddled there.

Things did not change because Juliette had witnessed Katarina going through a waking nightmare. Things did not change because Katarina was miraculously less abrasive. She wasn't. And yet the air had shifted.

It could be that they were heading into the first leaf showers of fall, and fall in Paris meant a special state of being. To most Parisians, it meant the slow meander toward winter, toward the end of the year. To Juliette and every other dancer, fall was the most wondrous season. One of being busy. One of running from class to rehearsal. One of watching young ballerinas from the corps painstakingly studying the call board, searching for their names.

On an early Tuesday, after a very light yoga class, Juliette found herself looking up at the call sheet that encompassed four shows and smiling.

Francesca was not messing about. They had barely started working on *Swan Lake*. The costumes weren't designed yet, and with a second main female lead, they'd have to bring something new to the table, something different from the ones the company used when they staged the production last.

And yet, here was the ballet. On the board. And here were the three names, one under the other, with Katarina's following her own and Gabriel's bringing up the rear of the top billing.

This made it official. Not that their first week of stumbling through the bursts of rehearsals was not official, but this felt real.

Behind her, a gaggle of corps dancers oohed and aahed at the board.

"Vyatka in *Swan Lake*?" A giggly voice could barely hold the girl's excitement.

"I wonder which part she is dancing, since Jett is Odile and Odette." The reply was polite and thoughtful. Juliette wondered if it was perhaps one of the soloists showing a greater familiarity with their Étoile, having had joint rehearsals and participating in the same productions.

A decidedly masculine guffaw sounded somewhere to her side, and Juliette inwardly cringed for what would follow.

"No idea, but Lucian-Sorel hates her. Bianchi, too. Everyone does. And there is no old crone part in *Swan Lake*, so there must be some kind of mistake."

Well, cringing was no longer an option, as Juliette's vision went red at the edges. She turned slowly and witnessed an almost cartoonish change of facial expression all around her. She had been right about the second girl speaking being a soloist. Marie Charles. She was dancing one of the smaller individual parts in *Don Quixote*, and Juliette remembered their evening tutoring sessions from years ago. She had been a nice kid and had grown into a decent dancer. Her face was a picture of horror and mortification, solidifying Juliette's good opinion of her.

However, Juliette had been wrong about the male voice. Michel Duval. Fucking Michel was leering at her from his six-foot-something height, very pleased with himself.

Why did Francesca keep him? Sure, competent male dancers were hard to find, and Michel wasn't necessarily bad. He understudied Gabriel for most productions and even had principal parts here and there, mainly during second lineup tours. But was he worth this aggravation when the most he brought to the table was harassment, gossip, and disrespect? Juliette loved ballet, but misogyny thrived in its wings, and no matter how drafty said wings were, the dust of it could never quite be aired.

For a moment, she stared directly at him, willing him to say something. He did not. If anything, his glee at his own remark only intensified. Juliette opened her mouth—

"How does that saying go? Violence solves nothing? Apparently it's correct, because here you are. Whole and hearty and thoroughly unafraid to spew hate. Your continuous presence at Garnier seems to be immune to the power of my violence, Monsieur Duval. Or maybe I didn't draw enough of your blood."

The voice managed to both raise the hairs on the back of Juliette's neck and for some strange reason dump an entire bucket of butterflies in her stomach. Which should have been a disgusting image, except Katarina was a vision.

Still in Juliette's ankle-length trousers and white shirt, the sleeves rolled past her forearms revealing pale skin and blue rivulets of veins, she carried her usual small bag with a change of clothes and a rather dreary-looking bouquet. If one could call the few well-past-their-prime flowers that.

And yet she might as well have held a scepter. Michel blanched. Marie and the other girl turned even more pallid, their eyes huge, their gazes fleeting from one ballerina to the next, to the next. Oh, this would be the talk of the company in no time.

"Ah…" Michel obviously had not forgotten the slap, and if Juliette looked close enough, his cheek still sported the scratch, now almost healed. Flustered, and visibly afraid, he wasn't ready for round two.

"Quite a comeback there, Monsieur Duval."

Katarina, while a head shorter, seemed to tower over Michel, who was now a rather pathetic shade of puce. Since blood had been mentioned and before it could be shed again, Juliette took it upon herself to intervene.

"Class starts in five minutes. I assume the *corps* will be joining us?"

Her deliberate focus on the word, despite him being almost a principal, would give Michel something to think about. After all, she had flashed her power in this building and this town a few weeks ago, and while liberating a defecting Soviet ballerina was a feat, demoting a troublesome dancer to corps would not be quite as big of an undertaking. By the look on his face—now a shade of purple, all puffed up in obvious anger—he knew it too.

Juliette took a few steps, expecting Katarina to wait for her, but she was already marching toward the classroom where the pianist could be heard warming up.

Short of running after her, which would be extra humiliating, Juliette had no recourse except…

"Katarina!" Several heads turned and stared, save the perfectly coiffed blonde one that Juliette was actually calling for. Still, in what could be seen as a concession, Katarina slowed down her stride, allowing Juliette to catch up with her.

"And now everyone will gossip about me chasing after you." Juliette could not hide the annoyance in her tone and did not care who heard it.

Katarina, unperturbed per usual, gave her a sideways glance.

"That would indeed go against the pervasive opinion that you hate me."

This almost stopped Juliette in her tracks, except she really did not want to chase after the woman again and cause additional whispers in their wake.

So she slowed down before quietly saying, "I don't know why you trust the words of someone you clearly don't respect and who even more clearly doesn't respect you. Michel Duval is not your best source of information, you know."

The right corner of Katarina's mouth turned up briefly before the impassive expression was restored to the sharp features. Juliette felt like she was in a twilight zone—in fact, that she had not left this very zone since last night—because surely Katarina Vyatka was not capable of camaraderie, or of a nervous breakdown, for that matter.

"If I don't listen to the masses, I am bereft of any sources of information."

"Do you need them?" Juliette almost wanted to smack herself on the mouth. Did she really have to go and say that? Katarina's smile disappeared, her eyes devoid of emotion yet again.

"We can't all be Juliette Lucian-Sorel, at liberty to listen to gossip in the hallways and not fear what she overhears."

Of course, whatever thaw Juliette had imagined was not happening. Twilight zone was gone and stark reality had returned. They were back to square one.

"They say nasty things about me too." Even to her own ears, she sounded defensive and therefore would not be believed. As if to prove the point, Katarina simply quickened her pace, and after a few seconds Juliette let her walk away, the wilted flowers bowing their little petals in rhythm with her stride.

The rehearsals went downhill from there. Well, that is to say, for Juliette. For everyone else it was smooth sailing. Francesca seemed happy, pleased with how even on the fly she was able to come up with things that the dancers themselves found innovative and exciting. The first act and the iconic pas de trois were not as reworked as the second act of the ballet, where the introduction of Katarina dancing the part of Odile separated the old *Swan Lake* from the new production.

As this was an entirely fresh choreography, the learning of the steps took longer, with Francesca being both demanding and ravenous for perfection. If Juliette was perfectly familiar with the classic *Swan Lake*, in this iteration Francesca allowed herself to really discard all the preconceived conventions of the profession and go all out.

And this is where the downhill began for Juliette. The white and the black swans' pas de deux was turning into her worst nightmare. Yes, it was extremely technical, but she reveled in that. Her movements were the gold standard of the ballet. And dancing with a partner such as Katarina, who was perfection in every single step, was quite a gift in itself. At any other time, Juliette would have relished this opportunity. As it was, she couldn't relax, couldn't focus, couldn't settle. Every time she and Katarina had to execute as much as an arabesque with their hands touching, Juliette would break out in goose bumps.

What would she do when they moved to the more complex and intimate support positions? And she knew for a fact—she had seen the choreography sheets—Francesca had envisioned them ending their pas de deux in a series of embraces. She shuddered at the thought that the most prolonged one required Katarina to fully encircle Juliette in her arms, supporting her backward bow before straightening them both and finishing the movement with them firmly pressed together, Katarina's arms holding Juliette from behind.

Juliette was beside herself with anticipation and apprehension. And she knew she couldn't entirely hide either of those emotions.

Gabriel teased her gently—and she loved him even more for the gentleness but really wished he'd not go there at all—about how Juliette would never wish to dance with him ever again.

"She has me beat, Jett. Next thing you know, you'll want to switch me off with her in *Don Quixote*, too! If she could lift, she'd be actually throwing you around, darlin'. I can sense all this pent-up animosity turning into something that would require the performance to be adults only."

He gave her a soft pat on the shoulder as she handed him back the water bottle she'd nearly dropped at his words and looked across the studio. Katarina was icing her left calf. The injury couldn't be too serious, since it had not slowed her down even for one millisecond.

Juliette—completely innocently, and not at all worried about the other ballerina—had asked their physiotherapist during her own visit earlier if Vyatka had introduced herself. Not only had Katarina not done so, she hadn't booked a treatment or a massage for the bothersome calf at all.

This didn't come as a surprise. After all, the issue of the révérence was still very much a thorn in their sides as it lingered between them like a ribbon of oil over seawater. Cleaning that up would require special care.

Care Juliette simply did not currently have. She was in the last stages of *Don Quixote* rehearsals. Even if she had danced this ballet four out of her seven seasons here in Paris, she still was unsure of herself. It wasn't especially technical and Gabriel was a steady presence, but she had never enjoyed it, and this year, with all eyes on her and the responsibility of carrying this performance square on her shoulders, it felt excruciating.

And so she watched Katarina ice her calf while leafing through a high school French textbook and wondered how the hell she had gotten here and how many more missteps she would encounter on her way to ridding herself of this woman who vexed and infuriated her and whom she really should dislike more than she did.

There were only two problems with that line of thinking. She didn't dislike Katarina at all, despite the "pervasive opinion" of the ballet troupe. Things would be so much easier for Juliette if only she hated the woman.

The second problem was last night. It weighed heavily on her, the tears, the grief of the sobs—even if Katarina had said nothing, it undid all the carefully laid work that Juliette had constructed day after day, brick after brick, into the wall around herself.

Katarina licked a finger and turned a yellowing page of the old textbook, and Juliette's palms went damp.

"I see I am already entirely outmatched. Literally been speaking the last three minutes, Jett, did you hear one word I said?" Gabriel sniffed theatrically and wiggled his eyebrows at her.

"That we need to work more on the last scene from Act One of *Quixote*?" Juliette finally turned away from Katarina and gave him a grin, and he smiled back. She knew her guess wasn't even close, but he let her get away with it.

"Oh love, we need to work on more than one scene in that cursed performance. I don't care what Cesca says, we should have stopped dancing this particular rendition of it a long time ago. And certainly not four years in a row."

"You think it will tank?" Juliette could hear her heart beating loudly in her ears. What would it mean for her if it tanked? What would happen if *Swan Lake* tanked as well? They'd chase her out on a rail.

"I don't want it to, but how does that saying go—the one about doing the same thing over and over again?"

Juliette wrapped her sweater tighter around her heated muscles and pretended she was shivering from the chilly draft. She could ill afford the centerpiece of the season to fail.

"But I was thinking that this one won't. Her Imperial Majesty and I had our first rehearsal together. Francesca has this idea for a scene where she seduces Prince Siegfried. I have to say, she's special."

His handsome face shone with honest pleasure. A pleasure that only people like them understood. Ballet nerds, both dancers and spectators, obsessed with the performances and the skills. His excitement was infectious, and she allowed herself to be genuinely happy for him. Gabriel was safe and secure in his position at Garnier. She dared not blame misogyny for always being singled out when their shows floundered, but Gabriel Flanagan rarely had to contend with the same level of vitriol lately poured over her and Francesca.

She made a face, and he—as always the perfect partner tuned to her every move and mood—touched her elbow.

"Jett, she's not after your job. We talked a bit, you know, like this, while cooling off or whatever, and she's actually kind of all right."

Juliette nodded and was glad that while he felt her disquietude, he misunderstood it. How to explain it all to him? How to convey her fear? Or her confusion?

And so Juliette said nothing for the moment, reaching out and tucking a too-long curl behind his ear. It sprung back almost immediately, making her laugh.

"Don't worry about me, Gabe." She deliberately used his boyhood appellation, which in turn made him grimace. A shrill whistle from the center of the studio interrupted their cozy tête-à-tête.

"Now, you lazybones, care to return to the issues at hand? Or shall I say feet?" Francesca laughed at her own joke, and Juliette stretched her back one last time before stepping closer. Gabriel clapped for her a few times and cheered as Katarina took her place in front of Juliette.

And then they were off to the races. The pianist's fingers danced over the keys, the centuries-old piano coming to life with the notes that were both so familiar yet so haunting to performers and audiences alike.

In the previous production of *Swan Lake* they had staged, Siegfried was ensnared by Odile, forsook his true love Odette, and picked the wrong swan. In Francesca's new, reimagined version, it was Juliette, the white swan, who was enchanted and ultimately seduced by the black one, and boy, did Francesca ever lean into the "seduction" part of the scene.

If Katarina was uncomfortable with how the choreography brought them together, into each other's space time and again, she never once showed it. In her role as the so-called aggressor, her arms tugged and pulled and encircled Juliette at times brazenly, at times shyly, and then toward the culmination of the pas de deux, once Odette surrendered and allowed herself to be taken by the black swan, they were just a hair away from openly sexual.

For those who wished for two women to all but make out on the stage of Garnier, they'd get the spectacle they desired. Katarina would sell it to them in a heartbeat. The person who turned crimson at the very mention of Juliette sleeping with women could apparently play gay quite convincingly.

By the look on Francesca's face, she was elated at their progress, and the entire room—the chosen soloists who accompanied them these days, Gabriel, and even Dione, their unflappable pianist—seemed mesmerized.

Juliette set her jaw and followed all the instructions precisely, though her mind was screaming that surely she was giving away too much, she was not doing her best to keep up appearances, she was being too obvious…

Perhaps reading the apprehension on Juliette's face, Francesca consented to something she rarely allowed in the beginning stages of the rehearsals. With one pull of the cord, she opened the heavy black drapes that shrouded the mirrored walls and the barre along them. As the room filled with her own reflection, suddenly Juliette could see why the audience seemed to be holding its collective breath.

She jumped, her split absolutely flawless, only to be followed by a mirror image of it from Katarina, dressed in a dark leotard and training tutu. Juliette executed a fouetté and then another jeté that almost brought her within Katarina's grasp, and then the form in black was slowly slithering to the floor in front of her, the incarnation of supplication, and yet, the way Katarina was playing it, it had nothing of submission and was all sly temptation.

In the mirror, her own face was suddenly so young, watching this ballerina at her feet, so credulous and a touch taken with the performance that she almost ruined it by wanting to drop the act and recoil.

This couldn't be. Katarina was acting. It was only a role. Juliette gritted her teeth and finished her steps, but as soon as the last note of the piano faded away and Francesca and the rest of the room exploded in applause, Juliette was like a bird set free from a cage, running out of the studio, not stopping to change her shoes, the pointes really not fit for the marble floors of the Palais Garnier.

Her back hit the bathroom door, firmly closed now, her body still on the adrenaline high from the performance, from Katarina's touch, and that look—

"Jett?" The latch rattled with the force of Gabriel's knock. "Are you okay?"

Juliette watched herself in the distant mirror. How to tell her best friend that she was so far from okay, they might not even be on the same planet?

She stepped farther into the bathroom and opened the cold faucet even as he knocked again and cracked the door just enough to stick his curly head in.

"Darlin'?"

Face splashed with water, she gave him a stern look through the mirror.

"Gabriel, I'm fine—"

"Then why did you—"

"It was hot there. Hot. I felt faint. It's fine. I'm fine. Don't you have your rehearsal with Her Imperial Majesty to get to? Please don't keep her, Francesca, and the rest waiting."

He huffed out a breath and gave her a long look that was too serious for eyes that always twinkled with merriment. They tended to never have conversations like these. The life-and-death kind. The "I think I am falling for someone who hates me" kind. And even if he didn't know it yet, here they were.

Juliette took a breath before shooing him again, but he beat her to the punch.

"I'll go, as I do have that rehearsal, and Francesca be damned, it's Her Imperial Majesty that I'd rather not piss off. But I am taking you out one of these evenings and we will talk this over, you and I. Whatever is happening with you." When she started protesting, he simply disappeared behind the door.

Well, turned out he did know something. She could hear his steps retreating. Belatedly, she realized she had allowed him to have the last word.

Juliette let her shoulders slump for a minute. Another long breath did nothing to calm her racing heart. Neither did the next one. Once her cheeks had lost their pallor, she dried off her hands and considered her course of action. She had indeed stormed out like a dramatic fool, and so she'd face more than Gabriel's genuine concern. There would be gossip.

She'd have to either go through the main studio, currently occupied by Gabriel and Katarina, which felt akin to a walk-of-shame level of humiliation, or take the side stairs to get back to the main rehearsal classroom and retrieve her belongings. Juliette shivered. She'd have to hurry, heated muscles or not. The drafts of Garnier eventually got to you, one way or another. In the distance, the bells of the Church of the Madeleine rang three times. Well, she was late for her massage therapy. Thierry wouldn't scold her, but his time was extremely valuable, and Juliette was one of the few who prided herself on never wasting it.

Running for the second time today, she pushed open the door to the emergency stairs. Dusty, a little too shadowy, and decidedly smelly, the stairs were seldom used. Which was a relief, because Juliette scrunched her nose as something probably not human made a scratching and then clunking noise ahead of her. Rats? Then behind her, the door opened and Michel stepped through it, cigarette and lighter in hand.

The series of events that followed felt like watching a car crash occur in slow motion. Juliette cursed, her words mere exhalations of air as she tried to keep it down, then took a few steps away from Michel, who was still focused on his cigarette, and then she felt the world spin, no longer in slow motion. In fact, it was all at double speed now. Double force, too, as her footing went and the stairs she was just thinking were rather disgustingly filthy smashed into her face.

The last thing she remembered was looking back to see if Michel had noticed her and the slippery and cold feeling of stepping on ice in pointe shoes. As her face met the floor, she thought about the damn ice and what a coincidence it must be, Katarina icing her calf through their earlier rehearsal. Katarina, who occasionally came down these stairs to smoke... Or avoid going through the busy corridors and studios of Palais Garnier... Just like Juliette had.

Eleven

Of Falls & Acrid Taste of Betrayal

Her face hurt, her right leg was bent at an uncomfortable angle, and fucking Michel Duval was touching her.

That last thought compelled Juliette to attempt to sit up, shrinking away from him. Michel was talking a mile a minute, and it took Juliette a while to realize that he was cursing and that there was quite a crowd around them.

A long-fingered hand reached forward from Juliette's side, and once the object it was holding came into focus, she recoiled. A small bag of ice. A little melted, yet ice nonetheless.

Katarina Vyatka was offering her own ice pack. Juliette blinked a few times, her brain working overtime to try and catch up to what was actually happening around her. Clearly unaccustomed to waiting, Katarina unceremoniously pressed the offering on Juliette's bent knee.

When their eyes met, Juliette laughed nervously, not knowing how to respond or where to even begin with this entire situation, and then hissed as her lip split further and she tasted her own blood.

"I don't have another one for your face. And you being you, I figured you'd want the knee taken care of before the cheek."

Katarina's matter-of-fact, detached tone betrayed nothing. She had been right, of course. Juliette cared very little if her whole head was smashed. But her knees were supposed to work. She had a busy season ahead. And speaking of the busy season…

"Would you help me up, please?"

Katarina smirked wryly at Michel, whose mouth was hanging open, and offered Juliette her arm. Mindful of not yanking too strongly on the slim limb, Juliette pulled herself up slowly. When she was finally on her feet, a harried Gabriel swept her up.

"Darlin'! Look what you did to my favorite face!"

Cooing and gently rocking her, Gabriel parted the crowd like he was Moses, and in the blink of an eye they were out of the dusty staircase and in the just-as-crowded hallway of the second floor. It seemed the entire company was there, ogling Juliette and whispering theatrically about how some people needed to be held accountable for this.

A resounding clap of Francesca's hands brought an end to it, however, and as Gabriel took the turn leading to the physiotherapists' office, her booming voice was the only one Juliette could hear.

"You are not being paid to gossip, no matter how juicy this particular event is. Now, off you go! There's a dress rehearsal in two days and a performance in four, so I better not see any of you wandering the hallways."

Waving her cane vigorously, Francesca followed Gabriel, and a few seconds later, the two of them were crowding the placid Thierry.

"Is she okay?"

"Fix her!"

Gabriel's question and Francesca's order did not seem to faze the physiotherapist, but his hands were less steady when he finally reached for Juliette's cheekbone.

"Jett, I thought you had grown out of your toddlerhood. After all, isn't that when we all learn to navigate stairs?"

He tried for humor, but Juliette could tell his heart wasn't in it and his eyes were concerned.

"I had help."

Gabriel stepped forward and laid a hand on her uninjured leg.

"I heard the rumors as I was running to you. They're saying it was ice. And I know what you're thinking, but it wasn't her—"

"How could you possibly…" The adrenaline rush having fizzled out, Juliette was in pain and quite angry at herself, first for being emotional enough to run away from her own rehearsal—not to mention in pointe shoes—and then for not watching where she was running to. And of all the people's help to accept upon coming back to her senses, for it to be Katarina? The one who caused her to—What did Gabriel just say?

"Okay, so yes, I was thinking exactly what you think I was. Granted."

"Thank you." Gabriel smiled and then shrank back from her slap on his bicep. "Ouch, what did I do to deserve this?"

"You don't have to do anything to deserve anything, Gabriel. You get everything for free. Love, hate, blowjobs, slaps."

Francesca came closer even as Juliette almost gagged on her words, and Gabriel made a valiant attempt to not laugh. Her hand on Juliette's leg was much less gentle than his. She tsked, looked her up and down, then tsked again. Thierry returned with a first aid kit and a big leather doctor's bag.

"I'd rather you fuss over her knee, Thierry. Her face and hands aren't of the highest importance to me."

"That's not what you said way back when." Juliette's attempt at humor fell flat, and so did Francesca's admonition, because Thierry went straight to dabbing her mouth with a piece of gauze and Juliette hissed again, this time from the alcohol.

"Is this really necessary?" Her lip felt on fire, and speaking was not easy with the cotton in the way.

"Yes, it is. Francesca here may not care about the most beautiful face in all of France, though I suggest she reconsider that based on her history, but I do care about infection."

Thierry's steady hands worked as he spoke.

"I thought you said I had the most beautiful face in all of France?" Gabriel actually pouted, and Thierry laughed. If the remark didn't serve as a huge neon sign that these two had crossed a few professional lines, then the laughter and lack of denial sealed it. Thierry had a bit of a reputation, but Gabriel had sworn that he trusted him. Juliette reasoned that she would have to as well.

As her mind wandered, the people around her kept making a lot of noise. Gabriel and Francesca bickered, and Thierry was still talking to her.

"I'm concerned about a possible cheekbone fracture and concussion. Can you look at me?"

Juliette did, and he poked and prodded at her cheek and forehead, all the while rubbing at her bleeding lip.

To distract herself from the stinging, Juliette pulled Gabriel's sleeve.

"You were saying?"

He patted her knee again before settling down more comfortably on the floor next to her.

"She was with me, we were rehearsing our pas de deux. Then there was a commotion in the hallway and people were screaming, 'Juliette, Juliette,' and she was out of the studio like Operation Barbarossa had been declared and the enemy was marching on Moscow. I've never seen her move so fast. She beat me to you by a good two—three minutes."

Francesca tsked a third time. "Why is this even important? So there was ice? So what?"

Both Juliette and Gabriel turned to face her, and she shrugged her shoulders before giving them the customary wave.

"I was in my office, about to join those two for their rehearsal, then all I heard were the screams, and by their volume you'd think someone was dead. And now we have this." She pointed at Juliette, palm up, and then tapped her foot on the floor. When neither Gabriel nor Juliette said anything, she rolled her eyes. "We have my prima injured and set to miss the opening night!"

Juliette and Gabriel's twin gasps were almost comical in synchronicity, and only Thierry's firm "She won't" seemed to bring everyone back to the present and away from the spiraling hysterics.

"Now, Francesca, I understand that dramatics are in your blood, but could you please keep a tighter rein on your Argentinian horses?" Thierry, clearly satisfied with what he'd done to Juliette's face, had moved on to her leg and was stretching it out. The maneuvers were largely painless, and Juliette managed to exhale as he continued.

"Unless you count her gorgeous, gorgeous visage being black and blue an impediment, the Princess of Paris will be there for the opening night of *Quixote*." Thierry bent and extended Juliette's leg to prove his point. "She doesn't have a concussion, from what I can tell, though if she suddenly develops headaches or balance issues, we will know differently. And her knee is probably fine, though it may be sore for a bit. The abrasions on her hands will be gone in a day or two. So basically, you dodged a serious injury. Still, how can you consider the mangling of this face not serious?"

He smiled and patted her on the uninjured cheek before taking a step back, making room for Francesca to come closer. However, she didn't, and Juliette looked at her, confused. When Francesca spoke, her words were anything but comforting.

"My entire season is hinging on you being okay, Jett. And you develop an affinity for stepping on ice?"

"Is this what passes for your bedside manner, Madame Bianchi?"

Juliette blamed her fall and subsequent discombobulation for knowing with absolute certainty that Katarina Vyatka was about to enter the room before she did so. The air changed, chilled. Juliette could have sworn that if she exhaled, her breath would come out as condensation. And there she was, walking straight, her shoulders proudly thrown back, no sign of a limp or favoring of the calf that had troubled her earlier. The Empress of Moscow had arrived to bestow her attention on poor little Juliette.

For once—and Juliette would choose to ruminate later on the reasons behind this very "once"—she did not mind the arrogance or the condescension. Katarina walked in, and while the air cooled, Juliette's chest grew warm.

"Mademoiselle Vyatka, as I asked the rest of the company, they are to return to work—"

"Madame Bianchi, I am—for better or worse—not exactly a welcome part of said company and here in Paris, as Americans say, by the grace of you and God, wouldn't you agree? And I know you would, since you revel in reminding me of that all the time." Katarina's smile was positively evil. Poison dripping from those full lips, she stepped into the space Thierry had vacated and Francesca had decided not to occupy.

"Mademoiselle Vyatka?" Francesca's eyebrows climbed all the way to her hairline. Gabriel's hand shook with suppressed laughter on Juliette's knee. Thierry made himself scarce.

"I was just wondering since when is it customary in your culture to accuse the victim? Surely, it must be your lengthy presence in France that is influencing your otherwise impeccable Argentinian lineage? Aren't the French supposed to be rude and the South American soulful and kind and caring? I've forgotten, truth be told, with representatives of both countries falling over themselves to prove to me all their negative traits."

Juliette bit her lip in the effort to hold back a smile and then had to suck it entirely in her mouth as it screamed in agony and blood dripped again from the new split.

Damn. And yet…

Francesca was in the wrong, and Juliette was about to tell her so, but that warmth in her chest, right under her fourth rib on her left side… Surely that must be gratitude, and comfort, due to being protected.

Her mind screeched to a halt at the word *protected*, because what the hell was she thinking? Wasn't she just a few minutes ago blaming this very woman for her fall in the first place?

Gabriel's words about Katarina being with him the entire time must've gotten to her after all. Alternatively—and that was another thing Juliette would have to consider when she had time to untangle her thoughts—she wanted Katarina to not be the one out to injure her.

Granted, that meant someone else must have been, or perhaps it was just a silly accident. Francesca was right. How many people walked around Palais Garnier icing some limb or another? Pretty much every other one. Dancers tended to baby their bodies all the time.

Francesca finally stopped sputtering, and Gabriel, probably guessing that she was about to launch into one of her tantrums, was off the floor and guiding her out the door in a matter of seconds.

"Coffee, coffee is in order, Cesca. Let's give your precious Étoile a few minutes to rest before Thierry sends her either to the hospital or home, and then we will return to the rehearsal, right?" His cajoling and not-so-gentle pushing and pulling worked, and soon enough their raised voices could be heard in the corridor becoming less shrill and then disappearing altogether.

In the room's quiet, Juliette could hear her own heart beating, harder and louder than the occasion warranted. Surely this wasn't even an occasion at all. So what if Katarina was sitting down, unlike Gabriel, on the edge of the treatment cot, clearly much more concerned with her own comfort and glutes than he was?

Oh my God, please, please stop thinking about her glutes!

It was too late, and if memory served—and it did serve quite well—Katarina had herself a pair of spectacular ones—

"I'm sorry."

The words were so unexpected they stopped Juliette's line of absolutely inappropriate thought dead.

"Now I'm even more confused."

Katarina lifted an eyebrow, and jealousy at such prowess fleetingly crossed Juliette's mind again.

"I'm sorry you fell."

Fell? Into… what? Oh God… Oh, of course.

Juliette almost slapped herself over the forehead. She really must be concussed, because her thoughts kept diverting to decidedly silly directions.

When Juliette finally got a firmer grip on her wayward mind, she shrugged. Did she actually believe for a second Katarina had come to confess? That earlier pang of wishful thinking that it be anyone but her returned. Along with it the dreaded feeling of wretched betrayal.

"Yes, this is why I am sorry. Because, once the rush dissipates, you'll feel it."

Juliette stopped worrying at her lip and finally looked into the shielded eyes. They were impassive as always, but after a few weeks of being around this woman, Juliette thought she could see something flicker in them.

"How do you know what I'm feeling?" She had to ask. She had to know for sure.

"Because I felt the same way. My second year as prima, I sprained my ankle as the result of a similar attempt at sabotage. Bolshoi is a meritocracy, to a certain extent, and 'you are who you know' to a much larger one. I did not fit in with the latter crowd. And my parents were dead traitors, or *enemies of the state*, as the government had them designated, so I had my share of ice on stairs, liquefied soap in my water bottle, glass in pointe shoes. And every time it happened, I felt wretched. Betrayal has an acrid taste, Juliette."

Katarina spoke slowly, her usual cadence on full display,

yet Juliette's mind was absolutely unable to catch up, so many questions and thoughts getting jumbled up like a bowl of yarn. She must've pulled on the wrong strand, because she went from wanting to ask about Katarina's parents to suddenly being completely tangled up in the sound of her own name falling from that perfect mouth.

Perfect mouth? If this wasn't proof that she was indeed concussed.

Either Katarina read the sheer level of foolishness on Juliette's face—and if anyone would, it would absolutely be this woman, as she seemed to read Juliette like a child's ABCs—or she remembered that she hated Juliette and stood up abruptly.

"I hope Thierry is thorough in his assessment."

With that, she was gone, the damn orange blossom the only proof that Katarina had even been in the room. Well, orange blossom and the few pieces of information Juliette now had tucked away like drying flowers in her book. She'd open it and examine them properly when the time was right, and she was not as breathless from Katarina Vyatka perfectly pronouncing every single letter in her name, as if she had been saying it for years.

Twelve

Of Failure & Perceived Weakness

Don Quixote failed.

No, to say the opening night of the ballet composed by the revered Ludwig Minkus and choreographed by the legendary Marius Petipa failed was to do both those icons a disservice. They were legends. Only the most grandiose epithets would do. If they couldn't have the very best, then the Parisian media—and thus the public that followed the media's lead—decided they would be given the very worst.

And so, *Don Quixote* bombed. The resoundingly humiliating reviews panning it completely were so numerous that Juliette was certain one could paper the entire Rue de Rivoli with them and there would still be column inches left to do a half-assed job on Rue Saint-Honoré as well.

Even Gabriel—normally shielded from the press's wrath by his gender and good looks, as unfair as that was—had been absolutely dismantled by the critics, from his technique to his interpretation of the character. And this time Juliette, studiously trying to ignore her own negative reviews, thought the public opinion was correct.

Not that it had been either of their faults. The issue lay much deeper and ultimately boiled down to one question:

What were they doing staging an 1869 version of a ballet that had been reinvented countless times since then, most famously recently by both Nureyev and Baryshnikov? Their versions were much more vibrant and modern without dropping the classism of the music or movement.

What the Paris Opera Ballet had staged was… passé. Petipa's vision was amazing. But he had had his time. And that time was the nineteenth century. The changes to the original choreography that Francesca had deemed necessary did not achieve the return to the classic roots she was aiming for. They just made it feel antiquated.

And yet, here they were. Sitting in Francesca's office next to Gabriel, who seemed entirely too big for the tiny uncomfortable chairs set up for this occasion, Juliette was not even remotely interested in hiding her thoughts. After all, she had been called "overrated, underused, and devoid of any emotional involvement in the proceedings surrounding her on stage" by *Le Monde*, with *Le Figaro* adding that she was "wooden and underserved by the lack of imagination of the stale production."

She knew her face, still black and blue despite the best attempts to cover up the bruises from her fall, spoke volumes, so she was not surprised when Lalande took one look at her and cursed.

"Merde!"

Juliette pursed her lips, felt the lingering sting of the yet-to-heal lip, and said nothing.

"Why are you cursing out Juliette? What does she have to do with it?" Clearly tired of the confines of the stiff chair and unaccustomed to being torn to shreds by the press, Gabriel was up like a bull seeing red. To his credit, the pinkish shirt Lalande was sporting deserved the derision.

However, pink shirt or not, the minister did not back down, even if he had to lift his face to look up at the six-foot-five-inch height from which the irate dancer was glaring at him.

"She, you, Madame Bianchi, Monsieur Lenoir, every single one of you has something to do with it."

Well, Juliette found no fault in this logic, though it meant that not even the poor seventy-year-old orchestra conductor, Victor Lenoir, was spared, and he had been with Palais Garner forever, was the soul of professionalism, and just played the damn music. He sat in the corner of the office silently, the only one yet to utter a word since they had all arrived at ten a.m. after getting both the evening edition and the first print of the morning papers.

"I disagree." Gabriel balled his fists before stuffing them in the pockets of his jeans. This had to be some kind of feat, because the garment was so tight on him, it must've been illegal in some places here in Europe and most certainly anywhere along the Bible Belt in the US.

"You can disagree all you want, Monsieur Flanagan, but you were rotten. You, Mademoiselle Lucian-Sorel—and no, I do not give a damn that she was underserved by the production. It was Dulcinea, for God's sake, a nothing part, and you fucked that one up too!"

It was Juliette's turn to see red.

"Too? Are you implying I have been messing up parts?" She'd be damned if she'd honor him with his title when he was being rude, sweary, and downright wrong. Gabriel made a move to stand in front of her, but she pushed him aside. "You are insulting. Every dancer has bad reviews. Bad days happen. Bad productions happen—"

"You've had nothing but bad days and bad productions for the last two years. This was marked as the be-all and end-all season. And I swear, I will end it all, right here, if nothing is done."

At Francesca's customary clap of hands, everyone turned toward the desk dominating the office as she slowly stood up from behind it. She was looking worse for wear, somehow ages older than yesterday, and smaller. Her cane was not in its regular spot by the door; she was holding on to it tightly, her knuckles white on the handle.

"I take responsibility." The buzzing of the overhead light, so much like an annoying mosquito, was the only sound in a room that, just a few seconds ago, had been submerged in chaos.

"I take *full* responsibility," Francesca amended, and when nobody protested, her fingers relaxed almost imperceptibly on the cane. "The choice of the choreographer, the call to switch scenes, and everything in between those decisions were mine and mine alone, Minister. My dancers execute my direction. I am the Director of Paris Opera Ballet. And I stand by my decisions, such as they are."

Nobody spoke. Francesca exhaled loudly and then lowered back into her chair. Outside, Paris was waking up, the sounds of people and birds, vendors and street sweepers, so familiar, so dear to Juliette, did nothing to soothe the abraded nerves.

"*Swan Lake* is the last chance you get, Madame Bianchi. *Swan Lake* is the last chance all of you get. And even then I cannot guarantee that I will not take matters in my own hands, since clearly none of you can." Lalande allowed his words to sink in and then left the room without a backward glance.

Through the door he left open, Juliette glimpsed him speaking softly to Katarina, of all people. What was she even doing on the third floor? And why was she talking to Lalande?

Except, it dawned on Juliette, she wasn't. The minister was whispering, accompanying his words with the classic gallic gestures of irritation and persuasion. Katarina's face, as always, showed nothing, but her eyes held that empty look, the look that Juliette had grown to know so well. Whatever he was selling her, she wasn't buying it—but wasn't saying so either.

Gabriel stood up and closed the door, and Juliette refocused her attention on the task at hand.

"What are we going to do?"

His voice was hollow, scratchy, his face a bit wan. He was so rarely sick, such an image of youth and vigor, that seeing him under the weather was unusual, and Juliette worried instantly.

"Dance, Gabriel. We will dance *Swan Lake* and we will dance it well. That's all there is to it. And after what just happened, what do we all have to lose?" Francesca spoke but didn't raise her eyes to meet any of theirs, instead watching the city below. Juliette had a sinking suspicion she was saying goodbye to Paris. To a city she had given over twenty years, arriving as an Argentinian political refugee after another coup spurred an exodus of intellectuals and activists.

Juliette knew history, loved it in school, and applied herself much better than the rest of the little ballerinas who were all too obsessed with dancing to bother with any other lessons. But even Juliette could not keep track of the Argentinian revolts. Francesca rarely spoke of her childhood. She had a brother somewhere. New York? Los Angeles? He was much younger, and they had been separated by their exile. Gonzalo? Gustavo? Something like that. Francesca spoke even more rarely of him.

Juliette's train of thought was interrupted by an irate voice from the shadows of the office.

"Madame Bianchi, you are too young to speak this way." Juliette smiled at the admonition clearly audible in Monsieur Lenoir's words. "I'm seventy, and I still have quite a lot to lose. This is Palais Garnier, for goodness' sake. You don't throw in the towel. You don't leave. They fire you, they murder you, or it all burns down. Those are the only options available. I, for one, refuse all three."

The old conductor stood up so forcefully that his chair overturned, but he made no move to pick it up. Instead, he shuffled out of the office and slammed the door. Francesca smiled.

"I love the French. They are so bloodthirsty. Everything is guillotine, fire, and bloodshed. Talk about drama. Lalande is the same."

Gabriel coughed in his handkerchief and continued to pace as he spoke.

"Lalande is serious, and you know it."

Francesca just waved him away.

"He is a bureaucrat. It's what they do. Threaten dismissals and then applaud and take all the credit during the opening night. We have an ace up our sleeve."

As Gabriel gave her an uncomprehending look, she simply pointed at Juliette and winked.

"Make it two aces. My swans will bring down the house."

***

The day dragged on. Juliette took class, trying to focus on her own steps rather than on the whispers that surrounded her, no matter how loud they were getting. And they were loud. Michel and Monique, the second prima, did not hide their glee. With *Don Quixote* scrapped faster than the morning newspapers were replaced with the afternoon ones, *Sleeping Beauty* was immediately put on the program for spring, Francesca and one of her choreographer friends working on the small changes to make it feel at least a tiny bit fresh to the public. Michel and Monique had danced the leads last year—since it was the lesser production and not the marquis ballet of the season—so it was no surprise that when Juliette approached the call sheet, their names were at the top.

Juliette told herself she wasn't bothered. Paris Opera Ballet staged multiple ballets every year, the program was extensive, and a single prima could never dance it all. Sure, as the absolute lead, Juliette performed the most, which amounted to four or five main parts in one season, but the rest had to be danced by someone too. Juliette may have been the resident Étoile, but Monique was good, and Michel, while nowhere near Gabriel's skill, wasn't awful.

As she sat on the floor under the barre, getting ready for

the run-through for *Swan Lake*, one of the last before the dress rehearsals, Juliette tried not to dwell on her resentment over the entire situation.

She pulled on the ribbon as she wrapped it around her ankle and couldn't help overhearing two soloists to her left, giggling.

"Do you think they will elevate one of us?"

Juliette's fingers fumbled the knot and bit her lip to stave off any possible reaction.

"Monique will gobble up all the parts, she's greedy that way. And Garnier has not had a French Prima Assoluta ever, since there are so few of them and they need some sort of presidential or governmental decree. I think they will give it to her, or at least elevate her to Étoile."

The brunette bent over to stretch her hamstrings and the ending of her reply was unintelligible. The follow-up question from the giggly blonde, however, was anything but.

"You don't think Vyatka will get it?"

"She might, but how many years does she have in her? Three? Four? She's a hag!"

Angry ringing filled Juliette's ears, and the room felt impossibly loud, as if Paris itself had stepped into it, with all its industry and traffic. She didn't know if it was due to the suggestion that Katarina would replace her or that Katarina, who was in her dancing prime, so to speak, was called a hag. She suspected, pathetic as it might be, it was the latter that upset her more and truly set her off.

Her vision glowing red at the corners, Juliette shook her head and got up, looking directly at the two ballerinas, who had the decency to look sheepish. She knew she should say something. It was a matter of principle. And a matter of principal. Turf wars were common, and the heads of the pack had to defend theirs quite often. It would not do to allow such disrespect, especially now that they understood she heard them. Except no words came to her, the cacophony still drowning cogent thought—

"Do you know what old hags do to little children, girls?"

Katarina, in a black leotard and tutu, stepped around Juliette and laid a hand on her shoulder. The long fingers glided up from where the skin was covered by the hastily thrown-on sweater, to the back of her neck, and then just rested there, unexpectedly warm and comforting. Though that last qualification was a lie. There was nothing comforting about the hairs at her nape standing up, the tingling sensations running down her spine, and the sudden evaporation of all air from the room.

Katarina was clearly unaware of her effect, as her fingers squeezed gently once, twice, before falling off, and her face morphed from placid to haughty.

"I may be a newcomer here, girls." She spoke the last word as if grounding it into dirt. Juliette shivered. "But no matter the ballet company, I know this. You have to have had your first true lead before you become scavengers on the hunt for the cadaver of a seasoned prima." Katarina was absolutely still, shoulder to shoulder with Juliette, but for all intents and purposes, she might as well have stood in front of her. Her eyes were chips of ice, impenetrable, the full mouth drawn into a straight line, nothing left of the earlier pathos and sarcasm. The soloists were now visibly trembling. Juliette wanted to fan herself.

Then, after her silence scared them both good and proper, the fake smile returned, the right corner of the mouth Juliette kept admiring lifting with nothing but arrogance.

"As for me, well, my dears, would you at least allow me to dance a few parts before you banish me to the old people's home? My teeth will be falling out any day now anyway. Old age and all that." Katarina's laughter was quiet, sardonic, and cruel. And attractive. Juliette's stomach clenched, the muscles spasming with one and only one sensation, and she wanted to smack herself over the forehead. Desire.

Really? What the hell is wrong with me?

A wave of Katarina's fingers and she turned away from the shivering dancers. "Now, shoo. Adults are talking."

The ballerinas were instantly gone, scrambling off, dropping shoes and water bottles in their haste to get away, before she'd even finished the last sentence, and despite having her back to them, Katarina's smirk widened the farther they got from her. Now both corners of that sinful mouth were upturned, the perfect set of upper teeth on display, as was the tiniest of imperfections—a slightly crooked lower left canine—and Juliette wanted to upend the entire water cooler sitting in the corner over her head.

Katarina, smile still on, a rarity that had the whole room staring at her, simply lifted Juliette's chin and held it up with two fingers before whispering, "Never let them see you down. Sensing weakness, they will stomp you into the ground."

Katarina settled into her place to begin the rehearsal and Juliette was left with only the feeling of warm, callused fingers, lingering on her skin, distracting her from things that mattered. Or perhaps becoming the only such thing.

Thirteen

Of Butterflies & Long Overdue Closure

Maybe she did have a concussion. Maybe that was the reason she was reacting like a smitten schoolgirl to a simple touch? All Katarina had done was brush her chin with her fingertips, and Juliette felt as if the entire population of butterflies from the National Museum of Natural History suddenly took residence in her stomach.

It was embarrassing. Yes, she had always been honest with herself, at least, that she found Katarina attractive. One might have said she'd maybe even entertained a few fantasies if not for two small—tiny, in the big scheme of things—details.

First, Katarina was straight to the point of being obviously disturbed by the displays or mentions of homosexuality. Her seemingly easy friendship with Gabriel didn't mean anything. He was a man, after all. He didn't count.

And the second detail, the one that was perhaps even greater than Katarina's heterosexuality, was that Juliette simply did not trust her. They weren't enemies, not in Juliette's eyes. Not anymore. But the ice incident. And the constant looking over her shoulder that Juliette felt she had to maintain due to Katarina's mere presence.

It could be argued that the latter was not the former Soviet ballerina's fault. Juliette allowed Helena, Gabriel, Agent Ivanov, the whole damn world to get into her head. She could still hear the slimy little man's words echo in the Place de l'Opéra all those days ago. Juliette chose to ignore them then. She fervently wished she could go on ignoring them.

"She danced over plenty of cadavers on her way to the crown. She will yet execute one of those grands jetés over yours."

Juliette sighed and tightened the jacket around her shoulders. Surely the shiver was caused by the chill of the late evening air and not the dreaded sense of premonition that had not left her since the summer.

She walked in the dark, her steps quick and sure, Rue de Rivoli as familiar as London's streets once had been. Juliette lifted her eyes at the signs of fancy stores and bakeries along the way.

She had become a creature of habit, her haunts, her routine, her little pleasures in life, more and more predictable. Like the same route she took every morning on Rue de Rivoli, Place du Marché Saint-Honoré, and then Place de l'Opéra.

Juliette had to smile at herself that the way back always took her through Place Vendôme and toward Rivoli. If she was entirely honest with herself, she knew exactly why she always returned home that way. Her own windows, the kitchen one especially, were on full display if she approached her building from that angle. And the little pink beacon light shining in her home was one of the few pleasures of returning to an empty apartment.

It had not been empty this past month. Yet the light still gave Juliette that warm, comforting feeling.

Like it did now. The butterflies fluttered their wings all at once, and Juliette felt she could fly. Katarina had left the light burning for her.

Juliette climbed the stairs to the fourth floor, avoiding the temperamental elevator, and carefully opened the door. The place was silent, the door to Katarina's room closed. It was just past nine p.m., but that was typical for her roommate.

Silently placing her bag and jacket in the hallway by the door, she washed her hands and stepped into the kitchen, still enveloped in the pink glow of the little lamp.

Her thoughts were chasing each other, so maybe it was the butterflies that they were after, but the chaos in her head matched the unsettledness she felt everywhere.

Her face hurt, and a pack of frozen peas did little to soothe it. The knee was sore, but Thierry was helping there, even if he kept admonishing her for favoring it too much when she didn't pay attention. And her heart? Her heart was in a world of its own. She didn't even want to examine it too closely. For goodness' sake, she had lost her breath over a chin lift. Such a damn cliché.

When the kettle boiled, Juliette poured water over the mint leaves in her mug and shook her head. She thought back to Ivanov's words, since they were another cliché. It was such a manipulative and dramatic speech to deliver to someone who had bested you. And she knew his purpose was to needle her, to plant a seed of doubt. But despite her own understanding of human psychology, none of it mattered. Those clichés were effective for a reason, and the one where ballerinas were at each other's throats and backstabbing one another for parts, for prominence, for attention and applause, was old as the ballet world itself.

"If Francesca thinks that staging that relic version of *Sleeping Beauty* will somehow go over better than her revamping that fossilized version of *Don Quixote*, she is mistaken."

Juliette almost dumped the hot contents of the mug in her lap. Only a last-minute hand from Katarina, catching it and scalding her own fingers in the process, prevented a new set of wounds.

There wasn't even a hiss as the now-empty cup was placed on the table, and Katarina just dropped into the opposite chair cradling her palm, which was turning red by the second.

Juliette stared dumbfoundedly at her companion. One second… Two… A breath… Another one, this one a touch labored, and then her brain finally caught up with her and she jumped up, grabbed Katarina's wrist, and dragged her to the sink where she opened the cold water, and now the labored breathing was accompanied by a whimper—only one, but it tore at Juliette's heart nonetheless. And that tear in her beating flesh allowed all the damn butterflies to find their way through. Sure, they vacated her stomach but found a home in a much more dangerous place.

And yet, looking at the pained features, at the lips contorted in agony, and at those always inscrutable eyes now full of suffering, Juliette felt that it was too late for her to mind this latest development. She'd learn to live with them and maybe even return the butterflies to the Museum of Natural History someday. But this look, this pain, she'd give anything to erase from the beautiful face.

They stood in place, their hands skin on skin under the running faucet, encased in that cherished pink light, and Juliette was suddenly battling tears. One must've escaped, because Katarina lifted her uninjured hand and dabbed a finger at her cheek, whipping it away with one of those crooked smiles, one that did not quite reach the sadness in her eyes.

"You're going to say that you're sorry, aren't you?"

Juliette sniffed and nodded, feeling like any words she might come up with would be inadequate. She was the one who was supposed to be cradling a burnt hand instead of Katarina.

"Setting aside the fact that I scared you into dropping the mug… I couldn't stop myself from catching it. I'm uncertain whether I knew how to stop."

The light of the lamp flickered and then the little bulb blew out with a tiny whimper of its own, surrounding Juliette and Katarina in a darkness interrupted only by the flecks of headlights of the rare car slinking down Rivoli at this late hour.

Her hand still holding Katarina's, Juliette felt her stiffen for a second, then gradually, as if very determinately, relax, confirming Juliette's earlier suspicion that she, too, might be afraid of the dark. And yet here she was, standing still, surrendering again to circumstances that were out of her control. For Juliette.

Under the cold water, Juliette bent her fingers slowly, parting Katarina's and intertwining them until they were palm to palm, the heat of their touch somehow negating the coolness entirely.

If her heart had been tearing earlier, it was stitching back together now, trapping all the butterflies. Juliette didn't care. As her eyes got used to the darkness, Katarina's face looked less impassive. A marble statue no more, emotions flickered in the dark depths, and when they welled up, it was Juliette's turn to lift a hand and wipe away the tear that trembled for so long on the wondrous lashes before falling down the pale cheek.

One breath… Another… A whimper again… Who was whimpering? Juliette suspected the pitiful sound of hunger, of need, of yearning emanated from her. Katarina's eyes were enormous, opening wider with every second, her lips parting—

The shriek of the phone was like a hammer to glass, shattering the moment, the intimacy, the dreamlike state, and the very possibility…

What possibility? How foolish.

Juliette watched Katarina's mask return to her features, and it was as if the moment never had happened, as if Juliette's fingertips—the ones that weren't still under the cold of the tap water—weren't holding the whisper of Katarina's tears.

The woman herself simply reached over Juliette's hand and turned the faucet off before wiping her hand on the nearby towel.

Juliette opened her mouth. To say what, she did not know, but something needed to be said. The moment had happened and it deserved its existence, it deserved words, dammit. But Katarina just shook her head, a brief motion of her chin in the darkness, before leaving the room.

The phone rang again, pulling Juliette out of her stupor. She almost didn't answer. It was too tempting to stand where she was and mourn the loss of whatever had been brewing for weeks between them. But Helena would try again, knowing too well that Juliette was home, and she wasn't yet ready for a conversation about why she was avoiding calls.

"You have awful timing, Moore."

Since Helena's late-night calls were becoming a habit of exorcism that never quite purged their demons, Juliette decided that attack was the best defense. Sun Tzu knew what he was talking about. The man lived in the fifth century BC and must have possessed the highest level of drama since he called his life's work *The Art of War*. Talk about over top. She'd give him credence for that alone. As a ballerina, she understood drama. She didn't like it, didn't enjoy it, as the call that was about to unfold would show, but she did understand it.

Helena's laugh was testament to the fact that she knew all too well what was coming.

"You're getting tired of me calling. And you're allowing it because you feel guilty. You think I am lonely and missing you and regretting my decision, and you have moved on. Survivor's guilt, Jett."

Juliette rolled her eyes.

"One day you will find a patient who will be so vexing, so difficult, so very bizarre and unreadable, Helena, that she will consume your waking hours. A puzzle of the highest order. And then you will be happy solving that puzzle. Sadly, I am not that patient. I'm not a patient at all, so please stop."

There was silence on the line, and Juliette finally allowed her shoulders to drop, feeling the tension of the day drain from her. She sat down, cradling the receiver to her ear, and listened to Helena breathing.

"I wanted to say…" Her ex paused for so long, Juliette thought they had been disconnected. Then the sounds on the other end of the line told her Helena was sitting down too, perhaps getting more comfortable. They'd finally tell each other what they needed to after all. It was time to cut this cord. There was a woman in the bedroom next to hers, a vexing, interesting, beautiful, confusing woman, and Juliette knew she had been branded for life by the ice thawing in those sad eyes.

"I miss you too, Helena." Now that her heart was shelter to this new emotion, Juliette felt that the truth was mandatory. Compulsory. They had lived in these pockets of half illusions about each other for too long. "But you left me. You made a decision. And it was the right one."

Juliette knew her words were sharp enough to cut the telephone cables sprawled on the floor of the Atlantic, but Helena said nothing, and the silence stretched again. When it was interrupted, Juliette released the breath she was holding.

"I do miss you. And I did make the decision. However, I miscalculated, and I'm the lonely one, not you. I have no right to ask you who it is. You're honest with me, and all I can do is repay you with the same honesty, the same kindness, and stop calling. These calls turned into something I never intended them to be, and I'm sorry for that."

Juliette sighed. Why did lesbians have to keep breaking up even after doing so several times already? Not everything was meant to be analyzed. Sometimes things were better left alone.

Granted, she could afford to think that way, her heart pounding in her chest at the very memory of Katarina's scent wrapping itself around her. And winners could be magnanimous, generous. But with every second, she wished she was anywhere but on this call. And by anywhere, Juliette knew she meant in the kitchen, holding Katarina's chilly hand, making sure she was okay and the burn wasn't serious.

"I hope—"

"Please don't say that you hope we stay friends." Helena's laughter was two-thirds hysterical, one-third sad. "We are friends, Jett. We were friends long before we were lovers. But I think I will stop calling for a while. I was indulging myself, you see, listening to your voice, imagining myself back in our room, just talking as we lay in bed about our days, the important and the mundane. Fuck, I do miss you, Jett. And I don't actually miss you enough to reconsider Columbia, or New York, or any of this."

And now when she laughed, it was sincere. Juliette smiled too, a sense of relief piercing her anxiety.

"The choices we make, right?" Helena's voice was so close, so near and yet so far, the words familiar, said so many times between them, holding so much truth.

"Yes, Hels. The choices we make."

"Be well, dearest. Don't jump too high."

Juliette could feel her smile growing wider at their inside joke. Helena could never outjump her, not when they were little girls and certainly not by the time they graduated. And so she concocted this silly little wish that they laughed at together, as Helena muttered it before every show Juliette danced.

"Oh, and dearest?"

Juliette's eyes were drooping, Helena's voice and the relief of having resolved their issues making her sleepy.

"Hmmm?" A murmur was all she could muster.

"Don't worry about the critics. I hear if Paris thinks it's too good for you, there's someone out there who will come calling very soon."

"Someone else wants me? Who? London?" Tiredness was fighting curiosity in Juliette's mind.

"That's for me to know and for you to find out, Jett. And soon, by the looks of things at Palais Garnier."

Unwilling to ask more questions and quite frankly too sleepy for riddles, Juliette said her goodbyes.

When she hung up the phone, a parquet board creaked somewhere in the quiet of the apartment and Juliette suspected that the last sentences of her conversation with Helena had had an audience. Did Katarina come out to talk to her? Had Juliette imagined the creaking board?

Everything was silent now, yet the absence of sound was not melancholy. Juliette was not lonely. The stirring in her chest was warm and welcome. As for the impending disasters, they were lulled to sleep by the Paris night and Juliette's knowledge that her nightmares usually showed their faces in the daylight anyway.

Fourteen
Of Dress Rehearsals & Glass

In her years as director at Palais Garnier, Francesca had taken every opportunity to eschew preview performances in favor of dress rehearsals. She took that road again for *Swan Lake*, forgoing any and all press exposure until the last possible moment.

"It's better this way, amor. Your first night in costume is in front of friends and not all the peasantry and rubble, and I gag at the thought of the critics sneaking in and seeing the performance before I deem it ready."

Juliette had never questioned Francesca's logic, chalking it up to one of her eccentricities, and why should she not do as she pleased? After over a decade of dancing prima parts under these lights, followed by five amazing years leading the company, Francesca had earned the right to do pretty much anything.

But the last two years had been abysmal, and Juliette wished Francesca had granted them more time and preparation before rolling out a performance. A preview night might not have been such a bad idea, especially after the *Don Quixote* fiasco.

She had said as much and was given the stink eye from a harried and disheveled Francesca before Gabriel pulled her away to avoid screaming. Not that it was really avoidable these days. Raised voices were everywhere.

When she made her way into the shoe room on the day of the dress rehearsal, Michel and Monique were engaged in a very public squabble involving a soloist and some alleged debauchery and, had Juliette heard right…debts? She had no idea Michel was a gambler, but Gabriel only shrugged a shoulder and Juliette let it go.

Francesca was in the middle of a good yelling session with Madame Rochefort, the reclusive shoe lady who ruled over the biggest bounty within the Palais. The room, which resembled a beehive with its honeycomb walls filled with shoes, named and labeled, for each of the one hundred and twenty dancers, was a marvel of architecture and a jewel in the crown of the French ballet.

Madame Rochefort was a jewel in her own right, renowned for having inherited the magic and knowledge of centuries of shoe masters. Juliette adored and feared her. Francesca was always in trouble with her, and their shouting matches were legendary.

As Juliette stepped into the gallery after class, she couldn't help but notice two things. Well, three.

Katarina was trying on a black pair, clearly getting ready for her Odile, two other sets lying next to her, already properly broken in and cut. There were strange, mangled flowers on Madame Rochefort's desk, and Madame Rochefort herself was stubbornly glaring at Francesca, who was yelling in Spanish. Judging by the level of noise, the purse of Madame Rochefort's lips, and the speed with which several other dancers vacated the premises—among them Michel and Monique, still quarreling—the fight was serious, and Juliette knew better than to get involved.

And what was more important, as she tuned out the screeching behind her, all Juliette wanted was to stare at Katarina, even though Katarina had not yet lifted her eyes to her.

Which wasn't that strange, Juliette told herself. In fact, she had been telling herself similar things all morning. When she had woken up, a bit later than her usual time, and decided to forgo her jog so she could enjoy a cup of coffee with Katarina, she had been greeted by an empty apartment.

Later, during class, Katarina did not take her customary place in the back of the room and stayed farther upfront, which ensured that Juliette was as far away from her as possible.

And now this. Not even looking up as Juliette plopped down on the floor next to her to check out her new shoes. Trying not to overthink things, she banged the little nail out of the first pair and went to town with the cutter, adjusting the height of the satin sides as her brain was in overdrive trying to figure out what was going on. They had shared something special last night, and if not for the phone call…

Damn, the phone call! And Helena.

For someone priding herself on being an intelligent woman, Juliette wanted to roll her eyes at her own blind spot.

"Helena will not be calling again."

The words fell out of her mouth before she realized that this was perhaps neither the time nor the place. The resulting glare from Katarina was utterly predictable. Maybe she had imagined the moment after all? Although this much anger over a phone call? Surely—

"I do not care about your escapades, Mademoiselle Lucian-Sorel. You are notorious for them. In fact, one of them is standing not ten feet away, showing off an impressive arsenal of curses for which her mother should probably wash her mouth with soap—"

"Vyatka, you prude, for your information I learned all of these from my sainted mother and she'd be so very proud of me. You, on the other hand, kept silent for a month and I liked you more then. Juliette, if you can get your longing and pining out of the way, I'd appreciate you leading the dress rehearsal in twenty minutes. Now both of you can get ready in your own dressing rooms. Juliette, try the other tutu when you get there. As for me, I need to murder Madame Rochefort and I'd like no witnesses to my crime. Scram."

Juliette blushed at Francesca's offhand remark about her yearning and kept her head down as she pulled the large canvas bag with her shoes from her cubby hole and exited the room, studiously avoiding everyone's eyes. Could Francesca embarrass her more?

Madame Rochefort was the only one she said goodbye to, receiving a rather sympathetic look in return.

Oh great, even the resident bog witch pities me.

Were all her emotions really written on her face? Katarina would probably be wise to avoid her since apparently Juliette was a lovesick fool. Absolutely unacceptable. Maybe if she herself stayed away for a bit, their pas de deux notwithstanding, she'd gain back either her wits, her dignity, or some semblance of control over her facial expressions.

As she took the stairs all the way down to the bowels of Garnier, where the dressing room she used on performance days was located, Katarina did not seem to have gotten the memo. The one about Juliette yearning. Back to the door and black pointe shoes on, she seemed to have beaten Juliette to her own dressing room. Why would she even be here in the first place?

"Ah, why—" Juliette was about to ask her that very question when Michel bellowed—again, why was everyone yelling at each other today?—that Gabriel was looking for her.

Katarina glared at Michel, murmured something decidedly profane in Russian, but otherwise did not move from the door to the dressing room.

"Um, I need to go see why Gabriel needs me," Juliette whispered, starting to feel like Alice once she stepped through the looking glass. The entire situation was now taking a turn toward the bizarre.

"I'll come with you."

Juliette knew her eyebrows had climbed perilously close to

her hairline, and she wished, as she often did, for the ability to raise a single one. That was such an expressive gesture. And just as the thought popped in her mind, Katarina proceeded to do just that, one perfectly manicured dark blonde eyebrow lifting regally up, giving Juliette a decidedly "move" command only an empress could impart without a word.

She shrugged, more for form than anything else, since shaking Katarina off clearly wasn't an option. Katarina who, a few minutes ago, wouldn't even look at her and now seemed glued to her side.

Gabriel was in his dressing room, which was usual. And he was wrecked by pre-dress-rehearsal panic. Which was par for the course as well.

"I am the worst dancer in the world, Jett! This will be awful. They will boo us off the stage. I'll be fired and never get another principal job anywhere in the world!" His eyes were brimming with tears.

Okay, so this was quite a few notches worse than Gabriel's norm. Was he really that affected by his first-ever negative reviews? Her own introductory one dated to two years ago and the callus that had formed over her heart was thick, yet even that very callus periodically had scabs torn off it and bled.

So, Juliette understood him. And because she loved him, and he was her only true friend in this city that was quickly turning hostile and nothing like the home they both adored, she lifted on her tiptoes and hugged him. Their usual peck on the lips should have followed, yet he grimaced slightly at the last moment and gave her cheek a chaste kiss.

"We have an audience, my heart. And I refuse to share our love with others." He booped her nose, the gesture allowing him to duck the light slap he knew was incoming at any suggestion that the two of them were an item.

"Ass." She shook her head at his antics, but her presence, and even that of the silent sentinel that was Katarina, quietly observing the two of them from the doorway, appeared to have lifted his spirit somewhat.

"Is your crisis of confidence over, Gabe?"

He nodded then leaned down and drew her in another long hug, rocking slowly side to side.

"Yes, darlin', thank you. I will see you on stage."

The day spun away from there. Everyone seemed to need her. Francesca for last-minute tweaks, Monsieur Lenoir for his usual double-check of the timing of her entrances, Monique saccharinely wishing her a successful dress rehearsal.

If one more person talked to her, Juliette felt she would just have to start pushing them out of her way. Or Katarina might, because for some incomprehensible reason, she had not stepped away from Juliette since intercepting her after the shoe room exit.

Even surrounded by people, well-wishers, ill-wishers, in-between-wishers, Katarina was at her side, never straying too far away. Though when Juliette tried to initiate a conversation, she couldn't get very far.

"Ah, I thought we could talk about what happened last night?" Juliette knew she sounded breathy and tentative and tried not to get mad at her own insecurity around this woman. She was Juliette Lucian-Sorel, and she was about to lead the Paris Opera Ballet into its revolutionary rendition of *Swan Lake*, which would break records or break careers. And yet, here she was stuttering in front of a beautiful woman. A beautiful woman she had almost kissed the night before. A beautiful woman who maybe, possibly, probably almost kissed her back?

"And what, pray tell, happened?" Katarina's eyebrow took its famous turn up, leaving Juliette to wonder why the divinity thought she was a strong soldier. How could anyone think she was a soldier at all, when all she wanted to do was take off her white tutu and wave it in surrender?

And why was she thinking about undressing? Of course, she

wanted to take the tutu off, the tutu and a lot more, because this woman was just unbelievably—

"Nothing happened, Juliette."

The finality in the soft, almost featherlike voice seemed both out of place and perfectly at home. If Katarina had filled a bucket of cold water and doused Juliette with it, that might have been a gentler letdown than her words. Or her tone. Nobody in Juliette's twenty-five years had been able to deliver indifferent and untouchable as well as Katarina Vyatka.

Even her name, the one she so rarely heard falling from those lips, was devoid of that intimacy Katarina bestowed every time she spoke it.

Juliette swallowed around the lump in her throat, surely a cliché of some sort probably employed by romance authors, but she had no better way of describing what it felt like, other than to maybe go fully dramatic and say that she was shoving down her feelings. As to what feelings, well, Juliette decided on the spot that they were of hurt and profound disappointment that even after everything they had been through together, not only was she still "Mademoiselle Lucian-Sorel" more often than not, but the gap that persisted between them only got wider.

They walked silently through the hallways of Garnier, Katarina's presence like a specter, like a thundercloud at her shoulder. Ignoring her wasn't an option, and talking to her made even less sense. Juliette had clearly imagined the flickers of care and affection in the icy depths of Katarina's eyes. There was nothing there, just as there was nothing between them. And most important of all, Juliette had a ballet to lead.

As they finally made their way to the main stage, Katarina in full costume and Juliette still lugging her shoe bag around, they were harried by everyone they met.

"You're late!"

"They are waiting for you!"

"Francesca already blew several gaskets!"

"You should've heard the screaming, go quickly!"

The stage was crowded, the full company involved in *Swan Lake* standing in a semicircle, listening to Francesca's last-minute words of what sounded like encouragement.

Juliette and Katarina pushed their way through the throngs of dancers to the very front.

"Oh, how kind of you to join us. Jett, I told you to be here twenty minutes ago! And my God, surely you are not yet in your dotage and remember that you'll have to have your pointe shoes on? Do you need someone to help you with those, amor?"

Juliette made a face at Francesca, who knew all too well that she had never been late to anything in her life and her delay was very much Francesca's fault to begin with for changing her mind at the last second about the tutu.

Rolling her eyes at the smirking and ribaldry around her, Juliette simply plopped down and opened her bag, pulling out the first pair she'd had Madame Rochefort trim to her customary specifications just yesterday. Breaking in new shoes during opening night was something Juliette never did, preferring to keep three pairs on hand during dress rehearsal and switching them out, one after another, thus having all she needed ready to go for the next evening.

Suddenly, several things happened at once.

Katarina all but jumped from behind her and snatched the shoes from her hands, the satin ribbons wrapping themselves around Juliette's wrist and pulling her closer, bumping them cheek to cheek.

Ninety people laughed in unison at their predicament.

Gabriel called out her name.

And something sticky and warm dripped down her hand and onto her thigh. As she lifted her fingers, still tangled in the ribbons, to touch her smarting cheekbone, blood was all she saw.

Her pristine white leotard, her slippers, the new shoes, were all drenched in crimson. Crimson that continued to gush... from Katarina's palm.

The laughter died in waves, first the front rows of dancers, the ones who were closer, then those behind them, until the silence was truly deafening, as only the silence of almost one hundred people rocked to their core could be. And in that silence, Katarina's voice, the same voice that had been so impersonal, so distant and cold all day, was anything but.

"Well, turns out she did need help with her shoes, Madame Bianchi."

Fifteen
Of Mint Tea & Being Known

Of course, the dress rehearsal was more than just a success. It was, in fact, a success of immense proportions. Standing ovation, encores, flowers, more applause, tears, and the look in Francesca's eyes that spoke volumes. After two barren years, Paris Opera Ballet had itself a hit. And not merely a hit, a masterpiece.

Yes, the shock of glass-filled shoes and the gushing blood, as well as Thierry being called to the stage to apply the necessary numbing and bandages, all delayed the performance, but once it was delivered?

Still riding the high of a job exceptionally done, of the heavy fear of another failure on her résumé beaten, Juliette, in her stage makeup, sat in Francesca's office once again. However, other than the setting, the opened windows overlooking Place de l'Opéra and the pigeons sleeping on the windowsill, nothing was the same. If there could be a duality of moods permeating the room, it would be this very moment. Elation and shock.

The former they'd be discussing many times, savoring every detail, especially after opening night, once every flaw underscored by the dress rehearsal was corrected, new stitches sewn into the now broken-in costumes.

And speaking of stitches. Katarina sat in her usual chair, her bandaged hand—and how did Thierry even find black gauze so quickly?—palm down and still on her knee. Her posture was perfect, spine ramrod straight and not touching the back of the chair. Francesca's chairs were famed for their lack of comfort. Juliette could relate.

Gabriel was pacing, alternating between looking worried and wanting to be anywhere but here. Juliette could relate to that too.

Monsieur Lenoir's face gave away nothing. And Francesca? Well, she was silent and motionless, both of which were quite remarkable in their own right. If not for the look she shot Juliette after the curtain went up and the audience—yes, friends and families, but an audience nonetheless—was on its feet applauding and clamoring for that never-ever-done-in-the-modern-ballet encore, Juliette would have been hard-pressed to say what exactly was on her mind.

As for herself, Juliette tried to push aside the sweet relief and the even sweeter success and focus on the fact that someone had intended to harm her. Again.

Finally, taking a deep breath, she closed her eyes, and what tumbled out of her mouth was nothing but the truth.

"You were right, Katarina, it does feel like betrayal."

The silence had thorns, and sandpaper, and Juliette looked up to everyone staring at her. Pity, sadness, compassion. And then there were the deep blue eyes looking at her with understanding.

"Because it is. No matter how you dress it." Katarina looked at the gauze on her hand and smiled at her own pun.

"For all we know, it was you."

Jacques Lalande, whom Juliette hadn't heard enter, spoke with a nonchalance that didn't fit the occasion. Neither of them, really. The success of the production or the injury. The minister crossed the office in three steps and unceremoniously plopped himself on top of Francesca's desk, blocking her view of the room. Instead of eviscerating him as Juliette expected her to, Francesca pushed her chair to the right and said nothing.

Gabriel coughed quietly, and as Juliette raised her eyes to him, his face spoke volumes. Shit was about to hit the fan, and not even Francesca was going to distract anyone from what was to follow.

Katarina lifted her injured limb then slowly undid the gauze, showing off the seven stitches.

"I assume you accuse me of doing this to myself on purpose?"

He waved at her, a gesture of dismissal so blatant Juliette could feel her jaw drop.

"Technically, you did do it to yourself, since you stuck your hand in the shoe all by your lonesome. What, did your plan go wrong, or did you have second thoughts?"

His voice was so full of disdain that Juliette recoiled. Gabriel stopped his pacing by Katarina's chair and placed his palm on her shoulder. She flinched, and Juliette's heart did that foolish thing it always did these days. It sped up, knocking maniacally on her rib cage as if wanting to break free. To get away? To get closer? Juliette suspected it was all of the above.

"Don't you think you're overdoing this bad gendarme routine, Lalande?" Gabriel hissed, all six foot five of him cutting a rather imposing figure when he chose to set aside the court jester persona. Juliette wanted to smile. Of course, out of the entire company, Gabriel would be the one to befriend and defend the outsider. Well, technically second. Since Juliette herself had friendly feelings toward Katarina. If you called wanting to kiss her senseless "friendly."

Lalande employed the same gesture to dismiss him as well.

"She was involved in at least five documented incidents with broken glass in Moscow. If anything, this is a modus operandi by now. Isn't it, Mademoiselle Vyatka?"

If he expected his knowledge of episodes from her past to shock Katarina, he did not succeed. She remained unmoved, Gabriel's hand still on her shoulder, her back still straight and her uncovered palm in her lap.

"Since you know something of my past, and my previous… experiences with broken glass used to maim dancers, Monsieur le Ministre, let me tell you one thing, and what you'll think of the incident and of me afterward is up to you." Katarina did not look at anyone in particular, her tone level and matter-of-fact. "If you want to deliberately injure a ballerina by interfering with her pointe shoes, simply sprinkling shards in one is not enough. It will be noticed. She will see it right away. Feel it as she adjusts it over her toes, if nothing else." Katarina patted Gabriel's hand, and to Juliette's surprise he instantly removed it, the two of them in perfect understanding of each other.

Katarina straightened her shoulders even more, if such a thing was possible, and then gave Lalande a decidedly dirty glance.

"Had you been a dancer, and not a bureaucrat, you'd know that in order to really harm someone using this particular method, you have to sew the glass in the toe box, so that the moment a ballerina steps on pointe, the sharp edges shred her foot—not before it, not after it, no. The damage, the blood and gore are delivered at the moment when the full weight of the dancer is on this tiny piece of cardboard and satin. And there's no stopping that. Gravity wins every time. And so does glass against skin."

There was a gasp, but Juliette could not tell to whom it belonged. She could not tear her eyes off Katarina, who had lost her pallor, her cheekbones stained pink in sharp relief against her black bodice and golden hair.

"And so, Monsieur Lalande, you see, me shredding my hand gives you a very important clue. Someone who, according to you and your sources"—she practically spat the word, all emotion now, a sight to see—"has been involved, as you said, in five of such experiences, would know all of this. And would surely not be this sloppy and this inefficient." She raised the injured hand for effect, and now only her rapid breathing could be heard in the room. Even the pigeons awoken by the kerfuffle were silent.

When she spoke again, it was as if the emotion of only seconds ago had been an illusion. Her voice, her face, her eyes, were all devoid of any trace of it.

"I heard something breaking right before a large group of dancers exited the shoe room and Mademoiselle Lucian-Sorel entered. When she opened the bag on stage, I thought I saw a shard falling out of it. As to why I had to sacrifice my palm to prove my suspicion right, well, there was no way of knowing for certain and no time to check. Does this explanation satisfy you?"

They looked at each other for what felt like an eternity and then, unexpectedly, Lalande laughed. "I don't know why I still think you would just spill all your secrets. Even our secret police, not to mention your famed KGB, informed us you are and always have been a tough nut to crack."

Something flitted across the marble features, and Juliette's heart squeezed painfully. This felt cruel. Unnecessary. They had offered her asylum, demanded a myriad of conditions from her, had her live with a stranger to prove good behavior, and made her take up roles that were beneath her. Did they really have to spy on her too? Cooperate with the Soviets to find out about her past?

Suddenly all eyes in the room were on her, and Juliette realized she must have spoken at least part of her internal monologue out loud. She winced and felt like a fool until she met Katarina's gaze and there was so much gratitude in it, so much wonder, Juliette was immediately elated.

Yeah, she was smitten, all right. Beyond smitten and not even hiding it, since Gabriel threw her a narrow-eyed stare before winking saucily. She'd have to deal with it—and him—but for now, she had asked a question.

"Well, we had to know who we were harboring…" Lalande trailed off, realizing that he had used the wrong word altogether.

Juliette was up and in his face in a second, and only Gabriel's arms pulling her back prevented her from doing something she'd probably regret later.

"She's not a goddamn criminal! She's a refugee! And if you had spent half of your energy trying to make things work instead of tearing them down, instead of tearing people down, you'd not be facing the issues at Garnier that you do. All you've done since you took over has been to sow discord and lord over us like we are inept children. It's insulting."

He had the decency to look sheepish, but there was no saving this meeting. They'd not be getting any new facts, nor would they be moving back to a constructive conversation. Perhaps sensing that, Francesca stood up and, banging her cane exaggeratedly on the antique parquet, exited the office, leaving the door wide open, exposing the dozen or so people standing there, too close to have been engaged in anything but eavesdropping.

Nauseous, feeling like she needed a shower and so exposed, her shawl not helping despite covering her entire upper body, Juliette followed Francesca and did not look back. She'd stepped over another line today. Applause, glory, respect, professional security be damned. She'd lose it all before she'd lose Katarina to these vultures.

As she raced down Rue Saint-Honoré, past shops and hotels on her way home, Juliette knew the only real question was whether she was prepared to lose anything other than Katarina. Anyone. The question was whether she was prepared to lose herself too.

When she came out of the shower, the apartment no longer felt empty. It was quiet, but Juliette could tell another person was in. As she wrapped herself in a towel and sheepishly exited the small confines of the old bathroom, she noticed the tiny things she had started to take for granted in the past few months since they had become roommates.

Her keys were on the hook and not thrown haphazardly

on the little table by the door. Her shoes were placed carefully, perfectly aligned with other pairs. Her wrap had been hung up in the hallway. Despite her being home, the little pink light was on in the kitchen, and the apartment smelled like mint.

She decided against dressing just yet, her curiosity too strong and, as always, so was the pull of Katarina. Especially this Katarina, the one puttering by the stove, making so little sound she might as well be a magician.

Perhaps she was. A witch. Surely only someone magical could look ethereal in pink light wearing oversized leg warmers and a sweater that reached mid-thigh, about a gazillion sizes too big.

"You changed the bulb."

Talk about pointing out the obvious. Juliette wanted to smack herself over the forehead for having the worst foot-in-mouth disease in the history of lesbians. Wasn't she supposed to be the experienced one? The one who could pick up any woman in a bar and take her home, all the while being the suave seductress all these people imagined her to be?

Clearly not where *this* woman was concerned. Katarina turned away from the kettle, holding a mug with her uninjured hand and balancing a teaspoon in her stitched-up one, and Juliette lost her breath, almost dropping her towel.

She grabbed the soggy cotton tighter and tried to look inconspicuous. Katarina's eyes were as inscrutable as ever. Her cheekbones were suddenly tinged with crimson, undoubtedly from the heat of the kettle. Surely not from almost seeing Juliette naked. Absolutely not.

The clock on the wall beat a steady tattoo and the intimacy of the domesticity enveloped Juliette like a cozy blanket. Had she ever felt this way? Like the apartment was more than a home, like the person standing in the middle of her kitchen more than just a stranger?

She couldn't even call Katarina a friend, though cutting her hand to ribbons for Juliette must qualify her for some kind of appellation. But the pink light was washing her in hope and tranquility, and Juliette did not have the words.

It was Katarina who finally broke the comfort of the silence. "I lied, earlier."

Juliette grabbed the towel and held it so tight her knuckles went white on the cream cotton. She tried not to jump to conclusions, not to assume what exactly Katarina had lied about, but the pause was giving her brain too much time to run away with the most painful scenarios. God, why was Juliette so desperate to believe her? To believe *in* her?

Katarina, finally glancing at her, must have noticed the confusion and panic on Juliette's face and immediately amended her previous statement.

"No, oh no, not about the glass or not being the one to drop it in your shoes. I didn't." Then she rolled her eyes, and the caring expression turned haughty on a dime. "Honestly, Juliette, that was such a poor job of trying to maim you, it's an embarrassing effort altogether." She tsked and placed the mug on the table, and then sat, still not touching the back of the chair.

Juliette lowered herself gingerly in the opposite seat, mindful of the towel, and reached for the tea. The scent of mint made her smile. Once she took a sip, her smile widened.

"What's so funny?" A raised eyebrow was supposed to be menacing and so was the tone, except the days when Katarina Vyatka could intimidate her with a single look were long behind them.

"You know the way I take my evening tea. Mint, half a sugar cube." Juliette was too pleased with the entire situation to react to Katarina's scoff and eye roll.

"Yes, well, it's been a few months. Anyway." Katarina waved her fingers at her as if turning the page, clearly done with Juliette's ridiculousness. It did not dampen Juliette's joy—in fact, it made her feel a touch giddy that being busted for paying attention to Juliette's habits made Katarina uncomfortable.

"Oh, for crying out loud." Katarina got up and poured another mug of tea, then turned back to Juliette and lifted her hands in exasperation. "You take you coffee with no sugar, you avoid carbs during the day but allow yourself more than your share in the evenings, you love peonies and pay way too much money to the lady on the corner who steals them from the garden behind City Hall. You don't care about the theft. All you want is for the lady to like you. She does. Begrudgingly, because she thinks you are too fancy, but she does anyway. She can't help it, you are very likable." Katarina accompanied each factoid with a bent finger.

"You knot your shoe from left to right, but you are a righty. Your hair smells of lavender, even though your shampoo is scentless, and it's because you add essential oil drops into it. And just like with the lady on the corner, you care too much about what people think. Even me, whom you don't like because you are afraid that I will steal your job."

Well, that was a refreshing spate of not just full sentences—since she had not heard that many words from Katarina in... actually, ever—but also honesty.

"I do. Care, that is." Juliette turned the mug in her hands in slow circles, not lifting her eyes to Katarina's. "And I do like you. Maybe a little too much for a person who is very much capable of taking my job."

Outside, an owl hooted in the Tuileries Gardens. Somewhere nearby, the wind was playing with the broken shutters, a rarity on Rue de Rivoli. The rich enjoyed their comforts, and the banging would surely wake up a few of them. Right on cue, a neighbor opened their own window and shouted. Then someone else joined in. After a few seconds of back-and-forth, the banging stopped, the owner clearly shamed enough by the neighbors' insults and complaints.

When only the wind could be heard outside, she finally lifted her eyes to Katarina, who was now the one smiling. If a tiny crook of the left corner of her mouth could be called that.

"When I was a girl, I dreamt of France. My father had traveled the world and Paris was his favorite city. He'd talk about the language, even if he never taught me French, about the people whose rudeness he found funny and refreshing. You'd never have this scene in Moscow. Or in Tallinn, for that matter."

"You're from Tallinn?"

Juliette wanted to swallow her words. Why oh why did she have to be so nosy? This was one of the most personal bits of herself Katarina was sharing with her, and she couldn't even stop herself from asking questions. She shook her head, but Katarina's smile just widened.

"Yes. I am from Tallinn. My mother was Estonian, my father Ukrainian. Hence the last name. And while it's not a secret, since neither the first nor the last name are exactly Russian sounding, Bolshoi has never openly acknowledged my motherland. And you know how big that entire country and its propaganda machine are on the concept. They even have a saying, 'My address is not a house, nor a street, my address is Soviet Union.' You aren't Estonian, or Ukrainian, or Armenian, or Moldovan. You are Soviet. Your identity, your culture is stripped away."

The smile lost its warmth and was all bitterness. But when she spoke again, Katarina's voice was neutral. Practiced.

"They wanted to change my name. Ekaterina Vyatkina. Now, that is very Russian. I refused. It was my one and only act of rebellion. And the first time I got glass in my pointe shoes, Juliette."

Damn, talk about full circle. When Katarina didn't add anything, Juliette knew the walk down memory lane was over. And it might as well have been paved with those shards, because Katarina's eyes were swimming in tears.

"You mentioned you lied?" Even as she asked, Juliette felt

an absolute fool. Surely, she was smarter than this. Why was this woman always reducing her intellect to the level of a turnip? Yes, change the subject, but maybe avoid the glass again since it was clearly a painful memory?

Katarina answered without hesitation, and after a blink, like magic, her eyes were dry once more.

"There was plenty of time to tell you I thought someone crushed glass in your shoes. I lied to that overgrown jackass minister about that. I wanted the entire company to bear witness."

Juliette's eyes widened.

"But why?"

"Because sabotage of this magnitude, as inept as the execution was, should never remain in the shadows. Mine was always hidden, my wounds bandaged, my absence explained with lies, to make everyone else feel comfortable." Katarina stood up, taking her mug to the sink. A quick rinse and she placed it on the drying rack.

When she turned back to Juliette, the usually composed features were filled with something akin to rage. There was no other way to describe it.

"I wanted them very uncomfortable, Juliette. All these people around you, in your life, in your bed, and yet none of them has any damn sense to keep you safe. I don't care if you're angry with me. I see that you are." Juliette didn't know what she was exactly, the emotion too complex to pinpoint with any accuracy, but the blows just kept coming. To her pride. To her heart.

Katarina dismissed her attempt to speak with a lift of her chin and went on. "This is the second time someone felt very confident in going after you, brazen even. Why? Because secrets and shadows breed that very brazenness. It was time to let them all know that hunting season on Juliette Lucian-Sorel is over."

Juliette blinked, her breaths, her anger, coming out in shallow puffs of air, and when she opened her eyes, she was alone with all the revelations, awash in pink light.

Sixteen

Of Love & Ballet

The people in her life? The women in her bed?

Okay, so the sentiment was nice, protective even, and it was true that Juliette had rarely been the subject of anyone's protectiveness. Helena was too cerebral for that, and Francesca tended to forget they had been lovers unless it suited her in one way or another.

But the gall to jump to all those conclusions. And to make it sound like Juliette had been sleeping around, when she had practically been a fucking saint. A nun! She had not had anyone since before the summer. Fine, so maybe there had been that woman in Monaco. Who cared? Katarina didn't even know she existed. Hell, Juliette herself had forgotten her entirely, including her name.

In the span of one day, Katarina Vyatka had saved Juliette's feet, signaled to everyone she was off-limits for sabotage, showed her that she knew her and understood her, shared a piece of her own past—something previously unheard of—and then insulted her to her very face.

Juliette would not take this. Not standing, not sitting, not lying down, not in any other way.

She had tossed and turned all night, consumed by her own foolishness—she had no other word for it. Katarina clearly didn't see her as mature, smart, discerning, or virtuous. Yet there she was, delivering swoon-worthy statements about the exact way Juliette liked her tea.

Damn her.

She left the apartment before sunrise, wandering the streets, aware that showing up too early at Garnier would earn her suspicious looks. And Juliette did not want the attention her status placed on her. She was Prima Assoluta, Étoile, but for once, she wished she was a corps girl.

The familiar street corner with its mainstay flower lady, Madame Broussard, beckoned. And yet Katarina's words came back to her.

"All you want is for the lady to like you. She does. Begrudgingly, but she does."

Understanding just how childish, how absolutely silly it was, Juliette turned around and took a parallel street. The last thing she saw was Madame Broussard's pursed lips.

And damn Katarina, but she cared about the flower lady's opinion. Why was that wrong? If Juliette didn't already feel totally foolish for walking away, she'd return. But it felt even more foolish to do so. And now that she knew that Katarina and Madame Broussard talked about her, she felt all the foolishness of the world suddenly descend on her shoulders.

One thing about this entire mess was that she had figured out how the janitors and the cafeteria ladies and even the indomitable shoe mistress, Madame Rochefort, got their wilted flowers every so often.

Saint Katarina.

Of course it was her. Who else would give away her money to make someone's day better, especially if that someone was always forgotten and underappreciated? Saint Katarina indeed, who burned her hands, cut them to ribbons, and stood up to bullies, all the while making Juliette so mad!

Juliette huddled into her sweater and walked the rest of her way, desperately trying to put Katarina, the flower lady—or the weight of the world's expectations—out of her mind.

The latter one proved to be impossible. Today was opening night. And the former had a similar fate. Not that she'd ever be able to forget about her dance partner, but the massive poster hanging off the facade of the Palais Garnier with her own silhouette, flanked by Gabriel's and Katarina's, was quite a reminder.

It seemed the entire universe was conspiring to remind her of Katarina. And of Katarina's patronizing attitude. Of Katarina's arrogance. Of Katarina's beautiful face—

No! Stop it!

A few hours later, in class, Katarina did not take her regular place out of Juliette's direct line of sight. Oh no, today of all days Katarina was a touch late, which was surely devious of her, because instead of focusing on getting her warm-up reps, all Juliette could do was look around and worry that her wayward roommate got hit by a taxi.

When she did arrive, Katarina was dressed in a splendid navy leotard Juliette had never seen before. It turned her skin translucent.

The hour went abysmally, because Katarina was not even ten feet away. She was right next to Juliette, the goddamn orange blossom driving her to distraction.

So Juliette didn't manage to get a decent warm-up, and with Francesca actually attending this class, as was her custom on opening night to ensure all her dancers were in good form before the most important performance, Juliette was left to redo most of the sequences and stretches by herself long after everyone else had gone to get on with their days and schedules.

She then went on to join Katarina and Gabriel for their last rehearsal, but being late by almost half an hour due to the extra warm-up time, she walked into a full-blown run-through. Except, it was interspersed with too much cutesy teasing.

Since when was Gabriel this smitten? No, she knew since

when. It had started the very first night he'd met Katarina. Traitor. He was supposed to be Juliette's best friend, not buddy to this... this... this woman.

"Oh, hey Jett!" Clearly not bothering to notice that she was upset, though even under torture she'd never confess to any such thing, Gabriel ran up to her once the music stopped and simply swept her off her feet.

It was a standard greeting for him, but Juliette pushed him away. He stumbled, one foot tangling with the other, catching himself at the last second.

"Hey, Jett, what the he—" He coughed once, twice, and then a few more times, as if he couldn't catch his breath.

Katarina patted him on the back and he straightened, his chest heaving and his face red and blotchy.

"Jeez, woman, do you want me dead or something?"

"She can't have you dead, Gabe. She needs you to lift her seventeen times tonight." Katarina gave Gabriel's back another pat, way gentler than Juliette thought he deserved, before stepping away to sip from her water bottle.

"Gabe? When the hell did this happen? She still calls me—"

"Mademoiselle Lucian-Sorel, the flower lady asked about you this morning. She said you were acting very strange. I believe her exact words were 'like a turkey,' or whatever the French use to describe such behavior. I told her I'd let you know."

The twinkle in Katarina's eyes was too much, and Juliette took a step closer until they were face-to-face.

"Would the two of you save your unresolved sexual tension for tonight? The performance so benefits from all this... estrogen." Francesca clapped her hands, and Juliette nearly fell over trying not to jump a foot in the air. And her own reaction to the words, to the entire ordeal, just made her even angrier.

She actually growled at Francesca, who sent a smirk her

way before there was more clapping.

"Okay, let's channel all this frustration into some dancing, shall we?"

And channel it they did. Into the last rehearsal. During costume and makeup. And then into the opening night performance.

It's a rarity when absolutely everything goes right for a production. Such a rarity, in fact, that it almost never happens. Their *Swan Lake* had seemed doomed by the opposition of the Culture Minister Gabriel's bronchitis in the middle of the mildest autumn in Paris, Juliette's series of strange sabotage-like events… And yet here they were.

A moment before the conductor's baton lifted and Lenoir commanded his orchestra into one of the most important battles for saving the Paris Opera Ballet season, Juliette closed her eyes and counted to ten. When she opened them, in the wing opposite her, Katarina was a serene presence, every perfect hair in place, her wounded hand bandaged.

Beside her, Gabriel was clearing his throat and joking. With a last glance to the audience, Juliette found Francesca, all focused energy, sitting next to a very familiar face.

Shannon Robbards. *The* Shannon Robbards. Second only to the Goddess that was Margot Fonteyn in London, Shannon Robbards was a deity in her own right. She had danced in London, behind Fonteyn, then in New York, leading that company for over a decade. She had returned to London in her later years, where she had retired. The thought crossed Juliette's mind that she had no earthly idea what Shannon Robbards did these days. She was always talked about as the next director for the Royal Ballet, but Rodion Foltin had been running that show after he'd defected a year ago.

For some reason, thinking about Foltin made Juliette want to hunch her shoulders. Katarina never talked about him, and that in itself was strange, since he had been her dancing partner for over a decade. But then, Katarina hardly spoke of anyone at all, so what else was new?

Juliette stretched her back and focused on the present. Shannon Robbards was now whispering to Francesca, whose face bore a strikingly worried expression.

Peeking one last time at the two dance masters, Juliette turned back to the dark stage. She'd have to ask about this exchange later. Something Helena said on their last phone call tugged at her memory, but Lenoir was raising his baton, the oboist was getting ready to play the famous first notes of Tchaikovsky's masterpiece, and Juliette knew it was time. Odette was about to step on stage, and the magic of *Swan Lake* would take over.

And take over it did. Sequence after sequence, step after step, jump after jump, Juliette's muscles sang and her heart beat a steady rhythm along with the orchestra.

To think that she had had doubts about this production. To think that she believed they would not be successful. To think that she assumed this interpretation was bound to fail.

When the curtain lifted for the second act, Juliette glided on stage and the audience held its collective breath. Instead of the Prince coming toward her, the Black Swan made her entrance in one jump. The weeks of rehearsals, the months of tension, of doubt, of yearning, had been worth it. And of course, the stage of Palais Garnier would be that place where the embers between them ignited.

The synchronicity, the angle of movements, the timing of the sequences. They were perfect. Juliette matched Katarina's every breath, every heartbeat.

When their hands met, Juliette could swear her skin caught fire. She burned, and the speed of the jumps and arabesques only fed the flame.

Francesca's choreography strayed from the original, and the pas de deux unfolded in an unwavering crescendo that took both the dancers' and the audience's breaths away.

By the time they were entwined, their embrace the culmination of the scene, Juliette was crying and Katarina's eyes were full of unshed tears. With Katarina's arms around her, her body supported and cradled, Juliette allowed the pressure of the last months—hell, of the last few years—to sweep her up and then away, like a summer thunderstorm, violent and then cleansing.

She closed her eyes and let her other senses take over. Touch was the one she chose to focus on most, as Katarina did not let go, her skin warm, her arms gentle. Opening her eyes, Juliette saw the luminous ones opposite her alight with so much emotion, so much tenderness, that she knew there was no coming back from this.

Katarina Vyatka dancing, living, breathing Tchaikovsky was a sight to see. A once-in-a-lifetime moment for every ballet aficionado. And surely the crowning achievement of every dance partner the Empress of Moscow chose to share the stage with. Juliette knew she'd never forget it. Would never be able to, not after being blessed by the light of these celestial eyes, burning with so much passion, so much pride and satisfaction.

A job well done, a ballet revolution, history made. Juliette turned her own hand, palm gliding over the arm holding her midriff, and Katarina's lips twitched before the dimples peeked and then fully blossomed on the heavily made-up face. Juliette was certain she heard gasps from the front rows. Maybe even swooning. Katarina Vyatka bestowing a full-on smile was a swooning occasion, after all.

Eyes on each other, chests heaving, they stood in their embrace for what seemed like forever, despite the music having to move forward. Lenoir, ever the experienced and savvy conductor, understood the moment too well and did not transition to the next sequence, where Gabriel would enter the stage along with the corps. Rather, he repeated the last thirty seconds of the pas de deux, giving her and Katarina time to collect themselves.

There should have been doubts and worries and missteps. Instead, they had danced like their lives depended on it. And they did. At least their professional ones.

Their eyes remained on each other, and Juliette could feel that whatever was happening, she wasn't alone. Katarina's own were filled with the same emotion Juliette knew was radiating from her. A heartbeat, another, and then the audience erupted, and they finally turned to the now-standing crowd of exaltation.

A rather gauche instance of interrupting a ballet with an ovation seemed only fitting this evening. The evening Juliette Lucian-Sorel and Katarina Vyatka broke convention. Annihilated boundaries. Revolutionized ballet. With a gentle squeeze of her hand, Katarina let her go and led her closer to the front of the stage, executing her famous révérence. The unthinkable yet so perfectly appropriate gesture of acknowledgment of the audience's reaction was met with more applause. Katarina's hand in hers trembled, and Juliette's tears started anew.

Tears of joy. Tears of pride. Tears of, dare she think it, love. Juliette lowered her head. Could it be all over for her? Was she in love? It felt immense. It felt like she was on the precipice of something poets wrote sonnets about. The kind kings abdicated their thrones for. The kind witches were burned at the stake for.

When she felt Katarina's hand gently tugging her up from her bow, the tenderness was painfully poignant, thoughtful, giving her the time to savor the applause yet communicating that they needed to allow the production to proceed. And Juliette knew she'd burn. There would be no turning back. This moment—of sharing the stage, the dance, the révérence with Katarina Vyatka—had changed everything. Juliette wasn't certain she'd do anything differently even if she could. It was too late anyway.

When the curtain fell for the last time, after being opened a record eleven times for ovations, Juliette finally allowed herself to breathe again. Fully. Unrestrained.

Her earlier anger long gone, she looked around for Katarina. They really should talk. Juliette had things to say. Life-altering things. Katarina surely couldn't pretend anymore. The pas de deux had revealed way too much for them to keep circling each other, acting like nothing was happening.

Instead, the moment Juliette entered the wings, arms full of flowers, Katarina disappeared and it was Francesca who caught her in a hug and kissed her firmly on the lips.

"I don't have to say it. But you are the best ballerina I have ever had the privilege to direct, amor. Never forget it."

Another kiss and Francesca was gone, the line of people clamoring for her attention a mile long. Resolved to find Katarina after the opening night madness subsided, Juliette turned her attention to her present situation.

There would be a line just as long, if not longer, waiting for Juliette and Gabriel and Katarina at the stage door of the theater. She was happy to share it with them, even though the public clearly felt compelled to crown her all over again. It was her night, after all. Odette wins. Seduced but not broken, she lives to defeat the temptation and get the Prince.

Juliette had been right about the sheer number of people at the stage door, young girls and autograph hunters alike swamping her with flowers and screaming out her name to sign the program, random scraps of paper, or their skin.

Juliette soaked it all in. In a few hours, the reviews would be in, but she knew this time she wouldn't need to hide from them, nor pretend she didn't care.

As the after-party with the important guests at The Meurice was winding down, Gabriel twirled her around the dance floor.

"Some folks are going to Le Palace to celebrate. Are you in? C'mon, Jett, you must!"

He looked good. She had been slightly worried about him lately, his cold lingering for a bit too long, but his eyes were shining, his complexion less pale, and he had had an amazing night, their chemistry and years of dancing together on full display.

"I'll go, absolutely. Who else is coming?"

Juliette took his arm and waved to Francesca, who was deep in conversation with Lalande and some people Juliette had greeted but whose names she cared not to remember.

"I guess you will just have to wait and see, darlin'."

He got them a taxi surprisingly quickly for all the hullabaloo surrounding The Meurice tonight, and before she knew it, the driver was opening her door in front of Le Palace.

A club with an unspoken predilection for a certain clientele, this was, above all, a safe place. The drinks were flowing and the dance floor was chock-full of ballerinas. Yeah, a jumping Le Palace meant only one thing: It was a successful opening night at Paris Opera Ballet.

It was a tradition of sorts to come here after a good performance, and it explained why Juliette had missed the club as much as she did. They really had not had an occasion to go dancing at Le Palace lately.

But tonight was different. Gabriel handed her a glass of something brown, the ice clicking in the small tumbler, and Juliette threw caution to the wind. She downed the contents in one gulp, what turned out to be whiskey sliding down her throat like honey, and then they were on the dance floor.

Around them, the bodies moved to the rhythm of a tune she did not recognize, yet it was driving the dancers to a frenzy.

Her body loose after three hours of performing, Juliette let go. She took off her shoes and allowed herself to simply be in the moment.

She had so much to deal with once this night was over, chiefly among them Katarina, who had disappeared off the face of the earth after they made their way to the after-party. Juliette would have to be brave there. Daring, even. She hadn't been surprised Katarina ran. After all, she was many things, but foolish wasn't one of them. Whatever it was that scared her—and Juliette assumed it was the moment they had shared on stage—they'd have to talk about. And if Juliette had to be the one to pin her down and finally broach the subject, so be it.

Images of pinning Katarina—to a wall, to a bed—made Juliette dizzy. Hot. Wanting. She shook her head, trying to dislodge thoughts of translucent skin and long naked limbs under her own mouth from her mind, but the whiskey was making her bold, hungry. The beat of the bass was like a throb in her blood, and she moved unbidden to it.

Gabriel was in and out of her line of sight, both of them swapping partners several times before reuniting and then splitting again. He brought her another glass and Juliette threw it back gamely. She'd pay for it later, but she'd be paying for so many things, what was one more?

She had danced with Monique, who seemed to be in Le Palace alone, and despite their differences, their past entanglements allowed them to have the time of their lives. When Monique spun her around and then into the arms of a stranger, a tall, lean, and muscular woman with an intriguing face and quick feet, Juliette thought she'd seen something in her peripheral vision. Someone. But the woman winked at her, took her hand, and spun her again, giving Juliette a pleasant little buzz, before bringing her close to her body.

The rhythm changed, slowed down, became a heartbeat, and the heady lighting, the cigarette smoke was making Juliette lightheaded.

The woman was gorgeous. Tall, strong, clearly interested, not Juliette's usual type but breathtakingly handsome with those immense eyes, and yet... These weren't the blue ones Juliette craved to have looking at her with this much interest, with this much desire. In fact, the same amount of interest and desire they'd looked at her with during their pas de deux.

Ah, Katarina, you liar... All these months... All these useless pretenses...

They swayed, their bodies bumping into each other, and it just felt wrong. These were not the curves and angles Juliette had gotten used to being around for the past months, dancing with, moving with.

Lightheaded, slightly disoriented in the darkness and the smoke, Juliette caught the decidedly invitational smirk on the woman's lips as they came close to hers, and she turned away. She smiled sadly and shook her head.

"Désolée, chérie. But I will be going home alone tonight." She caressed the chiseled jaw and the stranger bit her finger gently.

"Are you certain?"

Juliette merely nodded and dropped her hand.

"Whoever she is, the one who has you in knots, better be amazing." The stranger swayed her tenderly now on the bustling dance floor, ignoring the rapid music.

Juliette stopped, her thoughts in disarray and the club no longer cozy or welcoming. It was suffocating. She touched her sternum before murmuring, "She is."

Any other day, any other year, God, any other lifetime, Juliette would turn back and offer a hand to this stranger. Offer her much more than a hand. A bed, a body, an orgasm.

But she knew that none of this would be possible for her anytime soon. There was only one body she wanted. Only one person she craved to be near.

Katarina…

The universe surely was a perverse creature. The moment the name popped into her mind, that very something that had distracted her earlier when she'd stepped onto the dance floor crystalized, and with a sharp turn to her left, Juliette was met with the cold stare of a pair of angry eyes. Eyes that could belong to only one person.

Katarina.

Katarina, who was glowering at her from the far corner of

the bar, propped against the wall, nursing what looked like a glass of water. Or vodka. Her eyes were burning holes in Juliette. Then she turned slightly and gave the dirtiest of looks to Juliette's dance partner. Hell, Juliette was glad she was not wearing anything flammable, as that glare would most certainly set it on fire.

Anger. There was no other way to describe what Katarina was feeling. It must be anger. And that set Juliette's own banking coals of rage into overdrive. She missed a step and her partner caught her, bringing her even closer, smiling down at her, and Juliette smiled back before the sound of glass breaking made her turn. She knew immediately whose tumbler had shattered.

Katarina was already moving from her dark corner of the club to the exit, leaving behind shards of glass and gawking strangers. The curious, ogling, and leering stares just made Juliette angrier. The power Katarina had. Over strangers. Over her.

No fucking way. No fucking way this woman is going to do this to me. To ruin my night like this, in tantrums and hysterics.

In hindsight, as Juliette quickly apologized to her confused dance partner and chased in the club's darkness after Katarina, she might've realized that she had indeed allowed her night to be hijacked by this very woman, since here she was, on the sidewalk, looking both ways to determine which Katarina could have gone.

A taxi screeched to a halt right in front of her, and Juliette almost jumped out of her skin as a livid Katarina glared at her from the back seat.

For a heartbeat they just stared at each other, then, as Katarina lifted her chin in challenge, Juliette balled her fists and got in, slamming the door.

Katarina opened her mouth, whether to insult or admonish, Juliette was not certain and, honestly, not that interested. She had many things to say. Months' worth of things to throw at this woman who had become the bane of her existence. It was time to say them all. It was time to either embrace Katarina Vyatka or purge her from her mind. From her other body parts too.

"We'll talk when we get home," was all she said and was supremely satisfied when Katarina's face turned confused and then perhaps…concerned?

Good. Be concerned. Be very concerned.

Juliette was done with the endless silences and the unspoken longing. With the judging. With the patronizing. It would all end tonight.

Belatedly, as the driver turned his head to her and asked, "Where to, mademoiselle?" she realized she had called her apartment their home and wanted to bite her tongue. But the man was waiting, and all she said was, "Rivoli, corner of Rue d'Alger," before the car sped up into the night.

Seventeen

Of Bitten Lips & Confessed Fantasies

It was a truth already established that Katarina was good at silences. They suited her. They seemed to complete her. At any other time, Juliette would have reveled in how fitting absence of sound was.

As the taxi pulled to their apartment building on the deserted Rue de Rivoli and Katarina bolted up the stairs without saying a word, the silence just made Juliette angrier. She knew she was the one to decree they'd talk at home, but she also knew she had left her rational thinking at the dance club.

Not five hours ago they had shared a wonderful moment on stage, a moment that was followed by Katarina disappearing only to throw a jealous temper tantrum in Le Palace.

It didn't matter to Juliette that there were no witnesses to said temper tantrum. She knew Katarina enough to realize how immense the outburst had been, by her standards. And how ridiculous.

Well, enough of that. Enough of these unsaid words and half-acknowledged emotions. Tonight was the night they'd finally lay their cards on the table.

Just as soon as Juliette caught up with Katarina, who had suddenly found her third and fourth wind and was taking the stairs three at a time.

Fuck this…

Juliette pressed the button of the elevator she rarely used and stewed all the way to the top floor. She exited the old and loud contraption just in time to reach the door first, cutting off Katarina's access to a refuge. Oh, Juliette understood all too well that if she let her enter the apartment before her, Katarina would hightail it to her own bedroom and all Juliette's oaths of having conversations and explanations would be up in both the proverbial and not-so-proverbial smoke. Katarina would chain-smoke the night away and in the morning would pretend absolutely nothing had happened.

Fuck that too…

She entered the apartment first, leaving Katarina to close the door behind herself. Juliette stood her ground a step away, effectively blocking her from going any farther. With the *snick* of the lock Katarina finally turned around, and her eyes narrowed at facing an irate Juliette. The gesture, the familiar show of displeasure, only served to incense Juliette more.

She drew in a breath, noticing Katarina's chest rising and falling. Another one. In the quiet of the apartment, the ticking of the clock sounded like the timer of a bomb.

One second… Katarina's shoulders tensed, her eyes like burning coals, full of fire now.

Two seconds… Juliette gulped.

Three seconds…

Katarina grabbed her by the open collar of her blouse and their mouths met in a kiss that Juliette could only describe as violent. And then Juliette stopped wanting to describe anything. Her mind simply couldn't keep up with whatever was happening.

Lips and tongues and teeth. Katarina turned them swiftly, Juliette's back hit the front door, and she moaned, not in pain, but in exhilaration.

Fucking finally.

Katarina lifted her head, just a fraction, and gave her a wary look, but it was Juliette who tugged her back and they were kissing again.

Who'd have thought? The acerbic, occasionally cruel mouth was a delight. Soft and hard, sharp and soothing, tender and biting. Katarina's kisses were very much like the woman herself, and Juliette would probably need to wear makeup tomorrow to hide the more visible marks. Because Katarina didn't so much kiss as she branded. Juliette reveled in it. She remembered the very first time she'd seen this woman. The blood on her hands and slippers. The violence in her eyes. And the thought Juliette had then: *This woman would leave bruises.*

Accurate.

She dug her fingers in the blonde silky hair, tugging the pins out and sighing at the softness of it. At how it spilled over her skin. How her pulling at it caused Katarina to whimper, breaking the silence for the very first time since they entered the apartment. Katarina's knees buckling and her mouth losing focus only delighted Juliette. It made her even hungrier. It made her ravenous.

"You like it." Juliette couldn't help but bite the sharp edge of the jaw, exposed when Katarina threw her head back. She bit again, and the whimper turned into a moan. "Tell me you like it."

For some reason it felt imperative to know it, to have Katarina say it, and Juliette lifted her face to look into Katarina's eyes. Eyes that were clouded, unfocused, and half-lidded. Katarina swallowed, her throat working up and down, and Juliette wanted to bite again, right there on the alabaster expanse of skin, leaving a mark that even makeup wouldn't cover. When had she turned possessive?

Her mind supplied the answer as she watched Katarina finally look back at her.

"I don't." Katarina fisted her own hands in Juliette's hair and pressed their faces closer, whispering the words against skin. "I don't like it. I can't stand it. I can't stand anything that is not your mouth on mine. I can't stand all the women that are throwing themselves at you. I can't stand you being utterly oblivious of everything around you and how everyone wants you. And I can't stand you not seeing that I want you more than anyone."

Katarina licked from Juliette's neck to her ear and then sank her teeth into the lobe not too gently, sending shocks of sensation all the way to the very tips of her fingers. And into her already wet, wet panties.

Juliette bit her lip to hide her reaction but Katarina's thumb traced her mouth, freeing the tender flesh before biting it herself. Harder. Oh, the bruises... All the bruises...

"No, Juliette, I don't like your hands in my hair. Pulling, tugging. I don't like that it makes me imagine how you will do it when my mouth is all over your pussy. Eating you out. Is that an expression? I hope it is, because I want to eat you alive. I want to leave nothing for anyone else." Katarina sucked the now-bleeding lower lip into her mouth and flicked it with her tongue, the action so suggestive, Juliette shuddered. "No, I don't like it. I fucking love it, Juliette. I've fucking wanted you to do it forever. And I've just fucking wanted you forever."

This time, when Juliette pulled their faces close, they both moaned. They fit perfectly. Shoulders and breasts and pelvises. But above all else, their mouths. It felt like they had been kissing forever, the way Katarina would slide her tongue into Juliette's mouth, the way Juliette's would reach for it, suck on it. The way the lips nipped and the teeth bit. The exact amount of pressure, the precise amount of pleasure.

Juliette was so lost in the assault of sensation she barely realized that Katarina's hands were no longer in her hair, that the long fingers had dived under her skirt and nails were now dragging up her stockings, surely ripping them. Oh, but to have those fingers on her skin, on her thighs, inside her...

"You like it." Katarina's voice had the exact same inflection

Juliette's had when she'd uttered these words a few minutes ago. "You like it. Have you thought of me wanting you, Juliette?"

The wicked voice and the even more wicked fingers that trailed up her stocking-covered thighs, barely touching, were doing unspeakable things to Juliette's breathing. To her pulse. To her runaway thoughts.

Yes, she had thought of Katarina wanting her. Granted, she had never once allowed herself to believe it would ever come to pass. But she had thought of it, and here they were.

Juliette nodded and sensed Katarina's smile against the pulse fluttering in her neck. The smile was sharp enough she felt the teeth right before they plunged, and Juliette swore she'd come there and then.

"I need to hear you say it, Juliette. Now that you know I want you, I need you to say what it does to you. Say it!" Katarina bit again, and Juliette barely managed to clench her thighs together.

"Yes! Yes… I… It turns me on…" She panted more than spoke out loud, but Katarina smiled against her neck and then her deft tongue licked at the bruise that was surely forming.

"Good. So good. So delicious, Juliette. I wonder how delicious you are everywhere…"

The maddening fingers kept moving upward, skirting the very edge of the stockings now, tracing the frilly lace, teasing skin, giving just enough of a preview without giving away the show. Juliette thought she'd go mad. And that voice would be her undoing. The low, husky, merciless voice that kept talking.

"And I have wanted you, Juliette. Have wanted you every night…" Katarina's mouth was teasing her ear now, small puffs of air, gentle nips on the skin right beneath it. A turtleneck wouldn't save Juliette. Everyone would know. Juliette felt herself grow impossibly wetter at the thought. Everyone would know of Katarina branding her. Fucking her silly against the wall. Making her so weak, so powerless to resist, mad with want, desperate for the fingers that were tracing her naked inner thigh to slip inside and pound her pussy.

So wet. So fucking wet for her.

And Katarina kept winding the tightly coiled spring that was Juliette's core to impossible heights. Her mouth sucked another mark under Juliette's jaw, and she went on.

"I've wanted you, Juliette. And there have been nights when I couldn't stand it. Like tonight. I'd be so sick of all these women pawing at you, I'd be so jealous, so mad and so hot for you, I'd come to my bedroom and close the door…" She stopped speaking long enough to place a line of small kisses on Juliette's lower lip, mindful of the previous bites. Tender, gentle kisses. Juliette trembled.

Katarina's whisper was thoughtful.

"Hmm, I'm not certain you're paying attention, darling."

And then, before Juliette could so much as draw breath, the fingers that had been playing at the edge of her ruined panties speared her, the feeling of being penetrated exhilarating and overwhelming. The burn of the stretch immediately overtaken by the sheet exultation of the relief. So much relief that Juliette moaned, coming on the spot.

Katarina held her up, hand on neck and their hips fused, as she slipped in and out of Juliette's clenching pussy. The fingertips found the very root of her, unerringly, mercilessly, awfully, and Juliette was powerless, helpless, coming undone at the words, at the strokes, and Katarina just kept talking, kept placing tiny kisses along her jawline, her mouth, her brow, even as her hand pressed on her clit at every down stroke.

"I'd not even wait to lie down, Juliette. I'd drop my dress and tug my own nipples, imagining your mouth on them. How you'd bite and suck and torment me. How you'd make me beg. How you'd mark me and tease me. How you'd tear my underwear and get down on your knees in front of me. How you'd spread my cunt. You'd see how wet I'd be for you, how wet I am for you…"

Juliette actually screamed. The second orgasm slammed into her like a freight train, taking the last of her oxygen away, and the hand at her throat, despite not doing anything but hold there, made her vision gray at the corners.

The words... The imagery... Katarina, God, Katarina...
Who kept talking and stroking.

"And you'd lick me, Juliette, would you? In my fantasies you always licked me. You have such a beautiful mouth, it would look so pretty covered in my taste, covered in the desire for you. Don't you think so?"

Katarina withdrew her hand, fingers slipping gently out of Juliette, and the bereft feeling was almost too much, until Juliette opened her eyes and wished she hadn't. Or that she had the power to stop time. Katarina was licking her fingers. One by one, the teasing tongue was savoring. The feral, dazed eyes half-closed in ecstasy. Juliette bit her aching lip and clenched around nothing, pushing her hips into Katarina's, and then the wicked mouth smiled.

"I knew you'd taste amazing, Juliette. I can't wait to drink you up, spread you open, and devour you."

"Oh God..." Juliette felt more than heard her own gasp.

"No, he has nothing to do with any of this. Just you. Just me, Juliette. Just our fantasies about fucking each other. Have you had fantasies about me, Juliette?"

Katarina gave her own fingertips one last lick before lowering them again, except she didn't return them to where Juliette craved them most.

Clothes rustled, and then the hand was lifted to Juliette's face. Out of bare instinct, Juliette opened her mouth.

"Fuck..."

Katarina had dipped her fingers inside herself, and Juliette could taste their mingling flavors, tangy, sweet, unforgettable. She wrapped her tongue around the two fingers and sucked. It was Katarina's turn to moan.

"Such a good girl. Such a pretty, pretty mouth. Juliette…"

Juliette sucked harder, letting instinct take over again, and lifted her own hand, tugging and plucking at the tightly furled nipples separated from her touch by a sheer blouse and a bra. Almost nothing and yet too much. She threw caution to the wind and tore the silk, lifting the surprisingly demure cotton, and then pinched the erect buds. Katarina sagged in her arms.

"Yes, yes, just like that. That is how I imagined you, Juliette. That's what you'd do to me."

Juliette released the fingers in her mouth with one last nip.

"And then, what would I do then, Katarina?"

Katarina moaned and then laughed. A happy, honest sound. So joyful, so sincere. Juliette's heart stopped for a beat, then two, and when Katarina gave her a tiny peck on the tip of her nose, Juliette shuddered. No, there would be no recovery from this.

"Then you'd ravish me, Juliette. What else?" Katarina laughed again and then kissed her, a deep, sensuous connection of lips. Juliette tugged at her hand, and they stumbled into the direction of the bedroom.

"Well then. I have my instructions, madame. Let's see about putting my beautiful—was it?—mouth to good use. I can't let you down."

In the darkness of the apartment, Katarina's eyes were wide, her face unreadable as she murmured, "You can't, Juliette. You can't."

Juliette tried not to dwell on the fact that Katarina put all the emphasis on the word *you* and chose to kiss her instead. It was sweet, with an aftertaste Juliette couldn't identify.

Eighteen
Of Loss & Wasted Lives

Sometime between the second and third acts, they made it to Juliette's bedroom. The encore was even better between cool sheets.

Later, when the only sound was the rain beating a bluesy rhythm on the roof, they lay cocooned under the blankets, enveloped in each other. Katarina's head was on Juliette's shoulder. The sensation that no head had ever occupied this space before and seemed like it belonged was overwhelming.

Everything was saturated with this exact impression. No arm had ever wrapped itself around Juliette's waist and settled exactly this way. No breath had tickled Juliette's collarbone and felt absolutely perfect there even if it periodically sent shivers through her.

The sound and smell of rain, coming in like a welcome guest through the cracked window, had never been this magical. This perfectly timed.

Juliette wanted to shake her head at her own silliness and maybe a touch of whimsical, wishful thinking. But the world would intrude soon enough and shatter the wonderful pink glasses she had unwittingly donned. So why rush it?

On her shoulder, Katarina flinched, and her breathing changed, turning ragged. Juliette tightened her arms around the trembling figure. Just as with the night terrors she had interrupted earlier in their cohabitation together, she felt powerless and worried. In the twilight darkness, they lay in silence for a moment that transcended reality itself.

"The nightmares are the worst of it, really."

It was the voice of a very young Katarina, the one that occasionally disappeared into the closet, hiding from a bad dream, afraid to let the night in. Juliette had heard this tone several times now and recognized it, even as her heart broke every time it made its presence known.

"The fact that those don't seem to be nightmares but memories might actually be the worst of it, Katarina."

It wasn't her business. Juliette had told herself time and time again the same refrain. The life Katarina had led prior to their collision at that fateful party for the touring Bolshoi was none of Juliette's affair. And yet every single time, she felt compelled to act, to save, to intervene, to say things she had absolutely no place saying.

Katarina had mentioned only the smallest shreds of her past, the large canvas of it remaining a mystery. But even as sheltered as Juliette was, she had seen a slice of the world and had found this strong, independent, amazing woman in a ball of tears and terror in the closet enough times to understand that the canvas in question would be covered in atrocities.

"My mother was arrested when I was five. They tell you, in books and such, that children that young don't hold memories for very long. Yet, I am rather certain I'm not an outlier. In the orphanage, even in my short time there, I met toddlers who had recollections of their parents being arrested or murdered or tortured in front of them. And those memories never went away."

Juliette's arm tightened on the shoulder that seemed suddenly so fragile another ounce of pressure would surely break it. Snap it like a little bird's wing. She tried to relax her hold, but Katarina burrowed deeper into the space between her neck and collarbone, and Juliette held her close once again.

"She was tried and convicted of espionage. My father attended every hearing. He stood outside of every jail she was held at and waited for the truck that transported prisoners to pass by for a single glimpse of her."

Katarina's fingers reached for Juliette's and grasped firmly, as if she needed another anchor to get through this.

"She was a ballerina. Perhaps the biggest ballet talent Estonia has ever produced. She was allowed to travel outside of the Iron Curtain, and they say she was recruited by the US on one of the tour stops." Katarina's voice was growing more matter-of-fact with every word, emotion leaching out of it entirely.

"My father was an interpreter who worked for the government. Decoding things. Secret projects. Later, during his trial, they said she married him because she wanted to steal those secrets." Katarina made a sound, something Juliette could only describe as a scoff that somehow ended in a deep sigh.

"Every Saturday, she made him pancakes and he walked the dog and bought her flowers. There was always white cherry preserves, because it was his favorite, and she'd make it every summer, dozens of jars. And there were more often than not tulips, because after an entire life spent getting roses, she adored the simpler things. And they touched. All the time. You know, the way two people who cannot keep their hands to themselves do?"

Juliette nodded, trying to hold back the tears. She knew they'd spill; it was only a matter of time. Katarina's memories were already heartbreaking and she had not even gotten to the worst parts of them, Juliette was certain.

"I was a child, but it was such a wonderful feeling. Being in their presence. In the presence of love. It was everywhere. In little notes, in the hugs and kisses, in the late mornings in bed, where I'd find them wrapped in each other. And they taught me

English, since very early on. They made it a game, a celebration, and it was so much fun. It was something we did together, the three of us, and then just my father and me. He was adamant I learn. He was adamant I work on my accent, on my pronunciation, on my idioms. I think he knew one day I'd need it." Something wet fell on Juliette's skin, and despite Katarina's voice still sounding very much like a historian's might dispassionately recounting the facts, her tears spoke of a different story entirely.

"She killed herself in her cell. That's what they told my father. That it had been violent and therefore the body was in the most awful condition. He was persuaded to sign papers stating that he demanded no autopsy, no investigation. Said persuasion resulted in him coming home with broken ribs and blackened eyes. But he never relented. He kept going to all sorts of government institutions, to his and Mom's former friends. I say 'former,' because after a year of this kind of insistence, he became a pariah. All he wanted was to know what had happened to her." The tears kept dripping on Juliette's collarbone, each feeling like a paper cut, each deepening the wound.

"After three years of ringing every bell, accusing the prison officials of torture, he was institutionalized. They call it psikhushka. It's a place people go in and from which they never return. Long hallways with little white rooms, no windows, lights on at all times. Drugged-out-of-their-mind patients, living years on end with no trial, no sentencing, nothing that would allow them to ever leave. After Stalin died, the Soviet Union 'modernized.' Gulag was terminated. But the people who were still 'bothering' the powers that be—political prisoners—needed to be disposed of. Madhouses were a solution."

Juliette chewed on the inside of her cheek to stop the sob from escaping. The horror of the revelations, which only kept coming, was devastating. And Katarina didn't seem close to done.

"I was allowed to see him twice. The first time, I was nine.

I remember that corridor, the light of dozens of fluorescent lamps buzzing, some blinking. And the screams… The screams of hundreds of people going mad. I remember looking into each of the rooms and it was clear to me, even at nine, that the people who were insane to begin with were not the ones howling. The cries were of desperation, of impotence, of losing what vestiges of one's mind these people still possessed. Those who were ill had no reason to scream. The sane ones—every single one of those reasons. And the moment you stopped screaming? That's when you began to belong in the psikhushka."

Katarina sniffed, but Juliette was sure she hadn't noticed because her tone didn't change. She just kept speaking.

"I will hear my father till the day I die. His fear. His horror. His pain. They still institutionalize people against their will in the Soviet Union. All someone has to insinuate is that you're dangerous. And as you know, the danger is often in the eye of the beholder. Or an enemy."

Juliette bit her lip so hard, she felt her teeth cut the skin. The taste of blood in her mouth grounded her, allowing her to lie still and not get up to throw something, break things, scream herself raw at the dreadful size of the evils being described. So much about Katarina's life was becoming clear. When exposed to the sun, some of the demons she carried in her heart showed their faces, their reasons for existing.

"What happened to you?"

At the sound of Juliette's voice, Katarina sat up, her eyes swimming in tears, drowning in grief and remembrance. She looked down at Juliette as if she had forgotten she had not been talking to herself, that she had an audience.

A smile. A sad, lonely smile tugged at the corners of that mouth, slightly swollen from all the kisses. Katarina lifted a hand and touched Juliette's cheek.

She was telling her the most frightful things she had lived through, and still she was the one drying Juliette's tears.

Well, fuck, isn't it just like her? To take the full brunt of the pain? Of the sorrow?

Juliette caught the trembling fingers and brought them to her lips, kissing each one, pouring all the reverence she had for this woman, for the weight of the entire world on her shoulders.

"Nothing much happened to me." Katarina's smile was gone, and she looked down on Juliette with a forced nonchalance that did not suit the moment.

"Tell me, please." At Juliette's plea, the teary eyes closed. When they opened again, they were clearer, but that only made the sadness in them appear deeper, all-consuming.

"First, an orphanage. And honestly, that should be a conversation for another time. If it even should be a conversation at all. I don't think you want to hear about children being beaten with a leather belt, the sadistic alcoholic teacher trying very hard for the buckle to hit you every single time, to tear your skin and leave marks…"

"You never see Thierry." At the realization of why the prima, who was enduring a grueling season, had still not gone for physical therapy, Juliette finally let the sob out. And this time when the tears came, the flood of them could no longer be stopped, not even by Katarina's fingertips wiping them away.

"I was a ballet prodigy. Those genes, you see." Katarina gave Juliette a gentle kiss on the forehead before continuing. "My father, even in the agony of trying to prove that my mother had been tortured to death, took care of me and ensured that I had the best dancing opportunities. He took me to Leningrad and Moscow, showed me off to the most prominent ballet masters in both cities. So I was not an unknown. Somehow the news that I had ended up in an orphanage reached one of the people he had me dance in front of. Stepan Nikolayevich Marinov."

Something in the way Katarina said the name made Juliette smile even through tears. No, she did not know the man, but the voice warmed up so much, going from forced indifference to unrestrained affection, that Juliette's heart responded with a gentle thud. Someone had loved little Katarina. Surely this someone had been good to her.

"He risked his own career when he pulled all the strings to have me transferred to Moscow. I was the daughter of the Enemy of the State. Capital letters and all. My mother, even in death, was dangerous. And so was I, by association. A permanent brand on my skin. These associations could kill careers, stop promotions, cause a lot of issues in personal and professional lives. But Stepan Nikolayevich persevered. And he was my ballet master for almost ten years."

Katarina's smile was gentle when she paused and sad when she finally continued.

"He passed away when I was twenty—"

"After you danced your Giselle." Juliette could not hide the awe in her voice. It was the one grainy, copied-a-thousand-times video Gabriel and she had watched over and over again in London. Their own ballet mistress had shown them the wonders of the flawless performance, instilling in them the understanding of what ballet perfection looked like. "You were everything in that pas de deux." Juliette knew she sounded breathless. Ridiculous, even. She didn't care.

"Ah, so Stepan Nikolayevich wasn't the only one to have seen me in *Giselle*. Did they really smuggle the recording? I heard stories but wasn't certain. What did you think?" Katarina's face was amused, her voice playful. She was breathtaking.

Juliette rose up on her elbows, and when their lips were a breath apart, whispered, "I thought you were the most beautiful woman I had ever seen. And the most brilliant ballerina in the world."

Katarina laughed and then brought their mouths together, the kiss lingering, tender and sweet, full of promise and easy affection.

When they parted, Katarina traced Juliette's lower lip with

her fingertip before leaning in for a quick peck, seemingly unable to help herself. Good, Juliette was becoming more and more conscious that she would never be able to help herself where this woman was concerned.

"As for my mentor, yes, Juliette, he did see me in *Giselle*, and he was proud. And among everything that had been going on around me, it was the one event that was special and pure and worth dancing for."

Juliette expected her to say more, but Katarina remained silent, simply watching her, occasionally tracing her cheekbones or lips, apparently lost in her thoughts. Then she dropped her hand and lay back on the spot Juliette knew she'd never ever think of as anything but "Katarina's place"—Juliette's left shoulder.

The silence was not uncomfortable, and Juliette half hoped that Katarina would fall asleep, the last hour of reliving memories clearly taking a toll on her, but Katarina's fingers were tracing her clavicle and there was no sign that she might doze off.

"I bet you have a million questions." There was a smile hidden in that whispered observation, and Juliette felt her own bloom. But the things she wanted to ask were dark and full of fear, and Juliette held on tighter, refusing to allow the shroud of those nightmares back over Katarina's features.

When Katarina spoke, however, Juliette knew it had already blanketed her lover's heart once again, if it had ever lifted.

"I was never allowed to leave the country because my KGB dossier says 'daughter of the Enemy of the State.' You know, children, small babies who were sent to gulag back in the forties had those actual words on their files and were tortured into confessing that they were in fact conspiring against the country. Ten-year-olds, fourteen-year-olds. What could they have been conspiring against? Boiled vegetables for dinner? It's so absurd, so utterly incomprehensible, and yet so normalized, driven into regular people's skin like the smudged green of prison tattoos.

And life goes on, millions of souls snuffed. Millions of fates altered."

This time it was Katarina who held Juliette tighter, closer.

"You said you saw your father twice?" Juliette knew she probably should not ask this question. It was bound to bring new pain, but something was there, an essential piece of the puzzle to this entire horrific picture. And it felt imperative that she hear this answer.

"Six months before Bolshoi departed on this tour. I was not scheduled to be part of it. I never was part of any of them. As I said, the borders are closed for someone like me. But I bribed my way back to the institution that still held him."

She was silent for so long, Juliette felt that perhaps she had changed her mind and would not answer the question. Juliette would not fault her. How much pain could one person withstand?

"He stopped screaming, Juliette. He stopped screaming, speaking, he just stopped. My father, the one who taught me three languages, who read three hundred books a year, who brought my mother yellow tulips, was gone. A man with shorn hair and empty eyes, who I am told has no voice because he tore his vocal cords years ago, lies there in his place. He didn't recognize me. He knew not who he was, nor who my mother was when I showed him a picture. My father was gone, and the man I was allowed to see was dead inside. And I knew then that I needed to do everything I could to get out. For years, I entertained the silly dream that I could dance my father out of the institution. After seeing my dream get ground into a forced medicated haze, all I had left was to dance my way out of that godforsaken company. Or I knew I'd be next. And while my father screamed for years, I knew for a fact I'd never last that long. So I made a deal of my own, Juliette. With the man you know as Ivanov. A deal I'd rather never think about again. He pulled his KGB strings. And I…"

Katarina trailed off, her words dying in the warm air of the room, among their mingled scents. And they were just words, after all. Yes, ones hiding an unspeakable tragedy, but Juliette chose to close her eyes and honor Katarina's wish. There was no point in asking about the deal. Katarina was here now. She had done what was necessary and she was safe.

The tears did not come anymore, the abysmal powerlessness, the acidic grief taking their place, and Juliette again allowed the taste of blood to wash away the monstrosity of the memories that lived within this woman, who was light herself, who was art herself, and yet who seemed to have stigmata all over her soul.

Outside, dawn was breaking, its majesty—all royal purples and stately reds—breathing hope for the new day onto the horizon. Katarina's breathing evened, slumber finally claiming her, and Juliette lay quietly, her heart matching the beats of the one sleeping in her arms.

How had this soul survived to remain this gentle? How did it still thrive after all the horrors unleashed on it? And what had Juliette ever done to be the one afforded the privilege of holding it and letting it rest for a bit? She didn't know what the future held, but for now she herself held this future, skin on skin, and it looked amazing from where she was lying, bathed in those royal purples and stately reds of the Parisian sunrise.

Nineteen
Of Dances With The Devil & Paying the Price

They say that if you dance with the devil, be ready to get burned. Juliette knew the saying did not actually end like that. But in her mind, this was the only way it fit her situation. So, she went with it.

She also knew four months ago when she made the deal with Lalande that at some point the check would come and she would have to settle it.

Still, back then, it was all so nebulous. And he was just an insignificant little man, one of so many whom she saw periodically and forgot just as quickly. She barely remembered his name. She would not be able to pick him out of a lineup. What could he, in all honesty, do to her? How steep could his price really be?

Well, nobody tells you that you have indeed sold your soul to the aforementioned devil until he comes to collect. The collection for Juliette started the moment she and Katarina walked into Palais Garnier, hand in hand, three weeks after the *Swan Lake* opening night, and saw Madame Rochefort, of all people, hauling boxes full of knickknacks that looked disturbingly like Francesca's out the back door.

Before Juliette even opened her mouth, Madame Rochefort was shaking her fist in the direction of the third floor and mumbling curses.

Inquiries seemed impossible, and once the shoe mistress finished calling someone the son of the biggest prostitute in Paris—why do most swear words revolve around the probably innocent mothers?—she finally came closer to them.

"How can he do this when Francesca is not here? That bureaucrat fils de pute! She has not even woken up yet. Mais ce n'est pas possible."

And then, without another word, she turned on her heel and was gone, something rattling in the boxes she was dragging.

Katarina's face held that look again, the vacant one, the one that could turn into fight or flight at any moment. Juliette tugged on her hand, bringing it to her lips, and Katarina blinked as if startled out of her thoughts.

"How about we go check what's happening upstairs?"

Katarina's mouth twist could not even begin to be described as a smile. "I think, judging by the boxes filled with awards and trophies which Francesca treasured and would not allow to be discarded this way, that Lalande dismissed her."

Juliette bit her lip and tried to cajole her lover to follow her.

"Yes, but how about we not jump to conclu—"

"If the Empress's guess is that Francesca has been fired, she is dead on the money, darlin'. Give her the teddy bear, she hit the bullseye."

They both looked up, Katarina bending her entire body upward rather than just her neck. They had talked about so much during their three weeks together, but this one issue Juliette had no idea how to tackle. She had a feeling it was such a slippery slope that she'd need skis to descend it afterward.

She almost swatted at her persistent intrusive thoughts. Gabriel was hanging off the third floor's stairwell rail looking down at the two of them.

"I'd appreciate you coming up here. When you're done admiring my Adonis-like countenance, of course. Pretty please?"

He waved at them, his gestures jerky and so unlike his normal graceful self, Juliette hurried, taking two steps at a time.

The sight of a completely dilapidated office, one where she had spent so many hours, one where she had been chastised, praised, where she had made her stand to save Katarina—

"Ah, the culprit returning to the scene of the crime, Mademoiselle Lucian-Sorel?"

Lalande's voice was sly, the pleasure in it, the gloating, unrestrained. Next to her, Gabriel and Katarina looked uncomprehendingly between the two of them.

"I imagine you have already been informed, since you cannot set foot in this establishment without hearing entirely too much gossip, that Madame Bianchi has been relieved of her duties, effective immediately. The new Creative Director of Paris Opera Ballet is en route. I shall assemble everyone before morning class to introduce—"

"Shouldn't Francesca be present for a lawful dismissal?"

Juliette had no idea whether that was correct. But in order to process all the events occurring around her at the same moment, she needed to stall for time. Lalande was a talker who loved attention. A true stereotypical villain, pontificating before the demise, either his or his prey's.

"You are raising a wonderful point, and to answer your question, no, she does not have to be present. Technically, she could have come in this morning and found out that way, but I chose to proceed in a more expedient manner because we simply do not have time. The dysfunction of this company has reached epic proportions—"

"*Swan Lake* was named the production of the decade by *Le Monde*!" Gabriel took one step forward and Lalande instinctively mirrored him by taking one back.

"*Swan Lake*, in its current iteration…" Lalande made a pause after the word and wiggled his bushy eyebrows suggestively. "Is a niche show with a limited run time. The company may have 'a revolutionary ballet,' but it is scandalous and shall not be staged for long."

Juliette felt a tearing in her chest. Had Francesca known? Had she simply ignored the homophobia that had once again reared its ugly head and stopped art from reigning free? Had she chosen to ignore it?

Lalande coughed theatrically to hide his smug grin. "In any case, it will not fix years of negative reviews, mismanagement, and more importantly, budget issues that amount to millions of francs. It's a beautiful swan song. Pun intended." He grinned, and Juliette felt a chill run up her spine. "Who will answer for the massacre of *Don Quixote*? For staging and then scrapping a world classic? For butchering it to the point that it was unwatchable?"

The gallic gestures were in full swing, Lalande posturing and flinging himself from one corner of the room to the other.

"The new sets alone were thousands of francs! Who will answer for that? You think one successful ballet will suddenly drag this entire building out of the swamp and rot it had been dwelling in for years?"

"Paris Opera Ballet has been named the world's premier ballet company three times in the years you are drowning it in the swamp, Monsieur le Ministre."

Almost as soon as the words left her lips, Juliette regretted them. He had given her more than a fair warning. In fact, he had fired the shot across her bow the moment she had stepped foot into the office. They had a deal—this was the place it had been struck. He had held up his end of it, as shown by Katarina's cold hand gripping hers firmly. She was here. In Paris. Dancing at Palais Garnier.

And he could undo said deal with a snap of his fingers, because despite all the talk and all the column inches in the press, Katarina still hadn't received her new passport, or any other document for that matter. Every time Juliette asked, she'd get an anxious headshake as an answer and something about bureaucracy being a nightmare. Hell, Juliette remembered that it took her ages to get her working visa. And Katarina's asylum was a thorny political quagmire no matter who pulled which strings. And so Juliette had to honor her end of it now. She had, after all, promised to ask no questions.

His eyes, full of anger and, dare she say, hatred, scorched her, and she lowered her face, earning her a confused look from Katarina.

She was, however, saved from retracting her little rebellious comment by the arrival of the very person whose ransacked office was the main stage for this absurd melodrama.

"I'd repeat Juliette's astute remark, Monsieur le Ministre, but you heard it already. Did you not answer it because you have nothing to counter it with?"

Francesca stepped into the space, suddenly taking all of it, the room feeling crowded rather than the emptiness it exuded just a moment ago.

"I have sent a courier to your house with the paperwork. You are in breach of your contract, Madame Bianchi, and hence no longer need to be here. Someone will make certain your things are delivered to you."

Francesca took a few more steps into the dilapidated room then turned in a circle, as if taking it all in, her cane thumping loudly on the wooden floor.

"To say that I was not expecting a knife in the back, Monsieur Lalande, would be a lie. I expected you to do this. I even prepared for you to do this—"

"Now, Madame Bianchi, there's no need for scenes—"

"You are in the largest, best ballet company in the world, and you are telling me there is no need for scenes? Drama is in the blood here."

Francesca's laughter was loud and sincere. Juliette wanted to smile, but she couldn't bring herself to do so. In her hand,

Katarina's fingers tightened as if warning her about what would happen next. Well, it was unwarranted. Juliette knew that when all the theatrics and posturing was over, she'd be the one thrust center stage, and then she'd lose a friend. Francesca would be betrayed, publicly so, and would want nothing to do with her. How would Gabriel and Katarina react? Juliette squeezed the icy hand back and prayed.

"Madame Bianchi, if you think you can threaten me into changing my mind—"

"I am not threatening you. Merely underscoring that you only believe you have most of the power here. And you probably have some." She gave him a long look before taking another step closer. His lower lip trembled for a second, and he quickly sucked it in before looking directly at Juliette with something akin to a plea for help.

Francesca turned too, and her gaze was very different. Gone was the arrogance, the teasing. Francesca looked at her with so much pride that Juliette struggled to breathe around the lump in her throat. Was this how Judas had felt?

"The power I hold is the love of my people. You see, one leads a company by building loyalty. Affection. Respect. Why do you think Gabriel and Juliette are here? Vyatka too, though at the beginning there, I thought she'd either claw my eyes out or drop a piece of stage equipment on me."

Katarina's fingers fluttered in Juliette's hands before a razor-sharp smile blossomed on the full lips.

"Could've gone either way, Francesca."

Juliette blinked at the appellation. Katarina, who had rarely called anyone in the company by their first name, was using Francesca's. She was standing by her as much as she could despite still being an outcast, despite having almost no rights, an undetermined political status, and everything to lose. Katarina was taking a stand.

Juliette's heart fluttered in her chest, its chambers filling with blood and admiration. And love. She had felt the stirrings of it during their pas de deux just a few weeks ago, and yet it felt like lifetimes before. And now this feeling was coursing through her veins, flourishing and overtaking her.

Juliette was in love. And she was about to break every heart in this room, including her own. Because apparently her love came with those sonnets and those poems and those songs, but also with the sacrifices and the stakes and the infamy.

Wasn't it life's greatest joke to slide irrevocably in love in a moment like this? It was too big, too earth-shattering to discover in a place when their stage roles were flipping and Katarina was the hero, while in a matter of seconds Juliette would have to announce to the world that she was the villain.

Katarina and Francesca exchanged a few more friendly barbs before Lalande interrupted them, clearly having gathered his courage to finally end this spectacle.

"Madame Bianchi, if it is compensation you are seeking, I assure you, the legalities of a contract termination will be fully respected and your rights under the Collective Labor Convention properly taken care of—"

"Oh, my union. You have dotted every i and crossed every t, haven't you, Monsieur le Ministre?"

Lalande bristled, puffing up with what he surely saw as righteous anger. Between his and Francesca's justified wrath, the room was filled with so much rage it was getting harder to breathe.

"Screw you and your procedures and your lawyers and their bargaining agreements. She doesn't need any of that, Lalande." Gabriel lifted his fists. "She has more respect in this building than you ever will. If you fire her, we will all walk. Everyone in this room, everyone in the studios below!"

Gabriel did not say her name. Did not even look at her. His chest rose and fell, heaving, his voice raspy and breathless by the end of his tirade. When he let his fists drop, the room released a collective sigh of relief that he wouldn't beat Lalande to a pulp just yet. It would not be a fair match.

In the middle of the office, Francesca stood silent. When Juliette lifted her eyes for a second, she was met with a thoughtful stare, and what color was left in her cheeks drained. She could feel it leaking all over the floor, seeping through the parquet boards. She was a coward.

Another squeeze of her fingers, and this time Katarina accompanied it by a gentle touch to her elbow, and still Juliette said nothing, hiding her eyes, focusing on drawing air in and out of her lungs.

Juliette didn't need to be told in so many words what Katarina wanted her to do. She had taken a very public stand. So had Gabriel. It was Juliette's turn. To do something, to say something. Hell, Gabriel had all but bellowed her name.

But how could Juliette speak when it was becoming abundantly clear that she had made a deal which doomed Francesca to save Katarina? How does one vocalize that she was about to plunge the second knife into Francesca's back? Francesca, who had been nothing but kind and supportive and protective of her?

"Juliette?" Gabriel, still gasping, turned to her, his handsome, darling face, the face of her brother, of her only family for the last seven years, looking so earnestly at her. There was so much hope in those features. In those pained eyes.

Juliette straightened her shoulders. It was time to come clean.

"Gabriel, I…"

What was there really to say?

"Oh, Monsieur Flanagan, you fool. A gentleman, but a fool nonetheless. And oh, Mademoiselle Lucian-Sorel, how eloquent you are when you are throwing your erstwhile mentor to the wolves!" Lalande laughed and slowly clapped. One, two, three…

The buzzing in Juliette's ears intensified. She turned to Katarina, whose eyes were immense, full of that sorrow Juliette sometimes saw cross the cold blue and burn it into ash. Someone was speaking, but Juliette couldn't hear it from the noise of her own conscience drowning out everything else around her.

She really could sympathize with Judas, poor bastard.

"Juliette..." This time, when Gabriel spoke, his voice held a note Juliette had never heard when he uttered her name. Contempt. Well, what did she expect?

The massive antique doors swung with a resounding *bang*, slapping into the walls that held them, and then stayed open. In the halo of sunlight coming through the doorway stood a man, and Katarina's hand went limp in Juliette's.

"Welcome to Paris Opera Ballet!" Lalande all but ran to the newcomer. "How do you like your new office? I trust you will feel comfortable here."

The man, tall and slim, stepped forward, the sun no longer bathing him in its glow. Juliette knew this face instantly. Next to her, Gabriel's mouth dropped open. Francesca came closer to the door and laughed.

"I see I have been rather speedily replaced."

"I hope you will wish me well, Cesca, dorogaya?"

The Russian term of endearment grated like nails on a chalkboard. The newcomer bowed over Francesca's hand before she tugged it out of his long, slim, spidery-looking fingers.

"Never make assumptions where I am concerned." She gave him the fakest of smiles. "I would wish you to hell if that also didn't mean that I would wish my dancers there with you, and I'd never do that."

The man laughed, the sound just as abrasive as his words, and moved farther into the room, the draft of Garnier following him, filling the air up with dust and dread. Next to Juliette, Katarina flinched before becoming absolutely still.

Lalande chose that moment to jump in front of the man and give him an awkward handshake, a hearty pump answered with a barely there, limp-fish palm.

"How gauche of me! How gauche of me. We are in the presence of genius and I have not introduced you. Please forgive me, I have assumed everyone in this room knows who you are. Surely they must."

He executed a sorry excuse for a half pirouette before turning to the wide-open doors where quite a crowd had gathered.

"My dears, allow me to introduce your new Director of Paris Opera Ballet, Rodion Foltin."

In her peripheral vision, Juliette caught Katarina biting her lip, her eyes still vacant. In the pouring sunlight, in the crowded room, among the deafening noise of gasps and shouts, Juliette watched a tiny droplet of blood from the bite trickle to the corner of the now oh-so-familiar mouth and tremble there for a moment before disappearing as Katarina licked her dry lips.

As omens went, this one was rather self-explanatory, even to the only non-superstitious ballerina in the room. And as reactions? Juliette wanted to put her fist through the wall and howl from the sheer impotence. She had done everything to keep Katarina safe, including backstabbing her own most precious friend. And judging by Katarina's reaction to Foltin, it was all for naught. She didn't look safe. She looked in agony. Juliette had lost her dearest people, and it was all in vain. She closed her eyes and allowed the world to fall apart around her.

Twenty
Of Creative Reasons & Ice Cubes

It fell apart rapidly. Just as Foltin established himself in five minutes flat in Francesca's office—and Juliette's brain refused to call it anything else—her world kept subsequently crumbling in tiny little pieces.

First, Gabriel stopped speaking to her. He did not curse her out, unlike Madame Rochefort. But he looked at her with those bright eyes of his and the disappointment in them was so stark, so completely foreign to his angelic countenance, it hurt her to even stand in front of him.

And so, Juliette didn't. It was relatively easy, as it turned out. The one show they were both involved in, *Swan Lake*—the revolutionary production that was feted on the streets of Paris as the revival of rebellion in ballet and the push into modernism the stale old Palais Garnier needed—was paused after Francesca's ouster. Paused indefinitely.

"Creative reasons," Foltin explained to the company two days after turning Francesca's Louis XVIII desk into kindling. Granted, the man had been a rubbish king, when all was said and done, but the principle of things remained. When Juliette asked him about the public property and historical value of the antique item he had so cavalierly disposed of, Foltin smiled.

"Out with the old, my dear. Out with the old." He even winked at her, and Juliette felt the need to take a shower.

The company was assembled for the morning class, bodies lying in formless heaps here and there, others stretching at the barre, Gabriel and Katarina whispering in the corner, and Juliette studiously rolling up her leg warmers into neat little balls of wool. Surely her poor, thready garments had never been given such care, as she usually just threw them in the general direction of her bag. Whether they made it there or not was never a concern, she'd just pick them up much later.

"He is very loyal, and I hate that this dumb quality of his makes me like him more." Despite the neutral face, there was a smile in Katarina's voice as she caught up to Juliette after class.

"How is it dumb?" Juliette asked, barely lifting her head up. "It's admirable."

"Absolutes are not admirable, love, they are silly. He understands why you did what you did, and he still is mad. It's dumb. But then, he's a man." Juliette had to smile at that, and Katarina squeezed her fingers briefly. "He will come around. He's an idealist. And he loves you. He will come to understand that people sacrifice. Even other people. Our choices are just that, choices, and yet oftentimes the act of choosing is just a mirage."

Juliette sincerely hoped Katarina was right and Gabriel would see that in her case, there had been no choice.

Still, days went on, and the burden of being the pariah du jour was getting heavier. She wanted to ignore the world, especially since the world adamantly refused to ignore her. She wanted it to give her space and time, and all these people kept crowding her with their hate and their sneering and their judgment.

The papers, the whispers in the hallways, the finger-pointing. Her colleagues wouldn't talk to her, they wouldn't sit with her at lunch, not that she was in a particularly social mood. But her betrayal of Francesca made the rounds of the Palais

Garnier in a New York minute, which was probably just as fast as a Paris one.

Through it all, Katarina was her rock. Quietly efficient, endlessly thoughtful, she'd go about her business as usual. She had been an outcast since her arrival in Paris, and that had not changed with Foltin in charge.

She had, however, been forced to spend more time on the third floor, wasting entire afternoons in his office. It was something she clearly found difficult, if her face after every one of these sessions was a clue.

Juliette tried not to pry, not to ask too much. She had no right. It was none of her business. And yet, every time Katarina emerged from a meeting, she looked drained and weary. Withdrawn.

"He wants to know the lay of the land," was all Katarina replied once to Juliette's unspoken question, and they had never touched the subject again.

Juliette had no idea why she feared bringing it into the airy, bright lights that always seemed to surround them. Was she afraid of what Katarina would tell her? Surely she had heard the worst of the horrors. Surely?

She trusted this woman with her life, with her body. There wasn't anything she could do or say anymore that Juliette couldn't handle. And yet when she looked at the sunken cheeks, at the tired eyes, Juliette shrank a little, her heartstrings singing to the invisible chords of premonition. Hadn't they been through enough? Wasn't it time for the world to stop? Just for a moment?

But since astronomy, geophysics, and planetary science were not contributing to make Juliette's wishes come true, she ground her teeth and bore it all.

At home, Katarina treated Juliette as if she was wounded. The contrast to being shunned at work was rather stark. After two weeks of being babied and cared for, Juliette raised her face from the book she was pretending to be reading and finally gave voice to her fears.

"Are you feeling guilty? Is that why?"

Katarina put down the ice pack she had been applying alternatively to her own troublesome calf and Juliette's knee and looked up for a long moment before speaking.

"I feel responsible."

At Juliette's feet, Katarina took her left hand in hers, slowly caressing each finger as she looked out through the wide-open window into the darkening Paris sky. Another storm was coming.

"I should have guessed whatever deal you made with Lalande would backfire on you. And I should have known you'd make the deal anyway. For a stranger, no less."

"Who says chivalry is dead?" Juliette laughed, but even to her own ears it sounded false.

"Nobody says it. Maybe in a few decades, love."

Juliette let the word wash over her. They had not yet exchanged anything but the most basic of nicknames. But Katarina had taken to calling her *love*. To Juliette's tired mind, wretched by worry, the thought of love had been off-limits. It had been swelling in her chest for months. Perhaps from the first glance, when blood marred Katarina's fingers and shoes. Satin and crimson, and enraged eyes. How could Juliette ever dream of resisting? It seemed inevitable, really. Fated, perhaps.

But she hadn't said it out loud. Katarina had been so skittish, and they had been so new. Scaring her, losing her to haste and her own neediness wasn't something Juliette was ready to entertain. She'd wait. Just a little longer. And so when she spoke, she chose the most nonchalant of tones.

"I'd say it was chivalry, sweetheart, but I didn't think through the implications. And he double-crossed me. Please, don't ascribe much selflessness or thoughtfulness to me. Just foolishness."

Katarina waited for Juliette to look at her. For a moment they indulged in the softness of the connection, blue on amber.

"I don't doubt that he manipulated you. But I believe you knew what he was doing. Not realizing that my freedom would cost you a friend, the support of the company, and God knows what other repercussions isn't a strike against you, Juliette."

Juliette frowned.

"How does that not make me a fool?"

"It shows that you knew you'd have to sacrifice something and agreed without anticipating what it could or would be. Which seems like a more significant sacrifice, to be honest. Because I fully believe that if he had asked you on the spot to surrender what you ended up surrendering, you'd have done it. So you agreeing in the total dark of actual consequences means everything to me."

Juliette squeezed the hand caressing her palm.

"You give me a lot of credit. And you think me so much better than I am."

Katarina's smile was distant, as if her thoughts were no longer in this room.

"You *are* so much better than anyone I know. Better, kinder. And tender. You are so tender, despite the crowns, the fame, the trappings of it all. I'm afraid life will bruise you. It already has, and I am the one it used to dull your edges, love."

There was that word again. Juliette tried not to dwell on it.

"As long as it doesn't use you to shred me." She smiled as she spoke, however Katarina did not return her tentative mirth, just held her hand tightly and looked on, as if cataloging her features. As if committing this very minute and these very words to memory. Juliette leaned down and gave the full lips a lingering kiss.

"I'm just joking. I'm not shredded, sweetheart. I'm whole. And the company will come around. I am meeting with Francesca tomorrow. That gossip will make rounds quickly. And despite everyone bashing me and calling me a traitor, Francesca herself has said nothing."

Katarina rolled her eyes.

"That did not escape me. Weeks and she kept her counsel, enjoying your exile, while she is being feted around town as a martyr. I don't care for people who revel in victimhood."

Juliette's laughter this time was sincere. The aggrieved look on Katarina's face was extremely endearing.

"You just don't like her."

That got Juliette another eye roll.

"I don't. I never did. And before you jump to conclusions that it was because she was very cavalier with you and your career, yes, you would be correct. She wasted some of your best years, and I don't think she used you properly or to your advantage. However, you'd also be only partially correct. Mostly it's because she slept with you. There, how's that for honesty?"

This time they both laughed, and Juliette picked up the book she had been trying to finish for what felt like weeks now. Granted, she had been somewhat preoccupied lately. Still, she had been waiting for this particular one to be published, so why had it not held her attention?

Juliette balanced the novel in her hand, desperately trying not to watch Katarina. She needed to focus, to advance at least a paragraph, when the sudden feeling of an ice cube on her bare skin jolted her out of her already rattled composure. Juliette took a deep breath and, deciding to ignore the sensation for now, turned the page, staring at it blindly, valiantly not lifting her eyes in an effort to win this sensual game.

Katarina clearly had other thoughts. Gentle fingers drew the quickly thawing ice cube around Juliette's ankle, very carefully paying attention to every inch of skin before slowly moving up, the cold making her shiver and sigh.

"Is there something wrong with those pages, Juliette?"

Oh God... Oh dear God...

What book could ever hold a candle to this low, bourbon-over-gravel voice? Juliette felt herself getting wet instantly—and not just on her inner thigh toward which the almost completely melted ice cube was moving.

"Ah… Yes… No?" She blinked at Katarina over the top of the page and saw devils dance in those devious eyes.

The voice was amazing. Panty-ruining, even, if she borrowed the purple prose from the taboo romance novels she occasionally got her hands on. But the eyes? Juliette drowned in them every time. Their focus was completely mind-blowing. Be it a tendu, an arabesque, or fucking Juliette into the mattress, Katarina gave every task at hand her total attention.

Just like in that very moment, when Katarina was giving Juliette not just all of that aforementioned attention but so much more. She lifted Juliette's left leg, and even as her fingers caressed the thigh with the almost-gone ice cube, the hot mouth began to draw a trail of its own. Slowly, oh so very slowly, Katarina's tongue licked, her lips kissed, and occasionally her teeth bit Juliette's skin, traveling unerringly upward.

When mouth caught up to fingers, the ice cube was completely melted, and Juliette felt that she would spontaneously combust. Katarina kept placing little kisses along Juliette's inner thigh, and she found it hard to breathe.

"Oh, love, you sound in pain. Is there anything I can do?" The smug, fakely solicitous intonation made Juliette growl, and Katarina laughed. "Definitely in pain, then. I think we shall need more ice. A wound of this magnitude needs all the cold it can get."

And then, before Juliette knew what was happening, Katarina was dipping her fingers into the open ice bag and plucking another cube, this time placing it between her lips. Juliette's jaw dropped. It would have been comical to see, and she was certain in any other situation Katarina would've teased her. Instead, she just lifted that insouciant eyebrow and lowered her head.

When fire and ice connected with Juliette's skin

simultaneously, she thought she'd die. Perish on the spot. This should not be pleasurable. Cold and wet and everything she needed. Everything she wanted. One more second and she'd beg. Katarina dragged the ice cube upward still, tracing the line of hip meeting thigh, and Juliette trembled so hard she was afraid she'd come apart at the seams.

She had known sex. She had given and gotten pleasure. And yet, nothing in her life had ever come close to this. To how she responded to Katarina. To how Katarina read her like an open book and how she went on to satisfy every single desire among those pages. Every single fantasy. Talk about romance novels.

Her bathrobe was tugged apart and the mouth still holding a much smaller piece of ice traced her breasts. Juliette whimpered and bit her lip before realizing she had no reason to hold back. Katarina deserved to hear what she was doing to her.

Juliette moaned loudly, and when Katarina drew a nipple in, cold adding another dimension to the sensation, she grabbed the sun-kissed hair and held on, riding the wave almost to the very crest. What had she thought earlier? That she'd come apart at the seams? She'd be lucky if there were even any seams left when Katarina was done.

Katarina, who was clearly not done, gave the now tightly furled nipple a last little bite before she suddenly let go and the still-cold mouth moved downward. Swiftly, no more slow licks or gentle kisses. It was as if Katarina herself was too hungry to tarry anymore. In a matter of seconds, long fingers were opening Juliette, running through her soaked folds, splitting her open and slipping inside with ease. Katarina thrust once, twice, and then she was tasting her, licking her, drinking her in, again and again.

Juliette screamed. The feeling of insistent fingers, fucking her with ruthless precision, hitting the very root of her existence with every thrust, combined with the deft tongue wrapping itself around her clit, was almost too much.

The remnants of the ice and the hot, demanding pull of Katarina's mouth had driven Juliette crazy in minutes. She had always thought herself a rather difficult-to-please lover. And yet, this woman had been different from their very first time. Juliette had come fast and had come again and again, and it had been spectacular every single time.

And now, as always, Katarina was relentless, her eyes pure sin, leaving Juliette nothing to hide and nowhere to run. She pulled the silky strands she had been clutching, she tried to evade, it was all too much…

"Where do you think you're going, Juliette?" Katarina whispered against her wet and tender skin, and Juliette barely managed to stave off the orgasm. She'd come any second. She'd come and she'd be powerless to keep herself from saying the words. The words she tried to not burden Katarina with. It was too soon. It was too much.

But the wicked, wicked tongue licked the underside of her clit so insistently, so fast and hard and so hot. Juliette's fingers in Katarina's hair tightened. She was hanging on to the very precipice.

"Let go, love. Let go, *my love.*" Katarina lifted her face, and the eyes were so, so grave, so resolute that Juliette felt tears spill even as the orgasm overtook her, breaching the last vestiges of her good intentions, of her selflessness, of her self-preservation.

Still throbbing, muscles clenching around thrusting fingers, and heart beating out of her chest, she pulled Katarina up, kissing her, tasting herself on those love-swollen lips.

"I love you." They said it in one breath, in one voice, and Juliette knew the sciences, the seismic laws of physics had allowed them this moment. Just for the two of them. Just for this. The world had finally stopped. It would spin again, very soon everything would be in motion, but that would be much later. For this one fragment of time, they were happy, together, and everything stood still just for them.

Twenty-One
Of Patisserie Heart to Hearts & Blind Faith

Francesca waited for her at a pastry shop of all places. And she had what looked like half a baguette cut up in small tartines in front of her. She licked the jam off her thumb as Juliette entered the place and set down her espresso. For a second they just stared at each other, the crowded space, the people milling about, the smells of baked dough and coffee filling the silence between them.

Seven years, and it had come down to this.

"You've had two weeks from hell, I bet." The words, in the familiar heavily accented voice, landed like a blow. Or a caress. With Francesca, Juliette no longer knew the difference these days.

"And you've discovered the wonders of French bread? You who swore never to set foot in a patisserie? The one who drove the entire company insane with your demands on our bodies?"

"Ah, I get the fighting Juliette today?"

Then Francesca visibly deflated, the sarcasm and the slyness gone from her tone as she got up and reached for Juliette. The hug was tender and sincere.

"I'm sorry, amor. I really am."

"For what? I did betray you." Juliette held her for a second before letting go and sitting down. The server eyed her warily, obviously recognizing the Princess of Paris and just as obviously puzzled that she'd patronize such an establishment. Out of spite, if nothing else, Juliette pointed to the back of the place where food was being prepared and smiled.

"I'd love the same." She waved at Francesca's scrumptious meal. Oh, and a café au lait." She turned to Francesca after the perplexed server left and murmured, "Remind me to add sugar, while I'm at it."

"You going nuts on me, Jett?"

"You're not the boss of me, Cesca."

Then, after a lengthy beat, they both laughed.

"Oh, amor. This thoroughly blows. I hear they stopped speaking to you at Garnier, even Rochefort."

"You hear? Or you made sure they did?"

The silence that followed spoke volumes. Francesca tore a piece of the baguette then set it down on the plate.

"You chose her over me, Juliette."

Well, nobody ever doubted that Francesca was brilliant. Of course she had figured out the gambit immediately.

"Is that why you haven't said anything? Publicly? Or even to the people over at Place de l'Opéra? Is that why all you're doing is pouting and playing the martyred saint?"

"You don't think martyrdom is attractive?" Francesca's grin was sly.

The faint echo of Katarina's acerbic words, the ones saying it wasn't just yesterday, made Juliette smile before she said, "Not when you know the score."

Juliette's tartines were delivered with little flourish, as if the server was trying to hide it from the world. He was still giving her that incredulous look she deeply resented. Just like a man to have opinions about her life. What a damn ridiculous situation this was. Juliette tore one in half and dunked it into her coffee. She bit into the crust with gusto.

"Well, that shows us all now, Jett." Francesca stared then shrugged and followed suit.

They ate in silence, the absence of words a comfortable void. Life rushed outside of the windows, and inside they made theirs stop to nurse the hurts and the cuts they had inflicted on each other.

"Where will you go?" Juliette didn't really care what happened as long as something did. She had wronged this woman, and there was no way for her to fix it. Guilt was a strange feeling. She wanted her happy and she wanted her out of her own orbit to avoid choking on regret every single time they came across each other. She wondered if that made her incredibly selfish. Or incredibly human.

Still, it would be nice if Francesca landed on her feet. The luster of the world-class ballet director had been blackened by the abysmal performance of the Paris Opera Ballet these last two years.

"New York." The finality in the words and voice were immediately and immensely gratifying. Francesca had a sure thing on the line. Juliette felt her own shoulders relax in relief. "It's sweet that you were worried for me, amor."

"You knew I would be, Cesca."

Francesca gave her a sad smile. "I did. And I'm sorry I let spite get the best of me. I'll let Rochefort know to call off the dogs. I can't imagine it's easy for you under Foltin anyway. Not with Katarina there."

"Oh?" Something in the way Francesca spoke the name, something in the way she looked at Juliette, hinted at pity—and understanding. Of what, Juliette did not know.

"Amor, you cannot tell me that he has not been congregating with Katarina, seeking to promote her, seeking to push his own agenda. He canceled two of your performances. He gave her the lead in *La Bayadère*. And I hear she will be in *Sleeping Beauty* in spring? The one and only Bluebird."

It was a miracle, some sort of universal stroke of luck, that Juliette had not taken a sip of her coffee as Francesca delivered the final blow. Well, if she had sought to pay Juliette back for her betrayal, Francesca had succeeded. Katarina was dancing the Bluebird? And Juliette had absolutely no idea when that had happened and why nobody had told her. Why hadn't Katarina told her?

The pain did not come right away. Maybe it was the delayed reaction to the realization that Katarina had kept a secret from her. The moment she thought it, Juliette wanted to laugh at herself, at her own naïveté. Katarina kept secrets the magnitude of which Juliette had no grasp of. Her meteoric rise in Moscow, her battles to become the sole prima at Bolshoi, the fates of her rivals suddenly no longer standing in the way. Even her very defection. Why Paris? Why now?

Katarina kept secrets like people kept mementos of their loved ones. Collecting them. Guarding them. A veritable dragon with a golden hoard.

Still, Juliette told herself that an "I love you" meant very little in the big scheme of things when ballet was on the line.

And that was when the pain came. A stab under her fifth rib. A dagger to the heart, Francesca, with her touch of the theatrics, would say. But as she tried to draw shallow, inconspicuous breaths, Juliette thought back on her beginnings in pointe shoes. She knew she had always been an outlier in some aspects when it came to her life's work. Particularly because she didn't think it was. Her life. Just work.

Katarina lived and breathed ballet. It was everything, and existing without it was the greatest punishment. And for Juliette? Something that she adored. But not something she sold her soul to. Ballet was a fickle mistress, cruel and capricious, and Juliette wanted nothing of the unpredictability of her whip.

For the first time in her life, she felt that this difference actually mattered. The things we do for love. The things we do for ballet. Not the same for Juliette. One and all for Katarina, perhaps.

Juliette licked her suddenly dry lips. It was beside the point that she did not want the part for herself. Because Juliette didn't. Not really. Not even after so many of her own performances had been canceled or postponed to the springtime slots.

"Well, that's ballet…" Even to her own ears, her words held a hollow quality. Juliette added a shrug for good measure. Maybe Francesca would leave it be?

Francesca, being Francesca, did no such thing. What else was new? She reached out and patted Juliette's hand before simply covering it with hers.

"You were always the worst liar. Just absolutely godawful at fibbing. Granted, you never had to, amor. The world was your oyster. What will you do when the sea swallows you whole?"

Juliette tugged her fingers from under Francesca's.

"The level of drama, Cesca, honestly…" She thought she had at least managed to feign indifference rather truthfully.

"What is it with people trying to tone down the passion and the theatrics these days?" Francesca rolled her eyes. "I said it the other day, I am saying it again. Drama is inherent to our world, amor. It would serve you well to remember that. And to always act assuming something is afoot. Something dramatic."

When Juliette said nothing, Francesca just lifted her shoulder and added finality to her tone. "You are the biggest talent this side of the Iron Curtain, and yet you have zero comprehension of the intrigue and even less inclination toward the dramatic. I feel like I went wrong somewhere in your education."

"I chose to do my job." Juliette hunched her shoulders and didn't care how defensive she appeared. She was past caring. She had all these thoughts buzzing in her head, taking up all the space, leaving no room for her to sort through the wrinkles in the satin ribbons of the events. There were just too many. And by the look on Francesca's face, there would be more incoming shortly.

"Ah, there is the issue at the heart of it all. A job. It's life and death for these people. For your Katarina, it's life. And I mean it in the most precise way, because her talent is what landed her here, giving her all of these new beginnings. Paris, Palais Garnier. You."

Juliette blinked at Francesca echoing some of her earlier considerations. She had been prescient even as her heart did a little treacherous flip at hearing Katarina being called *hers*. Juliette tried to keep her face as neutral as possible. When did an outing with a friend become a game of high-stakes poker?

The friend in question, meanwhile, took a long sip of her espresso, her eyes never leaving Juliette's as if trying to gauge how real her own assertion was. Well, it was very real. Above all else, Katarina did have Juliette. For better or for worse.

Francesca set down her cup and her expression soured, her words dripping poison. "For Rodion Foltin, dancing is death itself. If you think he will not kill for it, you're mistaken. He assassinated my career, or damn nearly did."

Juliette watched as Francesca tried very hard to keep her voice down and to attract as little attention to them as possible. They were being looked at anyway, but it was a valiant attempt, and Juliette appreciated the effort it took.

"And yet, New York."

Francesca's smile was sad when she answered. "Yes, provisional position. But New York Ballet nonetheless."

"You'll love it, Cesca. And you will turn the entire provisional thing into permanent before I can finish dancing *The Nutcracker*."

Considering that *Nutcracker* season was around the corner, Juliette thought Francesca might not agree with the simile. But no disagreement followed, just a pursing of the lips and a thoughtful look.

"And you?"

Juliette's brow furrowed.

"Me?"

"Will it be London? The competition is stiff there, but they could use you. Shannon Robbards told me so. And Shannon would be better to you than he ever will be, especially with Katarina as his prima. As his Étoile."

First the gut punch of Bluebird, now this? Had Foltin really decided to name Katarina his Étoile? Was Francesca speaking from knowledge, or from wishful thinking? She had clearly been angry. Could she be this vindictive? Juliette's head spun. When had her life become this complicated? When had she lost sight of whom to trust?

The shard of premonition that had been cutting little pieces of her chest since the day she got on this carousel embedded itself deeper, her torn flesh singing with bittersweet pain.

"Is that why Shannon was at the *Swan Lake* opening?"

Francesca polished off her espresso and signaled for another before lowering her voice even more.

"She had come to warn me. Foltin had resigned that day. And I knew mine were numbered. Turns out the number was one. One day. That's how long it took for him to be named Director in Paris. He signed the paperwork while still in London. Lalande let *Swan Lake* play for the weeks it did because the run sold out after our opening night triumph and the Ballet needed the sales, but the plan to oust me was already in place, I just know it. But Shannon was also here recruiting. And while she couldn't offer me anything I'd bite on, she does have a special admiration for you, Jett."

"I am the Paris Opera Ballet Étoile, Cesca."

And this time, the look she received was filled with nothing but pity.

"You might be the company's one and only Étoile, but you are not his. And when he shows you the door, do call Shannon. Though I imagine she will reach out to you before you become desperate enough to do that yourself. Or smart enough."

They did not say goodbye when they hugged. They walked down the Champs-Élysées arm in arm, the crowds parting predictably in front of them. The silence between them was not comfortable anymore, the weight of secrets, guilt, and lies filling the spaces they always reserved for honesty. And the seed Francesca had planted was much too painfully shoved into the fearful ground of Juliette's mind to be ignored.

Yet, when she arrived on Rue de Rivoli, the light in the kitchen was burning pink and the betrayal of the unsaid, of the Bluebird part, of the suspicious meetings and long silences, was somehow palatable. Softer than Juliette expected it to be. And was it really a betrayal? Katarina did not owe her anything. She certainly did not owe her the courtesy of telling her when she had been given a new part. Bluebird wasn't even the main role in *Sleeping Beauty*.

Juliette let her head fall for a moment before she pushed open the door to the staircase. Why could she not cast aside this sharp little edge of doubt? It had been lodged in her chest since the first day she had seen Katarina. The premonition and the scintilla of distrust. She had swept both under the cover of love and lust. Under the glory of having Katarina in her arms. Of seeing adoration in those bright blue eyes. She could not be bothered about any role Katarina might take without telling her, but the uncertainty that existed now extended to what other trust her lover might be able to break without blinking an eye—and Juliette found that she just didn't care. Katarina was worth it. She mattered enough.

Her treacherous heart clung to the shadows cast by the pink lamp in her kitchen as she climbed the stairs to the woman whose secrets were so deep that Juliette was afraid she'd drown in them. And what scared her even more was that she didn't want the truth. She might just never recover from it. Why not choose the safety of familiar waters?

When the door opened, Katarina stood there in Juliette's

bathrobe, hair down and the apartment smelling of cinnamon and apples. And orange blossom. As Juliette fell into her arms, she knew she wouldn't ask about the Bluebird. Katarina would tell her when the time came. Juliette would have to deal with the fallout then.

They made love that night. Slow. Achingly tender. As if endeavoring to imprint their love on each other's skin, like ink. An endless tattoo of gentle kisses and silky caresses. Even the climax when it came was a wave, cresting to the sky, filling Juliette with warmth. And despite everything, despite the shadows dancing in the corners of the room, creeping slowly toward the bed, Juliette felt inexplicably safe. Was it her wishful thinking? Or was her heart seeing something nobody else had been able to see? That she was protected in these hands.

The hands that traced patterns in her collarbones, even as Katarina's head lay in its place on Juliette's shoulder.

"You are so…" Katarina paused, her voice like honey, sweet and languorous, looking for the word. "Admirable. Steady."

Juliette pouted, more for show, then kissed the blonde tresses.

"That sounds like a ship. Or a car. Steady is what you want from a ride."

She could feel Katarina's lips stretch in a smile against her skin.

"You did give me quite a ride, love." The mischievous note in Katarina's voice did wonderfully wicked things to Juliette's stomach.

But then Katarina lifted her head and looked her right in the eyes, a clear tell that something weighty and serious was about to be said.

"You face the world full-on. No reservations, no pretenses. The courage to do so comes from a place of security, yes, but also from your sense of self. You are whole, my love. And you face the world whole. Giving it your all. Your talent. Your art. Your joy."

Juliette drew the disheveled head back down to her shoulder, took the long-fingered hand in hers, holding it tightly, and they lay in silence for the longest moment. When she was certain the tears she had been fighting wouldn't spill, ever mindful of not placing more guilt on Katarina, who'd surely feel sad for making her cry, Juliette kissed the relaxed hand in hers.

"You see me with the eyes of a lover. And I think you believe I'm immortal. But it's the ovations that bestow immortality on people like us, you and I know this. It's the love that makes us who we are. Please don't take it away. And please be gentle. I've only ever given my all to the audiences and their faithful adoration. And I am giving you so much more than I have ever given ballet, Katarina."

Her eyelids were growing heavy, and Juliette fought sleep for the chance to hear Katarina's answer, but her lover was silent, the tender fingers still caressing her skin, lulling her deeper into slumber. Just before it claimed Juliette entirely, she thought she heard Katarina whisper, "Thank you."

Twenty-Two

Of Revelations & Grands Jetés

A ballet is a series of steps. Most of them are taken way before a single note of the music has even been played. From baby bunheads enrolled by their doting parents, to dancing classes, to nonstop rehearsals leading to opening nights.

It's positions, tendus, pliés. It's toes torn to shreds and the mangled satin of pointe shoes. It's the smell of resin and sweat. It's a steady string of events all building up to one. It's the raindrops, falling in sequence, building up to an entire deluge. A sea of steps, of emotions, of victories. A sea of falls, of tears, of failures.

In retrospect, Juliette should perhaps have applied herself to becoming a better swimmer. She wasn't a terrible, but by no means could she handle the rogue wave coming her way. To her credit, she had recognized it once it covered her whole, but by that time it was too late. She was sinking, and there was no reaching shore from that point on.

The opening night of *The Nutcracker* was one that Juliette always looked forward to. The anticipation, the children milling about, the soaring of the music being rehearsed by the orchestra, the general excitement for Christmas—all the small and big details that made this one ballet production feel magical. She had loved it as a tiny little girl in the corps in London, she had adored it as Clara, dancing her first solo part as a fourteen-year-old, and she had the time of her life headlining the ballet as the Sugar Plum Fairy.

With her, Francesca always made the part much larger than it normally was danced, and the entire second act transformed into a production of Juliette showing off. Grand jeté after grand jeté, split after split. The children adored it. And Juliette reveled in both the adoration and the opportunity to showcase movements that she usually did not get as much time to perform, as very rarely did a show require her to jump as much or as high.

The day had begun with love. They always did with Katarina, even if this one felt a touch desperate, her partner demanding and reckless in their lovemaking. Lying back after a mind-blowing orgasm, Juliette had tried to calm her racing heart and runaway emotions.

The heart that was living outside of her body, her lover, had stood up too quickly and almost ran out of the room. Katarina disappeared into the bathroom without a word. Juliette had closed her eyes at the *snick* of the lock shutting.

They'd talk. After tonight, they'd lay on the table all that had clearly been eating them from inside. Juliette had questions she had been so scared to ask. And clearly, by her behavior, Katarina had answers she was trying to avoid. But they would both do what they must. They were too precious. Like fragile, handspun glass. Juliette hugged it to her chest, afraid to break it, afraid to get cut by it to pieces.

But ballet went on. For as long as she remembered, Juliette had always watched the first act of *The Nutcracker* from the wings. The Sugar Plum Fairy did not feature, but she used the time to get into the spirit and the magnificence of Tchaikovsky. The soft spot she had for the long-suffering, torn-up, gay Russian in her heart often made her wonder if it was the drama of him that made his gift soar so high. The parallels with Katarina did not escape her, tragedy unspooling like ribbons off her arms, dripping with talent and secrets.

Standing in the dark, Juliette soaked up the music and the performances. A member of the corps, a girl in her early twenties whom Juliette had seen a few times but would have been hard-pressed to place, touched her elbow with the guiltiest of expressions.

"Mademoiselle Lucian-Sorel..." She stumbled through the full name, and Juliette took pity on the girl.

"It's Juliette. And you are?"

The girl gaped, stumbling even more, the two syllables of "Aimee" becoming six.

"What can I do for you, Aimee?"

The youngster blinked a few times, as if suddenly remembering that she was the one who had approached Juliette.

"Oh, Monsieur Foltin wants to see you."

It was Juliette's turn to be surprised.

"I'm about to go on stage after the intermission—"

"He said now, Mademoiselle Lucian... Um, Juliette."

Juliette rolled her eyes. She'd have to comply, since the girl was clearly terrified, and telling her to return to Foltin with any answer other than that Juliette was coming would cause her to faint.

"I'll be right there. And why don't you stay and enjoy the performance? They're about to do the pas de deux, and it's gorgeous."

The girl's face lit up like the Christmas tree from the set, and Juliette gave her a one-armed hug before making her way slowly behind the stage and to the stairs leading to the third floor.

Some things about the Palais Garnier she loved. The proximity of the studios and the offices to the main action was one of them. The way sound carried... was not.

"I did not ask for your opinion, Katya."

After weeks of rehearsals and meetings, Juliette would

know the high-pitched, out-of-place voice belonging to Foltin anywhere.

"Don't—"

Katarina's single word sent Juliette's heart into overdrive.

"What, suddenly you are too good for your Soviet name?" Foltin's mocking was coming through clearly even from this distance. Juliette hurried her steps.

"There is nothing sudden about disliking being called something that is entirely foreign to you." Katarina's voice held so much distress that Juliette almost vaulted over the secretary's desk on her way into the office. The beautiful vase full of yellow roses would surely have been a victim of her protective instincts. But her lover's next words stopped her dead in her tracks.

"You want me to betray Juliette, and you want me to do it when she has lost everything."

There was movement, steps and rustling fabric, and through the cracked-open door Juliette saw Foltin approach Katarina, whose back was so straight she feared it might snap at any moment.

"You and I want the same things, Katya, I think you've forgotten that this was the plan all along."

The spidery-thin fingers traced Katarina's jaw, and Juliette felt bile fill her mouth. She almost gagged and doubted she'd be able to hold it in much longer.

"Rodion, you have no idea what I want."

His laughter was like nails on a chalkboard.

"Oh, but I do. You could have defected in London, in Madrid, in Rome. And yet you chose Paris, with a vulnerable Étoile who is also a lesbian and would thus be easily hoodwinked. You've done it in Moscow, right before you threw Tatyana off the stairs. I heard that didn't work for you so well here?"

This time when he touched her, Katarina did flinch, and Juliette felt that movement like a blow straight to her solar plexus.

"I never—"

"Tut, tut, you never what? Never fucked Tatyana, or never pushed her? Never fucked Sorel? Never pushed her either?" Foltin stepped back, and Juliette could see Katarina's chest rise and fall in deep breaths. Too bad she could not say the same of her own. The nausea was so overwhelming she feared she would lose her lunch any second now.

"You are running out of 'nevers,' and I have no time for your excuses. You need to dance every single part the American is dancing. I have no time for her stubbornness. I have no time for her, period. She doesn't love ballet. She doesn't live it. And frankly, I just much rather prefer you, dorogaya. The company needs a fresh start."

Foltin sat behind his desk and placed his bony, creepy hands on the oaken surface, the contrast between the pale skin and the dark wood making the appendages appear even stranger and less human. His thin lips stretched into a smile as he went on.

"This is why Lalande wanted me. I am that fresh start and you are fresh out of a niche *Swan Lake* success. It was too gay even for the Gay Paris. But no matter. Your Bluebird will be spectacular. The city is at your feet. So is Sorel, and I commend you on some good taste, at least. Though if she will cause you issues, I advise you to get rid of her. And I know you've seen the vultures circling anyway. Bianchi will snap her up in New York. And Robbards is now back in London, picking up my discarded sloppy seconds there, as Sorel did here with you. She will fit right in…"

He allowed the line to dangle, the words unspoken but louder than a volcano eruption. Juliette closed her eyes to stave off the images of Katarina and Foltin. When it failed, she bit her lip, the taste of copper in her mouth doing more to ground her than to wipe away the pain of discovery.

Juliette was uncertain what hurt the most. The fact that she had been the victim of a conspiracy so simple as a lonely lesbian falling for a beautiful, unattainable woman? That Katarina had done it before to cement her place in a ballet company and hence had perfected her modus operandi? Or that Foltin was acting like whatever his relationship with Katarina had been, it was not in the past?

All of the above? Or that she believed—for once Juliette Lucian-Sorel believed another soul when she heard "I love you"? Hadn't she been told to beware? Hadn't she been warned? Hadn't her own mind kept some reservations about the events of the past few weeks? Hadn't she thought just this morning that they needed to talk?

Yes, she had doubts. And yet, the one doubt she should have had and never did, not for a single second, was that Katarina Vyatka loved her. That she had Katarina Vyatka's heart.

In the office, Foltin kept speaking, Juliette grateful her own thoughts distracted her enough that she'd missed whatever poison he was spewing. He must've said something vile because Katarina blanched and shook her head even as Foltin banged his fist on the new desk.

"Katya, I won't stand for this!" His screech was loud, stabbing her ears. "Time to get all the other shows on the road. It's always been business for you. So get down to business! The Empress takes the Paris crown…or the Empress goes home. So I will make it easy for you. I'm not even asking. I'm waiting on your yes."

Juliette didn't think Katarina could go paler than she already was. And yet, she achieved it. Juliette almost smiled. Sky was really the limit for this woman. And acting was in her blood. Or was it the blood that she put in her acting? Her and that of others? Juliette felt the first tear slip and fall down her cheek.

In the office, the silence stretched. Foltin banged both fists on the wooden surface of the innocent though worthless modern monstrosity of a desk that replaced the antique and then, as if in slow motion, Juliette felt her already crumbling castle raise a white flag.

Katarina's head dropped to her chest in a nod, and Juliette could not hold back her whimper. The vase of yellow roses Juliette had admired earlier was on the floor, the petals covered in shards of broken glass. She must've knocked it over in her shock.

Both Foltin and Katarina turned to the door, and for one horrible moment, Juliette could see their faces, their eyes. The utter satisfaction in his and the sheer terror in hers.

Then Juliette was running. There were screams behind her, Katarina's voice calling her name, someone else yelling at them for making so much noise with an ongoing performance on stage, Foltin bellowing for people to grab a mop and clean the mess Juliette had made.

She simply ran, not even feeling the pointe shoes, the unforgiving marble of the floors, the gawking dancers in the hallways. Katarina was behind her, she was not letting up, getting closer, and Juliette knew that no matter what, she could not get caught because what would happen then would surely cost them both their hearts.

Though, perhaps, Katarina did not have a heart. Tatyana must have been Belova, the famed "sad story" of Bolshoi of the last decade, who was supposed to dominate the stage for years—until a bad fall backstage cut her career short.

And propelled Katarina to take over...

Tears stung Juliette's eyes, her chest a dark pit of ichor. Desperation shouted in her ears a litany of instructions.

Turn around and tell her. Scream your pain. Let her have it.

But the audience was clapping for the second act to begin, and Juliette knew she was out of time. Out of options.

Dance. Entertain. Drown later. The wave is too big to survive it anyway.

The entire Palais Garnier was waiting, Gabriel standing in the wings for their joint entrance, his face awash with worry and confusion at seeing her running, Katarina on her heels.

The music soared. Gabriel gripped her listless hand and led Juliette out, Katarina missing her by seconds, stopping behind the curtain just in time to avoid being spotted on stage.

The face, that beloved face still held the horror, and now there was the guilt. Juliette knew this look. She had seen it before. Well, she had seen and heard enough to last her a lifetime. A lifetime of regret. A lifetime of agony over being so foolish as to believe. To trust. To love.

A pirouette. The wind instruments ominously setting the mood.

Gabriel, sensing her tumult and having danced with her for years, took over seamlessly, spinning her, supporting her through the more challenging parts, giving her time to catch her breath, come to her senses…

A lift. The percussion entering in support of the cellos, winding the atmosphere up a notch.

How to explain to this wonderful man that there would be no coming to her senses? That the stories she had once heard in the dormitories in London, of betrayal and intrigue, of drama and harm, of pain and ballet dancing forever arm in arm, were all true? And that now Juliette Lucian-Sorel was one of those stories, perhaps one of the most awful ones?

Well, she always did reach for the stars.

A series of supported jumps. The violins soaring with each one, the conductor's hands flying.

Gabriel held her through each leap as if she was fragile, as if she'd break.

Well, fuck this.

She let go of his hand and moved into the familiar, into the steps that were second nature. Her calling card. The first grand jeté.

The grand battement, the push off, and then, natural as breathing, the split at the apex. The first violinist solo shredding the short pause, a warning, a prophecy.

Gabriel, now a distance away, watched on, his eyes tinted

with so much worry, so much anguish. Juliette closed her own. She couldn't break for him just now. She was busy tearing her own soul to pieces. The initial jump was followed by a series, and Juliette took a deep breath.

She felt the shackles of her shuttered heart fall as she started the chain of leaps, the perfect split accompanied by the beginnings of thunderous applause. The second one was higher, her legs straighter, and the audience, perhaps sensing that something extraordinary was happening, was on its feet by the third one, and Juliette jumped again. And then again. In the wings, Katarina's face was now awash with tears, and at her right, Gabriel broke character and called her name. But she was no longer Juliette. She was a loose cannonball hurling to the zenith.

On the switch leaps, one jump flowed into another, and then another with the audience in a continuous ovation that drowned even the orchestra. Perhaps for the better, because Juliette had long since left the music in the dust, extending her part beyond the libretto.

In the pit, Monsieur Lenoir watched her with a rapturous and yet decidedly uncomprehending expression, keeping his strings and winds in check, making them repeat the melody, his baton tentatively tracking the beats.

Juliette landed on the opposite end of the stage after three switch leaps and then turned back. Gabriel and Katarina were now both on stage—which was madness, since the former was no longer supposed to be there and the later couldn't be there at all—and the sheer presumptuousness tore something in Juliette.

The hole in her chest opened, all-consuming, and all the anger, the rage, the pain of a heart ravaged by betrayal poured into the next set of leaps as she took the shorter, direct line to the front instead of the diagonal that would take her to Gabriel and Katarina.

It was the second grand jeté, as she was right in the center of the stage, at the very edge of it. With the music subdued and the ovation fading, the snap of the hamstring was particularly loud. An obscene sound of flesh tearing. For the longest moment, everything stopped. Then pain, late, like thunder after the flash of lightning was long gone, followed the tendon rupturing. It blinded her, and still in flight, Juliette felt as if she had been carved open.

Suddenly the world spun faster, trying to recover the lost seconds, and Juliette reeled from the fast-forward motion. In her periphery Katarina rushed the stage, Gabriel running past her, but even he wasn't fast enough to catch Juliette. If only she had taken the diagonal, she'd be closer to him, closer to his safe, sure arms. He'd have caught her…

Juliette landing on the leg with the torn hamstring meant only one thing. In an instant, that landing turned into a crumbling as her knee gave out, the speed and momentum too much for the injured limb to bear.

The cascading effect of her body failing her was truly overwhelming, as one after the other, her muscles, tendons, and bones shattered underneath her weight. And before her head hit the much-adored wooden floorboards, all Juliette saw was another beloved sight—Katarina's arms reaching out for her.

In a haze of pain, of her entire existence falling apart, of her life seeping like water through her clumsy fingers, Juliette frowned at the stream of tears pouring down cheeks that were even paler than usual. Katarina was saying something, her mouth moving, those full lips dry and trembling. Juliette desperately tried to understand, but the roar in her ears was deafening. She shook her head, the pain searing into her brain, a hot iron spear.

Katarina!

The stage lights were dimming, Juliette's vision blurring at the corners, and no matter how much she clawed to stay, to wipe those tears, she could only whisper the name over and over before the blessed darkness claimed her. At least in the pitch black, nothing hurt anymore. Not her leg, nor that place where the heart she had foolishly given away had been.

Coda

Twenty-Three
Of Awakenings & Rain-Washed Tears

There was no movie-like awakening. No slow awareness, no wondering where she was. Even before she came to, Juliette knew she was in the hospital. The pain in her right leg was such that her opening her eyes was accompanied by a scream and wrenching against the bed.

No graceful, ladylike recovering for Juliette. She almost laughed, except her throat was dry, her lips chapped and splitting immediately as she twisted her mouth, filling it with blood. What a familiar taste. And the arms that held her down were familiar too. Both sets.

"Well, you always knew how to make an entrance, amor." Francesca's words were teasing, but her tone was filled with worry. Juliette hated that. She fought the heaviness of her lids and almost won when the second voice joined in and Juliette immediately threw her eyelids open.

"Yes, however, she made an exit first, and that one will be remembered probably forever."

Helena, surrounded by the halo of the overhead lamp, looked changed. Tired. Somehow wrung dry. And her fingers were bloody.

"What is it with the women in my life and blood on your hands?" Her own voice sounded broken to Juliette's ears.

"I don't know, dear, but this is yours. Your mouth is bleeding." Helena dabbed at her lower lip with a piece of gauze Francesca had handed her and then stood back, giving Juliette a long look. The pursed lips were par for the course, as was the incoming lecture, but the gaze was sad, and Juliette knew. She just knew. Still, she had to ask.

"Am I done?"

Helena and Francesca exchanged a telltale glance, and whatever Juliette's previous knowledge was, it solidified. She kept silent, waiting for the words that would end her career.

Francesca teared up and turned away. Helena took her hand and looked her in the eyes.

"Yes." She laid the word on the bed next to Juliette like a live grenade.

There was silence after that, Juliette realizing her mind had gone completely blank. She didn't have any questions. The pain was ravaging her entire right side, even her teeth were singing with it, the intensity of it taking over her thoughts for one blessed moment. She didn't have to think at all. Not about Katarina. Not about the fact that she'd never dance again.

"Hamstring, anterior cruciate and medial collateral ligaments, tibial shaft… Dear…" Helena seemed lost for words. Juliette could sympathize.

When Helena gave up on explaining, Francesca took over, waving her away theatrically. A touch too theatrically. "They repaired the tendons, and the bone will heal. Moore is pretty hasty here with her diagnosis that you're done, amor. If anyone can recover from this and dance, it's you." But she did not sound sure, and the tremble in her voice, the scratchy false note, abraded Juliette's senses.

"It's okay."

Helena's laughter held even more of that falseness. The choked whimper it ended on said as much. "Look at you, Jett. You are consoling us from your hospital bed."

Juliette allowed her lips to stretch into a facsimile of a smile. The taste of blood returned, as did Helena's gauze.

"I don't know what you two are doing here. Of all people..." She let the end of the sentence dangle, leaving Helena and Francesca to exchange looks again. This time, it was the latter who answered.

"In true lesbian tradition, amor."

Juliette felt her chest shake in what surely was a pathetic reaction to such a good joke. This entire situation was ridiculous.

"How long..." The shake turned into a wheeze. She coughed, then coughed again, trying to catch her breath. The pain overtook her, the lack of oxygen making her lightheaded. The lights dimmed again.

Waking up the second time was like finding herself in a sealed tomb. She blinked once, twice, and then the panic set in, the surrounding darkness smothering her, swallowing her whole. Juliette tried to open her eyes, her hands desperately clawing at her face, at everything around her.

"Juliette! Stop, stop! Please, I'm here."

Helena... Helena... Not dead.

Helena was alive and so was Juliette. She was not dead. She would just never dance again. When Juliette opened her mouth to speak, it was a choked cry that came out, and then another, and then her face was wet, hot tears soaking her hospital gown and Helena's shoulder that had somehow materialized in front of her. Everything was pain, even those very tears, but Juliette allowed them both to flow. She'd fight later. For now she let go, clutching Helena's sweater in her swollen fingers, her nails digging into skin underneath.

The third time, Juliette simply opened her eyes. The winter light, gentle and weak, filtered through semi-drawn blinds. Helena sat in the chair in the corner and Francesca paced the length of the room, her cane measuring her steps. *Thump.* One.

Juliette inhaled the daylight and the numbness in her right leg. *Thump.* Two. Juliette exhaled at the sight of a wheelchair by the door.

Well…

"How are you feeling, Juliette?"

"Like I fell off the Eiffel Tower." Was this hoarse mess her voice? The thought crossed her mind and evaporated into the void of the soft shadows and softer lights of the sparsely furnished room.

"Oh, her so-called wit is back. I thought maybe the fall would knock that out of you. Seems not even three surgeries could fix it though, amor." The false note was back in Francesca's tone, as if she could not quite pull off the teasing.

"Three? Pfft, you had more on that ankle of yours, Cesca."

Helena stood up and brought her cool hand to Juliette's forehead.

"The surgeries will resume once your fever goes down. You've gotten yourself a case of hospital bed pneumonia, dear."

Juliette gaped. "How many days have I been here, exactly? Pneumonia seems like something I'd need time to develop."

The exchanging of looks was back. Juliette gritted her teeth. Finally, Francesca spoke up.

"It's the end of the third week, Jett. We had some trouble getting you to wake up after the third operation, and then the fever set in. You've been out the past four days."

Juliette reached for humor again, the numbness and the tingling scent of disinfectant making her nauseous. "I hope I'm setting some records or something, otherwise this has all been for nothing."

"What has this been for, dear?"

Well, Juliette knew she'd have to answer questions, but Helena latching on to her inadvertently double-edged phrasing so soon wasn't her plan.

"How about you give her some space to at least sit up,

Helena? The rest can wait." Francesca's cane thumped furiously, as always attuned to its mistress.

"We have been keeping the 'rest' you are talking about, Cesca, at bay for three weeks. This 'rest' will not wait forever. And I don't think it will wait for her to sit up, either. So, Jett—"

"Oh, for fuck's sake, Helena. Do you ever just stop? So she's outside, so she will stay there for as long as we say so, and if you ask me, she can stay there for eternity. What the fuck was she even doing on stage? Why was Jett running from her?"

Katarina!

The sensation of her vision darkening returned, and Juliette shook her head, making herself dizzier in the process.

"She can't come in, Helena. Katarina can't come here."

Helena took her hand, rubbing soothing circles on her forearm.

"She's not coming in, dear. She didn't try. Breathe. You can't have coughing fits again. The last one knocked you out, Jett. Please, breathe."

Juliette took a carefully deep breath, then another and another, feeling the fluttering of her own pulse under Helena's fingertips.

"I don't want to see her, okay?"

Francesca crossed her arms over her chest. "You won't. That's the last thing you should worry about, amor."

In the ensuing silence, Juliette listened to her own breathing and tried to process what she had heard.

Katarina was outside. Katarina had been outside. Katarina had not tried to come in.

She closed her eyes and counted to ten. Then to another ten. The bitter taste of the impending panic attack slowly receded.

"She and Foltin planned this all along. Your dismissal. Her taking over as prima, perhaps becoming an Étoile. She defected here because I was an easy target. A desperate, sad, naïve lesbian." Juliette shouted the words and the room spun, the scent of roses fighting with the hospital disinfectant, so real, so strong, so cloying she felt she would gag at any moment, her senses going into overdrive on the sheer intensity of the memory.

"Jett…" Francesca's cane clattered to the floor. Well, wasn't that Juliette's very reaction to the news three weeks ago? To crumble down? She had simply done it in a more dramatic fashion.

Helena's fingers on her hand tightened, the pain a welcome distraction.

"I wanted her. She wanted my crown."

The buzzing of the lamp above filtered through the ringing in her ears.

"Well, dear, you had her. And she is now wearing your crown. She opened *Onegin*, Foltin's mesh of opera and ballet, on Tchaikovsky's score last night. The reviews are all raves. The queen is dead, long live the queen, and all that garbage. Honestly, these people couldn't even wait till you were out of the hospital."

A sniffle from her side distracted Juliette. Francesca so rarely cried.

"I hoped to keep you from this, amor. I so hoped to spare you."

Something in the wording, in the way Francesca spoke so carefully, made Juliette struggle to sit. Helena helped prop her up.

"Keep me from this? From what, Cesca?"

A sudden gasp from Helena was confirmation enough. Juliette felt the world around her narrow down to Francesca's next words.

"The farce that had been going on for two years now, Jett. Also known as the game to oust Francesca Bianchi from Paris Opera Ballet, authored by one Jacques Lalande. You might have an acquaintance with him, no?"

Francesca's voice broke with her own sarcasm, but she carried on.

"Everything was sabotaged. Small details to production-wide issues. Performances in the corps and solos. Dancers falling ill, transferring suddenly at the very last moment, understudies being a no-show. Decorations being delivered damaged. Nothing was working as it should have been. He and his cronies were out on the warpath to get me fired. They asked me to resign when Foltin defected two years ago. They wanted him to lead our ballet company. His name, the scandal around him, the prestige. I guess they thought it would elevate Paris Opera Ballet more. As if Paris needs elevation!" Francesca smirked, then set her jaw. "I refused. The reviews started tanking pretty much right after."

Francesca sniffed again, her hands balled, her knuckles white. "No matter how high you jumped, how many fouettés you performed, how well Gabriel lifted you. Nothing worked—the papers were destroying me. And dragging you along to hell. Collateral damage. As a woman you took the brunt of it, but once it became clear that I was not going to give in easily, Lalande decided to take aim for Gabriel as well."

She unclenched her fists and took out a dainty handkerchief, drying her eyes. There was pity in them when she looked at Juliette.

"Amor… I'm sorry. I'm sorry I didn't tell you. I'm sorry I tried to keep you out of it. I knew you'd run to the president, or do some other foolish grand gesture to save me from Lalande—"

"Cesca, but how can he have so much power?" Like little pieces of the bigger mosaic, things were falling into place. How had she not seen this sooner? He was at the center of everything. A despicable man, with big ambitions and a pocketful of intrigue and lies.

Francesca shrugged, but her face was anything but indifferent. "He was with the Finance Ministry for years. Budgets were his authority, including the one for Paris Opera Ballet.

And illustrious mass media. Some of the newspapers are owned by his friends. But that's not even the point, Jett. It's that in this city, in this country, everyone owes him."

Juliette felt her hands go cold. Was it really this easy to ruin a life? It certainly seemed so. So many questions now had answers.

Still, Francesca kept speaking. "He had ambition. Once. But God gave him no talent to dance. And apparently a hatred for women. Why do you think Gabriel was initially spared? No, at first it was all on me. And then on your head too. And I couldn't bear it. The productions weren't as awful as they painted them, Jett. You know it. You danced them."

"But if you read more and more bad reviews, you start to believe them. The public did. Soon the company did too. Mission accomplished. From a psychological point of view, a brilliant scheme." As she spoke, Helena crossed her arms over her chest and stepped closer to the window. Her face showed nothing, and when she didn't carry on, Francesca began again, her tone beseeching now.

"Amor, I never wished for you to be in the middle of any of this." Juliette wanted to laugh at the assertion, but Francesca kept speaking, words just pouring out. "I couldn't see how to stop any of it. The press, Lalande, and when Katarina defected, I knew what would happen. She was the match that lit the fuse of my demise. I figured they'd perhaps marginalize you once I was gone, maybe add her as the second Étoile, make you split your parts. But for the life of me, I didn't foresee Katarina betraying you this way. I could've sworn, I thought she loved…"

Francesca trailed off, letting the unspoken "you" hang in the air, a loose feather of a bird long gone.

"Good thing neither of us had to swear then, Cesca. I'd hate to break a vow like that." Juliette allowed the words to fall to the ground and closed her eyes.

"I'm so sorry, amor. For everything." The tears kept falling, Francesca now hiccupping with every word.

"You know you could've shared some of the burden instead of going about making as much drama for everyone." Helena sounded like she wanted to either hug or slap Francesca. Juliette worried her lip, opening the unhealed split, welcoming the metallic taste.

"I don't blame you, Cesca. You told me to expect the drama. I guess it was very much in character." Juliette smiled, feeling the warm blood drip down her chin. A curious and strange sensation. Her eyelids drooped.

"Jett?" Both voices lifted in alarm, and Juliette could hear the cane thumping away, Francesca leaving the room, surely in search of a doctor. Good. She wasn't feeling all that well. Someone should probably check her out.

"Jett, love, talk to me, stay with me, please!" Helena sounded panicked.

"See… I am your love… And she is mine… And isn't that a tragedy?"

The image of Katarina standing outside of the hospital swam in her mind before Juliette closed her eyes and drifted off.

***

The actual sight of Katarina standing in front of the hospital was nothing like the one had Juliette imagined as she convalesced for two more weeks and underwent another surgery. The antibiotics cleared her pneumonia, though her cough was still a rather painful memory for her ribs. Along with her lungs, her mind gained some of its clarity back. And so the sight was particularly jarring.

Of course it was raining. It should have been snowing. February in Paris was usually reliably cold.

"Guess I can't even count on Paris." Juliette belatedly realized she had murmured her thoughts out loud when Helena, who was pushing her wheelchair out the side door and toward the limo waiting at the curb, stopped.

"What did you say, Jett?" And then Helena jerked the wheelchair and Juliette knew she would not have to answer. "What the fuck is she still doing here?"

Helena phrased it as a question, but all Juliette heard was the finality of war being declared and lines being drawn. Katarina was not coming anywhere near her. Well, by the look of her. Hair soaking wet, matted to her face, clothes clinging to her body that somehow looked so much thinner than the familiar willowy form, making her seem frail and fragile, driving Juliette's treacherous heart to beat faster with worry.

The speeding up of her heartbeats angered Juliette. All the rage returned, at herself, at this damn woman who stood in the rain looking foolish and reckless.

Helena pushed the wheelchair and Juliette turned away, refusing to meet the once beloved eyes that looked on beseechingly.

"Juliette!"

Well, she had some gall. But then bravery was always something Katarina had in spades—Juliette had to give her that.

"No fucking way, Jett. Get in." Helena growled near her ear and handed her the crutches, then opened the car door.

Juliette stood up, wavered, then gritted her teeth. She would not give Katarina the satisfaction of seeing her weak. She bit the inside of her cheek and straightened, resting her weight on her left leg and the crutches now tucked under her arms.

But when she finally turned to Katarina, who was now much closer, just a few steps away, there was no satisfaction on the rain-washed face. Just pain. Goddamn pain. Would it ever end?

"Juliette..." One word, a lifetime of heartache. Juliette allowed herself to meet Katarina's eyes. She clenched her jaw hard at the sight. Wan, somehow bruised, as if she was the one who had broken all her bones, the one whose future was as uncertain as the Parisian weather this winter, Katarina looked sick.

"Juliette…" Even her voice was broken, the vowels subdued and the consonants unnaturally harsh.

"You need to stop saying my name as if it is the answer to everything." Juliette herself knew she did not sound whole, or remotely like herself. But it felt imperative that she speak. She was still alive. She was moving on.

"It is… For me. Please…" Katarina stopped, gulped, and Juliette realized the rain was washing tears off the angular face, the unusually dull pale blue eyes swimming in them.

"Please what?" Juliette heard herself whisper, and then her own vision blurred. The tears infuriated her all over. God, why could she not stop surrendering?

"Please what?" And this time the shimmer of tears was gone, and she was screaming. "What else can I give? You took everything. Was any of what we had true? Was any of it real? Is this?" Juliette gestured with her chin to the distance between them, fingers gripping the handles of the crutches. Next to her, Helena put a hand on her shoulder. As restraint went, it was a feeble attempt.

"Standing here every day, crying in the rain. You're no romance heroine, Vyatka. You're the villain of this book. And I am the fool who loved you, despite everyone telling me you're hiding a knife under your pillow and that I will wake up one morning with it in my back. Enjoy your throne, Your Majesty. Seems like I can't sit on it anymore anyway."

The tears were choking her now, and Juliette felt that one more word would make her cry uncontrollably. And despite her earlier assurances that she had nothing else to give Katarina, she'd already given her more than she intended. The hysterics would be too much.

Juliette drew in a desperate breath. Just a few more words and then she'd be done, then she'd allow Helena to put her in the car.

"Are you here to soothe your guilt but getting wet in

the cold Parisian rain? How romantic." Juliette spat the last two words as if they tasted foul. She was certain they would be there tomorrow morning for the street sweepers to throw away. "You've accomplished some of that. As for guilt? You always carried enough of it, so what's a little more, *sweetheart*?"

Juliette knew the term of endearment was a bullet. She didn't care. She loaded it in the empty barrel and spun it. Fate of the Russian roulette had it that out of everything she had said on this sidewalk, it was this word that seemed to hit Katarina square in the chest. She swayed, her arms falling to her sides, hands shaking, knuckles white as if she'd been wringing them.

When the smoke from the metaphorical gun settled around them, the rain washing it away, Juliette drew a long breath in. She could have sworn there was a whiff of gunpowder in the air.

"Remember how I asked you to be careful with my love?" Katarina's gasp was her only answer before Juliette spoke again. "All the lies, the scheming, the intrigue. And for what? You didn't need to sleep with me to get what you were after. Did you do it because I was…what? There? Lonely? Desperate? I loved you, Katarina Vyatka. I deserved a gentler goodbye from you."

As the words spilled, opening her heart to this woman one last time felt natural. She knew her smile was distorted. Ugly. Her own tears would follow suit soon, and she didn't want to give the satisfaction of being seen crying. She'd indulge later. Alone and broken.

Still, Juliette allowed herself one more look. Wet, cold, shivering. No, seeing Katarina like this did not please her, did not take away her pain. In fact, speaking to her, hurling all those words at this fragile figure swaying in the wind, only made Juliette feel like a cad. She turned sharply, Helena's arm saving her from a face-plant, and maneuvered herself into the car.

Katarina still trembled on the sidewalk as the limo pulled away. Juliette's tears came then. Hot and bitter.

Twenty-Four
Of Strange Apartments & Misplaced Trust

"I can't believe you let her have your apartment." Helena washed the cup under the steady stream of water for much longer than she needed to. But Juliette had been sitting in the small kitchen of the rental and Helena had been finding reasons to occupy the same space. Which meant only one thing. There was about to be a conversation. She had been trying to pin Juliette down for days now. And only Juliette's claims that she was tired and sleepy or in pain made Helena back off.

Well, they might as well talk. Juliette had been silent for what seemed like ages. She had gone to the hospital. She had come back here. The place Helena got them was warm and cozy and so foreign. Juliette wanted to close her eyes to avoid noticing all the details that were just wrong.

The windows were smaller, the windowsills too high, the shower too narrow, and the doors opened in the opposite direction. And it was not her space. But then, nowhere was. Not anymore.

"I couldn't go back, Hels." Her voice sounded rusty, husky from unuse.

"You and I shared the Rue de Rivoli apartment for much longer than you and she did."

Juliette bit her lip. How to tell Helena that the years they had there were nothing compared to the scant few months that had ruined her life? That had reshaped her entire existence—and not just in the way that broke her bones and tore her tendons.

When she lifted her face, Helena was watching her with such regret that Juliette figured she didn't need to say anything out loud. The thing about her former lover—she was one of the greatest psychologists of her generation. Juliette smiled, and Helena blinked uncomprehendingly.

"I love you, Hels. I'm sorry we never worked out. And I'm sorry you're wasting your time here with me when Columbia clearly thinks you're the next iteration of Sigmund Freud and probably wants you back yesterday."

Helena's laughter was music to Juliette's ears. The terrible feeling she'd been wallowing in this past week, of being unable to do anything right or say the correct words, had not been something Juliette was used to.

"Oh, my dear, do not insult me, as I'd rather be compared to Anna Freud myself than to that ghoul. And as for being missed, you are the golden child. The sheer sea of flowers that people bring to Palais Garnier steps every day…" Helena sighed, and Juliette waved her sadness away.

"You'd think I'm dead. Though I might as well be."

She got up and leaned heavily on her crutch. She had learned to maneuver quite competently, wielding only one in the past week. A caged animal, she limped to the living room before letting herself fall to the leather sofa, which creaked pathetically under her weight, mimicking the sound Juliette imagined her own heart was making these days under the pressure of depression and gloom.

"Juliette…" Helena stepped into the room and then just stood there, clearly unable to decide what to say or what to do next.

"You want to believe I'm wrong, but we both know I'm not.

Foltin made it clear that my forced vacation is permanent. He can't fire me, but then, I can't dance. And even if I ever recover enough to do so, Juliette Lucian-Sorel will never be who she once was."

"Juliette—"

"Hels, you were right to tell me I was done in the hospital. I will never disrespect the stage by giving it anything but my very best. And it's something that I can't ever reach again. Funny, I always thought I was very pragmatic about ballet. It was a job. Well, I was wrong. It was more than that, but it doesn't matter now, since I will never have it back. I know I should be glad to even walk, but you and I both know I don't give a fuck about that."

Helena nodded and finally gave in, sitting down next to her, the small sofa making their proximity much closer than Juliette felt comfortable. After all the poking and prodding and touching she was enduring at the hospital almost every day, she wanted none of the human contact. She ignored the treacherous thought that she did indeed want contact from one particular human.

"I know. And I also know that being all stoic about this entire ordeal is something that you need. But you can lean on people, dear."

Juliette smiled even though it tasted bitter on her lips.

"I have you, Hels."

"You have Francesca. She's in New York, but you have her. And you have Gabriel."

Juliette rolled eyes. Gabriel…

"He never once visited the hospital. Over a month spent there. And I've been here two weeks now—"

"He's coming today, soon…" Helena trailed off but her face said so much more, and Juliette's heart sped up. Was this the conversation Helena had been gearing up to for days?

"Hels?"

"He… Jett… Just… be nice, okay?"

A knock on the door interrupted them, and Helena suddenly looked panicked. A second, two, and then the familiar composure was back on her face and she gave Juliette a side hug. She got up and left the room.

Her heart in her throat now, Juliette pushed herself up, flailing for a moment, her crutch falling out of her hands and clattering to the floor with a sound that seemed to go on forever. In the middle of the cacophony, Gabriel appeared in the doorway Helena had disappeared through.

And suddenly, Juliette knew. Ghostly pale, his eyes almost lifeless, Gabriel stood stooped, wringing his hands. Her Gabriel would have been at the hospital with her. He'd have been there every day. Her Gabriel would have leaped from the threshold to pick up the crutch. Her Gabriel had never been afraid to come close to her.

The little shards of reality she hadn't allowed to penetrate her life for the last six months had finally cut through her selfishness.

"Gabriel." She breathed his name and tears fell, rolling down parchment-white cheeks, yet he continued to stand feet away from her, clutching a scarf. Her scarf, one she had forgotten somewhere years ago and he had adopted because he thought it was fashionable and claimed it suited him much better than her.

"Gabe…" And now a wretched cry escaped him, and then another and another and she hobbled toward him, jumping on her left leg. She stumbled and knew she was going to fall, was ready for it. Juliette closed her eyes and gathered her arms at her chest as she'd been taught in school to avoid breaking her wrists.

He caught her. Two steps and his arms cradled her to his unexpectedly much bonier frame. And then he was trying to lower her to the floor and Juliette was clutching him with everything she had.

His sobs turned into whimpers, his shoulders shaking, his hands gripping her tighter. And through it all, Juliette knew. It had been right in front of her face this entire time. She fucking asked about this very thing all those months ago. When summer was ending and he was happy and sated and fresh out of someone's bed.

"Jett, if I can't trust this man, I can trust no one." He had said that then. And Juliette brushed it aside, believing him. Believing in some nameless, faceless man. Believing Gabriel was invincible. Hell, she herself had been just as naïve back then.

And now they were on the floor of some apartment on the wrong side of the Seine. Nothing at all was right. She might as well have lost her leg, and Gabriel—

"I have the plague, Jett. I got the gay plague."

They were both crying now, tears like a flood taking it all, washing all the hubris, all the nuisance hurts, the nonsensical fights.

Gabriel tried to push her away, but Juliette only held him tighter.

"I'm not afraid, silly. Stop fighting me. Is this why you stayed away from the hospital?"

He nodded, hiccupping.

"Katarina figured it out. Of all the people, she took me aside after *Swan Lake*."

Well, it seemed she was destined to be haunted by the specter of Katarina even like this.

"How would she..." Juliette trailed off, remembering that Katarina used to joke that there was no sex in the USSR and how everyone was so closeted. It was such a taboo, in fact, nobody would mention it nor discuss it, and people just disappeared...

Gabriel shrugged.

"She said a dancer, some soloist who she knew was gay and had been touring with the company in the US, one day never came to classes or rehearsals and nobody ever talked about him. Katarina being Katarina went and checked on him, and he was in bad shape. Coughing, you know..."

Juliette once again marveled at how sheltered she had

remained and how involved in the world Katarina had been. How present. Despite the detachment, the coldness, the appearance of being too good to even share a room with a member of the corps, here she was looking up people who stopped coming to work.

"Well, thank goodness for Saint Katarina." Juliette couldn't keep the bitterness out of her tone, and Gabriel turned his hand palm up and threaded their fingers.

"I don't know what to say about her, Jett. She went with me to talk to a doctor and then she fucked you over. How can both of those things be true? How can both of those people be her? She held my hand and told me how much she cared about you—"

"Stop!" Juliette wrenched her fingers out of his and covered her face. What was it about this woman who was so embedded in all Juliette was surrounded by that she could not escape her? Katarina was everywhere, taking everything, leaving Juliette on the floor of a damn apartment in a strange part of town…

Gabriel wrapped his arms around his torso, and they sat in silence for a while, the clock on the wall measuring the time and fear unspooling between them. A spiderweb of emotions, pain, terror, all-consuming anxiety being weaved by the ticking of little black hands on a white plastic panel.

Juliette took a deep breath and pushed through the resentment and the pain of betrayal, still as vivid as the image of Katarina shivering under the cold Paris rain.

"Was it what's-his-name?" She didn't particularly care, there wasn't anything to be done now, only to move on, but she had a feeling this was the first time Gabriel had the chance to speak about any of this at length.

He closed his eyes and leaned back against the sofa, and she could see he was struggling with words.

"I was coughing, you know I was. Though, damn, Garnier is draftier than usual this season. And then I noticed a spot.

On my pec. Just one. But you know how it is. You remember Ziggy?"

"Vaguely, Gabe."

All she did recall was that he had died so quickly, all alone, and that initially no hospital in Paris wanted to care for him. She squeezed Gabriel's forearm and tried to force the horror images out of her mind.

"So when Katarina mentioned the possibility of the virus, I kinda knew already. I was afraid to come to the hospital." He wiped his eyes and held on to Juliette's hand as if it were a lifeline. Perhaps it was. "I went to see Thierry. Our Thierry. Can you imagine? The one we all trust with our bodies."

Juliette closed her eyes. Hadn't she seen Gabriel and Thierry teasing each other, looking for all intents and purposes as lovers? It had never crossed her mind that Thierry…

"I confronted him, Jett." Gabriel's tone was full of confusion. "And he admitted it. He knew. Thierry knew all along and he told nobody. He knew, Jett. How could he do this to me?" His shoulders shook again, sobs interrupting his words, and Juliette gathered him in her arms.

"He told me to keep my mouth shut and to go fuck myself, that he would deny everything. I slapped him and ran. I just ran and I went to Pont au Charge—"

"Gabriel! What the hell? You went to the bridge Javert jumped from? Were you—"

Gabriel actually smiled, and Juliette smacked his arm.

"You moron! You scared me!"

"Shhh, darlin', I wasn't going to jump. Well, the thought crossed my mind, but damn, I don't know how one even does that. The bridge seemed rather low to achieve anything but cripple you…"

He trailed off and laid gentle fingertips on her bandaged leg.

"I'm sorry, darlin'. I'm sorry. I'm just so damn sorry about everything."

She placed her hand on top of his much larger one and watched his eyes fill up again.

"What am I going to do, Jett? I'm sick… What the fuck am I going to do?"

Juliette gripped his hand tighter and tried to keep her own tears at bay. "We. My poor darling, we. What are we going to do? I can't walk, and you're sick. And neither of us can dance anymore. But we'll figure it out, Gabe, together."

She lifted his chin and pushed his face into her neck, holding him as he tried unsuccessfully to calm down, his hiccups interrupting the silence of the room.

The sound of a throat clearing from the door made them both look up.

"Well, Francesca is on the phone, and I think she might have the solution. For both of you."

Twenty-Five
Of New Seasons & Emergency Contacts

People often said that Manhattan in the fall could rival Paris. For sentimentality, if nothing else. Too bad Manhattan and its quirky worldly beauty was lost on Juliette. She missed the leaves falling off the chestnuts in the Jardin du Luxembourg with a pain as acute as if she had been sitting on those benches and felt the foliage on her own shoulders just yesterday.

She missed so many things. Which was the real loss of her life? The winding streets or the bright boulevards? The gardens and bridges? The City of Lights itself?

Or the dancing? The ability to command the entire audience with one move of her fingers? The ovations? The curtain calls?

She squeezed the handle of the polished black cane that had kept her company for all these years since she and Gabriel had left Paris.

Seven years ago. Seven more surgeries. Some hope of returning to the stage despite her own better judgment. Francesca offering to wait for her to recover and begin anew with the New York Ballet.

And Juliette had begun anew, just not as a dancer anymore. Because of the cane. Well, because her knee never quite recovered, but who cared about those semantics? So instead of the new face of New York's most prestigious ballet company, Juliette Lucian-Sorel had become the one who made them all dance by accepting the position of Head Choreographer under Francesca's directorship.

Seven years on, and they had gone from success to success. Juliette sipped her impeccably brewed coffee and leafed through the overnight copy of the *New York Times*, the arts supplement all aflutter with enthusiasm and superlatives about yesterday's opening night of *Don Quixote*.

"Took us all these damn years to finally stage it right."

"Are you talking to yourself, Juju?"

Juliette turned around and smiled. Her former roommate looked good. Very good, if she were to judge, and who better than her, since she had been by his side through it all and knew every wrinkle on his handsome face.

"I kinda miss this place, darlin'. Mostly I miss your coffee, though." He reached for her mug, snatching it from her fingers. Juliette just shook her head and poured herself another one.

"I should be mad that you moved, but you and Gustavo are seriously adorable."

Gabriel smiled, his eyes going soft.

"Who'd have thought, Jett? Francesca's little brother and me?"

Juliette bused his clean-shaven cheek and wrapped her arms around his body, muscular and sturdy as ever.

No, not as ever. But as in the days before…

"You're the catch here, Flanagan."

He sighed and hugged her back. They stood in the quiet kitchen, cars speeding below on the busy street the only noise interrupting their gentle swaying.

"Did you think, sitting on the cold floor in that empty rental in Paris, you hobbling around on one leg and me crying and scared of dying of AIDS, that we'd be here?"

He whispered the last part of his question, the reality of his disease still an ever-present fear despite how far they'd come.

"Well, I had no idea we'd get you into the first-ever trial for antiretroviral therapy. Then again, you were always such an overachiever. Once you were in, I knew you'd excel and be their model patient."

They laughed, an easy, relieved sound, though both knew that Juliette was lying through her teeth. The trial was rough, Gabriel's body taking time to respond to medication and Juliette nursing him through a myriad of side effects. But then, a new cocktail of pills, another medical breakthrough, and one day Gabriel's color had returned. Suddenly, he could run up the stairs. His strength returned. He quietly got a job on Broadway as a backup dancer and teacher.

And life went on. Francesca's younger brother, Gustavo, a theater set designer, was an unexpected development, but once he arrived, he was the most welcome occurrence. He didn't care about the disease, he only had eyes for Gabriel. His "beautiful boy," as Gustavo called him, and honestly, Juliette teared up every time she saw the two of them together.

Gustavo had some strange friends, including an up-and-coming film director, a severe-looking woman with purple eyes who acted like she was better than all of them and whom Francesca secretly and not so secretly despised.

And life went on still. Out of all the scenarios into which Gabriel's story could unfold, this one—them, happy, employed, and on their feet—had been the least probable seven years ago. She put her palm on his cheek. Clear, smiling, joyful eyes met hers, and she smiled back.

Gustavo had a ring. He had dragged Juliette all over town to pick it out. He would propose tonight, and Juliette couldn't wait for Gabriel to burst in tomorrow morning and scoop her up, twirl her in circles as he was prone to, screaming with joy that he was going to get married.

And no, it wasn't legal, but they'd have a wonderful ceremony.

Francesca already had everything planned, the venue, the guest list. The fact that nobody spoke the one name with a question mark in front of it—despite being one of Gabriel's earliest supporters—was not a surprise.

Not a single soul mentioned Katarina Vyatka around her. No one alluded to Paris Opera Ballet. It would mean speaking of her, because of how immense she had become at Palais Garnier. She was now synonymous with it. The president had named her Prima Assoluta. Only the second one of a kind in France.

It had been seven years. Juliette had not moved on, and everyone around her knew it. How embarrassing.

"Darlin'…" Of course Gabriel would see through her. He lifted her chin, a gesture so familiar Juliette had to squeeze her eyes shut to avoid tears spilling.

"I'm sorry. I'm thoughtless…" He bit his lip.

"No, you're silly. And you're happy. I'm the one who is sorry for being maudlin." Juliette gave his cheek a peck.

"Shh." He gathered her back at his chest. "I wish… God, I don't know. I wish for so many things. I wish you'd forgive her. I wish you'd forgive yourself. I wish you'd allow yourself to move on."

Juliette felt her mouth fall open.

What the hell…

"You wish I'd forgive her? How dare you!"

He gingerly stepped away from her and looked around warily, as if judging whether she'd throw something at him, then, perhaps deciding that the risk was worth it, simply sat down at the kitchen table.

"It's been seven years and nobody knows what happened and nobody is happy."

Juliette felt the knife twist in her chest.

"She lied and she used me and she used all of us to get my job, Gabriel. Have you forgotten?" Juliette felt the world tilt, her anger making her see red.

"I haven't forgotten, Jett. But there are two sides to every story and then there's the truth. And you, of all people, are the one who told me that. You are the fairest person I've ever known. The most open-minded. You've wallowed in your pain for seven years and you don't even know why."

Juliette actually growled. She set her cane down very carefully, lest she'd do something she might regret. Annoyingly, he didn't even flinch when she pushed it aside.

"Saying that nobody knows what happened doesn't make it so. We know very well what happened. She defected in Paris to get my position. And she got in my bed to make sure she had me sufficiently distracted to not notice her machinations. Nobody knew? Everyone knew! You, Francesca, Helena, all of you told me she was after my job. That I should not trust her. That I should be careful. Now you tell me, how am I not being fair? How am I not being open-minded? I think opening all the doors for her, including the one to my bedroom, to my fucking heart, was more than fair and open-minded."

She felt more than heard her own voice rising to a scream at the end of the sentence, and yet Gabriel sat silently, watching her, pity and chagrin stark in his eyes.

"Gabriel, honestly, just go already. I never forbade you to speak to her. If you miss her, you should call her, for crying out loud."

He shook his head, then got up and squeezed her shoulder gently.

"Now who's silly, Jett? I'd never do anything to cause you pain. She's allowed to come to my funeral, nothing else. You are my friend. My darling one, who was by my side when hardly anyone else was. Who nursed me, washed my bedding, and changed my bandages when I needed them. I love you. And I'm sorry I even brought her up. I just heard…"

He trailed off, and Juliette sighed.

"You heard what?"

"Paris Opera Ballet revived *Swan Lake*. Francesca's version. And they are taking it on the road."

Juliette closed her eyes. The memory of Katarina and her dancing the pas de deux together, the gentle arms around her, those fingers in hers, the exhilaration of performing a seduction on stage in front of hundreds of people, wanting those lips on hers…

When she opened her eyes, Gabriel's brimmed with tears.

"I hate this, Jett. I hate that you are stuck."

"I'm… I feel like I lost myself, along the years, in between cities, among all the regrets."

She reached for the cane and stepped away from him. Her leg suddenly leaden, Juliette moved slower, her own tragedy, the reminder of everything she had lost, her career, her legacy, all dead, on various operating tables, in bloody clumps of white sponges and bandages, all wailing along with the damaged ligaments of her knee.

"But I'm not stuck, Gabe. I had a date just yesterday." Technically they'd had coffee, but he did not need to know that.

His scoff was answer enough as to his thoughts on the hour she'd spent drinking subpar brew with someone Francesca had set her up with.

"I'd ask you what her name was, but you'll make one up to cover for the fact that she was entirely unremarkable."

Juliette allowed a small smile. He wasn't wrong, but she wasn't going to admit it so easily.

"Don't you have to go, you goof?"

"Ha, I knew I was right." He raised his arms and did a little hip shimmy. Juliette felt her smile widen. Well, if anyone could change her mood after pissing her off, it would be him.

But then his face turned serious again, and she sighed. He could be like a dog with a bone.

"I want you happy, Jett. Life is circles. They're all around us. You said goodbye to the most promising career modern ballet has ever known. You've established yourself as the most exciting choreographer in the US, if not in the world, and yet you go on dates with women whose names you can't even make yourself remember the next day. And Katarina Vyatka is coming to New York."

He exhaled loudly at the end of his long list.

"Which one of those bothers you most, Gabriel? I won't start a fight with her when she performs on my stage. Are you that afraid of my reaction?"

He rolled his eyes. "It's the first one. That one hurts me, darlin'. That you aren't happy. And I'm not scared you'll fill her pointe shoes with glass… Shit." He slapped himself over the forehead and fell silent.

"You know that has never been my modus operandi. Maybe Katarina's, if Rodion Foltin and everyone else is to be believed—"

"I never believed that. And you never should have believed him, darlin'. He's a user. He wrung Paris Opera Ballet dry, and he did it for his own selfish egomaniac reasons. Nothing he has ever said was without an agenda."

"Gabriel…" Juliette felt the years of memories press heavily on her shoulders. "He said what he said, and she never once contradicted him."

"We don't know that. You don't know that. She was a survivor, above all else. And she was afraid—"

"Do we have to do this now?" Juliette touched his sternum, her own chest almost caving in from the pain of reliving. "I don't care enough to do anything to her, so don't worry about glass. I'm sure I will run into her at some reception or another." Juliette wisely sidestepped the issue of Gabriel's upcoming wedding since he didn't yet know about the proposal nor about Francesca burning the phones to Paris to request the presence of all his friends. Juliette wondered if Francesca would invite Katarina. Gabriel, loyal to a fault as he was, clearly loved her and was also grateful to her for being the first to guess his condition, to see his secret and embrace him instead of shunning him.

A thought for another day.

"You will be late for your date, and poor Gustavo is going to be impatient." She motioned with her cane toward the door, and he nodded.

"Now who is being silly and not subtle? That man will wait for me forever, haven't you heard? I'm his beautiful boy!" He said it with the biggest grin, and Juliette felt her own lips stretch in response.

"Yeah, yeah, I heard." She winked at him and bit her lip. He did not need to know how Gustavo had talked her ear off about how much he loved this gorgeous creature during their day of hunting for an engagement ring. Oh, she would tell him all about it soon, and she would tease them both so much about how utterly ridiculous they were in their sappiness. But for now, she pushed Gabriel to the door and kissed his soft, smooth cheek.

"Think of what I said, Jett."

It was her turn to roll her eyes.

"You've done nothing but talk for hours. Go already."

He gave her one last hug, a long warm one that seemed to envelop her whole and cushion the blow of his next sentence.

"You've been grieving someone who's very much alive, Jett. Are you sure the wake you've been holding for years isn't for your own heart?" He kissed her brow and quietly closed the door behind himself. She could hear him whistling as he skipped down the stairs.

Juliette sat down in the chair he had vacated and allowed his words to seep into her skin. Then she lowered her eyes and confessed.

"*She* was my heart, Gabriel."

***

You never quite know when your life, like brittle bone, will shatter all over again. And you never really think it will be a phone call and a stranger's voice asking if your name is Juliette Lucian-Sorel and informing you that as Gabriel Flanagan's emergency contact you should come to the Presbyterian hospital.

"How is he? What happened? I'll be there immediately! I'm just a few blocks away—" Juliette shouted into the receiver, only to hear a sigh on the other end of the line. The sirens in the distance sounded like crows. Juliette's heart was a drum in her ears. And then, it paused. In total silence, the thread of fate was snapped.

"I'm sorry, ma'am. There's no need to rush anymore."

Twenty-Six
Of Unannounced Visits & Ruination

Funerals are such peculiar events. People come, bring food, talk about the dead, and then they leave and you pick up the pieces and life goes on. As if you didn't just drop six feet of dirt on top of a huge part of it.

Juliette watched the long line of people pass by the casket. Some touched it, some placed flowers on it, some cried, some didn't. On her right, Gustavo had not stopped shaking since they'd arrived at the graveyard. He had been doing so well until then, but she guessed he had reached his limit. Francesca held his arm as tears streamed down his cheeks.

The enigmatic, haughty, very young, and very aloof woman with violet eyes stood by his other side. Blackthorne something or other. Juliette hadn't caught her first name. Her demeanor reminded her too much of Katarina. Entirely unapproachable.

So Juliette just nodded at the stranger and did not speak to her. There was no need for words. Words fixed nothing. She closed her eyes, and when she opened them, Rodion Foltin was placing a large bouquet of pink roses on the casket. Juliette sighed. He actually struck a pose before moving on, and she felt like slapping him. She gripped the handle of her cane tighter.

Motherfucker.

And then words she thought she had not needed simply

died in her mouth. Katarina Vyatka stood at the side of the crowd. She held a red carnation, her face was bowed. And she was everything.

She must've flinched, because Helena, who had just arrived due to some emergency at the hospital and had missed most of the funeral, touched her arm inquisitively.

"Jett? What is it?"

Juliette shook her head, but Helena followed her line of sight, and then cold fingers were clasping Juliette's skin tighter before relaxing their grip.

"I wondered if she'd show."

Juliette blinked.

"You did? It genuinely did not occur to me at all."

"Just because you wanted her to disappear, Jett, didn't make it so. And he loved her."

Juliette felt tears sting the backs of her eyes.

"The last words we exchanged were about me forgiving her. He was so adamant, Hels."

Helena said nothing, just squeezed Juliette's arm one more time.

Returning to her empty apartment was an unpleasant shock. Gabriel had moved out weeks ago and yet the place still held so much of him. Juliette fought tears. Pictures, slippers, a sweater she had commandeered and he graciously never took back. He was everywhere.

The knock dragged her mind to the present, and she swiped at her eyes hastily. It was probably Francesca or Helena, who had a key and never really knocked. Still, today was such an odd day.

She opened the door and the day got stranger. But also more beautiful. Overwhelmingly so. Juliette wanted to slap herself for even thinking it, but who was to know? She'd never tell a soul.

Katarina Vyatka was standing on her doorstep, holding a folded piece of paper and an envelope. And she brought all the beauty with her. Time had been powerless over her. She was a vision still.

No crimson blood, nor white satin to echo the first time Juliette saw her. In a simple, demure black dress, and without saying a word, Katarina opened every scar Juliette had spent years sewing back together.

The blue eyes were so wide, so bright, as if she had been scared of who might be on the other side of the threshold, as if she had been afraid that the door would open at all. Katarina's right arm was raised halfway, perhaps about to knock again, and Juliette watched it fall to her side in slow motion.

A second passed, a day, a week, a month. A year. And then seven and they were here, in a place that wasn't theirs, in a city that never slept and that had never been as full of light as the one they both belonged to.

Katarina's face was translucent. She seemed thin. Much thinner than she had been years ago, and she was willowy even then. Her angular cheeks had taken on a sharp quality that looked almost gaunt in the dispersed light of Juliette's doorway.

She had to say something, because this staredown had gone on for eternity and Juliette knew she'd start crawling out of her skin if it continued for a moment longer.

Except Katarina spoke first, and Juliette felt her own shoulders relax at the sheer sound of the silence breaking like glass between them.

"I apologize for showing up unannounced."

Juliette watched this almost stranger bite her lip, fingers crumpling the envelope in her hands tightly, paper crinkling under them. Well, at least she wasn't the only anxious one.

Words were stuck in Juliette's throat. She had no idea what might come out of her mouth if she let them. Seven years was a long time, and seven years was a blink of an eye. And it turned out that no matter how many times she imagined this meeting— and to her credit, she was woman enough to admit that she had done quite a lot of imagining—Juliette had not been ready for it.

She moved aside and gestured to Katarina to come in. The

wide eyes followed the motion of the black stick with something too close to pity for Juliette's comfort, and so she very deliberately set the cane down by the door, the wood making a satisfying sound against the sideboard.

Katarina drew a deep breath and took a step in, then another, and in no time at all Juliette watched as the one person she had never expected to cross this threshold stood in the middle of her living room.

"Life is so bizarre." She didn't bother explaining herself even as she regretted that these were her first words to Katarina.

Her fingers pushed the door closed and, willing her legs to move, Juliette crossed the space she had called her home for the last seven years, trying not to see it through Katarina's eyes. She had a feeling it would be found lacking, and that made her irrationally angry.

The rooms were New York small, nothing like their place on Rue de Rivoli with its airy, tall ceilings and massive windows letting in the gentle Parisian morning light.

Belatedly, it registered that she had thought of the Parisian apartment as theirs, and she cursed herself for a fool. Seven years and this woman still held her in the palm of her hand.

Katarina's impossibly wide eyes seemed to widen even more at the cursing.

"I'm sorry… Juliette… I'll go."

But she did not move from the spot where Gabriel had stood just five days ago, and Juliette felt her chest simply cave in. The armchair was the closest harbor for her tired body, and she sat down gingerly, wondering if even a tiny flinch would shatter her bones. Where had this fragility come from?

"Why are you here?"

It seemed like a fair question to ask someone you'd not seen for a lifetime, and yet it also felt like the most foolish thing to say out loud. Tears threatened, screams too, and Juliette clamped her lips tighter, desperately clinging to whatever social graces she still possessed.

Katarina appeared to fight an inner battle of her own, as she kept standing motionless in the middle of the room. Juliette's worry about what she might see and what she might think about how she lived now was in vain, as Katarina looked at nothing but Juliette herself.

The eyes gleamed with sadness. But then, they always looked sad. Except this time they were almost lifeless, and as someone who just came from a funeral, that angered Juliette more. How dare she? How dare Katarina Vyatka be here and look like she had been buried for the past seven years?

"Gabriel wrote to me a few months ago. He gave me your address." Katarina unclenched her fingers from around the envelope and Juliette recognized the familiar chicken scratch. Gabriel's cursive had always been atrocious.

Well, isn't this swell.

Her dead best friend from beyond his early grave sent her the ex she had grieved for years. The ex who broke her, who ruined her life, who took everything from her.

Juliette smiled and then let out a peel of laughter. It sounded a touch hysterical. The second one was no longer just a touch so. The desperation and loneliness rang loudly.

Tears came then, laughter tuning into a cry on a dime, and in an instant Katarina was on her knees in front of her. Juliette bowled over, folding over her own chest, her own grief, and Katarina's trembling hands, cold, always so cold, were on her neck, on her forehead, her lips at her ear, whispering something as utterly foolish as, "Please, my love, please…"

"How can I be your love? How can I be anything to you when you did this? All of this? Tell me? How many KGB files are there in Moscow with my name on them? How many of them have you studied to know your mark before defecting, Comrade Vyatka? I loved you, and you lied to me and you played me like a toy, and then exactly like a toy you broke me—"

"And I ruined myself in the process!" Katarina finally found her voice, the hoarse whisper gone and the rusty shout escaping. So unexpected, so undignified, so unlike the Empress of Moscow Juliette knew. Their tear-filled eyes met, and Katarina looked away before continuing speaking, no longer bothering with how loud she sounded.

"I never lied to you. Yes, I defected to Paris because I knew Juliette Lucian-Sorel had been getting bad reviews for years and was vulnerable. And then I saw you… There wasn't anything vulnerable about you. You were the best dancer I'd ever laid eyes on, you were the perfect ballerina, and I had no chance to ever upstage you. And I never wanted to."

Juliette tugged her fingers out of the ice-cold ones gripping them like a vise.

"Could've fooled me."

Katarina's hands, now empty, fell to her lap, and the feel of that skin on hers, the familiarity of it despite only knowing it for such a short time, infuriated Juliette all over again.

"You were the love of my life, Katarina. And then you were the ruin of it."

Katarina glanced at the cane by the door, and Juliette sighed. She could throw many stones, many faults at Katarina's feet, but this wasn't one of them. Juliette pushed up, giving her all to not falter.

"No, you can flagellate yourself about a lot of things, but my career will not be on your conscience." The lump in her throat was threatening to choke her, yet Juliette went on, determined to end this conversation that was draining the life out of her.

"My heart, my job in Paris, my trust, my ability to hold on to a normal relationship. Yes, for all of those, you are solely responsible, Your Majesty. But that cane? The fact that I never danced again?" Juliette threw her head back and laughed. The hysteria was not far off.

"You didn't break my tibia, nor tore my knee, or my hamstring. And I guess I could've come back from one of those, maybe two, but not even the great Lucian-Sorel could overcome her tendons simply shredding underneath her no matter how many surgeries followed. And trust me, I had so many my knee has more scar tissue than skin these days."

She was breathing far too fast, the vein in her neck fluttering so hard Juliette had to cover it with her fingers.

"Juliette—"

"No! Why did you come? To seek forgiveness? To buy an indulgence? Well, it's free. I absolve you. You didn't take ballet from me." The sound of her exhalation echoed in the room and Katarina's tears finally fell, off the butterfly lashes and down the gaunt cheeks.

Juliette was almost certain Katarina had no idea she was crying, so focused those eyes were on her. Still, Juliette wasn't finished. And wasn't it strange that in a day that started with her having no words, she couldn't stop spewing them now when she perhaps should leave herself some of that armor of silence?

Katarina looked away, and Juliette realized that she couldn't have that. Not while she had her here. In this space. In this sanctuary she had created for herself. In this nest Juliette had woven out of broken bones and broken promises.

She took a step, and they were inches apart. That feeling, Katarina's body heat, was like a punch of whiskey to an empty stomach—painful, sly, teasing, pleasurable, and ultimately deadly. Orange blossoms enveloped her. The scent of home, the scent of her. Her own tears threatened.

Juliette lifted her hand and touched Katarina's chin, raising it till they were eye to eye again. Katarina's trademark gesture, Katarina's trademark gaze. The years between them were erased and only pain remained. Hers. Katarina's. And all the guilt. Well, some of it Juliette could heal.

"I ruined ballet for myself, Katarina. And now I get to create it and watch it but never dance it. I am at peace with it. I hope you can be too." Juliette allowed herself one more indulgence, one more forbidden pleasure. Her fingers traveled down Katarina's neck, where the aorta greeted her with a fluttering very much in sync to her own, and she smiled. God, they had destroyed each other ten times over and yet they were still here, one breath away, one whimper away from burning each other's world all over again.

Katarina's face showed nothing, the fingers at her throat seeming to not even register as the right corner of her mouth lifted in a sarcastic smirk.

"Peace?" Her tone, hoarse, measured, a touch insane, scraped Juliette raw. "The biggest talent to have ever danced will never step on the floorboards of a stage. The love of my life will never know how much I regret the circumstances of everything that happened between us. And the world keeps turning. I keep performing. And you keep seeing nameless, faceless people who will never love you the way you are loved. Here."

Katarina's closed fist connected with her chest, the *thump* like a detonation making Juliette's ears ring.

"You have no right to speak of these things." Her own voice nothing but a snapped string, Juliette panted through an impending panic attack.

"No, Juliette. I'll have my say. I have been silent for seven years and I'd still be silent if that gorgeous fool hadn't gone and broken everyone's heart by getting hit by a fucking truck. He survived the virus and a goddamn drunk driver took him. And he had the gall to send me a sermon on forgiveness and how short life is. And when I didn't answer him, he went and died on me, on you, on that man who will never be the same, because Flanagan was right. Yes, damn him, life is short. So here I am, Juliette. Scream, yell, curse, but listen to me. And forgive me."

Juliette gritted her teeth.

How dare she!

"Get out, Katarina. Not everything is about you. Not his life, not mine. I have lived without you for seven years. And you were just fine without me as well. Prima Assoluta, Étoile, success after success, rave reviews, performance after performance, Paris at your feet. Did I tick all the boxes? What else have you ever wanted?"

"You! Flay me for understanding too late that all I ever wanted was you. And before you say again that I was just fine, have you tried watching everything you've ever dreamt of be snatched away from you because you yourself are too weak to fight for it? I was scared, damn you!"

Katarina's cheeks were finally burning, and Juliette was mesmerized by the fire.

"I was being blackmailed and I couldn't go back. I'd be dead. If not by their hands, then by my own. I could never go back there! To that country. To that place. To those people, who hunted me and tormented me and made me dance like their puppet on a string. And you were leaving! Shannon Robbards was about to make you an offer and you never told me!"

Leaving? Shannon?

Juliette blinked, the barrage of information sweeping her up, but Katarina wasn't done.

"You were leaving, and you were leaving me behind." Katarina swallowed jerkily, coughed, then closed her eyes. When she opened them, her voice was quieter, the panic gone. Only sorrow remained.

"I had a moment of weakness. The one you witnessed. I said yes to Foltin. I said yes to stop the deluge of threats. To give myself some time." Katarina licked her lips, and then her smile was all sharp edges of regret. "Turns out I ran out of time in the exact three minutes it took you to flee to the stage and break your leg. And there has never been a second that I haven't blamed myself for that weakness, Juliette. For letting his lies and his viciousness scare me. Plant doubt in me. I blame myself with every breath. Every class. Every tendu. Every fouetté. Every ballet I dance. It should be you, and I should be watching from the audience, adoring you."

Juliette felt more than heard her own whimper. Katarina reached out, her fingers no longer cold, and wiped away a stray tear. Juliette almost leaned into the touch. Almost.

"And so I lost everything. I lost you, Juliette. And I lost ballet. Even if I keep dancing, the joy, the life of it is gone from me. And every day I am alone in the place we shared, and all I think about is that I am the only one to blame. Juliette, have you tried blaming yourself for seven years for making a choice so wrong it destroyed two lives?"

Juliette gulped down her sorrow, the pain making her back teeth sing. This was all too much. She needed to punch something—and preferably do it while she was alone, lest she broke another bone in Katarina's presence.

"You need to leave, Katarina. You'll be back in New York soon enough. I'll be polite. You'll perform *Swan Lake* and dance Odette, as you always wanted, and I will pretend that it isn't my part. You'll get your grand reviews and five curtain calls. And we will both pretend we don't know each other. Life will move on. And I need you to move on too."

Katarina gave her a strange, faraway look before nodding and taking a few steps toward the front door. Juliette heard the door open, and then Katarina's words reached her before the sound of the door closing did.

"I dance on your stage, I look in your mirror in your dressing room, I sleep in your bed in your apartment on your street. I have nowhere to move on, Juliette. I've given up trying."

Twenty-Seven
Of Chain-smoking & Last Bows

The door shut, the words like mustard gas slithered to the floor, heavier than air, poisoning everything around them. Juliette closed her eyes and then opened the window. Greenwich Village was full of conversations and tidings of fall, and after a few deep inhalations, she decided the poison was better.

Other people were their own hell, and autumn was a reminder of all her "nevers." The opening of a new ballet season she'd never dance in. Or a tour she'd never go on. Or Katarina Vyatka, whom she'd never see again.

Katarina Vyatka, who dared to walk through life as a martyr. Who lived wounded, who tore her own muscles and tendons and never quite allowed any of those wounds to heal. How dare she? And how dare she come here?

Juliette flung herself to the sofa, then remembered Gabriel sitting exactly there, just a few days ago, looking at her with pity. Because it was her, Juliette, who was swearing up and down a Manhattan afternoon that she had moved on, went on dates, and had a full life.

Well, he sure showed her. Writing to Katarina, begging her to attempt a reconciliation, chipping at Juliette's armor, pointing to her how utterly ridiculous she had been, and then going out and getting himself killed. And here Juliette sat in the damn room that still smelled of the tobacco he favored and still held his last mangled butt in the ashtray.

Juliette reached over and plucked a cigarette from the limp pack with a shaking hand. Said shaking made the lighter take forever to flicker to life, and every single unsuccessful *snick* got Juliette madder.

In fact, she had been enraged since the call from Presbyterian. Maybe for seven years, but for the purpose of exorcism of this particular demon, she'd settle on this timeline.

The smoke enveloped her in the familiar fog, and Juliette prayed it would erase the orange blossom lingering in the air.

How dare Gabriel write to Katarina? And how dare he die? After they had survived so much, after she had gone with Gustavo and bought him a ring? And how dare Katarina come to New York? This was Juliette's city now. Juliette's street, Juliette's apartment. And now she was chain-smoking to drive the scent of Katarina deeper into the cracks in the walls. It would resurface in the middle of winter nights and haunt her dreams, her waking hours, lacing everything like arsenic.

She looked down at her fingers and realized she'd snapped the cigarette in half. When she reached for the pack again, it was empty. And wasn't that a fitting last drop, last straw, last everything that broke all the backs, filled all the cups, and she screamed, allowing her throat to take the brunt of her impotence to do anything but love this one woman who for some reason would never just leave.

Juliette stood up and lifted the phone from the hook. She couldn't yell at Gabriel for going behind her back, for dying, for leaving her to face all of this alone, but she could do something about Katarina.

When a tired hello greeted her on the other end of the line, Juliette knew that this was a sign indeed. Francesca had never been home at this hour in all the years she had known her.

"Cesca, where is Foltin staying in New York?"

There was rustling and then a sound of things falling, making Juliette pull the receiver away from her ear. More coughing, and then a Zippo lighting and Francesca inhaling. After two drags, Juliette heard her drink a sip of something. She tapped her fingers on the coffee table and tried not to lose her temper yet. She needed it for later.

"Four Seasons."

Two words. No questions. No commentary. Another long drag and another sip. More clothes rustling. Francesca said nothing more, and it was Juliette's turn to exhale.

"Thank you."

"You're welcome. Tell Bernard the concierge I sent you, and give him twenty dollars. He'll tell you the room number you actually need."

It was the *actually* that made Juliette bite her lip. Of course Francesca knew all too well whom Juliette needed to see. The fact that she basically rolled out the red carpet for her to find Katarina spoke volumes.

"I… I should go, Cesca."

"You really should, Jett. It's been seven years. You really should." The sadness in Francesca's tone only made Juliette angrier.

She nursed her anger all through the taxi ride to Madison Avenue, through the lobby and the painful search for a tiny man named Bernard who, despite being an entire foot shorter than her, still managed to look down his nose at her and the extended twenty-dollar bill.

The slow elevator, all opulence and useless flowery, enhanced the fury, and by the time she was standing in front of the room with an ornate plaque showing 1259, Juliette was certain steam would be coming out of her ears any moment.

The fact that Katarina opened the door before Juliette could give it a good knock was like a starting gun.

"Juliette—"

"Do not Juliette me!" She pushed past Katarina, who didn't even have the decency to be surprised by her presence. Juliette had turned predictable. And she was being foolish. Gabriel must have been nodding sagely up there on his cloud, or perhaps laughing his excellent angel ass off, since he would be more prone to the latter than the former.

"What would you want me to do to you, Juliette?"

And the question, the sheer exhaustion in it, the finality of that misery, tore at something in Juliette, and she stepped to Katarina and then into her.

Their lips crashed together, teeth clashing, Juliette tasting blood, not even caring if it was hers or Katarina's. If anything, the coppery tang only enhanced the taste of her. The one taste she had never been able to find no matter how many women she kissed.

Katarina hissed in pain and Juliette let go immediately, only for two cold hands to grasp her shoulders and pull her back. Juliette grabbed the collar of that ridiculously attractive blouse and tore. The buttons spilled all around them, revealing a stunning lace bustier, and Katarina simply pushed the magnificent garment down before dragging Juliette's hands over her skin to cover her breasts.

It was like lightning, one they had ridden before, and they moaned in unison, the sound obscene and entirely too perfect. Their mouths fused together, Juliette pushed Katarina into the door she had just walked through, and the satisfying rattling noise was accompanied by another moan. They were greedy, anxious, desperate.

Juliette couldn't get enough of the bloody lips under hers, and Katarina matched her kiss for kiss, lick for lick, bite for bite. When Juliette left the impossible temptation of the swollen lips and moved to the exposed neck, Katarina sighed and plunged her hands into Juliette's hair, fingers pulling and tugging in rhythm with the bites. And Juliette made sure to leave many, sparing not an inch of skin.

The bite to the junction of neck and shoulder, as always, caused a whimper, and Juliette smiled against the sensitive spot, the bruise blooming like tulip petals. She left another one right next to it before noticing once again how slim the shoulders had gotten. How under her hands Katarina was all bone and sinew, somehow smaller, fragile, painfully so.

Her face must've shown exactly where her thoughts had gone, or maybe her hands on Katarina's rib cage, going slack, revealed the true story, because Katarina gripped her chin, and the old gesture was neither affectionate nor gentle.

"In your apartment, you told me not to pity you. Well, same goes, Juliette. Fuck me or leave me."

Juliette knew she was given a choice, but the hand on her face was not letting go and the other in her hair still clutched as tight as a second ago, and she was only human. It had been seven years of wanting this. Of regretting this. Of loving Katarina and hating her and cursing her and missing her more than the ruined knee. More than ballet.

Juliette dove in again, their lips relinquishing none of their violence, drawing pain and drawing pleasure, and she let go. Of caution, of anger in the name of anger, of her own heart that had betrayed her all those years ago and still yearned for the one it could never quite have and settled to execute Katarina's order.

Fuck me.

Juliette could do that. She allowed her fingers to drag the tatters of the shirt down the lanky arms and slapped Katarina's helping hands from her skirt.

"No. You said to fuck you. So I will. Fuck you. And you'll take it."

A feral look crossed Katarina's face before she threw her head back, banging the door yet again, eliciting a smug smile from Juliette as she dragged her fingers down her abdomen.

"Tell me you'll take it, Katarina. Tell me you want it. Otherwise, why did you sleep with me for months when all you had to do was push me down the fucking stairs? Tell me!"

Juliette couldn't recognize her own voice, or even the intention behind it. This was not what she had come here for. She lowered her face, and when she lifted it up again, Katarina's eyes were looking at her with that knowing expression, of seeing through her, and Juliette leaned in one more time and kissed her with a tenderness that belied the moment.

"I want you now." The words came as soon as their lips separated and Katarina's hand rose to Juliette's cheek yet again, mirroring the gentleness of the kiss. This time like all those other times. Exactly like those other times. Juliette gritted her teeth against the onslaught of memories and the agony of regret.

"And I wanted you then. It's as simple as that, no matter how much I messed it all up for both of us."

Juliette wanted to ask, to respond, to contradict, but Katarina was having none of it, and the kiss that followed seemed to go for ages, from rough to tender, from her lip being bitten and sucked on, to their tongues meeting and tangling in slow motion. Juliette's head spun, and Katarina's hands on her face, their mouths together, were the only points of connection she felt she had to this room, to this life.

She allowed Katarina to push away from the door.

"We always ended up vertical somewhere. Do you ever wonder why it was standing wall sex for us?" Katarina's voice was teasing, but Juliette heard the past tense and the melancholy and wanted none of it. She also didn't want any more questions, or words.

She had no business being here, no business talking to Katarina Vyatka. And so she walked them backward in the direction of what looked like the doorway to the bedroom, and once Katarina fell on top of her, Juliette flipped them, prompting one of the low moans that always turned her insides to fire.

She moved past the remains of the blouse, the bustier she had dragged down, licking and biting, leaving a trail of little angry marks in her wake. Katarina seemed to revel in the roughness, writhing on the fresh-scented cotton, her fingers tangled in the sheets, seeking purchase.

Juliette did not bother with the skirt, simply pushing it up, and the garters and stockings waiting for her underneath took her breath away. She let her head drop on the satin ribbons for a second, breathing Katarina in, drinking in the scent she knew so well. Katarina wanting her. Katarina wet for her. Katarina desperate for her.

And Juliette knew it was all mirrored in her. She wanted, she was wet, and she was desperate. She pushed the drenched silk to the side and licked.

Katarina screamed, Juliette licked again, her tongue firm, her fingers clasping the pale thighs, leaving bruises.

The taste she knew she'd never be able to forget—now on her tongue and all over her face, as she kept licking and sucking on the tender flesh—brought back the memories of the simple happiness, of the joy and the love they had shared on Rue de Rivoli, and the magic of these memories erased the years between them. She was Juliette Lucian-Sorel, and Katarina Vyatka was her lover. They were in love, they were successful, they had the world at their feet.

Juliette spread Katarina's legs wider, and this time her impatience drove her to rip the panties, making Katarina let out a peel of laughter that ended on another moan as Juliette ran a finger slit to clit and then back down, spreading the wet and the hot desire, before leaning down again and inhaling her. Katarina panted, and Juliette smiled against the trembling flesh.

She drew the straining clit into her mouth and then slowly slid one, two, three fingers into Katarina, who covered her mouth with her palm, biting her own hand.

Juliette's smile turned to a smirk and she lapped harder,

curling the fingers in rhythm even as the thighs trembled and the body she held down bowed back like a string. When she let go and resorted to quick, firm flicks to the very tip of the clit, Katarina came.

The ice blue eyes watched hers through climax, never closing, the muscles around her fingers clamped tight and the hands tangled in the sheets gripped so hard that Juliette could have sworn she heard the cotton tear, and yet, Katarina made no sound. Her mouth opened in a silent cry, she slumped back on the bed, and for the next minute or two their breathing and the Manhattan traffic were the only sounds permeating the room.

When Juliette finally raised her face, Katarina's eyes were closed and her mouth was bleeding, the tiny rivulet of blood marring the perfect skin.

Why did they always make each other bleed? Hadn't Juliette bled enough for the two of them? She shook her head at the foolishness of her own thoughts and sat down, her back to Katarina.

This resolved nothing. As much as she delighted in still being able to make Katarina surrender, in the big scheme of things it meant nothing, and if anything, the chasm between them was wider than ever.

She sat motionless, arms on her knees, bent over the edge of the bed. Behind her, the rustling of clothes told her Katarina was setting herself to rights.

She settled down next to Juliette, promptly crossing her legs after sliding the mangled pair of underwear off them. She dropped the ruined lace between them like evidence of a crime slammed by a prosecutor on the table for the defendant to confess. Juliette bit the inside of her cheek to keep from speaking.

What could she say anyway? That she loved Katarina and had loved her for the past seven years? That she had come here to exact punishment for breaking her heart and yet she only hurt herself in the process? That she wanted Katarina to make love to her more than anything but knew she couldn't allow a single caress because Juliette felt she'd die if Katarina touched her again?

And yet Katarina sat still, that grace in repose she possessed on display to its full perfection. That grace she used to outwait and outwit her rival. Juliette felt the tears sting the back of her eyes. They had always been rivals, no matter how many times they fucked.

It was Katarina who lifted her face and looked straight into the nothingness of the empty hotel room wall and spoke first.

"I had surgery, Juliette."

The sentence seemed so out of place, and yet… Funny how years later and still Juliette knew exactly what Katarina was talking about.

"Cervical hernia?" There was no *I told you so* in Juliette's voice, just an honest question, and Katarina nodded before drawing in a deep breath and venturing a reply.

"I have had it since I was a child." She smiled, but her eyes were distant and cold. "When they came to arrest my father… They had to hold me back. I strained too hard against the arm of the agent trying to stop me from running to him. And I was afraid that it would prevent me from dancing. The more I danced, the better I got. And the worse my neck got. Ironically, it became my calling card to the world. Katarina Vyatka's révérence. I was too scared to—"

"To have it treated because you thought it would stop you from dancing. And if you weren't dancing, you thought you'd not be needed anymore. And that you'd not be able to escape. I'm sorry, Katarina."

And she was. Juliette felt the confession like a blow to her solar plexus. Was anything in the life of this woman not marred by the pain and horror of where she came from?

"I hated you so much for guessing it. For seeing through my bow, for seeing through me. I hated you because I was afraid of you, Juliette. Afraid you'd expose me. I guess I was right to be scared. Even if for other reasons."

Juliette felt the walls of the small room close in on her, the ceiling threatening to choke her any minute. She wanted to say something. How Katarina should never have been afraid of her, that Juliette would never hurt her. Except she had. And Katarina had been right all along.

"I take it you're done, Juliette." There was no question mark at the end of the sentence. And the way it echoed Juliette's own question at the hospital, about being finished with ballet… Well, it made sense. She was done with both.

Juliette had no idea what to say to that, and Katarina went on. "Is this what you came here for? To prove to me you can still have me? I don't think there was any doubt of that."

Juliette licked her suddenly dry lips, the taste of Katarina lingering. A blessing and a curse. Perhaps more the latter than the former. And the sheer truth of how much she wanted more, how much she wanted to let go and reach for Katarina again lit another match under the banking coals of her regret.

The show was over. It was time for the révérence. The last bow. There would be no curtain calls.

"I'm sorry, Katarina."

Juliette got up and picked up the cane, Katarina's "So am I" following her out of the room.

Twenty-Eight
Of Violence & Long Overdue Confrontations

The words would have actually followed Juliette right to Greenwich Village, except today wasn't done being a very strange day. She had buried a friend. She had damn near buried herself in a lover that had never quite become an ex.

And it seemed the universe was conspiring to make her face her mortality, her love, and her regret all in one fell swoop.

At the elevator bank, desperately clinging to her cane with one hand and pushing the button with the other, Juliette heard the light clearing of a throat behind her and knew instantly that whatever plans she had for this evening, they'd have to be delayed.

She wasn't done, not by a long shot. As she turned with as much grace as she could muster toward Rodion Foltin, Juliette knew that out of the many mistakes she had made over the years, everything she had done and especially abstained from when it came to this man had probably been her worst.

Because instead of standing her ground when he kept taking swaths of it upon his arrival at Paris Opera Ballet, Juliette had surrendered. Her role as the Étoile, the first Prima Assoluta of France, her parts in all the productions, her place in the history of French ballet, and most importantly, she had surrendered Katarina.

In the fog of anger and sex, Juliette had not considered Katarina's earlier words. The earnest confession at her apartment. That while Katarina had indeed betrayed her, she had not done so willingly. In the moment, and even now, with time and pain between them, the distinction hadn't mattered. A betrayal was still very much a betrayal.

But looking into the smug face of this man, Juliette knew she had been wrong to dismiss said distinction out of hand.

"Mademoiselle Lucian-Sorel." Foltin took a step forward, eyes gleaming with something akin to the self-satisfaction of a job well done. Well, he had indeed done a job on her years ago.

Cufflinks sparkling blindingly, he extended that spidery-fingered hand to her, and Juliette balled hers.

Same voice. The heavy-accented Russian attempting French, shooting for intriguing and falling straight into grating. The same tone. Going for mysterious and barely managing palatable. The man himself, tall and slim, almost bald, with an unfortunate combover that hid absolutely nothing yet served the purpose of pretenses.

Just like him. The con man, teetering on the verge of villainesque, was simply a regular fraud.

For years Juliette had thought him evil incarnate. Sure, Katarina was the other side of that villainous coin in her mind, but Foltin… Well, Foltin was the fulcrum of all her sorrows.

And yet, standing in front of her, that conceited smile on his face, Juliette could not for the life of her understand why she had let this man ruin her life.

Though… Had he?

The elevator beeped its arrival behind her. Foltin stretched his lips in an even more unpleasant imitation of human emotion, and Juliette had an epiphany.

He passed by her, clearly amused by her confusion and stupor, and she watched him go. Watched him press the button to the ground floor. Watched the hundred-year-old doors slowly close.

"What do you think you're doing?"

And now, when Juliette stuck her cane in the gap between the elevator doors and they sprang open for her, when she faced him full-on, when she took a few steps into the brightly lit square space covered in mirrors that oddly reminded her of the dancing classroom, Juliette heard what she had so wished to hear back in Paris.

The violence of steel hitting her trusty dark oak sounded in the quiet, luxurious air of the hotel, and the note of fear in the voice of a man whom she hated with all her heart settled something inside Juliette.

This man terrorized Katarina. This man was the one whom Juliette had allowed to make a mockery of her career and her prestige. And whom Juliette had blamed for the longest time for destroying all of it.

"Except, I ruined it all by myself…" Juliette murmured to herself before raising her voice to be heard. "I have nothing left to lose now, Foltin. Do you know what people who have nothing to lose do to others?"

She tilted her head to the side and gave him the slowest once-over. He took a faltering step back, his thin form reminding her of a roach, all mustache and filth. She held the cane firmly and moved closer to him. The doors closed behind her, and with her free hand she pressed the STOP button.

They tell you to take a deep breath before you begin the thirty-two fouettés, the series of fast, continuous spins on one leg being one of the most complicated movements in ballet. So difficult due to their exquisite technique, but also because they demand perfect balance. Juliette marveled at the simile. So much like her own life.

She took that prerequisite deep breath. Foltin yelped and lifted a hand in front of himself.

"You're mad!"

Juliette smiled and remained silent. Some things she did

learn from the best. Katarina and her silences disarmed better than any blow ever could. A second. Two. In her mind, Juliette spun into the first fouetté. She could do it with her eyes closed. In her sleep. Three seconds. She missed ballet so much. She missed her life. Her fingers tightened on the dark handle till they went white.

Foltin screeched and shook visibly, his eyes never leaving Juliette's hand. She took another step. Would it really be this easy? Had it been this easy all along? The taste of regret was bittersweet. This man had been nothing but a scheming coward.

"What do you want? What do you want from me? You… you…" He trailed off, his voice rising to a high pitch of impending hysteria before trailing off, perhaps recognizing how unhinged he sounded. For a moment his loud, hiccupping breathing was the only sound in the elevator. Not even background classical music interrupted the wheezing inhalations. He sucked air greedily, as if Juliette was about to take it all away.

"Fine! Fine! Stop this. Press the damn button. You win. God dammit, you won this years ago. No matter how I cajoled, pleaded, begged—"

"Threatened." Juliette's word jolted him out of his blubbering, and he finally raised his watery eyes to meet hers. He gulped loudly, and when Juliette thumped her cane on the tiled floor, he lifted his hands in surrender.

"Yes, yes. Did it do me any good? No. You broke your leg and she broke her heart and she still was never mine!"

All his limbs shook, all veneer of sophistication wiped away. "We were supposed to be married. In Moscow. She had agreed. She said yes, for God's sake! She was to be my bride."

The familiar sensation, the one Juliette had felt back in the secretary's office listening to Foltin talk to Katarina, returned tenfold. The disgust. This man should've never been allowed anywhere near Katarina. Her name should never have left his mouth. He wasn't worthy of breathing the same air she did.

"Did you browbeat her into that too?"

She was years too late, but when he nodded, hiding his eyes from her, Juliette knew that she was finally catching on.

"She was sleeping with Belova, I caught them. And she agreed! The scandal had been hidden then, and she was mine, we were unstoppable."

The tragic Tatyana Belova, she who had fallen down the stairs and whose position as the lead of the company Katarina took. Tatyana Belova, whose name Juliette had heard in conjunction with Katarina's forever. And for whose loss of a career Katarina had always been blamed. Even Gabriel had alluded to it on that fateful first day when Katarina drew Michel's blood.

A memory resurfaced and tugged at the ends of Juliette's consciousness. Something Katarina had said years ago, something Foltin spoke around, with innuendo and rancor. And this something was so important that Juliette, who so rarely dissembled, allowed herself to bluff.

"Back then, you insinuated that Katarina had tried to injure me, that everyone knew it was her because of the things she had done in Moscow. Because of Belova. And yet… Something tells me it was you who threw Belova off the stairs. What, Katarina didn't forget her? Didn't leave an old love in the past? So you took matters in your own hands."

He stood a touch taller, his back still against the mirror of the elevator, and shook his head.

"You can't prove it."

Juliette smiled.

"Do I have to prove it?" He recoiled from her words, from the meaning behind them, the gesture obscene in its swiftness.

"You're crazy. I'll call the police!"

Juliette smiled wider.

"And tell them what? That a ballerina who can barely walk beat you up? A strapping man such as yourself? And would you even want to attract attention to yourself, a KGB, or whatever they're calling it now, asset in America? Are the French aware of you, or are you still pulling the wool over Lalande's eyes and his blinding ego?"

She had thrown that last assumption out as a wild guess, but his jowly face turning impossibly pastier told her everything she needed to know.

Foltin kept shaking his head, even as she lifted her cane, tossed it up, and caught it, holding it like a baseball bat.

The seventeenth fouetté always crept up on Juliette, her eyes focused and her feet working like clockwork, like an expensive mechanism, drilled by time, experience, talent. She was in the middle of the movement, all speed. Precision, and yet, mostly instinct.

And it was instinct that was guiding her. The one she was indulging. The instinct that meant spewing words, because if she set her true wish free, Katarina's little bloodletting in the classroom at Garnier would look like a paper cut by comparison. Years lost to this worm. Years, careers, health, hearts…

Juliette clutched the cane harder. Foltin actually squealed.

"I should've done this seven years ago. I should've seen through all the lies, through all the intrigue, through all the games. I should've known that this was never about ballet. And always was about having Katarina. About owning her. Possessing her."

Foltin's head was still swaying, but now his lower lip was quivering as well.

"I should've confronted you that evening instead of running away. You see, I blamed you for ruining my life. You and Katarina. And all this time it was me. My fear, my inability to trust fully. I should've entered that fucking office of yours where you were threatening her, where you were blackmailing her, and I should've stood by her. And maybe I should've also slapped you silly. Granted, I had no cane back then to do much damage. I do now. Ironically, thanks in some tiny measure to you and your pathetic spy games."

She took a small step closer to him, the wood warm and tantalizing in her hand. He shrank so far into the wall, he almost dissolved into it. What a coward. Bullies always were.

"Are you afraid of me, Foltin?" Her own voice sounded foreign to her. Juliette had forgotten the last time it had held this note of authority, of self-confidence. Well, it had taken her long enough and it had taken her stepping all over this sorry excuse of a man to gain herself back. Wasn't that what she had told Gabriel just a few days ago? Circles everywhere. She was on her last, thirty-second fouetté. And it felt glorious.

"Are you afraid of me?" she repeated, tone lower, deadlier, and watched him squirm. When he shut his eyes tightly and turned his head away from her, she closed the distance between them and whispered into his ear, "You should be."

Juliette remembered how ages ago Francesca had pontificated about drama and how it was everywhere in their world. This entire scene, so over the top, so beyond everything that had been normal in her life, so far from who she had been, was a fitting end for a character arc.

Juliette breathed in the stench of his fear, so very real, so palpable she thought she could wring it like a rag and let the dirty water of this whole sordid affair drip between her fingers, poison leaving the wound.

Then she stepped back and pressed the button for the ground floor. She left him cowering in the corner of the elevator even as Madison Avenue opened up in front of her, full of people, of hope, and of new beginnings.

Twenty-Nine
Of Good Intentions & Wine-Stained Floors

When she found her apartment unlocked, she knew she wouldn't be able to take the shower she didn't particularly want but was aware she needed. With Katarina's scent all over her face and Foltin's fear on her hands, Juliette felt she was going slowly insane.

Juliette closed the door and allowed herself to lean back against it for a second before she took off her shoes and set her cane in the corner.

She drew in a deep breath and ventured toward the light and the scent of coffee coming from the kitchen. Dusk was settling outside, yet it felt like the perfect time for it. Sleep wasn't really an option anyway.

"Does your girlfriend know where you're spending your evenings, Helena?"

In scrubs of all things, Helena puttered around the small space looking decidedly at home. For all the time she had spent in Juliette's apartment, she might as well have been.

"She thinks I'm working late at the hospital. Having shifts at the psychiatry ward down at Staten Island has its benefits."

Juliette leaned against the doorjamb and stuck her hands in the pockets of her slacks.

"Like lying to an unsuspecting woman who worships the ground you walk on?"

Helena finally turned, and her face was serene.

"She can't remember how I take my tea, Jett." There was no bitterness in Helena's matter-of-fact observation. "And I am not above lying. Especially when I get a panicked call from Francesca that Juliette is likely murdering Katarina at the Four Seasons, and my girlfriend emphatically doesn't approve of Juliette to begin with."

Juliette smiled at the non sequitur of the explanation.

"What are you going to do?"

"Probably dump her. It's tiresome, trying to deny that your mind is somewhere else all the time. But what am I saying? Of course you know exactly how that feels."

Juliette's mouth dropped open before she stumbled over words to refute Helena's assumptions.

"Hels, you don't think of me and I don't think of Katarina. C'mon—"

Helena laughed and set her mug down.

"Oh God, Jett. Talk about jumping the gun and showing your hand. Please calm down. I meant that my mind would rather think of my practice and patients than about her. And she knows it. Hence her jealousy over anything and anyone. However, you denying for seven years that you don't think of Katarina is just as absurd."

Helena gave her a long look before speaking again.

"I assume you went there to murder her, and since your blouse is covered in stains of a different nature, I also assume you've not actually proceeded with your plan."

It took all of Juliette's discipline not to fall for the obvious bait, and she did not pull her hands out of her pockets to cover her collar.

The sounds of a door banging open and then closing shut with considerable force saved her from further exploration of the embarrassing subject. It could herald the entrance of only one person. Juliette bit the inside of her cheek to avoid tearing up, because yes, there was just one friend left who could simply barge in. Gabriel was gone, and Francesca whirled into the kitchen with the power of a cyclone hitting shore.

"Oh good, no blood. Did you read her the riot act already, Helena? Or were you playing shrink games and bitching about that useless girlfriend of yours?"

Helena and Juliette exchanged a look and burst into laughter. It felt wonderful. There had been so many tears lately.

Francesca pulled out a bottle of wine from her immense canvas purse and lit a cigarette. Helena rolled her eyes and placed an ashtray in front of her before pulling the cork out and pouring three glasses.

"Why do I always turn into your maid, Cesca?"

"Because you cannot stand mess and I am chaos personified. Your tendency to fix things is propelled into action every time I am around. Or she is, for that matter." Francesca pointed with the lit cigarette in the direction of Juliette.

"Are you after my job, Bianchi?" Helena handed them their glasses.

"God, this fucking day. I think you could fit a decade into this fucking day." Francesca's voice sounded tired.

"I'll drink to that." Helena tipped her glass, and they sipped in silence, the wine settling heavy in Juliette's empty stomach.

She set the glass down and finally allowed herself to breathe, clambering on the counter next to the sink, the farthest she could from both women in the small space. For some reason, she couldn't stand the thought of being touched. Not when the only hands she wanted on herself were the ones that had been tangled in her hair just two hours ago.

"This fucking year. Maybe even these fucking seven." If Francesca's voice had sounded tired earlier, her own was downright wrung dry by exhaustion.

"For you more so than for others, Juliette. I take it tonight went lousy?" Helena did not come closer as she spoke, and Juliette appreciated it.

"Was there any way to keep my affairs private, Cesca?" Juliette was sick of being the permanent subject of conversation between her friends. They meant well, but being the "wounded" one was getting tedious.

"Ah, so now there's an affair?" Francesca lifted her glass and gave Helena a knowing look.

Juliette rolled her eyes.

"There has always been an affair, no matter how much you hated her, Cesca."

Francesca's eyes widened. "I never did! What are you talking about?"

Juliette shrugged. "It always seemed that way. And you were constantly cautioning me back in Paris that she was after my job—"

"And she was. I didn't even do a half-assed jig when I turned out to be right."

Helena's laughter was quiet. "You can't do a jig, Cesca, half- or full-assed. And I was just as convinced that she would betray you, Juliette. And just as sorry when she did."

"She did. Granted, the more I allow myself to think, to see, to listen, the more I understand that she had to. But sleeping with me still was a rather extreme way to get my parts." Juliette took another sip of her wine and her stomach roiled.

In her misery, Juliette almost missed the long look Francesca and Helena exchanged. Almost missed, as she turned back to them just in time to catch the former drop her gaze and the latter purse her lips.

"What?" She gripped the edge of the counter, her knuckles whitening with the force of her hold. There was some kind of weight in the air, one that could only be a secret unexposed for years and about to be revealed. Juliette braced herself even as she knew her heart was about to be ripped out of her near-mended chest. God, she had so painstakingly placed every stitch back in those ribs, desperate to be able to breathe again.

"Juliette, what really happened the night of *The Nutcracker* opening?"

Helena's tone was cautious, but Juliette was thankful to her friend for not reverting to her clinical professional voice. She couldn't stomach being psychoanalyzed tonight.

"I thought you knew." She wiped her suddenly damp and cold palms on her slacks and looked from Helena to Francesca. "I was in the wings waiting for my cue, and some kid told me Foltin expected me. Which was so unusual I almost sent her away, but she seemed so scared of what he'd do to her if she didn't fetch me…"

She ran her fingers through her hair, the knots and tangles Katarina had put there catching on her knuckles, and for some reason this small reminder of where she had been and what she had done made these memories even harder to recount. What she'd had, what she'd lost…

"So I went, the door was open—"

Francesca's curse was loud, filling the kitchen with ire so palpable Juliette felt as if she could reach out her hand and catch the rage like a flaming butterfly in her fingers.

"Foltin had his hands on her face, caressing her, I guess." Bile rose to her throat, and she sped up her account, desperate to get through this part. All the parts, really. Not a single memory about that night was palatable, if Juliette was honest with herself. The wine was making her nauseous. Or the recollection was. She swallowed hard to tamp down the urge to purge herself of both.

"And he was reminding her how the reason she defected in Paris was because it was the one main company in Europe where the prima was vulnerable. And that she had already laid the groundwork, albeit sloppy, of getting rid of me with the glass and the ice."

Francesca blanched and looked at Helena. Juliette ignored them and took a deep, deep breath, trying to calm her racing thoughts. Some of the threads of that conversation, of what she had overheard, sounded different in the light of what had happened in the Four Seasons's elevator.

"He also accused her of doing the same to Tatyana Belova in Moscow, but I know now that was a lie." She needed time and space to process it all. Things were happening too quickly, and she had been too crowded to even begin to unravel the mess in her head.

"Anyway, after a back-and-forth full of threats and denials, he told her that she would be taking over, and she said yes. I told you that much in the hospital. The rest is history, as they say. And as they write in my medical chart."

Juliette smiled at her own joke, but Francesca just closed her eyes and Helena covered her mouth with her fingertips as if trying to keep words from escaping.

"What is happening?"

Finally, after what seemed like forever, Helena dropped her hand. "Juliette, why didn't you tell us all this years ago? Why didn't you tell us Foltin accused Katarina of the sabotage?"

Juliette shrugged. "Does it matter? It's water under a burned bridge anyway."

And how to explain that talking about it now was like pulling her own nails from her fingers? That she would have gladly never mentioned Katarina's name at all? How to express how the betrayal shaped her entire being, not just in the form of her broken leg and barely functioning knee, but never allowing her heart to let anyone else in—and wasn't that a life of deprivation much larger than her inability to ever dance again?

"Juliette, it was never her. Amor, had I known you blamed her, I'd have told you much sooner. It was never her." Francesca's words like bullets shattered the glass pane of Juliette's silence.

Helena laid a hand on the agitated shoulder as Francesca struggled to get up.

"It was me, amor. The ice, the shoes… It was me all along."

Juliette heard the sound of her glass shattering, the remnants of red wine splattering on the tiles. Had she dropped it? Had Francesca tried to sabotage her last season at Garnier?

"But…"

Juliette had no idea but what. Or but why. Did it matter? Her closest friend. The person she trusted.

"I told you in the hospital that Lalande had been after me and my name and my projects for years after I refused to resign to make room for Foltin. And I suspected that with him as Minister of Culture and his power over Paris Opera Ballet unchecked, he'd remove me. And he'd destroy everything I had built. Out of pure spite. His hyenas in the press nearly ruined you for two years with their awful reviews. Why, do you think? You were mine, my Étoile, my star. Our names were linked. Two women leading the Paris Opera Ballet. And you know how much he hates women."

Francesca could not seem to stop speaking. Gone was the reticence. Gone were the hints. Truth was bubbling to the surface, pouring like champagne at a funeral. Out of place and much too late. Seven years too late. Juliette closed her eyes and let it wash over her anyway.

"I tried to remove you for short time frames, just long enough to spare you the awfulness of the press and the association with me, thinking the new director would allow you to remain if they believed you were not part of Bianchi's most recent failures, like *Don Quixote*. I wanted you to stay in Paris. To keep triumphing."

"And yet you worked on Shannon to invite me to London?" Juliette found her voice even if she wasn't at all certain she truly cared about this one question.

"That was me, dear." Helena's answer was barely audible, and it was that whisper that tipped the scales of Juliette's heartbreak. She touched her own sternum, as if holding her hand there would salvage what was left of her needlework. The stitches twanged with the intensity of her pain.

Seven years. Seven years, and much of them a lie? The road to hell and the good intentions that paved it swam up in her mind, but she shook her head.

"Anything else?" Juliette could barely push the words out of her mouth. When both Francesca and Helena remained silent, Juliette allowed a little of her anger to escape. "Any fucking thing else? How else have people been running my life without asking me once for my opinion? Do I have agency in this manuscript you are all weaving? You almost broke my legs to spare me, what? Bad reviews? And you made me think I had to forsake Paris and bought me a safe passage to London, for what? All I had to do was stay and fight for my place!"

Francesca bit her lip, and when she spoke her tone was pacifying, which only made Juliette more furious.

"Amor, that isn't quite true—"

"How is it not true?" Juliette jumped up at her own shout.

"Because, no matter how much Francesca wished you to keep dancing at Palais Garnier, you'd have not kept your place. That's not how the world works, Jett. And Cesca should've known better, but that's not the subject of this conversation." Helena threw her friend a decidedly evil glare. "You, Jett… You were the best dancer, but it didn't matter. Hence Cesca's attempts to shield you, idiotic as they might have been. Hence me asking Shannon for a favor, though I assure you London would have jumped at the chance to hire you. But maybe being the best always has sheltered you from the reality that talent alone means nothing. Life isn't fair."

Helena crossed her arms around her chest and went on.

"Katarina is the best Soviet ballerina to ever grace the stage of Bolshoi. And it still didn't matter. They marginalized her and treated her like shit. You don't get what you deserve, Juliette. You get what they give you, and a ballerina is dispensable. Someone is always more talented, someone is always willing to do more to fight for the prize. Fight dirty. You had never done anything but dance. You, with your chivalry, kindness, and your wholesomeness and your unbeatable jump…"

Helena stumbled over the last word, perhaps realizing what she had said, and Juliette's cane by the front door, visible from the kitchen, was an eyesore.

Juliette wiped away the bitter tears. It felt imperative that she speak, even if she couldn't keep the sarcasm from her tone.

"Well, there's no more kindness, wholesomeness, and certainly no more jumps. As for chivalry, there's not a day that passes that I don't regret that I saved her."

"Do you? Juliette, she was the love of your life—"

The peel of laughter Juliette let out scratched her throat raw.

"And now she is the ruin of it. What good did love ever do me? You never loved me enough and she—"

Another peel of laughter that dissolved in the air and fell like hail to the floor. Helena grabbed her by the shoulders and actually shook her, startling her out of the hysteria.

"And she might have loved you too much. Maybe all these unsaid truths that we have kept from you are what was truly ruinous. We wronged you, dear." Helena stopped and gulped, and the tears she had been fighting ran freely down her cheeks now. "I did. And as for loving you? It was never an issue. You and I are a regret I've nursed quietly for years and will probably carry forever, and Cesca… Well, if dragging you to New York, saving you from joblessness, and giving you a new lease on life is not atoning every day for her utter awfulness, I don't know what is. As for Katarina? I sense that her silences hold a much bigger meaning than ours ever could."

Helena stepped out of the kitchen and extended a hand to Francesca.

"I think we will leave you now, dear."

"But we need to talk, amor—"

The buzzing in her ears intensified. She felt like a badly written character. One who was led around the script by her nose, events happening to her and nothing being in her control. Maybe it was time to take some of that agency back from the author penning the story of her life.

"I do need to talk, Cesca. But not with you. You've done and said more than you should have. You propped me up for years. Both of you, and Gabriel. He's gone, and you need to let me stand on my own two feet, no matter how unsteady I literally am. I'm grateful to and for you. But enough now."

Both Helena's and Cesca's faces showed surprise and resignation, and Juliette felt the weight of her words sinking, the meaning of them impacting her friends. A brick to the storefront window of their friendship. They would either replace it later, patch it up with cardboard, or let the entire thing sink. But those questions were for another day.

The door closing told Juliette that for the first time in seven years, she was truly alone. And the blood-red wine on the kitchen floor was a lousy companion for a broken heart. But it also felt like the one companion she had actually chosen herself. And wasn't that a wonderful feeling?

Thirty

Of Returns & Yellow Chrysanthemums

Rue de Rivoli was quiet, and the absence of sound soothing. Paris met her with rain and silence, and Juliette knew this had once been her true home. It was also the home she'd never be able to return to, not fully. One couldn't enter the same waters twice—the Seine, a stone's throw away from her, was testament to that, the river ever changing. But damn if she could breathe with her full chest for the very first time in seven years.

Her cane beat the steady tattoo of her steps on the empty sidewalks. Her hands were full of chrysanthemums. A fall cliché if she had ever seen one, and yet their color and vibrance did not grate. They felt like the missing piece in the puzzle that had been her trip to France.

If the customs officer at Charles de Gaulle airport was surprised that a lone woman coming from JFK had no luggage bar a small purse, he did not bat an eye. In fact, he gave her the longest look, and when he finally spoke, it was to say, "Welcome back" instead of "Welcome to Paris," and Juliette's heart, already working double time, went into overdrive.

She took the most circuitous route possible, asking the taxi to drop her off at the Tour Saint-Jacques. And gave herself some grace. To just wander aimlessly the streets whose every cobblestone and every crack in the asphalt she had known. Some of those had been fixed, new ones formed in their place. Life went on.

And some things remained the same. Madame Broussard, the flower lady on the corner of Rue Saint-Honoré, had gazed at her above her glasses, and Juliette could have sworn a smile was playing in the dark hooded eyes.

"The usual?"

That one question hit Juliette in the center of her chest and had her on the ropes like nothing else on this trip. Not the Louvre, not the Opera building, and yet here she was fighting a losing battle with tears and reaching for her wallet.

"Non." The arthritic hands plunged into the plastic bucket and pulled out an immense bouquet of yellow chrysanthemums.

"I… Madame… I can't…" Juliette's arms were suddenly filled with wet flowers as she instinctively accepted what was handed to her.

"It's autumn in Paris, mademoiselle. And it means only two things. Chrysanthemums and ballet season. And the latter is you."

Juliette gulped and forwent wiping her eyes.

"Not anymore, madame." She juggled the bouquet into a more comfortable hold and gripped her cane harder, trying to steady herself as much as her emotions.

"You are Juliette Lucian-Sorel, ma jolie, a stick doesn't change that."

With that the woman waved her away, turning to another customer, and Juliette was left floored on the corner of Rue Saint-Honoré, arms full of flowers, water dripping down her sweater.

From there, it seemed she had no other way but to Rivoli. Past the Louvre, past the Tuileries. She entered the almost-deserted Angelina, so rare, and ordered a cup of their famous hot chocolate. The maître d' greeted her by name, and so did the server. They took care of her flowers and sat her in the back, away from the wandering eyes of the handful of patrons.

The thick liquid slid down her throat like a blessing, and yet as she sipped Juliette knew she was just stalling. The darkness was falling on Paris, and she had a hunch the staff was allowing her to lollygag instead of pointing to the door. Her second cup was making her queasy, and she acknowledged it was time.

Drunk on Angelina's chocolate… Such a lightweight, Juliette…

She said goodbye with the air of someone being taken to the guillotine. Well, Place de la Concorde wasn't all that far from here.

Under the arcades of Rivoli, Juliette took a few steps to the corner of Rue d'Alger. Just a few more and she'd be in front of the entrance to the building that had been her home for seven years. The building that still held her heart.

It was late and dark, but she had a feeling Katarina would be home. And wasn't that a kick in the teeth that it was she who now called the apartment where Juliette had spent seven years her home. But then they were seven apiece now, so their claims to the airy space would probably be moot at this point.

As she stepped from under the awning, Juliette couldn't help but glance up, and her heart flipped over in her chest and some of the stitches she had so painstakingly placed around it tore. Figures that it wouldn't be pain that undid them. Simply love. And yet there was nothing simple about it.

On the top floor, the pink light illuminated the kitchen windows. The sole bright spot on the entire block, it was reminiscent of the lighthouse beam. The little lamp. Juliette's guide home. A tear escaped, and Juliette let it slide down her cheek as she bit her lip to stem the tide of the coming flood.

The elevator that Juliette never used to take before sounded like a dying man in excruciating agony. Juliette could sympathize. Seven years and she had been wandering the world half-blind and angry, and yet the light shone through the night for her. She had a feeling it had been shining since the day she left.

"I always look up from the street, and seeing the light on makes me imagine someone is home. And that someone left the light on for me. In that moment, I matter. I matter enough to make an effort…"

She remembered her own words and the sensation of Katarina's eyes on her. Watching her with something remarkably like understanding. As if Juliette indeed mattered. How had Juliette been so oblivious of the simplest of truths? She had been loved from the start. And she had been the one who wavered. The kitchen light shone on, and Juliette thought how much she had to atone for. Years, words, broken hearts.

She hoped she'd be given the chance.

Juliette took a deep breath and clutched the flowers tighter to her chest. She exited the elevator, and before she was ready—though how could one ever be truly ready to face one's destiny?—she was standing in front of the yellow apartment door. Her thoughts were running amok, a jumble of anxiety and overthinking. And maybe hope. Was it a fresh coat of paint? If so, the shade was exactly the same as the one she herself used to cover the sturdy oak all those years ago. She had broken all the French rules when she dared to paint it, but Juliette didn't care. She'd had yellow splatters on her fingers for ages—

Katarina flung the door open, and then nothing else mattered. Not the paint, nor the twinging in Juliette's knee.

She was beautiful. But then, she had always been ethereal. Framed by the door and the pooling light behind her, her face gaunt and tired, hands clutching the same old shawl around that thin frame, Katarina was sheer perfection. She took Juliette's breath away. Still. She also took her sanity away, because of all the things to say, Juliette stumbled through the awkward "Hello" and Katarina's eyebrow lifted, the move so familiar Juliette felt the second tear trickle down.

Katarina bit her lip and after only a moment lost the fight

with the smile that had come on the heels of the raised eyebrow, and when she reached out a steady hand, Juliette wanted to scream. Her own hand on the cane shook, making the wood rattle slightly and the flowers in her other arm tremble.

"Tears and chrysanthemums, Juliette. Do you know the French deem them death blossoms?"

Juliette grimaced. She had forgotten. Katarina smiled gently.

"Good thing they also symbolize neglected love and a rebirth for pretty much all other nations. Should we go with that meaning?" Juliette nodded, and Katarina's smile widened. "And all of this at almost ten in the evening. For someone who has never been dramatic, my love, you sure embrace it when making your entrances."

Juliette couldn't tell what exactly did her in—though she suspected it must've been the oh-so-natural "my love" slipping off Katarina's lips as if she had been saying these words for seven years—but her legs gave out and her heart shredded the rest of the stitches and she fell to her knees on the threshold by the yellow door, the chrysanthemums, mirroring the exact same color, falling all around her.

And the flood came. The tears, the unstoppable release of all the years of loneliness, of pain, of loss, all poured out of her and she bent over, shaking so hard she was afraid she'd simply shatter—surely the very fabric of her being would rend, her very bones crumble. They had before. From heartbreak, so why not from regret?

But they didn't. Two cool, slightly calloused hands lifted her face and cradled it in the crook of a shawl-covered shoulder, where the scent of the orange blossom welcomed her home.

Katarina sat on the floor next to her, rocking them, murmuring soft incantations that for once had no edges. Warm skin, short nails, tickling wisps of golden hair.

"I've come back home. Will you forgive me?"

Juliette's words fell even as the tears abated, and she raised her head to see one of Katarina's fluttering on those still impossibly long butterfly lashes before she flicked it away with an impatient hand.

"I've been waiting for you. You were forgiven years ago."

Katarina could hide the tears, but the voice betrayed her, an ocean of emotion overflowing in it.

"I'm sorry I made you wait all these years." Juliette ran her fingers over the tips of Katarina's disheveled locks, and it felt like dipping them in gold.

"I didn't mind the wait. As long as you were coming back, my love."

Juliette traced the sharp jaw, the divine craftsmanship on full display.

"How did you know I would?"

Katarina caught the wandering fingertips and kissed them, one by one. Juliette's skin felt like a branch covered in ice that the sun touched for the first time with the coming of spring. The thawing a physical sensation, Juliette blinked and savored both the warmth and the simple pleasure of being held, hearing the sound of the voice she thought she'd never hear again.

"I didn't, my love."

Katarina looked down just as Juliette's eyes flew open in surprise.

"Then why—"

"Because you asked me to keep the light on for you, Juliette. Because you… God, you're everything. You always have been. And love doesn't stop even if it doesn't know if it will ever be needed again. Love goes on, like this light. It shines without any expectation that it will serve anyone, yet it shines anyway. Hoping."

Juliette gulped the heart-wrenching realizations away. She'd atone. She'd atone for every single thing she'd broken and all the mess she'd made.

"I'm a fool, Katarina."

The exhalation was barely audible in the shadowy hallway.

"So am I."

"You tried to tell me. You tried to warn me about Foltin, about the KGB, about everyone, and all I heard was your reasons to betray me."

Katarina shrugged.

"I also accepted taking your roles, Juliette, believing that you were departing to London and leaving me behind. And despite having my freedom here in Paris, I was still afraid—"

"I didn't see that part, and I can't believe that even after everything you told me, I didn't understand how immense your fear was. How it molded your decisions, your entire life."

Juliette felt tears threaten again. Katarina did not shrug this time. In fact, she did not move a muscle. When she finally spoke again, her voice had that faraway quality Juliette detested, because it meant some of the fear was worming its way into those notes of perfect English.

"We talked so much, Juliette. And I shared so much of myself with you. And yet, I held so much back too. I suspected you were wary of me at the beginning, but I was so certain you had beaten back those whispers by the time we got together. It almost killed me knowing that I never earned your trust fully."

"Oh, sweetheart, I didn't start with trust. Everyone was warning me against you, but I fell apart as hard as I did, breaking everything, us, myself, because of how much I wanted to trust you. The weakness was mine all along. I let my own insecurities take over. I was so ready for the one I loved most to betray me, and yet so absolutely convinced that you would never, so when I thought that it had happened? When I saw him put his hands on you, to see you allow it, agree to his schemes, essentially oust me… I allowed the deception and the anger to take over and my tendons to snap underneath me, because I believed you despite everything else I was being made to see and to hear. And I thought it was my worst mistake, to believe you."

And now Katarina let her tears fall freely too.

"I see you falling every time I close my eyes. I will keep seeing it over and over as long as I live, my love. Gabriel failing to catch you by just a second and your face as you realized what was happening… The awful sound of your hamstring snapping. I will never forgive myself, Juliette."

"And that was my own foolishness yet again. Had I stayed, had I made him talk to me, had I exposed him for the fraud that he is… I bet he set it up so I'd be at his office door listening in at the exact time he was getting you to agree to his schemes."

Juliette almost slapped herself for not seeing so many angles of the entire charade sooner.

"He did. He kept bragging about all of it, how masterfully he dealt with you and how fate gifted him your injury to get rid of you once and for all. Well, he didn't brag for very long."

Something in Katarina's gaze sparkled with brutal satisfaction, and Juliette wished she could close her thighs. Since when had Katarina's violence become so attractive? Then Juliette laughed.

"Scratched his eyes out, did you? Oh God, blood and ballet and you. Always you. You are completely irresistible to me when you are covered in wrath and bloody satin and putting weak, useless men in their place."

Katarina's smile was sly. "Only then? I shall see about slapping more people." They giggled like schoolgirls sharing a dirty joke. "Speaking of weak, useless men. I hear I am not the only one with a propensity to put them in their place." And now Katarina's face was all exuberance and not a little schadenfreude. "Foltin ran to my room the minute he could get out of that elevator, my love. He blubbered about you brutalizing him. It was glorious. And led to several confessions. And some decisions."

Juliette's curiosity piqued.

"I always thought he was a whiny small man. What did he say?"

Katarina's fingers played with her hair, and Juliette felt a smile bloom against her temple.

"That you almost blew his cover, but he may salvage it still, since you weren't certain. So I made sure he knew that if you didn't go to the French or American authorities, I would. He's resigning on Monday. I don't know if he works for the Russian secret police now that the Soviet Union fell, but he was an active agent for the KGB for years. None of the governments he has been in good standing with will like that. The Brits would be made fools for granting him asylum only for him to turn spy, and the French hate being duped, and they invested in him the most."

"So he's gone? Katarina, you vanquished him?"

"My love, you're very easy to impress." Katarina laughed but did not deny anything, and Juliette felt incredibly proud. She picked up one of the fallen blossoms, the yellow like a ray of sunshine in her hand, and offered it to Katarina.

"No, don't dismiss this. It's huge. You faced him. And your fear, and you beat him."

Katarina took the flower and tucked it behind Juliette's ear before slowly kissing her forehead. The world was suddenly brighter, the shadows nesting in the corners of the hallway disappearing. Juliette burrowed deeper into the scent and the skin and tried very hard not to cry.

"I should have faced him sooner. I should have faced so many things sooner." Katarina sighed, the weight of the exhalation palpable in the air. "I went back, you know. The new government allowed me. Welcomed me, even. So strange. But I wanted to go. To see what was left. I visited Tallinn, and it's beautiful. It's small and quaint and utterly amazing. It's my mother's city. I walked the streets, and I swear I could hear her voice and her steps."

Juliette held tighter, feeling this particular story did not have a happy ending. And how could it? So many people were dead, so many lives wasted, tormented, cut to pieces. As if echoing her thoughts, Katarina whispered, "I found out that my father died about the same time as I defected. I stood where his marker stands now, and I finally felt at peace. That he didn't suffer for much longer after I left. You know, they passed a law recently, it's called something about rehabilitation of Soviet Union political prisoners, declaring innocent all the people who perished in gulag and afterward in many prisons and institutions."

Katarina's whisper was almost inaudible now, Juliette straining hard to make out her words.

"As if a paper could ever bring them back. Years of pain. Ruined lives. For what?"

"I wish I had gone with you, Katarina."

As if coming out of a trance, Katarina jolted, then smiled down, staring into Juliette's eyes, fingers still running through her hair.

"It's okay. It's something I had to do by myself. To say goodbye to both of them. And to my fears. But you can come with me, if there ever is a next time. Certainly to Estonia. To say hello. Will you?"

Juliette sat up, not breaking their eye contact for even a second, because it felt imperative that she hold this serious ice-blue gaze. Because Katarina was asking for so much more than a chance to visit a faraway country. Katarina was asking for everything.

"I will. I will go with you anywhere. You will never have to ask. And you'll never have to go alone."

Katarina's smile was serene, pure unrestrained joy before she reached out and traced Juliette's cheekbone.

"And if it's to Paris, Juliette?"

There was a slight hesitation in the words, as if Katarina was still not fully accepting that Juliette was back for good. It was an easy concern to erase.

"To the ends of the earth, sweetheart. To the moon and back."

"Just to Paris. With Foltin gone, there's no telling who will get the directorship, but I would like to dance for a few more years…"

Katarina's eyes filled with tears suddenly, and Juliette knew exactly what she was thinking.

"I would love to watch you dance. Days, months, years. As long as you want. You are my favorite ballerina, after all. My beloved one."

Juliette shifted slightly. She had more to share, more to promise, and Paris… Paris was a dream she had never stopped weaving every night in her sleep. They had so much to talk about, so much to say. Her heart was so full, so warm, even if the cool floor was making her knee ache. She shifted again, and Katarina caught herself immediately.

"Oh, my love. This is so silly of me. Come, the kitchen is cozy and there's mint tea. Have you eaten? I'm afraid there are only eggs, but I can make you something—"

At the thought of food, or interrupting this conversation, or even leaving Katarina's arms, Juliette panicked.

"No, no, I had hot chocolate. I had two. I'm going to be sick. And if you stop holding me, I'm going to be lonely, so can we go to bed instead of to the kitchen?"

Juliette flashed her the most winsome smile, and Katarina rolled her eyes.

"First, it's Angelina's special and nobody gets sick on it, it's marvelous. I have faith that you can handle two hot chocolates. And second, you never have to ask me to hold you. Though, I never did stop calling that room *your* bedroom."

This last confession was said with so much sorrow, so much shame. Juliette shook her head, trying not to succumb to the same emotions, and did the only thing that had always brought solace. She reached out her hand and touched the downturned pale lips of the person who held her entire world in the palms of her chilly hands. Then, as Katarina's eyes widened, Juliette slowly closed the distance between them.

Yes, she was home. This was home. This mouth, this scent, and this woman, above all, was her home. They tasted each other as if anew, and yet every move, every flick of tongue was familiar, was theirs, was a return to themselves, to the love they had shared once, the love that still bloomed between them.

When they parted, Katarina drew Juliette up and over the threshold, quietly closing the door behind them. In the quiet of the apartment, with the scent of orange blossom in the air, Juliette couldn't hold on anymore, the words falling off her lips unrestrained.

"I love you, Katarina Vyatka."

"And I love you, Juliette Lucian-Sorel."

As they moved in the light of the little lamp, the world taking on a joyous, serene pink hue, Juliette heard Katarina whisper, "Thank you" before their lips met once again.

Yes, thank you. Thank you, Paris, thank you, ballet. Thank you for this peace, this forgiveness, this joy of having and holding. In the bedroom doorway, Juliette closed her eyes and savored her happily ever after as Katarina's arms wrapped her in love.

Thirty-One
Of Curtain Calls

"Juliette, you did it!"

The exclamation and the sound of hurried footsteps in the hallway distracted her from the task of choreographing the next movement, and she lifted her head from the notebook where she had been meticulously drawing out the steps of the pas de deux.

Juliette shifted her now-considerable abdomen and wished the weeks would pass sooner. Hadn't she suffered enough? It had been eight months. Whoever said pregnancy was magnificent either hadn't been pregnant or had one of those ridiculously, awfully, horribly, disgustingly easy ones.

Juliette had not had one of those. Getting pregnant had turned out to be the easiest-peasiest piece of cake in the history of cake. Or the making of babies. Turkey basters rocked.

It was the months that followed the joy and the happiness and the euphoria of those first few days that neither rocked, nor rolled. More like waddled.

Katarina was setting up the nursery the moment the doctor told them they were expecting. All yellows and greens, and Juliette vomited the very first time just thinking about everything that would come.

What came were seven months of morning sickness. Again,

whoever said nausea was the joy of only the first trimester had been the biggest liar. Juliette had been sick every single day, sometimes twice a day, and nothing had helped. Nothing. Crackers, ginger ale, chanting, praying. Nothing.

She had cursed, she had cried, she'd had Katarina drag her from doctor's appointment to doctor's appointment. The consensus was that the symptoms would stop. Eventually. Juliette had cursed some more.

"Of course it will all stop. When I'm dead!"

Katarina had held her hair away and patted her back over the toilet bowl.

"I see the little one is finally bringing out your dramatic side, my love. Ballet couldn't and yet the baby did. It's a miracle."

Juliette had gagged, heaved, then laughed.

All the grumpiness aside, it was a miracle. This baby was a miracle. Juliette and Katarina, together, happy, sappy, in Paris, were a miracle. Katarina still dancing at the age of forty-five and Juliette being named the Director of Paris Opera Ballet after being its chief choreographer for two years, was also a miracle.

As she sat back and ran her fingers up and down her belly, Juliette smiled. Miracles everywhere. Under her palm, the baby kicked.

"So you agree, little one?"

From the doorway, Katarina looked on, her eyes radiating calmness and peace. Another miracle.

"You were saying, sweetheart?" At the customary nickname, Katarina's lips crooked upward, the half smile sweet and familiar.

"The reviews for *Don Quixote* are in. It's a rave." Katarina took a few steps into the office and embraced Juliette from behind before settling in the visitors' chair, holding open what looked like a brand-new copy of *Le Monde*.

"'The newest iteration brings life and magic, whimsy and joy to the old, stale classic. What failed for years has been reborn as a must-see performance. Vyatka is magnificent in Lucian-Sorel's direction, and the latter is the breath of fresh air Paris had been craving since, well, since she herself walked the floorboards of Garnier. We are all witnessing history. Long Live The Queen.'"

Katarina put down the newspaper and gave Juliette an indulgent, half-smirking glance.

"I shall even overlook that they are perhaps slighting me, insisting that Paris Opera Ballet needed fresh air, considering I have been their prima for years."

Juliette tsked and extended her hand for the paper. The baby kicked again, harder this time.

"Ugh, sweetheart, these people have no idea what they're saying. Except for you being magnificent. That one is perfectly true and probably not even good enough, since you were above magnificent. You were superb. Ethereal. All the superlatives."

Katarina laughed. "You charmer. I already got you pregnant, there's no need to sweet-talk me. And speaking of, is she being too active?"

"First of all, she? Although, the more you say that it's a she, the more I feel that you're right. Only a dame would be this demanding and insistent on having her way, even in the womb. Second, she is your daughter—it's all grands jetés today. And third, did you see they finally promoted me? Princess forgotten. I'm the Queen of Paris."

Juliette struck a pose, somewhat inhibited by the belly. The baby chose that very moment to press on her bladder, and she winced.

"Not long now, love." Katarina got up again and massaged her shoulders gently. "And yes, I shall get you a crown. An impressive one, worthy of the Queen of Paris."

Juliette relaxed into the tender ministrations. "As long as it doesn't come with the guillotine. The French and their monarchs…" She rolled her neck, then they were quiet for a moment before Juliette spoke again. "What *Le Monde* fails to mention is that this is not my first successful *Don Quixote*. I staged it in New York to similar raves. Gabriel helped me with the choreography then."

Katarina's hands stilled on her shoulders, and the silence filled with sadness.

"I miss him every day, love. He was such a light." Katarina lowered her face to Juliette's temple and kissed her as she spoke. The movement of the lips tickled. The gentleness and the memory made Juliette tear up.

"He was light." The evening sun shone into the wide windows of the space that had seen everything begin. Once Francesca's office, then Foltin's. Now Juliette's. Circles. She thought of Gabriel standing there, by the window, hamming it up to make her smile, defending her, supporting her, pushing her to do what was right. He was so real then, in her memory, in this office, the setting sun playing in his blond curls.

"I know what the baby's name will be, sweetheart. Because she is light too."

Katarina lifted her head and looked into Juliette's eyes, the happiness and wistfulness of the moment unspooling like cotton candy, sweet, sugary hope between them.

"Gabrielle." Juliette set the name free like a little bird, and it spread its gentle wings, greeting the world.

"Gabrielle." Katarina's voice trembled. It sounded absolutely perfect spoken in her serene tone.

Outside, Paris was settling into an evening of autumn leaves, ballet performances, and tranquility. Inside, Katarina and Juliette embraced, the baby kicking joyfully between them.

Afterword

Of Political Repressions & Knives Under Pillows

When my grandmother was fourteen, her father was declared an Enemy of the State. He was arrested and whisked away by men in leather coats in the dead of night. His family didn't know it yet, but he would be executed very shortly after his arrest, for the crime of being an educated, well-read, well-informed man. A mayor of a small town and a public notary. An intellectual. The Soviet regime did not want intellectuals. After all, the Soviet regime did not tolerate free thinking. Intellectualism was the root of evil, the root of unrest, the enemy.

My grandmother and her mother were put on a freight train car with hundreds of other family members of arrested Enemies of the State and sent to a place they had never heard of.

Gulag.

A few months after arrival, typhoid swept the camps. At the age of fourteen, my grandmother was an orphan, having watched her mother die with no medicine and very little food and water.

By the time she reached eighteen, my grandmother had been held in nine prisons. And her captors had meticulously and systematically tortured her to obtain a confession. That she, a mere child, had been indeed conspiring against the State.

If it makes no sense, if it sounds like a made up horror story, if it feels like this could have never happened because of how monstrous it is… Well, it makes no sense, and it is monstrous and yet it did happen. And in places very close to where she was born it is happening again.

With Stalin's death the gulag system was closed and my grandmother returned home. She lost everything, her family, their home, but despite the horrors she had endured, she remained the most loving person.

She raised me, she was my rock and she never once spoke about her time in either the prisons or the camps. That she occasionally slept with a knife under her pillow was something she pretended nobody noticed.

When she died we requested her KGB files and found out about the sheer atrocities that had been done to her, a child, whose only crime was to have a father who could read, write and think for himself.

I love you and I miss you every day, Grandma.

Afterword
Of Plague & Science

Some of you know that I started my career in HIV programs, working with sex workers, men who had sex with men and injecting drug users. I was so young, I had no idea that those were the World Health Organization's terms for the beneficiaries of the services provided to people living with HIV.

In fact, at the age of twenty two years old, I had a very vague idea about the virus or the people who lived with it. That changed. In the subsequent years I learned a lot about people. But not about those who lived with HIV. No, I learned much more about the people who didn't. About those who worked with them. About those who lived with them. And about those who did everything in their power to forget that these people existed.

I got what you'd call an education. On ignorance, on indifference, on malice, on sheer evil of governments, bureaucrats, neighbors... I learned that there were entire swaths of people who could have helped. Entire administrations who turned their backs on thousands of suffering and dying. Entire governments that spread hate and misinformation. That did nothing. Or worse, did everything, to turn others against those who were in need of help.

And again, if this sounds like something out of a horror book, well, no, these were just the '80s in the US.

In "Reverence" I use terminology that is appropriate for the time, the disease having been called "the gay plague" by many back then. And because of that terminology and open, blatant homophobia, so many men were not helped, were turned away, and were left to die alone.

The timeline used in "Reverence" is historically accurate too. The trials for the antiretroviral therapy were piloted in the US in 1985 and the FDA approved the medication for use in 1987, so Gabriel could have been part of one of the successful ones and he could have lived to see that nowadays HIV is not a death sentence and that people live full happy lives. And they do so because science was not influenced by politics, because science was not swayed by homophobia and discrimination, and because science remained true to its purpose, serving all people.

Acknowledgments

This book was almost left without the Acknowledgements section. Mostly because I have been very careful this past year to tell the people to whom I'm grateful exactly how grateful I am for the fact that they are in my life.

But just as telling people that you love them is important, it's also important to tell them often. And so here goes!

To my grandmothers. The one who lived through the gulag and the one who lost half of her family to it. The one who believed I can move mountains and the one who trusted me to know better and not strain myself. To the one who always knew I was her baby and the one who always thought of me as her partner in crime. Thank you for your love. It still shines, despite you being gone for fifteen years.

To my mother. You often say you don't really support what I do. Yet you keep the copy of my debut novel on the shelf, proudly displayed next to my baby pictures, and what is that if not support? You believed in me when I told you I am writing a book that will feature the horrors your own mother lived through. Not only did you believe in me, but you kept pushing me and offering advice and love. And for that, as well as for always loving me, no matter how many curve balls I throw your way, I will forever be grateful.

To Jenifer Prince who came through like an absolute champion and did not laugh at my sketches, and understood my vision. And then made everything so much more beautiful than I could ever imagine. You're amazing. Thank you for taking a chance on me! I can't wait for our future projects!

To Heather Flournoy, who was the cavalry over the hill when I did not have faith in the manuscript. You always believed, even if you did nix the butterfly and the needle. I will get even for that one day, though you might've been right. Thank you. And to many more deadlines I'll try to meet!

To Jude. To Kathryn. Thank you.

About the Author

Milena McKay is a Lambda Literary and Golden Crown Literary Society award-winning sapphic fiction author.

Milena is a romance fanatic, currently splitting her time between trying to write a novel and succumbing to the temptation of reading another fanfic story.

She is a cat whisperer who wears four-inch heels for work while secretly dreaming of her extensive Converse collection. Would live on blueberries and lattes if she could.

Milena can recite certain episodes of The West Wing by heart and quote Telanu's "Truth and Measure" in her sleep.

Her love for Cate Blanchett knows no bounds.

www.milenamckay.com

Printed in Great Britain
by Amazon